THE SEVEN UNDERGROUND KINGS

AND

THE FIERY GOD OF THE MARRANS

by
ALEXANDER
MELENTYEVICH
VOLKOV

Translated from the Russian by
PETER L. BLYSTONE

RED BRANCH PRESS
Staten Island, NY
2009

Published by Red Branch Press
Staten Island, NY 10306

The Seven Underground Kings
    First published in Russian 1969
The Fiery God of the Marrans
    First Published in Russian 1972
    Translations ©1993 by Peter L. Blystone

Publisher's Cataloging in Publication

Volkov, A. (Aleksandr)
    The Seven Underground Kings, and, The Fiery God of the Marrans: two novels/ by Alexander Volkov; translated from the Russian by Peter L. Blystone.
—

    p. cm. – (Tales of Magic Land; 3-4)
    Summary: Chaos results when a certain magical spring goes dry in an underground realm that is ruled successively by seven kings, and Ellie, an ordinary little girl from Kansas, is called upon to set things right. In the second story, a wicked man recruits an army of conquest from among a primitive people who lack fire, by passing himself off as a sort of fire-god.

    ISBN 978-0-578-01707-5

    1. [Fantasy] I. Baum, L. Frank (Lyman Frank), 1856-1919. Wizard of Oz. II. Title: The seven underground kings. III. Title: The fiery god of the Marrans. IV. Series

    PZ7.V6   [Fic]

    Library of Congress Catalog Number 93-83409

To

MICHAEL T. LOSCHIAVO

whose support and encouragement
have made this a better book,
and whose friendship has (I hope)
made me a better person!

— PLB

TABLE OF CONTENTS

THE SEVEN
UNDERGROUND KINGS 11

TABLE OF CONTENTS

TABLE OF CONTENTS

Part IV
THE SILVER CIRCLET 333

THE
SEVEN
UNDERGROUND
KINGS

Chapter 1

HOW MAGIC LAND
CAME TO BE

In the olden days, so long ago that no one even knows when it was, there lived a mighty wizard named Hurricap. He lived in the country that at a much later date would be called America, and no one in the world could match Hurricap's skill when it came to accomplishing wonderful things. At first he was very proud of this , and he was most happy to grant the requests of people who came to see him: he gave one man a bow that shot without ever missing its mark; he made another so fleet of foot that the man was able to run a stag down with ease; on yet another he conferred invulnerability to the fangs and claws of wild beasts.

And so it went on for many years. But then the people's requests, and their gratitude as well, began to get on Hurricap's nerves, and he decided to withdraw into seclusion, where no one would bother him.

Long did the wizard wander about the as-yet-unnamed continent, and at last he found a suitable spot. It was a remarkably nice country with thick forests, limpid rivers that provided irrigation for green glades, and marvelous fruit trees. "Just what I needed!" said Hurricap joyfully. "Here, I can live out my old age in peace. All I have to do now is to arrange things so that humans will not come here."

13

To a magician as powerful as Hurricap, this was nothing at all.

One! — the land was now surrounded by a range of impenetrable mountains.

Two! — beyond these mountains there now lay a Great Sandy Desert which no human being could ever hope to cross.

Hurricap reflected about what might still be lacking to him. "Let it be summer here all the time!" commanded the sorcerer, and his wish was granted. "Let this land be magical, and let all the animals and birds here have the power to talk like humans!" exclaimed Hurricap.

At once, an unbroken chattering could be heard everywhere: the monkeys and the bears had begun to talk, as had the lions and the tigers, the sparrows and the crows, and the woodpeckers and the titmice. All of them were most bored from their long years of silence, and they made haste now to express to one another, in no uncertain terms, their thoughts, their feelings, their wishes...

"Not so loud!" commanded the wizard angrily, and the voices were stilled. "Now my life of peace and quiet can begin, without any meddlesome people around," said Hurricap with satisfaction.

"You're mistaken, mighty wizard!" resounded a voice near Hurricap's ear, and a jaunty magpie perched on his shoulder. "Excuse me, if you please, but there *are* people living here — and lots of them, at that!"

"But that can't be!" exclaimed the wizard in vexation. "Why didn't I see them?"

"Because you're very big, and the people in our country are very small!" explained the magpie with a laugh, and it flew away.

It was true: Hurricap was so tall that his head was on a level with the tops of the highest trees. His eyesight had grown weak with the onset of old age, and in those days, even the most accomplished wizards had not heard of eyeglasses.

Hurricap found himself a broad clearing, and he lay down on the ground and turned his gaze into the thick of the forest. There, with difficulty, he indeed made out a multitude of tiny figures hiding fearfully behind trees.

"Hey, you there," commanded the wizard menacingly, "come here, little people!" His voice reverberated like a clap of thunder.

The little men came out into the clearing and looked timidly at the giant.

"Who are you?" asked the wizard sternly.

"We're the people who live in this land," answered the men, trembling, "and we've done nothing wrong."

"I'm not blaming you for anything," said Hurricap. "It's just that I had to look really hard to find myself a place to live. But what's done is done, and I'm not going to do anything to nullify the sorcery I've already performed. Let this land remain Magic for all eternity, and I'll simply find myself a corner that's as secluded as possible..."

Hurricap betook himself to the mountains, and quick as a wink, he built himself a splendid palace and took up residence there, strictly forbidding the inhabitants of Magic Land even to come near his abode.

This command was heeded throughout the centuries that followed. Then the wizard died, and his palace fell into ruin and gradually came tumbling down. But even then, no one had the courage to approach the spot.

After that, the very memory of Hurricap was lost. The people who resided in that land, cut off as it was from the rest of the world, came to believe that it had always been thus, that the World-Encompassing Mountains had always surrounded it, that they had always had a never-ending summer, that animals and birds had always talked like human beings...

Part I

THE CAVERN

Chapter 2

A THOUSAND YEARS AGO

The population of Magic Land grew and grew, and there came a time when a number of different states emerged within it. In those states, as is usually the case, kings rose to power, and along with the kings came courtiers and large numbers of servants. Then the kings created armies and began to fight with one another over the borders of their kingdoms, and thus did wars come into being.

In one of these states, which was located a thousand years ago in the western part of the land, there ruled a king named Naranya. He reigned for such a long time that his son Bofaro grew tired of waiting for his father to die, and he got it into his head to oust him from the throne. By making tempting promises, Prince Bofaro attracted several thousand supporters to his side — but they never had an opportunity to do anything, for the conspiracy was uncovered! Prince Bofaro was brought to his father's tribunal. The king was seated on his high throne, surrounded by his courtiers, and he gazed severely upon the rebel's ashen face.

"Do you confess, unworthy son of mine, that you plotted evil against me?" asked the king.

"I so confess," replied the prince boldly, never once lowering his eyes before his father's stern gaze.

"Perhaps you intended to kill me, to gain control of the throne?" Naranya went on.

"No," said Bofaro, "I never wanted that. Your fate would have been merely imprisonment for life."

"But fate has decided otherwise," remarked the king. "What you had in mind for me will now be the lot of you and your adherents. Do you know the Cavern?"

19

The prince shuddered. Of course he knew of the existence of the enormous underground Cavern, which spread out deeply beneath their very kingdom. People sometimes looked down into it, but after standing there at the entrance for a few minutes and beholding the strange shadows of unknown beasts, both on the ground and in the air, they would turn back in terror. Actually living in it seemed nothing if not impossible.

"You and your supporters will go into permanent exile in the Cavern," decreed the king solemnly, and even Bofaro's enemies shuddered. "And that's not all! Not only you, but your children and your children's children — none of you will ever return to the surface, to the blue sky and the bright sun. My successors will see to that, for I'm going to take an oath from them that they carry out my will scrupulously. Perhaps you have some objections to raise now?"

"No," said Bofaro, who was as proud and unyielding as Naranya himself. "I've earned this punishment because I dared raise my hand against my own father. I ask only for one thing: let us be given equipment for farming."

"You shall have it," said the king. "And we'll even supply you with weapons so that you can defend yourselves against the predatory beasts that inhabit the Cavern."

The despondent columns of exiles, accompanied by their weeping wives and children, headed underground. The exit was guarded by a large detachment of soldiers, and not one of the rebels would be able to come back out.

Bofaro, with his wife and his two sons in tow, was the first to descend into the Cavern. An amazing Underground land spread out before their eyes: it stretched as far as their eyes could see, and its even surface was broken here and there by low hills covered with growths of forest. In the center of the Cavern shimmered the smooth surface of a large, round lake.

Autumn appeared to predominate on the hills and in the meadows of Underground Land. The foliage on the trees and the bushes was crimson, rose, and orange, and the grasses on the meadows were yellow, like grass mown down by a harvester's scythe. Underground Land was in semidarkness: only some goldenish clouds swirling about beneath the roof of the cave provided a little illumination.

"You mean *this* is where we'll have to make our home?" asked Bofaro's wife in dismay.

"Such is our fate," replied the Prince, downcast.

Chapter 3

SIEGE

The exiles walked on for a long time, until they reached the lake. Its banks were strewn with rocks. Bofaro climbed onto a large slab of rock and raised his hand as a signal that he wanted to speak. Everyone fell silent and listened.

"My friends!" Bofaro began. "I've done you a very great wrong. My own ambition has drawn you into misfortune and caused you to end up under this dreary vault. But there's no way to bring back the past, and staying alive is better than dying. Before us lies a harsh struggle for existence, and we must now elect a leader to guide us."

Loud cries resounded: "You shall be our leader!" "We elect *you*, Prince!" "You are the descendant of kings, and you shall also rule, Bofaro!"

Not one person raised his voice to express disapproval of Bofaro's selection, and his melancholy face lit up in a weak smile. He would still be a king, even if only of a subterranean kingdom.

"Listen to me, my people," he addressed them. "We've earned a rest, but there can be no rest for us yet. While we were walking through the Cavern, I observed the dark shadows of enormous beasts following us from afar."

"We saw them too!" added others, bearing out his statement.

"Then to work! Let the women put the children to sleep and take care of them, and let all the men build a fortification!"

Bofaro, setting an example for the others, was the first to roll a rock over to a large circle that they had drawn on the ground. Forgetting their weariness, the men dragged the rocks and rolled them forward, and a circular wall began to rise higher and higher. Several hours went by, and the wall, which was wide and sturdy, had stretched up to twice a man's height.

"I think this will be enough for now," said the king. "We'll build a city here later."

Bofaro placed a guard of several men armed with bows and spears, and all the other exiles, who were exhausted, lay down to sleep beneath the uneasy light of the golden clouds.

Their sleep did not last long.

"Danger! Everybody up!" shouted the guards.

The frightened people climbed up the stone steps that had been constructed along the inner edge of the wall, and they saw several dozen strange beasts approaching their place of refuge.

"Sixpaws! Those monsters are Sixpaws!" echoed their cries.

Indeed, each of the beasts had six, rather than four, stout, round legs that supported long, rotund bodies. Their fur was a dirty white, and it was thick and shaggy. The Sixpaws stared with their big round eyes, as if bewitched, at the fortress that had risen so unexpectedly in their path.

22

Chapter 3: SIEGE

"How horrible they are!" the people said to one another. "It's a good thing we're protected now by walls."

Men who were sharpshooters with the bow took up
their battle stations.

The beasts approached, sniffing, looking, shaking with
annoyance their great big heads with the short whiskers.
Soon they had come to within firing range. Bowstrings
twanged, and arrows whizzed through the air and landed
in the beasts' shaggy fur. But the fur was too thick for
them to penetrate, and the Sixpaws continued to approach, growling softly. Like all animals in Magic Land,
they had the power of speech, but they talked badly, for
their tongues were too thick and moved around with difficulty inside their mouths.

"Don't waste your arrows on them!" ordered Bofaro.
"Get your swords and spears ready! Women and children
— move into the center of the stronghold."

But the beasts did not choose to go on the attack.
Rather, they formed a ring and surrounded the fortress,
never once taking their eyes off it. It was a true siege.

Bofaro realized that he had made a blunder. Being unfamiliar with the habits of the denizens of the Cavern, he
had not bothered to order anyone to stock up on water,
and now, if this siege should be a long one, the defenders
of the fortress faced the threat of death by thirst.

The lake was not far away – no more than a few dozen
paces — but how was anyone to break through to it past
the chain of their enemies, who, despite their apparent
clumsiness, were really agile and quick?...

Several hours went by. The children were the first to
begin to ask for drinks of water, and their mothers were
unable to keep them quiet. Bofaro was already preparing
to make a desperate sortie.

All at once, a noise was heard in the air, and the be-
leaguered people beheld a flock of amazing creatures approaching in the sky. They were reminiscent somewhat

of the crocodiles living in the rivers of Magic Land, only much larger.

These new monsters were flapping enormous leathery wings, and powerful feet armed with sharp claws dangled beneath their dirty-yellow, scaly bellies.

"We're lost!" cried the exiles. "Those are dragons! Even our walls won't save us from those flying creatures!..."

The people covered their heads with their arms, expecting those dreadful talons to be plunged into them at any moment. But instead, the totally unexpected happened: with a screech, the flock of dragons swooped down on the Sixpaws. They aimed for their eyes, and the beasts, who were clearly accustomed to attacks like these, tried to bury their snouts in their breasts as they waved their forepaws in front of them, standing up all the while on their hind legs.

The dragons' screeching and the Sixpaws' roaring deafened the people, but they watched this amazing sight with the keenest curiosity. Some of the Sixpaws rolled themselves up into balls, and the dragons bit at them savagely, tearing out huge clumps of white fur. One of the dragons, which had carelessly placed its side within reach of the blow of a mighty paw, was unable to fly away, and it crashed down on the sand...

It all ended with the Sixpaws dashing away helter-skelter, pursued by the flying reptiles. The women, who had meanwhile picked up vessels, ran down to the lake, and they gave drinks of water to their crying children without delay.

Much later, after the people had made themselves at home in the Cavern, they learned the cause of the hostility between the Sixpaws and the dragons. The reptiles were egg-layers, and they buried their eggs in the warm ground in secluded spots; to the beasts, these eggs were a great delicacy, and they dug them up and devoured them. That is why the dragons attacked the Sixpaws whenever they could. Of course, the reptiles were not free of sin either: they tore the Sixpaws' young to pieces if they caught any that were not under their parents' protection.

And so it was that the enmity between beast and reptile saved the people from death.

Chapter 4

THE DAWN OF A NEW WAY OF LIFE

Years went by. The exiles became accustomed to life underground. They constructed a city on the shore of Central Lake and surrounded it with a stone wall. To provide for their sustenance, they began to till the soil and to sow grain. The Cavern lay so far below the surface that its soil was warm, for it received heat from the underground fires. From time to time, there were even light rainfalls from the golden clouds. Thanks to this, the wheat did ripen, albeit more slowly than it would have on the surface. But the people found it extremely taxing to drag the heavy plows as they tilled the hard, rocky soil.

One day, an aging hunter named Karum came to see King Bofaro. "Your Majesty," he said, "our plowmen will soon be dying of sheer exhaustion. I therefore propose that we begin harnessing Sixpaws to the plows."

The king was dumfounded. "But they'd maul their drovers to death!"

"I know how to tame them," asserted Karum. "I used to have to deal with the most savage beasts of prey when we still lived up above. And I always handled them."

"All right, go ahead with it!" Bofaro gave his assent. "I suppose you'll be needing some aides?"

"That's correct," agreed the hunter. "But instead of men, I'll be calling on dragons to do the job."

Again the king was surprised, and Karum explained calmly: "Don't you see? We humans may be weaker than either the Sixpaws or the Flying Reptiles, but we have intelligence, which those beasts lack. I'll tame the Sixpaws with the help of the dragons, and the Sixpaws, for their part, will help me keep the dragons in a state of subservience."

Karum went into action. His men captured some baby dragons, ones that had barely even hatched from their eggs. Being reared by humans from their very first days, these reptiles grew up to be obedient, and it was with their assistance that Karum was able to capture his first batch of Sixpaws.

It was not an easy matter to subdue those savage beasts, but he managed it. After hunger strikes lasting for many days, the Sixpaws began to accept food from the hands of humans, and then they allowed harnesses to be put on them and began to pull the plows.

The first period did not pass without unfortunate incidents, but everything worked itself out after that. Tame dragons carried people through the air, while Sixpaws plowed the land. People could breathe more freely, and crafts began to develop among them quite rapidly.

Weavers wove cloth, tailors sewed garments, and potters fashioned ceramics. Miners dug ores from deep mines, founders extracted the metals from them, and metalworkers and lathe-operators produced all the essential goods from the metals.

Obtaining the ores required the most work of all, and many people went to work in the mines. For this reason, the entire territory came to be called the Land of the Underground Ore-Diggers.

The Undergrounders had to answer to no one but themselves, and they became extremely inventive and resourceful. The people began to forget about the upper world, and children who were born there in the Cavern had never seen it and thus knew about it only from their mothers' stories, which eventually became almost like legends...

Life became settled. The only drawback was the creation by the ambitious Bofaro of a large staff of courtiers and numerous retainers, and the fact that the people had to support these idlers.

So although plowmen diligently tilled the land and sowed and reaped grain, though farmers cultivated vegetables, and though fishermen caught fish and crabs with their nets in Central Lake, their produce quickly began to run short. The Underground Ore-Diggers eventually had to enter into barter with the inhabitants of the surface world.

In exchange for grain, butter, and fruits, the inhabitants of the Cavern offered their own products: copper and bronze, iron plows and harrows, glass, and precious stones.

Trade between the lower and the upper worlds gradually increased. The spot where it took place was the Blue Land exit from Underground Land. In accordance with King Naranya's command, this exit, which was located near the eastern border of Blue Land, had been closed off by sturdy gates. After Naranya's death, the guards outside the gates were removed, since the Underground Ore-Diggers had never made any attempt to return to the surface: after many years of living below ground, the cave-dwellers' eyes had grown unaccustomed to sunlight, and now the Ore-Diggers could come up to the surface only by night.

The midnight tolling of a bell that hung by the gate announced the beginning of a typical market "day." In the morning, the merchants of Blue Land checked and counted the merchandise that the Undergrounders had brought up to them during the night. After that, hundreds of workers brought in wheelbarrows filled with bags of flour, baskets laden with fruit and vegetables, and boxes of eggs, butter, and cheese. The next night, all these things had disappeared.

Chapter 5

KING BOFARO'S WILL

Bofaro ruled Underground Land for many years. He already had two sons when he first descended into it, but five more were born to him after that. Bofaro loved all his children very much, and he had no way of choosing his successor from among them. It was apparent to him that if he designated any one of his sons as his heir, the others would be deeply insulted.

Bofaro changed his will seventeen times, and finally, weary of the squabbles and the intrigues between the would-be successors, he came up with an idea that brought him peace of mind. He designated all seven of his sons as his successors, and ordained that they should reign in turn, each of them for a month. Hoping to forestall any and all quarrels and civil strife, he made his sons swear an oath that they would always live in peace and that they would adhere strictly to the order of succession

[The day finally came when King Bofaro breathed his last.]

But the oath did no good: dissension began immediately after their father's death. The brothers quarreled about which of them would rule first.

"The order of succession must go by height," insisted Prince Vagissa. "I'm the tallest, so I shall rule first."

"Nothing of the sort!" objected fat Gramento. "The one who weighs more also has a bigger mind. Let us weigh ourselves!"

"You've got plenty of lard, but no mind," cried Prince Tubago. "It's the strongest who can best deal with the affairs of kingship. And I'll take on any three!" Tubago waved his mighty fists.

And so a fight broke out. When it was over, some of the brothers were missing teeth, while others had black eyes and dislocated arms and legs...

After they had fought with one another and made up, the princes wondered why it had never occurred to any of them that the arrangement least open to dispute would be to rule the kingdom in accordance with their ages.

Once they had settled on the order of succession, the seven underground kings decided to build themselves a single palace for all of them, but to make it in such a way that each brother would have a section of it to himself. On the city square, accordingly, architects and bricklayers erected an enormous building with seven towers and seven separate entrances that led to the apartments of each king.

The oldest inhabitants of the Cavern still recollected the magnificent rainbows that sometimes shone in the sky over their lost homeland. They decided to perpetuate this rainbow for their descendants in the walls of the palace. Its seven towers were painted the seven colors of the rainbow: red, orange, yellow, green, blue, indigo, and violet. The skilled craftsmen succeeded in making the shades of color stand out with amazing clarity, and the hues were in no way inferior to those of a real rainbow.

Each king chose as his primary color the color of the tower in which he had settled. Thus, everything in the green apartment would be green: the king's festive attire, the clothing worn by his courtiers, the livery of his lackeys, the paint of his furniture. In the violet apartments, everything would be violet... The colors were distributed among the princes by lot.

There was no alternation of day and night in the underground world, and time was measured by hourglasses. Therefore, the kings decreed that special high officials — the Time Keepers — would keep track of the regularity of the rotation of the kings.

King Bofaro's will had some dire unforeseen consequences. To begin with, each king, suspecting the others of hostile intentions, provided himself with a retinue of armed guards. These guards rode around on dragons. In the same manner, each king had his own squad of flying overseers to keep an eye on the work in the fields and in the factories. The guardsmen and the overseers, as well as the courtiers and lackeys, had to be fed by the people.

Another misfortune arose from the fact that the land had no fixed laws. As soon as the residents got used to the requirements of one king in the course of his month of rule, these were replaced by others.

The etiquette of greeting produced an especially large number of annoyances. One king demanded that when anyone met him, he get down on his hands and knees, while another had to be greeted by the person's placing his left hand, with the fingers spread apart, to his nose while waving his right hand over his head. With a third, it was necessary to hop on one foot...

Each monarch tried to think of something a little more remarkable, something that none of the other kings would be likely to hit upon. And the Undergrounders groaned loudly at each of these inventions.

Every resident of the Cavern had a set of pointed caps in all seven colors of the rainbow, and on the day when the king changed, it was necessary for each person to change his cap as well. This matter was watched closely by the soldiers of the king currently on the throne.

On one thing alone were all seven kings in agreement with one another: they were constantly coming up with new taxes. The people strained themselves at their work so that the whims of their monarchs could be satisfied — and there were many such whims.

Each king, when he ascended the throne, gave a splendid banquet, for which the courtiers of all seven kings were invited to the Rainbow Palace. They celebrated the birthdays of the kings, their wives, and their children, and they commemorated successful hunts, the hatching of another baby dragon at the royal dragon farm, and many, many other things... It was a rare day when the palace was not resounding with the shouts of banqueters treating each other to wine from the upper world and singing the praises of whatever monarch was currently ruling them.

Chapter 6

A DAY WITH NO REST

It was now the 189th year of the Underground Era (as reckoned from the time when the rebellious prince Bofaro and his supporters were banished to the Cavern). Several generations of Undergrounders had come and gone during that period, and the people had adapted to life in the Cavern, with its constant half-light so reminiscent of twilight on the upper earth. Their skin grew pale, and they became leaner and more spare; their large eyes grew accustomed to seeing well in the weak, diffused light from the golden clouds swirling about beneath the high, rocky vault, and they could no longer tolerate the full light of day in the upper world.

The term of kingship of King Pamelia the Second was coming to an end, and it was time to transfer power to Pampuro the Third. But Pampuro the Third was still a baby, and he was under the regency of his mother, the widowed Queen Stafida. Stafida was a power-hungry woman, and she was in a hurry to take Pamelia's place on the throne. So she sent for her Time Keeper, who was a stocky, gray-haired old man with a long beard.

"Urgando," she commanded, "set the clock on the main tower ahead by six hours."

"I shall obey, your Excellency!" responded Urgando with a bow. "I know how anxiously the subjects are waiting for you to ascend the throne."

"Fine!" interrupted Stafida. "Now go, and don't stand here talking!"

"Not on your life!" smirked Urgando.

He carried out the Queen's bidding. However, the Time Keeper to King Pamelia, a young man named Turrepo, received a directive from his monarch to set the clock *back* by twelve hours: Pamelia, for his part, wanted to *prolong* his period of kingship.

Chaos soon prevailed, in the City of the Seven Monarchs and in all the land. Hardly had the townspeople closed their eyes and become submerged in their first pleasant slumber, than the palace bell tolled six A.M. — the signal for reveille. The people, sleepy-eyed and unable to understand what was going on, nevertheless crawled out of bed and prepared to go to work.

"Hey, neighbor!" the tailor called out to the shoemaker after being thus awakened. "What's happening? Why did the bell toll at such an untimely hour?"

"Who can figure these things out?" answered his neighbor. "The kings are the most knowledgeable about time. Get dressed, and don't forget to put on your green cap..."

"I know, I know. Last time around, I caught it good by walking into the bakery wearing the wrong cap. Had to spend twenty-four hours in confinement..."

The people coming out onto the square heard a dreadful noise and howling from up above: it was Urgando and Turrepo fighting up on the clock tower. Turrepo was trying to push Urgando away so that he could put the clock back to the time that he had set previously, but the old man proved to be the stronger of the two, and he threw his opponent down the stairs.

Turrepo lay on the lower landing for several minutes, and then he rose and climbed back up the steps. Once again Urgando threw him down. But Turrepo would not give up. In their third skirmish, he contrived to grab his adversary in a bear-hug, and they tumbled down the stairs together. Urgando hit his head on one of the steps and was knocked out.

Turrepo made haste to set the clock back and to toll the curfew bell. Town criers ran about the city, directing the townspeople to go to bed, while soldiers in yellow saddled their dragons and set out for the villages and communities to report to the people that the ones in green had awakened them ahead of time.

Immediately, the green caps were replaced again by yellow ones.

The victorious Turrepo went home to bed, forgetting all about Urgando, who was still lying there unconscious. The latter, who came to himself about an hour and a half later, went back up the stairs and sent out his own messengers to awaken everyone in the city and in the land.

So that day, the residents of the Cavern had to get up and go back to bed seven times, because the stubborn Turrepo would not yield to his adversary. It was announced at last to the people that his Excellency King Pampuro the Third had ascended the throne. The people quickly took off their yellow caps and put on their green ones for the last time that day.

Chapter 7

A SIXPAW HUNT

Another century passed. The situation in Underground Land became worse and worse. To satisfy the insatiable appetites of the kings, the courtiers, and the soldiers, the commoners now had to toil as much as seventeen to twenty hours a day. The future held nothing for them but foreboding.

But then an amazing event occurred which brought relief to the residents of the Cavern.

It all began with a Sixpaw hunt.

Tame Sixpaws were very useful in the country's economy. They drew the heavy plows and harrows, the mowers and the reapers, and they turned the wheels of the threshing machines. It was they that operated the water wheels that diverted water from the lake to the City of the Seven Monarchs, and they drew up baskets of ore from the deep mines.

The Sixpaws were omnivorous beasts. They were fed on straw and hay, on fish from the lake, and on leftovers from the city kitchens... There was only one problem: to replace Sixpaws that died of old age, it was necessary to capture new ones in the rocky labyrinth that surrounded the Cavern. This labyrinth was designated a royal preserve, and none of the residents of the Cavern dared hunt there, for the penalty was death.

It was quiet in the royal preserve. Not a sound broke the silence of the underground chambers and passageways.

In one of the caves, by the wall, stood a Sixpaw. Its shaggy white fur glowed weakly, throwing light on objects for two or three paces all around. The beast was contentedly licking huge snails off the rocky wall of the cave and swallowing them down, shells and all.

It had been indulging in this delectable pastime for a long time when all at once its keen hearing picked up a distant sound. The beast began to listen; it lapped up fewer snails from the wall, and it nervously turned its enormous shaggy head.

What was alarming the beast? That riddle was soon answered. In the distance there appeared some indistinct spots of light, swaying back and forth in the air. Then human forms became visible, with headdresses enhanced with little glowing balls. The light from these was similar to that given off by the Sixpaws' fur, but it was much brighter, and it illuminated objects for twenty paces around.

These tall, graceful humans in leather outfits drew near the Sixpaw's retreat, remaining at an even distance from one another. They carried before them a long net, which stretched the entire width of the cavern. A few of them had rods with nooses at the end.

The Undergrounders were on a hunt, and the Sixpaw was their quarry.

"Silence, my friends!" said the leader of the royal hunt, an accomplished trapper named Ortega. "I sense a beast not far ahead. I've picked up its scent."

"We smell it too," replied Ortega's subordinates in confirmation.

"Keep your main strength at your flanks," directed the royal huntsman. "Sixpaws always try to break out along the wall."

"We've got our torches ready," said the torch-bearers. "We'll scare it with our fire."

Softly as humans were conversing, the beast still heard them, and it darted noiselessly into the narrow corridor at the opposite end of the cave. But the huntsmen were masters of their craft, and their knowledge of the lie of the labyrinth was excellent. The second exit leading from the cave was likewise blocked by a net, held by other men.

With a howl, the Sixpaw leaped back and began to dash to and fro in the cave. The huntsmen gave out a cry; they lit their torches and stamped their feet, and they banged their rods against the stone floor. This fiendish racket, made even louder by echoes, so terrified the beast that it charged forward and, thanks to its poor eyesight, it became entangled in the wide pockets of the net. The ropes began to snap beneath the mighty blows from its paws, but the huntsmen continued to wind the net around the beast, and the Sixpaw was quickly captured.

The second party of huntsmen appeared from the passageway. Their faces beaming, the men congregated around the Sixpaw. "We should receive a good reward for this beast," the hunters said to one another. "Just look at how enormous he is!"

The function of the rods with the nooses now became apparent. Carefully disentangling the monster's feet, the trappers threw nooses over them and tied its legs together in such a way that the Sixpaw could take only small steps. They placed a strong leather muzzle over the animal's head and tied some ropes to its neck. When all this had been done, they removed the net from over the Sixpaw with a dexterity that bespoke long experience, and several of the men undertook to remove the beast from the premises.

The huntsmen set out for home. The huskiest and strongest of them dragged the Sixpaw by the neck, and when it balked, others jabbed it from behind with the sharp ends of their rods. The beast calmed down and trudged along behind the men.

"Take this baby to Sixpaw Corral number four," said Ortega, turning to the trappers, "and you, Zelano, can have the job of taming him! You guys can go on ahead. I'm going to take a walk around the labyrinth, for I have the feeling that there's more easy money waiting for us in these precincts."

Chapter 8

A MYSTERIOUS SLEEP

The huntsmen offered Ortega a torch, but the trapper declined: the ball on his cap would be more than sufficient for him.

The trappers moved off, taking the Sixpaw with them, and Ortega began to walk about the labyrinth by himself. After he had searched it diligently for about two hours, the huntsman was convinced that this region of the preserve harbored a rare prize: a female Sixpaw and her young.

The trapper set out for home. His path took him through a part of the cave where he had not set foot for a long time. All at once he observed a reflection of light in a basin that previously had always been empty.

"Let's have a look at that!" said Ortega in amazement. "A new spring has opened up. There was never any here before, as far as anyone can remember."

After so much continuous walking, the hunter very much wanted a drink of water. Dropping to his hands and knees beside the spring, he scooped up a handful of water and drank it down with relish. The water had an especially pleasing taste, and it foamed and fizzed. Ortega wanted to drink a little more of it, but he found his whole being overcome by some species of lethargy.

"Hey, Ortega, Ortega!" the hunter rebuked himself. "You must really be getting old and weak! Would a walk like this ever have tired you out so much before? All right, I'll rest a little..." He stretched out as comfortably as he

could on the rough stone, and closed his eyes in irresistible sleep.

Ortega's disappearance caused his family no concern
until the second day was nearly ended: long absences on
the old hunter's part were a way of life with them. But
when he was still gone even after the third day, his wife
and children, not to mention his fellow huntsmen, became
downright alarmed.

What could have happened to the hunter? There was
no way that he could have gotten lost in the labyrinth,
for he knew it as well as he knew his own five fingers.
They could only assume the worst: either an attack by a
hungry beast, or a cave-in. But the Sixpaws had long been
acquainted with man, and they tried to keep as far away
from him as possible.

King Ukonda, who was on the throne that month, ordered a party of hunters to set out on a search. It was led
by the huntsman's assistant, Quoto.

The men carried bundles of torches and a large stock
of provisions, since the searches might last a number of
days. And indeed, it was only after prolonged efforts that
they found Ortega at last, lying in a cave that none of
them was too familiar with, near a small circular depression in the floor. The depression looked very much like
the basin of a pool, but there was not a drop of water in
it.

The hunter seemed to be sleeping peacefully, but no
traces of breath were apparent. They placed their ears
against his chest: there was no heartbeat.

"He's dead!" cried one of the huntsmen.

"And he must have died just a short time ago," added
Quoto. "His body is still completely supple and warm.
But how could he have lasted for two weeks without any
food and water?..."

The doleful procession bearing Ortega's body stopped
before the portico of the indigo wing of the palace, the
one in which Ukonda lived. The king himself came out

onto the portico to pay his last respects to his faithful huntsman.

"When are you thinking of burying your husband, ma'am?" he said, turning to Ortega's wife Alona, who was bowed with grief.

"In accordance with our fathers' custom — tomorrow!" she answered.

"Ha, ha, ha!" A sharp laughter rang out, and Doctor Boril, his blue cape hanging down from his shoulders, pushed his way through the crowd. "Are you really going to bury a live person?... Just look at his fresh face, untouched by the finger of death. And how about this?" The short, fat doctor lifted Ortega's arm, and it fell gently back onto the litter.

Alona looked at Doctor Boril with both hope and doubt, while the doctor continued to demonstrate that Ortega was alive and merely in a deep sleep.

"Rubbish! Nonsense!" resounded a thunderous bass voice, which pronounced every word in a staccato fashion, and the very tall, skinny Doctor Robil, wearing a green cape thrown carelessly over his shoulders, approached Ortega's body. "This! man! is! dead! as! a! rock!"

A fierce argument ensued between the two doctors, accompanied by scientific proofs. Alona alternated between giving way to despair and feeling renewed hope, depending on which of the two had the upper hand at a given moment. However, it was Doctor Robil who came out ahead in the end, thanks to his penetrating voice, and he looked down from above on little Doctor Boril.

"I! maintain!" he thundered, "that! this! man! must! be! buried! tomorrow!"

But at that very moment, the "dead" man stirred a little and opened his eyes. The astonished crowd surged to the side, while Alona collapsed on her husband's breast and tearfully covered his face with kisses.

"Ha, ha, ha! Ho, ho, ho!" Boril burst into laughter. "So the highly learned Doctor Robil almost buried a live person! That's how his learning shines!"

39

Robil, though disgraced, would not give up: "It's! still! necessary! to! prove! that! he's! alive!" And he flounced angrily off the square, wrapping himself majestically in his green cloak.

Some of the spectators laughed at Robil's last words, but Doctor Boril looked most anxious. Though Ortega had regained his senses, he did not utter a word. He did not recognize anyone, not even his wife, nor did he understand the expressions of concern that King Ukonda himself was addressing to him.

"Strange, very strange!" muttered Doctor Boril. "Ortega's eyes are wandering, just like those of a newborn baby, and the movements of his arms and legs are equally uncoordinated." Then he snapped back to life. "It's interesting, very interesting! This occurrence may prove very valuable for science. My good woman," he said, turning to the huntsman's wife. "I'll take it upon myself to treat your husband, and entirely free of charge."

Without even listening to Alona's expressions of gratitude, the good-natured doctor directed the hunters to take Ortega home, since the latter could not take even one step on his own two feet. Boril walked along behind the bearers.

Chapter 9

THE SOPORIFIC WATER

Doctor Boril spent days and nights by Ortega's bedside. The huntsman was indeed very much like a newborn baby in every way. He did not know how to eat, and he had to be fed with a little spoon. Ortega could not utter a single word, and merely babbled meaningless sounds. He did not understand any words that were addressed to him, nor did he respond to his own name...

Chapter 9: THE SOPORIFIC WATER

"What an amazing case!" mumbled the bewildered Boril. "What a report I'll make about it to the doctors up above. I'll wager my life that they've never seen anything like it before!"

But Ortega regained his lost faculties with surprising speed. The very first evening he said "papa" and "mama" (which was downright comical coming from a grown man with a beard!), and he took his first timorous steps, holding onto his son's arm.

On the second day, his speech became fully connected, and his perception cleared. The huntsman's assistant, Quoto, conversed with him for hours on end, telling him about various incidents that had taken place on the hunt, and all of this reawakened Ortega's memory. After one more day of intensive care, the huntsman, after Doctor Boril had led him before the king, related his amazing adventure in the labyrinth.

"But when we found you, the basin was completely empty!" exclaimed Quoto, who had accompanied the hunter there, and he was quick to add: "I ask your Excellency's pardon for my breach of propriety!"

"What's that you say? Empty?" Ortega asked his assistant once again.

"There wasn't even one drop of water in it!" insisted Quoto.

"But that's impossible!" the huntsman raged. "Are you saying I dreamed it all?"

"It's! not! impossible! that! you! dreamed! it," commented Doctor Robil spitefully. "You! are! quite! strong! and! you! slept! a! long! time."

An expedition was dispatched to the labyrinth; it was led by Ortega, who by now had fully regained all his faculties. In addition to the huntsmen, he was accompanied by King Ukonda's Ministers of Farming and of Industry, as well as by Doctors Boril and Robil.

Ortega felt an astonishment that was unheard-of when the basin proved indeed to be dry. "But how could all

41

this happen?" he mumbled. "I remember quite distinctly being overcome by sleep after drinking water from this basin."

The men were already about to leave. But Doctor Boril gave voice to an idea which eventually led to a profound change in the way of life in the Land of the Underground Ore-Diggers. "Maybe water appears and disappears here?" he said. "It could come out of the rocks at certain times and then disappear back into them!"

Doctor Robil derided this surmise at once, and Boril, affronted, proposed that they put it to the test. "Let's stay here for a week, or two weeks, or even a month!" he exclaimed.

"Why! not! a! year?" asked Robil scornfully.

"If no water appears in the course of a month, then I'll admit defeat," Boril announced boldly. "And as a sign of submission, I'll even go around the City of the Seven Kings on all fours!"

"Agreed!" smirked Robil.

The two doctors remained to keep a vigil by the vanished spring, and to prevent them from becoming bored, the two Ministers also stayed with them, since they had taken an interest in the controversy. This was most convenient, for the presence of four of them made it easier to indulge in gaming with the dice that were in the pocket of one of the Ministers, an inveterate gambler.

"But what about your ministries?" asked Ortega.

"They'll get along even without us," replied the Minister of Agriculture in a flippant manner.

The Ministers ordered that beds be brought to the cave, along with everything essential for a prolonged sojourn in the labyrinth: provisions, wine, and fruit. It was necessary for others to come and see them after a day to replenish their supplies.

Ortega returned to the cave five times, and each time, everything in it was just as before. The basin was empty, Doctor Robil was taunting Boril and advising him to learn in advance how to walk on all fours, and Boril was becoming more and more dispirited with each passing day.

But on the sixth visit, Ortega and his fellow huntsmen beheld an amazing picture: the two doctors and the two Ministers were lying motionless on the floor of the cave, with no breath and no heartbeat. The dice were lying between them: the game was unfinished. And again the basin was empty!

When the four sleepers had been borne away to the indigo portico, King Ukonda said: "Everything's quite clear now. This water, which appears and disappears in a mysterious manner, is soporific. My Ministers and the two doctors showed great lack of discretion when all four of them drank the miraculous water at the same time. Well, what can we do? We'll just have to wait till they wake up. Take these sleepyheads to their houses, and report to me every day about their condition."

Ortega the Huntsman had slept for two weeks. But two weeks went by now, a month, and a month and a half, and there was no change in the sleepers' condition: their bodies were warm and pliant, but no one could detect any breathing, and their hearts didn't beat.

The first to awaken was Doctor Boril. This happened on the fifty-third day after he had drunk the Soporific Water. As with Ortega the Huntsman, Boril was just like a newborn babe in every way. But in his case, this was truly a misfortune.

Underground Land had only the two doctors; a third doctor would have had nothing to do, and there would be no practice for him. The doctors passed their knowledge on to their offspring, from father to son. But Boril's and Robil's fathers had been deceased for a long time. Who was there now who could teach medicine to the two former doctors?

The seven kings were infuriated when they realized that they would now have to go without medical assistance. They even considered hanging Ortega for finding the confounded spring in the first place, but then they

43

thought better of it: such a step would do nothing to help matters.

Boril mastered the art of walking and talking after three days, but all his medical knowledge had evaporated completely from his head. Fortunately, his father's writings had been preserved in his house, as well as Boril's own lesson books. After two weeks, Boril could again cure sick people to some degree.

By this time, Robil was awake. "I'll train him!" said Boril, and, quite understandably, no one offered any objection.

Now that his enemy and rival had been delivered into his hands, the chubby doctor sought to derive as much benefit as possible from the situation. When Robil began to talk and was alert once more, Boril began to make suggestions to him: "Do you know who I am? I'm the celebrated Doctor Boril, luminary of science, your sole mentor and patron, without whom you're doomed to remain forever a dolt and an ignoramus. Do you understand? Now repeat it after me!"

And lanky Robil, bent almost double and looking down from above on his instructor, his eyes filled with admiration, said: "You're the celebrated Doctor Boril, luminary of science, my sole mentor and patron. Without you, I should remain forever a dolt and an ignoramus..."

"Exactly right! Remember that always, and don't listen to anyone who tells you anything different."

The Ministers, who had drunk a larger quantity of the water than anyone else, reawakened simultaneously three months after dropping off to sleep. King Ukonda, who was incensed both at their unauthorized absence from their duties and at their long sleep, ordered that suggestion be made to them that, prior to their sleep, they had been lackeys in the palace. Members of their families, under threat of severe penalty, were forbidden to tell the poor devils anything about their real pasts. This daring experiment was a total success. Both Ministers had for-

44

gotten their past lives completely. Dressed in their livery as lackeys, they ran energetically around the palace with trays; they swept the floors, they cleaned shoes, they served meals...

Chapter 10

A BRILLIANT INSPIRATION

At the time when these strange events were taking place, it was a certain Bellino who stood out among all seven of the Time Keepers in intelligence and integrity. His sound advice was heeded and carried out not only by the other Time Keepers, but by the kings as well.

And now, after the spring of miraculous water had come to light, this Bellino got a remarkable idea into his head. "Suppose we put the kings to sleep during the times when they're not actually ruling?" said Bellino to himself, looking around fearfully as he said it: might someone not have heard him?

At first, this idea seemed impertinent and unfeasible to the Time Keeper, but the more he thought about it, the more he liked it. "Indeed," he reasoned, "right now the people are feeding seven kings and their families, along with seven staffs of courtiers, seven rowdy bands of lackeys, seven detachments of soldiers, and seven gangs of spies. That's over a thousand parasites. But if my idea were put into practice, then the people would only have to put up with 150 or so idlers, while all the others would be in deep and dreamless sleep, without the least worry about their stomachs."

Old Bellino pondered this plan by himself at first, and then he shared his ideas with fat little Doctor Boril. Boril was delighted.

"I swear by all the mustard-plasters in the world!" he exclaimed, "that idea is truly ingenious!" Then he added thoughtfully, "The only thing is, will our monarchs be willing to go to sleep? Well, I know we'll be able to convince them!"

Before they could do anything, it was necessary to investigate all of the Soporific Water's mysterious properties. Bellino set out to do this, along with Doctors Boril and Robil.

They learned that the miraculous water flowed from the rocks but once a month. It filled the small circular basin, remained there for a few hours, and then returned again to the unexplored depths of the earth.

They collected the water in vessels that they had brought into the cave, but it lost its soporific property after twenty-four hours. In order for a person to go to sleep, it was necessary that he drink the magic water quickly after it had appeared.

It was a while before they succeeded in measuring out doses of the water that would put a person to sleep for exactly six months — no more nor less. These experiments took a great deal of time for Bellino and his assistants.

With the permission of the seven kings, who still had no idea of what all this was leading up to, the doctors put some of the artisans and plowmen to sleep. The latter agreed willingly, since a long, quiet sleep would give them a rest from their wearisome labors.

At last the experiments were completed. They had determined and measured off the precise quantity of the magic potion necessary to put an adult male to sleep for exactly half a year. For women, less of the potion was needed, and for children, very little.

Chapter 11

THE SUPREME COUNCIL

When all the preparatory work was complete, Bellino made a request that the kings assemble at the Supreme Council. In accordance with custom, *all* the kings and their families, along with their ministers and their courtiers, attended this Council.

The Round Hall in the Rainbow Palace — the meeting-place of the Supreme Council — offered an extraordinarily colorful spectacle. The hall, which was brilliantly illuminated by garlands of little phosphorescent balls, was divided into seven sections, one for the court staff of each of the kings. And what variety there was in the attire of the Underground Kings and their courtiers!

One section shone with every possible shade of green, from the deepest hues to the palest emerald. In another there was a striking play of red in remarkable combinations. Elsewhere one could see deep indigo and violet, sky-blue, sunny yellow... The very rainbow would have turned pale with envy here, if there had been any way for it to come down from the sky into this huge subterranean hall.

The eye, weary of the monotonous brown, ochre, and dark red shades that predominated in nature in Underground Land, was soothed and pampered by this lush feast of bright color. How clear it was that wise King Carvento had done the right thing two hundred years before when he passed a law mandating that the most colorful patches possible be grafted onto the sparse coloration of Underground Land. In accordance with Carvento's mandate, the walls of houses, the columns that enclosed plots of land, and the road markers were painted in bright turquoise, blue, and pearly shades.

47

The last belated king entered with his wife and two sons, and so it was possible finally to begin the meeting.

With the permission of King Asfeyo, whose turn it was to rule that month, Time Keeper Bellino took the floor. He began by talking about the grievous situation that the country was in. For ever so long now, there had not been enough hands to do all the work; every year, revenue from taxes dwindled more and more, and consequently, it would be necessary to impose limitations on the luxury enjoyed by the royal courts...

"A disgrace! A scandal!" resounded exclamations from the spots where the kings were sitting.

"I agree that it's necessary for us to put an end to this," Bellino concurred calmly, "and it appears that I've found a means of doing so."

"Hmmm, sounds interesting," grunted King Asfeyo. "Let's hear it."

So Bellino expounded his amazing idea. A long, agonizing silence followed, as people thought over how they should react to this outrageous proposal. But Bellino began to tempt the kings with the advantages of the new plan.

"Just think, your Excellencies, how convenient it will be for you! Right now, you rule for one month at a time, and then you languish in idleness for an entire half-year until it's your turn again. As a result, there are all kinds of quarrels and intrigues. But now, the time between one session on the throne and the next will go by as if it were but a minute. Your whole lives will be just one continuous reign, broken only by periods of magical sleep that will pass unnoticed. And you do sleep part of every day as it is!"

"That's a sound notion!" exclaimed one of the kings.

"Of course it's sound." Bellino picked it up, pleased at this show of support. "And along with everything else, I and the esteemed Doctors Boril and Robil" — at which point both doctors stood up and bowed to the assemblage with an air of importance — "we have established that this sleep, though lasting a long time, has no influence whatever on the person's longevity; time merely stands still for him during it. So instead of the sixty years allotted to you by nature, my lords, you will each live four hundred years, with your life-span increasing sevenfold."

Stunned by such an alluring proposal, the members of the Council were silent for a long time. Then King Ukonda cried out with delight: "It's settled! I'll be the first to be put to sleep."

"Why should *you* be the first?" exclaimed King Asfeyo jealously. "My term of rulership expires this week, which means that *I* shall also be the one to be put to rest! You, your Excellencies, will have to wait your turns!"

Queen Rinna asked: "Would the courtiers and lackeys have to be put to sleep as well? It may be that there won't be enough of the magic water to go around for everyone?"

There's enough water," Doctor Boril assured her. "And besides, what would the courtiers, the soldiers, and the spies be doing while their kings were asleep? Coming up with various seditious ideas, perhaps?..."

"No, no!" shouted all the kings and queens with one voice. "Let's put them to sleep, let's put them *all* to sleep!..."

Chapter 12

THE NEW SYSTEM
IN THE CAVERN

The first day when the magical water flowed again, King Asfeyo was put to sleep, along with his entire family, his courtiers, his servants, his soldiers, and his spies.

It was strange to watch: first the king himself, then his wife and children, drank doses of water (which the doctors had measured out precisely) from crystal goblets, and they lay down at once on a soft carpet, overcome irresistibly by sleep. After that came the turns of the courtiers who served him, his soldiers, and his spies. The lackeys of King Ukonda, who had replaced Asfeyo on the throne, joked and laughed as they carried the sleepers off to a special storage area and stashed them away on shelves arranged in several tiers. They sprinkled them with powder to keep moths away, and in order to prevent the sleepers from being bitten by mice — of which there was a multitude in the Land of the Underground Ore-Diggers — they placed in the storage area two tame owls, which took the place of cats in the Cavern.

Month after month passed by — and new parties of sleepers began to fill up new storage places. The land's populace began to feel some relief: there was less demand for their produce at the royal palace, and more was left for the commoners.

But the people realized the full benefit of Bellino's great idea only when half a year had passed, and six of the seven towers in the Rainbow Palace, normally so noisy, had grown quiet and empty, with only one of them yet bubbling with life. Banquets still went on there, music rang out, and drinking songs could be heard, but it was immeasurably easier to live with it now than it had been before, when merriment was being indulged in at all seven royal courts at once.

Bellino the Time Keeper found himself the object of uncommon veneration. Whenever people met him, they would bow down before him, all the way to the ground — an action which, though he was modest by nature, he did nothing to suppress.

Needless to say, Bellino himself did not drink any of the magic potion and fall into the enchanted slumber: he had been given the job of keeping track of the order of

50

succession of the kings. And he did that so well that the people decided: "We don*t need any seven Time Keepers, for they'd only make a mess of things now. Let Bellino alone be our permanent Time Keeper, and let him choose whatever assistants he pleases. When his time comes to pass on, the people will elect a successor for him from among the most honored and respected citizens of Underground Land."

And that's how it was done from that time on.

The most troublesome periods for the Time Keeper and his assistants came on days when the next group of sleepers awakened, and it was necessary to teach them to walk and talk, and to restore their memories, all within some three days...

Then, for that group that had just emerged from their sleep, there followed a month of uninterrupted waking. In their half-year of rest, they had accumulated so much stamina that they had no need to sleep every day, and so they gave the whole month over to pleasure. A banquet would be followed by a Sixpaw hunt, then a long outing, a fishing expedition, a ride on the backs of the winged reptiles, and then another banquet...

The king had no time to govern the country and to issue new laws. The burden of rulership, and all governmental concerns, passed imperceptibly to the Time Keeper, and the kings were left with only their prestige and their titles.

Bellino still took care of the maintenance of the spring, which received the designation "Sacred Spring." Then the very cave in which it was located came to be called the "Sacred Cavern." The basin into which the water flowed was enclosed by a beautiful round tower constructed of multicolored bricks, and guards always manned the entrance to it.

The Soporific Water was declared government property, and anyone who wanted an allotment of this water for himself had to obtain permission from the Time

Keeper and the two doctors, who were Boril's and Robil's descendants. Such occasions occurred when quarrels and dissension broke out in one family or another. Husband and wife would go to sleep for a few months, and when they awakened, the past would all be forgotten.

And so century after century went by in that land, separated as it was from the upper world by an enormous layer of earth and linked with it by a single exit, at which spot trade was carried on between the Ore-Diggers and the residents of Blue Land.

As the ages passed by, the Undergrounders' character changed drastically: they grew suspicious, and fearful of malevolent designs on the part of the surface people. Guards, their bows and arrows in readiness, flew continually beneath the roof of the Cavern on the dragons' backs, on the lookout for enemies.

Centuries passed, and many generations of commoners came and went in Underground Land. In the Rainbow Palace, however, life proceeded with extreme slowness; in seven hundred years, reckoned from the Day of the First Sleep, there were only two complete turnovers in the seven kings, their courtiers, and their servants.

Mentally, these people did not alter throughout all their long lives. When awakening after their latest round of sleep, they had forgotten everything they had previously known, and it all had to be relearned. And how much can really be taught to a person when his entire course of study lasts only three or four days?

The people were already beginning to have doubts as to whether the country even needed these seven kings, who slept and held banquets but did nothing to take care of affairs of state. However, they still felt too much reverence for the monarchs that the people had inherited from their ancestors, and very few of the inhabitants gave any serious thought to the idea of getting rid of the kings and living without them.

Then an unexpected event occurred which destroyed the system that had been established for centuries in Underground Land, and everything was disrupted.

We will relate that in due course, but we must continue first with events that happened before it.

Chapter 13

A FEW MORE PAGES FROM THE HISTORY OF MAGIC LAND

An astounding event took place one day in Magic Land. It occurred exactly three hundred years and four months after Ortega the trapper discovered the Soporific Water in the labyrinth.

There were four sorceresses living in different corners of the continent which, by that time, had already begun to be called America; two of them were good, and the other two were wicked. The good witches were named Villina and Stella, and the wicked ones were Gingema and Bastinda. The two wicked witches were sisters, but they were constantly quarreling and did not want to maintain any contact. Human settlement was moving ever closer and closer to the witches' retreats, and at last the sorceresses, like the mighty Hurricap in an earlier day, decided to change their places of residence.

It's a strange thing that all the fairies should have gotten this same idea into their heads, but stranger things have been known to happen in the world! The witches consulted their magical books, and they all took it in mind to resettle in Magic Land, which was cut off from the rest of the world by a Great Desert and by impenetrable mountains.

Their books likewise told them that the land was inhabited by peaceable little peoples who would be easy to subdue, and that not a single witch or wizard lived there with whom it would be necessary to contest their power.

But the four fairies were unpleasantly surprised when, after reaching Magic Land by different routes (and not forgetting, of course, to bring all their magical belongings with them!), they came face to face with one another.

"This is my country!" screeched Gingema, who was all wizened from her perpetual wickedness. "I was here first!" Indeed, she had preceded her rivals by a whole hour.

"Your appetites are too ravenous, witches," the beauteous Stella, who commanded the secret of eternal youth, remarked derisively. "There's plenty of room for all of us in this huge country."

"I won't share it with anyone, not even my sister Gingema!" declared the one-eyed Bastinda, her black umbrella under her arm. (This umbrella carried the witch around from place to place in the manner of a flying carpet.) "Keep it in mind, fairies, that if it comes to blows, you'll get the worst of it..."

Kindly, white-haired Villina did not utter a word. She drew forth from the folds of her clothing a teeny-weeny little book and blew on it, and the little book expanded into a huge tome. The other witches looked at Villina with awe: they were not able to manipulate their own magic books in this manner, and carried them around just as they were.

Villina began to thumb through the pages of the book, mumbling: "*Africa, apricots, bananas, bandages, bun*... Ah, here it is! *Battle*" The sorceress read several lines to herself, and then she smiled triumphantly. "So you want to fight? All right, go ahead!"

Gingema and Bastinda were cowed. They realized that a direct confrontation would be a serious business, and that in all likelihood, Villina's Magic Book portended defeat for them. So the four fairies settled the matter amicably.

Of course, their books told them that a certain Cavern existed, but none of them wanted to go there. They cast lots, and from this, Gingema received Blue Land; Villina was awarded Yellow Land; Bastinda got Violet Land, while Stella ended up with Rose Land. They left the central region free, so that it would form a buffer between their dominions and they would not have to run into one another so often. The witches even agreed that no one of them would leave her own domain for any length of time, and they took an oath on this. Then they departed — with each of them going in a different direction.

By that time, royal authority in Magic Land survived only in the Cavern: it no longer existed anywhere on the surface. The people had had all they could take of kings, who were constantly quarreling with one another and waging wars. They rose up in revolt and expelled the tyrants. Swords were reforged into sickles and scythes, and the people began to live in peace.

The tribe of people who had previously occupied Blue Land migrated elsewhere, and in their place appeared a diminutive race of people who had the amusing habit of continually moving their jaws, as if they were munching on something. For this reason, they were called Munchkins.

It was an evil day for the Munchkins when the witch Gingema made her first appearance in their land. She climbed up onto a tall rock and began to screech in such a penetrating voice that the residents of all the villages in the area heard her and gathered in response to her summons. Then, looking at the trembling little people, the evil old woman said: "I, the mighty sorceress Gingema, hereby declare myself the ruler of your country. My power is limitless. I can conjure up storms and tornados…"

Disbelief showed on the Munchkins' faces.

"Ah, so you still doubt me?" cried Gingema in a rage. "Well, see for yourselves!"

She spread out the folds of her black cape and began to mumble some words that no one could understand:

Pickapoo, trickapoo! Loricky, yoricky!
Toorabo, foorabo! Scoricky, moricky!

At once a strong wind arose, and black clouds appeared in the sky. The cowed Munchkins fell onto their knees and acknowledged Gingema's authority.

"I won't interfere in your affairs," said the witch. "Sow your grain, and go on raising your chickens and rabbits; but you must pay me tribute: gather mice and frogs, leeches and spiders for me — for those are the delicacies that I dine on."

The Munchkins were dreadfully afraid of frogs and leeches, but Gingema herself was far more dreadful, so they burst into tears and resigned themselves to it.

Gingema picked out a large cave as her dwelling place, and she hung clumps of mice and frogs from the ceiling and summoned the Great Horned Owls that lived in the forest. The Munchkins never even came near the witch's cave.

However, they still needed metals for their scythes, sickles, and plows, as well as precious stones to use for ornament. For this reason, they continued to maintain their trade relations with the Underground Ore-Diggers, and on the appointed days, they gathered by the Market Gate to await the sound of the midnight bell.

The Munchkins never saw the Ore-Diggers themselves. In the course of the centuries, the Diggers had grown so unused to the light of day that they could appear on the surface only in total darkness, when the Munchkins were asleep.

Bastinda had as easy a time as her sister in asserting her authority over Violet Land, home of the peaceable, hard-working Winkies — who had received this designation from the fact that they winked their eyes unceasingly. The witch ordered them to build her a palace, and she holed up inside it with several servants and lived there, unseen by anyone.

The denizens of Yellow Land and Rose Land, however, were fortunate, for their countries were taken over by the kindly Villina and Stella, respectively. These sorceresses did not oppress their people — on the contrary, they helped them in every way possible and endeavored to improve life for them.

And so things continued in Magic Land for centuries on end, and then an event occurred which seemed insignificant at first glance but which was to have portentous consequences.

In America, in Kansas, there lived a loser named James Goodwin. He was not a loser on account of laziness or stupidity — he was merely unlucky in life. No matter what business he undertook, he met with no success. Finally, he bought himself a balloon, and he began to make ascents into the air during carnivals, for the amusement of onlookers, who paid him money for his performances. But on one such occasion, a windstorm came up, and it snapped the rope that was attached to the balloon. The wind seized it and bore it all the way to Magic Land, with Goodwin still in it.

Fortunately for Goodwin, the tornado set him down in the central part of Magic Land, which was free of the sway of the witches. But when the people who ran forward saw that he had come down from the sky, they took him for a mighty wizard. Goodwin was unable to convince them otherwise.

Throughout the next few years, he built a splendid city, trading with the Undergrounders for a multitude of emeralds with which to embellish it. Goodwin named his city the Emerald City, and after construction work on it

57

was completed, he secluded himself away from other people in his magnificent palace and spread the rumor that he was the most powerful wizard in the world and capable of performing the most extraordinary miracles.

To visitors, Goodwin appeared in various outlandish forms, which frightened the people. And his voice, which came from the side in a mysterious manner, said the same thing to everyone: "I am Goodwin, the Great and Terrible. Why do you disturb my wise meditations?"

Goodwin tried his utmost to promote his fame as a mighty wizard, and in this he succeeded admirably, but he made one crucial mistake: he got it in mind to take over Bastinda's domain. The resulting war was a short one. The Winged Monkeys, which the evil fairy had at her beck and call, quickly smashed his army, and they came near to taking Goodwin himself prisoner; but he was able to make an escape. Many years passed after that, and this one failure was forgotten: in fact, even the fairies regarded him as a mighty wizard.

Goodwin was finally exposed by a little girl named Ellie, who had found herself by chance in Magic Land. Here is how it happened.

Chapter 14

ELLIE'S FIRST TRIP TO MAGIC LAND

Ellie and her parents lived on the broad Kansas prairie. A light trailer, whose wheels had been removed and which lay flat on the ground, served as their home. One day, the wicked Gingema decided to destroy the whole human race, and she conjured up a tornado of awesome force, strong enough to carry even to Kansas. But the good

Villina rendered the tornado harmless and allowed it to pick up only the one trailer from the Kansas prairie: her Magic Book told her that this one was always empty whenever a storm was raging.

But even Magic Books don't always know everything: Ellie happened to be in the trailer, for she had run in after her dog, Totoshka. The house was borne away to Magic Land, and it fell down on the head of wicked old Gingema, who had been watching the storm with admiration. The witch perished.

Ellie found herself alone in a strange land, without any friends, unless one counts Totoshka, who suddenly began to talk there in Magic Land, to his young mistress's great surprise.

But to Ellie's aid came Villina, the Good Witch of Yellow Land. She advised the girl to go to the Emerald City to see the great Wizard Goodwin, who would send her back to Kansas, to her Mom and Dad, provided that she — Ellie — helped three creatures attain the fulfillment of their fondest wishes. That is what her Magic Book said. Then Villina disappeared: she flew away back to her own dominion.

While Ellie was talking with Villina, Totoshka, who had been poking about the neighborhood, came upon Gingema's cave, and he removed from there, in his teeth, the beautiful Silver Shoes that were the witch's most prized possession. The Munchkins who had assembled at the place of Gingema's death, assured the girl that there was magic power contained in these shoes, but what it was, they didn't know.

The Munchkins supplied Ellie with provisions; she put on the Silver Shoes, which fit her perfectly, and then she and Totoshka traveled down the Yellow Brick Road to the Emerald City.

In the course of her journey to see Goodwin, Ellie found some new friends. In a wheat-field, Ellie took

Strasheela down from a pole; he was a man of straw, who could walk and talk and whose fondest wish was to receive some sharp brains for his straw-filled head. Strasheela went along with Ellie to the Emerald City, to see Goodwin.

In the deep forest, Ellie and Strasheela rescued an Iron Woodman from destruction. He had been standing for a whole year next to a tree, with his heavy ax still raised, because he had been caught in the rain at a time when his oil-can was back in his hut, and his iron joints had rusted. Ellie fetched the oil-can and oiled the Woodman, and he was good as new. He, too, went along with Ellie and Strasheela to the Emerald City, in the hope that Goodwin would give him a loving heart for his iron breast — for receiving a loving heart was the Woodman's fondest wish.

The next to join this strange company was the Cowardly Lion, whose fondest dream was to acquire courage. He likewise joined Ellie to travel to Goodwin.

On their way to the Emerald City, Ellie and her companions had many perilous adventures: they vanquished an Ogre, contended with the dreadful Saber-Toothed Tigers, crossed a wide river, and found themselves in a Deadly Poppy Field, where Ellie, Totoshka, and the Lion almost went to sleep forever from the scent of the poppies. During this last adventure, Ellie met and became friends with Ramina, Queen of the Field Mice. Ramina gave the girl a magical Silver Whistle, which was to stand her in good stead later.

But they put all these obstacles behind them, and Ellie and her companions arrived at Goodwin's magnificent palace. At the entrance to the City, green spectacles were placed over their eyes, and everything sparkled before them in different shades of green.

Goodwin admitted the strangers to his presence so that they could make their requests, but each was obliged to see him without the others. To Ellie he appeared in the form of an enormous Animated Head, whose voice seemed to be coming from somewhere on the side. The voice said: "I am Goodwin, the Great and Terrible. Who are you, and why do you seek me?"

"I am Ellie, the Small and Meek," replied the little girl. "I have come to you from afar for help."

Ellie told the Head about her adventures, and she asked him for assistance in returning to Kansas, to Mom and Dad. When the Head learned that Ellie was from Kansas, its voice grew almost tender. Yet the Wizard demanded of her: "Go to Violet Land and free its residents from the wicked Bastinda. *Then* I'll send you home."

Goodwin placed this same condition — freeing the Winkies from Bastinda — on Strasheela, the Iron Woodman, and the Lion, when they in turn went in to him to ask him to grant their wishes.

The dejected friends set out for Violet Land, though they had no hopes whatever of defeating the powerful Bastinda. And yet the wicked witch had to go through all her magic before she was able to overcome the dauntless travelers. In obedience to her command, the Winged Monkeys, who were subordinate to her, unstuffed Strasheela, threw the Iron Woodman down into a ravine, and bore Ellie, the Lion, and Totoshka away to the Violet Palace.

There, they languished in captivity for the longest time, with no hope of liberation. And this liberation, when it finally came, was wholly fortuitous. As it happened, the Witch was afraid of water: for five hundred years she had not washed herself or brushed her teeth, and she never let her fingers touch water, because it had been predicted to her that it was water that would be the death of her.

And it came about that Ellie, in her rage, doused Bastinda with a bucket of water when the latter tried to steal the magical Silver Shoes from her. Bastinda melted, and Winkie Land was free of her domination.

The delighted Winkies mended Strasheela's outfit and stuffed him with fresh straw. As for the Iron Woodman, they took him apart and put him back together again, repairing all of his limbs and polishing him to an almost unbearable luster. The Winkies took such a liking to the Woodman that they asked him to become their ruler, and he promised to return to them after Goodwin had given him his heart.

The friends returned victorious to the Emerald City, but Goodwin took his time about carrying out his promises. The indignant company burst into the Throne Room, and there, Totoshka exposed a little old man in striped trousers, concealed behind a screen.

Ellie and her companions were most disappointed when it turned out that this timid little man was Goodwin, the Great and Terrible Wizard. Goodwin told them his story and confessed that for years he had been misleading the people, but he concluded: "I will indeed fill your requests, my friends. I've been a wizard for so many years that I've learned many things."

Goodwin removed Strasheela's head, shook the straw out of it, and filled it with bran, mixing in needles and pins. "Now you have an extraordinarily sharp mind, my friend," said Goodwin, "but you must find out how to use it for yourself."

"I'll find a way to use it, never fear!" cried Strasheela in ecstasy.

Then Goodwin cut an opening in the Woodman's iron breast, suspended within it a red silken heart stuffed with sawdust, and he soldered the hole shut. The heart throbbed inside the cage formed by his breast, and the good soul was moved to delight.

As for the Lion, the sham Wizard gave him a drink of courage from a large platter, and the Lion declared that he had now become braver than all the animals in the world.

In this way, the fondest wishes of the three friends were granted, which meant that the time had come for Ellie to return to Kansas, as predicted in Villina's Magic Book. But this ended in failure, although Villina's book was not at fault.

Goodwin announced that he had had enough of playing the role of Wizard, and that he wanted to return to Kansas with Ellie. For this journey, he fixed up the balloon in which he had first flown to Magic Land. Unfortunately, when the time came, a gust of wind bore the balloon away before Ellie could get in, and the girl was left behind in Magic Land.

Goodwin had put Strasheela the Wise in his place as Monarch of the Emerald City. The new monarch called his friends together, and it was decided that they would travel in a group to see the good witch Stella, in the hope that she would assist them.

And indeed, Stella did assist them. The travelers went through many more dangerous adventures before they even reached her, but, through assisting one another, they were able to overcome them.

Stella revealed to Ellie the secret of the Silver Shoes. It turned out that all one had to do was wish, and the Shoes would take him to any place in the world. "If you had known the Shoes' power," said Stella, "you could have gone back home the very first day the tornado brought you to our country."

"But then I should not have had my wonderful brains and become Monarch of the Emerald City!" cried Strasheela. "I'd still be scaring crows in the wheatfield!"

"And I should not have had my loving heart," said the Iron Woodman. "I should have stood there in the woods and continued rusting until I crumbled to dust."

"And I should still be a coward," said the Lion, "and not have become the King of Beasts."

"I have no regrets that everything turned out this way," said Ellie. "I'm very glad I found you, my dear, faithful friends, and that I helped you in the fulfilment of your fondest wishes."

Then the girl said a tearful farewell to Strasheela the Wise, the Iron Woodman, and the Courageous Lion, and, thanking Stella for her kind help, she clasped Totoshka in her arms and commanded: "Now, Shoes, take me to Kansas, to Mom and Dad!"

Everything melted together before her eyes, and the sun stretched out in the sky like a fiery arc. But before Ellie had time to be frightened, she found herself in the yard before the new house that her father had built to replace the trailer carried away by the tornado.

Ellie's Shoes had been lost during the third and final step that she took toward the house, but there was nothing surprising about that: in Kansas, after all, there's no place for marvels.

Chapter 15

ELLIE'S SECOND TRIP TO MAGIC LAND

During the period when Blue Land was still under the dominion of Gingema, a crafty, malicious joiner named Urfin Jus lived there. He did not like his fellow Munchkins, and he built himself a house in the woods not far from Gingema's cave. Then he went into the witch's service and helped her collect her tribute from the Munchkins.

Several months after Gingema's death, a storm broke out in Magic Land. It dropped the seeds of an unknown plant into Urfin's garden, and the plant quickly filled up all the vegetable patches. The more Urfin tried to get rid of the weeds, the more thickly they grew, so great was their vitality. Finally, Urfin pulled them up by the roots, cut them into small pieces, and dried them out on iron baking trays.

The brown powder that the joiner collected from this turned out to have the power of conferring life. Jus accidentally spilled a pinch of it on a bearskin — and the skin came to life, and began to walk and talk. Urfin brought a wooden clown to life, and it bit its master in the finger.

Jus then conceived an ambitious plan: to construct mighty wooden soldiers, bring them to life, and then, with their help, make himself monarch of Magic Land. Urfin was a skillful joiner, and he made this idea a reality. With his army of Deadwood Oaks, he subjugated first Munchkin Land, and after that the Emerald City itself, which was ruled by Goodwin's successor, Strasheela the Wise.

Urfin found his conquest of the Emerald City far from easy. Strasheela, Din Gior (the Long-Bearded Soldier), Faramant (Guardian of the Gates), and a large number of armed townspeople gallantly repelled every attack by Urfin Jus's Deadwood Oaks. Then Jus turned to cunning. He sent Guamoko, a Great Horned Owl who was one of his supporters, into the City with the mission of winning over a certain traitor that the Owl had previously found among the citizens. The turncoat was the envious and wealthy Ruf Bilan, who had harbored dreams of becoming monarch of the city himself. At night, Ruf Bilan opened the gates to the enemy, and the Emerald City became the foe's prize.

Ruf Bilan received a reward for his treachery: King Urfin made him his Prime Minister. Several other traitors turned up in the city, and Urfin gave them the rank of counselors.

Strasheela and the Iron Woodman became Urfin's prisoners. When they refused to become the self-styled king's vassals, Jus placed them at the top of a lofty tower located not far from the city. There, they would have to remain in captivity until they submitted to Urfin.

But the friends did not even think of submitting. Their good friend, Kaggi-Karr the Crow (the selfsame one who had first advised Strasheela to get himself some good brains) penetrated the bars of the cage to where they were. The captives decided to send the Crow to Kansas to enlist Ellie's aid. Using a needle, the Woodman scratched a letter to Ellie on the leaf of a tree, and Kaggi-Karr set out on the long, perilous journey. She succeeded in finding the girl and delivering the letter to her.

At that time, Anna's brother, the one-legged sailor Charlie Black — a jovial, enterprising man — was staying as a guest on the Smith farm. Ellie became close friends with Uncle Charlie, and she told him about her adventures in Magic Land and confessed secretly that she missed the dear friends whom she had left behind there. Then all at once there came a line to her from them, announcing that Strasheela and the Woodman were in trouble!

Ellie entreated her parents, and they gave her permission to set out again for Magic Land with Uncle Charlie. Ellie also invited Goodwin, who now kept a little grocery store in a nearby town, to come with them, but he refused point blank. "I'm fed up with wizards and witches and everything pertaining to magic!" he said. "I had enough of all that to last me till I die!"

Ellie and Charlie Black set out together, taking Totoshka with them. When they reached the edge of the Great Desert, Uncle Charlie, who was a jack-of-all-trades, took tools from his knapsack and constructed a land-boat with four broad wheels. After raising sail on it, the travelers traversed the desert, though they came near to dying of thirst when they were trapped by Gingema's magic Black Rock. Then they crossed the mountains and found themselves in Munchkin Land. There, Ellie and the Sailor learned for the first time that they were faced with the difficult task of defeating the malign Urfin Jus and his wooden soldiers.

But they were undaunted, and they called on the Lion for assistance and traveled to the Emerald City via the Yellow Brick Road. Ellie and her friends encountered many dangers in the course of this, just as they had the first time around, but the Sailor's resourcefulness helped them to overcome them. When they were near the Emerald City, they found that there was no way to get into it, since it was surrounded by Urfin Jus's soldiers and policemen.

Ellie blew on a little silver whistle, and before her appeared the fairy Ramina, Queen of the Field Mice. Ramina told the little girl that an underground passage began not far away, and that it led right to the prison tower on whose summit Strasheela and the Woodman were confined. But the Queen of the Mice warned Ellie that this passage led past the Land of the Underground Ore-Diggers, and she advised her to be careful and not pry into their affairs.

This warning was well given. Ellie nearly paid for her curiosity with her life when she looked out on the wonders of the underground world through a window that they fortuitously discovered. A guard, flying on a dragon beneath the ceiling of the Cave, shot an arrow at her, and only by a miracle did the girl come out unscathed.

While these events were taking place, Urfin was ruling Emerald Land. But his life was not a happy one. To amuse himself, he arranged banquets, but none of the townspeople attended them, and listening to the obsequious speeches of his ministers got on the king's nerves.

Urfin heard about the arrival in the land of Ellie and her uncle, whom the diminutive Munchkins termed "the Giant from Beyond the Mountains." In preparation for doing battle with the newcomers, Urfin constructed new squads of wooden soldiers, and brought them to life with the magic powder. This work was most exhausting in itself, but then the Powder of Life ran out. In spite of all the vigilance of the policemen and the Deadwood Oaks, Ellie and Charlie Black liberated the Woodman, Strasheela, the Long-Bearded Soldier, and Faramant, Guardian of the Gates, and all of them headed for Violet Land. There, they armed the Winkies and set out with them to take on the wooden army of Urfin Jus. The Sailor's main hopes were placed in a wooden cannon bored out of a stout log, for which Charlie Black himself had prepared the gunpowder.

The cannon did not let them down: its single shot decided the outcome of the battle. The wooden soldiers were afraid of fire, and when burning rags and red-hot coals rained down upon their heads, the Deadwood Oaks fled in panic.

Urfin Jus fell into captivity. He was tried and sent into exile. The warlike Deadwood Oaks were transformed into gentle, dedicated workers when, at Strasheela's suggestion, their savage countenances were replaced by happy, smiling faces.

The disloyal townspeople who had served Urfin Jus were punished, but the biggest traitor of all, Prime Minister Ruf Bilan, disappeared somewhere.

And once again Ellie Smith, the little girl from Kansas, said goodbye to her devoted friends...

Chapter 16

CATASTROPHE

Ruf Bilan was running. His short, fat legs were wobbling, and his breath burst with a wheeze from his wide-open mouth. A lantern swayed back and forth in Ruf's trembling hand, feebly lighting the path before him.

If he could only stop and rest!... But the heavy footsteps of the Iron Woodman resounded behind him. Overwhelming fear drove the fugitive along once more.

Chapter 16: CATASTROPHE

News of the decisive engagement and the defeat of the wooden army had been conveyed to Ruf Bilan by fleet-footed policemen who had fled from the field of battle. The other royal counselors, Bilan's colleagues, had decided to make their peace with the people and to beg for leniency. But their misdeeds were insignificant compared to Ruf's crime. How could he ever hope for mercy for his detestable treason? So Ruf Bilan determined to go into hiding.

But not one person in all Magic Land would shield Bilan from the wrath of the people. "I'll hide in the underground passageway," decided Bilan.

The traitor was in such a hurry to leave the city that he took along nothing to eat, and grabbed only a lantern with an oil-lamp inside: after all, it was perpetually dark in the underground passage.

Ruf Bilan stole furtively into the basement of the tower, on the upper platform of which the Woodman and Strasheela had been held in captivity. This basement was separated from the tunnel by a solid door. But Charlie the Sailor had sawn an opening in this door when he, along with Ellie and her friends, had come here to set the prisoners free. The Woodman and Strasheela had made their way to freedom through this opening, and the plump Ruf Bilan squeezed through it with difficulty now.

The fugitive hurriedly kindled a flame, lit the wick of the lamp, and plunged into the blackness of the tunnel. Before long, he heard the heavy tread of the Iron Woodman behind him. "Come back here, you madman!" the latter called out. "There are monsters in the Cave! Destruction awaits you!..."

But to someone as blinded by fear as Ruf Bilan was, anything would be preferable to returning to the City that he had betrayed to the enemy. Sheer terror drove him on and on, and finally, noticing an opening in the wall of the underground passage, Ruf rushed into it without even thinking. A narrow, winding tunnel opened up before him, and Ruf Bilan, trying not to make any noise, crept further and further. He could no longer hear the footsteps and voice of the Iron Woodman: the latter had clearly lost the fugitive's trail.

"I'm safe!" gasped Ruf Bilan, and he tumbled down onto the rocky floor and lost consciousness.

The lantern fell from his hand, and the lamp flickered and went out, leaving Bilan enveloped in impenetrable darkness.

Ruf Bilan awoke. He could not tell if he had been lying there unconscious for a long time or not, but his arms and legs had grown numb, and it was with difficulty that he rose to his feet. But now he understood completely the horror of his situation. He was all alone, without any food and water, and he would soon be without light as well, because the supply of oil in the lamp was barely enough to last three or four hours...

"I'll go back and give myself up," decided Bilan. "That way, I may have a chance of staying alive, while here, I'll die of hunger and thirst in excruciating agonies..."

He lit the lantern and began to walk. But after his fainting spell, Ruf Bilan no longer knew which direction was the right one, and he was no longer approaching the main passage that he had left, but walking away from it. He realized this some time later, when the narrow passage suddenly widened and opened out into an extensive circular cavern, in whose walls several more openings could be seen.

Without even taking time to think about what he was doing, the fugitive walked into the center of the cavern and took a look about. "I wasn't here before," said Ruf to himself, and the weak sound of his voice, echoing from the walls again and again, became unexpectedly booming. "That means I took the wrong direction. But what passage did I come through to get here?" His blood froze now in dread — for he could not recognize which corridor he had just come out of!

70

Since he had lost the faculty of thinking it out, Ruf Bilan headed into the first opening that struck his eyes. Ten minutes of frantic running brought him to a bare wall: the passage was a dead end!

When Ruf had returned to the now-familiar cavern, the first thing he did was to place a rock by the opening that he had just emerged from. "I'll mark every passage I go into," said Bilan. "At least then I won't pass one and the same way twice..."

After resting for a few minutes, he plunged deeply into the corridor next to the first one. When this passage divided in two, the fugitive chose the right branch. But it wasn't long before Ruf was again called upon to select one of two directions. The further he walked, the more intricate became the interweaving pattern of wide and narrow passages, high and low ones, and straight and winding ones. These passageways connected caverns together, some of which resembled enormous banquet halls, so lofty that the feeble light of the lantern would not reach to the top; others reminded him of round bowls with water in the bottom, while still others were heaped with mineral deposits that had dripped from the ceilings...

Several hours were spent in aimless wandering. How many? Bilan didn't know, but he did notice that the lamp in the lantern was beginning to go out: the oil was almost gone. The fugitive now faced the worst ordeal possible: traveling in a totally dark labyrinth, being able to move only by crawling on all fours, feeling his way with his hands...

Then Bilan unexpectedly encountered something new there, below the ground: his way was barred by a wall constructed of multicolored bricks.

The work of human hands! That meant that there were people in this mysterious labyrinth! And they might even be here now and would rescue the wanderer from death.

Ruf Bilan stopped. The faint sound of voices reached him from behind the barrier. Yes, no mistake about it, there were people here, and they would help him... Ruf took a look around: a rusted pickax that the bricklayers had forgotten about lay to the side.

Intoxicated with joy, and with strength born of desperation, the fugitive began to chop a hole in the brick barrier. "Faster, faster!" he thought. "I've got to get in there! The people will leave, and I'll be left all alone in this impenetrable blackness..."

Indeed, the wick of the lamp did sputter and go out, and darkness did envelop Bilan. But at that very moment, the wall gave way beneath his violent blows; he heard the bubbling sound of water flowing, and then loud shouts.

Before Ruf Bilan spread a small round chamber, illuminated weakly by miniature phosphorescent globes that hung down from the ceiling. Bilan saw a basin in the floor of the chamber, and it was rapidly draining. A door opened on the opposite side, and in ran three men wearing sharp-pointed caps with lights attached to them. The men's faces were pale, and, filled with alarm, they looked at Ruf with enormous black eyes.

"Woe!" shouted one of the Undergrounders. "The Sacred Spring has emptied!"

Ruf Bilan shuddered. He didn't understand yet what he had done, but he felt a chill. It was evident that he had committed some serious crime, and that the threat of punishment was upon him.

"Who are you, and how did you get in here?" asked one of the newcomers in a stern voice; he was no doubt their leader, judging by his imperious deportment.

"I'm an unfortunate exile from the upper world," replied Bilan, trembling. "I was being pursued, and the threat of death was hanging over me, so I hid in this tunnel."

"We know that the surface-dwellers believe in justice," the leader of the guards observed astutely, "and you must have committed some evil deed if such a punishment awaited you."

"Yes, exactly so!" Bilan confessed, and he fell to his knees. "I aided an enemy in gaining admittance to my native city, which they were besieging without success."

"Ah, so you're a traitor!" exclaimed the leader contemptuously. "And to that one heinous crime you've just added a second one here: you've fouled up the basin of the Soporific Water at the very moment when the water was rising up from the bowels of the earth."

"Ah, woe is me! woe is me!" Ruf Bilan began to moan. "I was in my second day of wandering through the labyrinth, and all hope of rescue was fading, when suddenly I heard the sound of your voices. Don't you understand?... I lost my head!"

"I'm afraid you'll be losing it permanently," quipped the leader gravely. "I'm taking you now to King Mentaho, outsider! And you, my friends," he added, turning to his subordinates, "stay here and keep an eye on the spring. And one of you speed straight to the city if water should appear again. Only I fear that's not going to happen..."

"Go ahead, Renyo," answered the ones remaining behind. "Everything will be taken care of."

Chapter 17

THE ROAD TO THE CITY

The passageway through which Renyo was leading his captive, divided into two from time to time. Ruf Bilan noted that whenever this happened, the commander of the guards directed his steps by following arrows painted in red on the corridor walls. "If only I'd noticed those marks," thought Ruf Bilan, "perhaps I'd have been able to get out of the labyrinth without destroying that confounded wall. But why do they set such great store by that water?"

Had Ruf Bilan known at that moment how vital the Soporific Water was for life in Underground Land, the hair on his head would have stood straight up in fright. But the thing was still a mystery to him, and thus he felt some degree of calm as he walked along, hoping that he might yet manage to extricate himself from this situation.

"The Underground Ore-Diggers have no right to punish me for things I did above ground," the traitor reasoned. "And as for the wrecked basin... What's the big deal about that?... I can repair it with my own hands..."

The road sloped downward, growing ever steeper and steeper. They frequently found themselves descending staircases, stone steps that had been chiseled by human hands. The way was a long one.

Presently, the floor of the passageway leveled off; its walls opened out, the glow of the ball on Renyo's hat dimmed, and a feeble light materialized in front of them, similar to the twilight that comes when the day is done. Ruf Bilan beheld a colossal cavern, illuminated by golden clouds swirling about high above. Hamlets were visible here and there on hilltops, and in the distance, a city enclosed by a wall could be vaguely discerned.

"So *this* is what it's like, the legendary Underground Land that I heard so many amazing tales about when I was a child!" said Bilan to himself. Addressing his guide, he said: "Tell me, my esteemed Renyo, what's the name of this city you're taking me to?"

But instead of an answer, he received a shove in the chest, a shove so violent that he was barely able to keep his footing. "If life has any value for you, you won't go asking questions about anything," said Renyo menacingly. "In our country, the lowly do not have the right to ask questions of the highborn."

Ruf Bilan's old arrogance began to stir within him. He wanted to counter with a haughty remark about the exceptionally high standing he had enjoyed in the surface world, but he caught himself in time. "It's evident that here, I'll have to rely solely on my eyes and my ears," thought Bilan, and he began to look about attentively.

He saw many interesting things. The road ran through fields, and here and there it wound around hills. It was bordered by small columns set up along the roadside, painted in shades of bright green, blue, and gray. How pleasant it was to rest his eyes on these after seeing the faded, gloomy colors in the passage...

In one of the fields, which came right up to the road, plowing was in progress. A beast with six legs was harnessed to an enormous plow. Ungainly as its steps were, it was pulling the plow with ease, and broad layers of earth were rolling aside beneath the plowshare. Behind the plow plodded a plowman wearing a burlap jacket and rolled-up trousers, and walking barefoot. On his head was a green cap topped with a tassel. A second farmer was leading the Sixpaw by its bridle, turning it around when the plow reached the outer edge of the plot.

This sight astonished Ruf Bilan: in the upper world, he had never even suspected the existence of such outlandish beasts. Ruf wanted to ask his guide if they had many such tame beasts in their domain, but he recalled his recent lesson in etiquette, and he bit his tongue.

Then he saw a sight that made him turn numb with terror and drop to the ground with a shriek. An enormous dragon with a slippery white belly and yellow eyes the size of tea-saucers, flapping its mighty webbed wings noisily, was swooping down on them from above. A man wearing a leather suit and a green beret was seated on the creature's back.

The man flying toward them on the reptile had a long bow and a quiver of arrows on his back, while in his hand he held a spear. His long, pale face with its hooked nose stared at them severely.

Ruf Bilan could tell that this was an overseer charged with keeping his eye on the workers, because no sooner had he made his sudden appearance than the two plow-men, who had been taking a break in the middle of the field, jumped up and went back to work. The overseer rebuked them soundly for their laziness, then flew away. At this same time, a second reptile with a man on its back flew into view high up among the clouds.

Renyo conducted his prisoner through the Cavern for a good two hours, but the twilight never ceased. The clouds continued to glow up above, the horizon looked as gloomy as ever, and up there on the hilltop, the city loomed dark — the city that the two foot-travelers were now approaching.

The fields came to an end, and the terrain became rocky and elevated. On the left side of the road there appeared a structure which turned out to be a long embankment fitted up with toothed wheels and large pulleys. Ruf Bilan, in spite of his dismal frame of mind, could not help smiling when he saw that this complex system was in motion through the actions of two Sixpaws walking one behind the other. Heavy buckets of ore were inching up from the depths of a mine, above which a hoist had been erected, and these buckets were being dumped out in a large cart, with tremendous din. Ruf Bilan observed a Sixpaw harnessed to the cart, and as it waited there calmly for the loading to be finished, it was amusing itself by shaking its big round head.

Chapter 18

THE KING'S JUDGMENT

The city lay beside a broad lake enclosed by level banks. As they walked along the bank, Ruf Bilan was convinced once again of the Undergrounders' inventiveness. In the water, they had set up enormous wide-bladed wheels, far removed from one another. The wheels were rotating, because a Sixpaw was clambering upward from blade to blade, trying to escape being overtaken by the rising water. The beast was tired and was breathing heavily, and clouds of foam were issuing from its wide-open mouth.

"It serves you right, you miscreant!" Renyo turned maliciously in the creature's direction. "You mauled your drover, so now you're pumping water for the City of the Seven Monarchs!"

"Aha! so *that's* what they call your city!" Bilan gloated to himself. "Clearly, a person can learn a lot here by keeping his ears as wide open as possible. Now I know that your country is divided into seven regions, and each of them has its own king. Your kingdoms can't be very large!"

The little group stopped at the city gate. The walls of the stronghold were composed of bricks that had turned brown with the passage of time. Renyo pulled on a rope hanging down from above. The moment the sentry on duty recognized the escort, he opened the gate and admitted the newcomers. He looked with great curiosity on the outlander, but he did not dare ask any questions.

"This means that Renyo must be senior to him in rank," Ruf Bilan decided.

The city was not large. Its winding little streets were lined with houses painted in quaint fashion, with tall, narrow windows and strong doors. Curious women in green bonnets were looking out these windows, and they riveted their eyes on the stranger.

The street led them to a central square, and in the midst of the square rose the palace with its seven towers. Ruf Bilan saw before him three adjoining walls, painted in hues of blue, indigo, and violet, hues of such amazing brilliance that the colors began to dance before his eyes.

Each facet of the building had its own attractive portico with a massive door. It seemed strange to Bilan that there was no traffic in their vicinity, and that the doors were tightly shut. "Could it be that no one lives there?" thought Ruf.

Above each door hung an hourglass of unusual construction, an hourglass unlike any that Ruf Bilan had ever seen in the upper word. There, wealthy people had hourglasses, but they had servants to look after their progress. When all the sand had flowed from the upper section down into the lower, the servant inverted the hourglass and announced the time in a loud voice.

Here, however, there were two glass funnels connected with one another, fastened vertically over a large circular dial. It's unlikely that Ruf Bilan would have understood how this clock worked, but as chance would have it, the last grains of sand flowed from the upper section into the lower just as he was passing by the indigo door; when that happened, the apparatus inverted itself with no outside assistance, and the dial moved one division from the right to the left, so that the arrow affixed to the hourglass now pointed to the next hour. A bell tolled softly inside the clock. "These Undergrounders are amazing craftsmen," thought Bilan with admiration.

They passed by the indigo wing of the palace, and Bilan surmised: "There's a violet wall before us now, then a red one, an orange one, a yellow one, and a green one, the way we're heading now. It's evident that Mentaho, to

78

whom they're taking me now, is the Green King — that's clear from the color of these people's caps."

Ruf Bilan was not mistaken in his assumptions. They took him to the green portico, and Renyo conducted his prisoner into the green reception area, passing a sentry dressed in a green tunic.

There were no windows in the vast reception hall, but it was brightly illuminated by shining globes located beneath the ceiling and on the ceiling itself. Courtiers, dressed in stylish green outfits and wearing caps adorned with precious gems, were strolling about the hall.

The moment the courtiers set eyes on this person, who was unlike anything that had ever been seen in Underground Land before, the courtiers dashed over to Renyo and began to bombard him with questions. They had the right to do so, since they ranked higher than Renyo. The Guardian of the Spring said: "My lords, I have no time to talk with you — I must report to the king at once about a dreadful occurrence. The Sacred Spring has just been damaged, and the water flowed directly back into the ground."

Exclamations filled the air. "But that's impossible!" "Our section is due to go into sleep tonight!" "What's going to happen now?"

Renyo turned to one of the courtiers, a stately older man with a gray moustache and beard: "Lord Minister Coriente, please go quickly and request an audience for me with his Majesty."

Coriente disappeared at once. A few minutes later, a door swung open at the other end of the reception hall, and a haughty Master of Ceremonies announced: "His Underground Majesty, King Mentaho, commands that the captive outsider be brought to the throne room of the Rainbow Palace!" Ruf Bilan followed timidly behind the courtier.

Phosphorescent globes — gathered into clusters, hanging in strings, and affixed in chandeliers — provided the throne room with remarkably bright illumination, yet they did not hurt the eyes, and the strange lamps did not cast shadows of any object. There was no heat from any of them — they shone with a cold light.

Later, Ruf Bilan learned that every dwelling in Underground Land had shining globes like these, for the windows admitted too little light into the houses. The number of phosphorescent lamps bespoke the person's wealth. In the houses of the aristocrats, they numbered in the dozens, while the pauper's hovel shone dimly with but a single globe the size of a cherry.

Bilan would discover these things at a later date, but right now, he turned his eyes toward the far end of the hall. There, on a dais, lay the royal throne. On an enormous divan with a multitude of carved ornamentation sat a tall, stout man with a large, shaggy head. A robe embroidered with green flowers hung down from his shoulders. Bilan's frightened gaze was riveted to the king's face.

"Tell me everything, and don't hold anything back!" commanded Mentaho sternly.

Bilan, embarrassed and stumbling on every word, told him of the position that he had boasted in the Emerald City, how he had fled to the world underground to escape punishment, and what he had been up to in the Labyrinth.

Mentaho listened, frowning more and more as he did so, and then he spent a long time lost in thought. A silence fell over the hall, and even the courtiers ceased their whispering: everyone realized that the man's fate hung in the balance.

"Here is my verdict," said the king at last. "You did behave despicably toward your fellow-countrymen, but the doings of the upper world do not concern us. However, you have damaged our Sacred Spring. That is a dreadful misfortune, and it's difficult as yet to foresee all the consequences of this. Such a crime, if committed by any Undergrounder, would have warranted his execution. But you are not an inhabitant of the Cavern, and you com-

80

mitted your evil deed in ignorance of the death penalty. For this reason, it would be unjust to put you to death..."

Ruf Bilan was about to give out a cry of exhilaration. "I'm going to live! I'm going to live!" He experienced a fleeting sensation of ecstasy.

"I'll even give you a position at court," continued Mentaho, "so that you won't be eating our bread for nothing. But don't think that you'll be obtaining the rank of courtier merely because you were administrator to Urfin Jus. I hereby designate you assistant to the fourth lackey, and you will lodge with the palace servant staff..."

The traitor fell at the king's feet and began to kiss his embroidered emerald slippers. Mentaho drew his feet back squeamishly and grumbled, "This person has the heart of a lackey, and his true place is among the servants."

Ruf Bilan emerged from the throne room beaming. The main thing was that he was still alive, and now he could endeavor, whatever it might cost him, to scramble to the top of this little world.

Chapter 19

CHAOS

On the day when the Spring of the Soporific Water dried up, and in the days that followed, there was a mighty commotion in the City of the Seven Monarchs. King Mentaho, his family, and his court were due to go into their sleep, but the magic water had flowed back into the bowels of the earth, apparently never to return.

Mentaho's children wandered after their father in a little file, whining: "Daddy, daddy, we want to go to sleep!"

"Go to sleep, then!" answered their father in vexation.
"But we don't have the water..."
"So go to sleep without the water!"
"We can't..."

And indeed they couldn't — nor could their parents, nor any of the courtiers and servants. They were unable to sleep in the ordinary manner because, in the course of centuries, they had never gone to sleep except by magic.

People exhausted by lack of sleep followed in droves behind Time Keeper Rujero and his assistants, beseeching them to find some way out of the dilemma. But the latter merely brushed them aside: Rujero was having a hard enough time of it instructing the court of King Arbusto, which had just awakened. They could not lose even one hour now, because little attention had been paid to the newly-reawakened during the first days, and they had remained total idiots... "It's about time!" sighed Rujero when he heard King Arbusto say: "Daddy, Mommy, give, me, hot..."

But nature took its course at last: after four days of sleeplessness, sleep of the normal variety began to come to King Mentaho, his family, and his court. But not a single room in the palace had any beds in it — as we know, people put to sleep by the Soporific Water had been sheltered in special storage rooms. But not everyone who succumbed to sleep was able to go there now. People fell asleep wherever they happened to fall, in the most curious postures. One snored away while sitting in a chair with his head hanging down, another was in a standing position, leaning against the wall, while a third curled up right on the doorstep... The green section of the palace looked just like a fairy-tale kingdom that had been enchanted.

When these occurrences had been reported to Rujero, he came and gazed upon this laughable sight. "At long last, they'll be leaving me alone!" said the Time Keeper with a smile. "Now they'll be just like other people. The only thing I'm afraid of..."

But whatever else Rujero was afraid of, he didn't say: he merely hastened to go and take care of King Arbusto.

The two kings, Mentaho and Arbusto, met one another after Mentaho had caught up on his sleep and Arbusto was still undergoing his course of treatment. Each of the monarchs had been around in the world for about three hundred years, but not once had they ever met... Whenever one of them went into his sleep, the other was already awake, his mind that of an infant. They now confronted one another in the throne room, with all their courtiers present, and they exchanged glances that were full of curiosity.

"Greetings, your Majesty!" said Mentaho first. He was a little younger, about thirty years or so.

"Greetings, your Majesty!" mumbled Arbusto. "I'm very happy to meet you. We're related in some way or other, though not very closely. Wasn't your grandfather second cousin to my mother's uncle?"

"No, my grandmother was grand-niece to your father's aunt... But if anyone really wants to understand all the fine points, let him go digging in the old chronicle books for himself..."

"Absolutely!" said Arbusto in agreement. "We'll simply call each other brothers — after all, we're both descended from the glorious Bofaro. Are we agreed, brother Mentaho?"

"Agreed, brother Arbusto!" And the kings shook each other's hands amid general approbation.

To celebrate this congenial new fellowship, a lively banquet was held in the palace, with the retinues of both kings taking part. Rujero the Time Keeper was also present at the feast. Everyone in turn offered him goblets of wine, but the old man pushed them to the side, stroking his white beard sullenly.

Chapter 20

THE SITUATION GROWS
MORE INVOLVED

As the next few months went by, what had been troubling the wise Rujero became all too clear. One after the other, the kings and their courts awakened, and one after another, the sections of the Rainbow Palace that had previously been empty and hushed, came alive. No magic water was forthcoming, and so there was no way of putting the kings back to sleep after they had finished ruling.

Ruf Bilan, who had shattered the centuries-old system of Underground Land, was now serving as a lackey in the Green Section under King Mentaho. He kept himself quieter than water and lower than a blade of grass, and he performed all his duties with uncommon fervor, striving to avoid catching the eye of the king and his grandees. "It'll mean calamity for me," thought Bilan, "if they should be reminded that I'm the cause of all this turmoil."

One morning, the Manager of Bread Bakeries came to see Lasampo, Minister of Stores to King Mentaho. "I have the honor to report to your Excellency," he began despondently, "that the reserve of flour that's left to me will last only three weeks. If we don't get a replenishment, it'll be necessary to close down the bakeries and confectioners' shops."

"Replenishment! replenishment!" the Minister interrupted him with annoyance. "Where are we going to get one?"

"I was thinking," murmured the official, "that we'll have to hold Market Day ahead of schedule..."

"You're out of your mind!" howled the Minister. "What a market day that would be! Have you forgotten that we've already traded away everything we had available, and that we've got no new goods ready yet?"

"Then what are your instructions, your Excellency?"

"Just get out of here!"

No sooner had the bewildered official withdrawn than in walked the Inspector of the warehouse where dairy products were stored.

"Your Excellency," he began with a confused air, "I have only enough butter and cheese in my storehouses to last two weeks."

"And what do you expect me to do?"

"Well... maybe... at your command..." the frightened Inspector mumbled.

"Here is what I command! Butter is to be denied to the confectioners! No butter is to be given to military cooks Provisions are to be refused to the spies altogether!"

"But they'll die of hunger... Who'll get after the dis-contented? And there are more and more of those all the time..."

"That is a problem... All right, put the spies on half rations, as long as they can drag their feet. Is that under-stood?"

"It's understood, your Excellency," replied the Inspec-tor as he backed toward the door.

He ran into the Royal Wine-Scooper. The Minister fell down in a faint the moment he saw the consternation in the latter's face.

"You too?" asked the Inspector of Dairy Products, his voice low.

"Yes," responded the Wine-Scooper, his voice equally low. "There's only enough wine left for a week."

They set about reviving Lasampo, and the moment the latter had regained his senses, he dashed off to see the ministers of the other kings. It became apparent that the same catastrophic situation obtained everywhere with regard to provisions, and it was decided to convoke the Supreme Council. This had not been summoned for centuries, and everyone had forgotten how it was done. They had to turn to the ancient chronicles.

The Council was presided over by Barbedo, the king who was reigning that month. He turned the floor over to Rujero the Time Keeper.

Rujero stood silent for several minutes, looking over the participants at the council and at their outfits shining in all colors of the rainbow. His face was somber. At last he spoke: "Your Majesties, my Lord Ministers, Courtiers! You are all aware of the grievous situation that arose in our land when the Soporific Water ceased flowing. It is with sorrow that I must report to this assembly of the distinguished, that all excavations by our craftsmen have proven fruitless. The Sacred Spring has dried up forever." The speaker paused to catch his breath.

King Barbedo said: "You're talking about things that everyone already knows. It would be better to report on something new."

Rujero continued his speech: "Our misfortune lies in the fact that we have too many mouths to feed, and that our workers are totally insufficient to keep up with them. I have read in the ancient chronicles that it was thus also before the Day of the First Sleep. At that time, the people likewise could not feed the kings and their courts. The Soporific Water saved the situation by reducing the number of idlers by a factor of seven..."

"What are you suggesting?" cried the Minister Coriente sarcastically. "That we kill off all the extra people?"

"Why kill them?" countered the Time Keeper calmly. "They can just as easily feed themselves. Each of the seven kings has his own staff of ministers, counselors, and courtiers, totaling no fewer than half a hundred people. They help their monarch run the government only one month out of seven, and for the remaining six months they live in idleness. Why can't there exist but one staff, which would transfer its loyalty from one king to the next with each change of monarch? That would mean the immediate release of three hundred pairs of helping hands, which are so badly needed in the fields and factories..."

Rujero's outrageous proposal dumfounded the members of the Council. Many of them leaped to their feet right where they sat, to voice their objection to it. A dreadful uproar ensued. The kings' relatives were particularly enraged — all the uncles, cousins, and nephews. But the law prohibited anyone from interrupting a speaker until he had finished all that he had to say.

King Mentaho restored order, and Rujero continued: "If my proposal should be adopted, the kings could release the greater part of their palace attendants, which now overcrowd the palace and wait not only on the kings and their families, but also on the ministers and courtiers. And I think that when this is done, there will no longer be any need for men-at-arms and spies, for all grounds for discontent among the people will have vanished. I have calculated that no fewer than six hundred idlers could be put to useful work. And when all these parasites stop living for free off the land, then our resources will be more than enough."

As Rujero concluded his ardent and convincing speech, a storm of indignation broke loose in the hall. Ministers and courtiers shouted and waved their fists, and cries like the following rang out: "The very idea of us walking behind a plow, us, the descendants of the glorious Bofaro!" "Roasting beside the smelting ovens!" "Giving up the privileges we've inherited from our ancestors and joining the ranks of the common people!" "The Time Keeper is out of his mind!"

After Rujero had finished, many of the ministers and counselors had their say. Every one of them rejected the Time Keeper's plan, and they held forth that what was really needed was to get more work out of the craftsmen and the farmers. If the factory workers put in more of an effort, they would produce more goods, and it would be possible to trade them for more provisions from the surface-dwellers. And there was no way the men-at-arms and the spies could be dismissed, for they alone could keep the people in subjection.

The last orator's presentation was interrupted by an unexpected event. The head of the city's men-at-arms burst into the throne room and said, gasping for breath: "Your Majesties! A courier has just flown in with the news that two outsiders are approaching the City of the Seven Monarchs!"

The meeting adjourned at once. Amid shouts, shoves, and bickering, the kings and the courtiers dashed out of the palace. The robust Mentaho rushed along in front of all the others.

A motley crowd ran out through the gates, and then everyone stood still in amazement. Two individuals were approaching the city: a tall, dark-haired boy; and a little girl clasping to her breast a shaggy little beast of a species never before seen.

Part II

AN EXTENDED OUTING

Chapter 21

A LETTER

After her victory over malign and crafty Urfin Jus, Ellie Smith said goodbye to her loyal friends Strasheela, the Iron Woodman, and the Lion, and then Uncle Charlie transported her back over the Great Desert in his land-boat. That boat was waiting for its passengers by Gingema*s Black Rock, and it was in perfect working order.

The return journey passed without incident, because the Black Rocks could detain only those who were heading *toward* Magic Land. They posed no obstacle to those who were *leaving* it.

Mrs. Anna hugged her daughter, once Ellie was home again. "Well, my child," she said, "I hope you aren't planning to leave us any more? We were so worried about you, and we expected..."

But John Smith mumbled, as he puffed on his pipe: "You've had enough of these magical adventures, and it's time to get to work. A school has opened two miles from us, and you're going to go there. Friendship with fairies and other magical beings may be delightful, but it's no substitute for an education."

Charlie Black the one-legged Sailor sat down at the table with his relatives as they celebrated, and he boasted about the huge emerald that he had received as a gift from Strasheela the Wise. "What do you think, John, is it valuable or is it valuable?"

John Smith examined the stone from all sides, and he weighed it in the palm of his hand. "Yes," he said, "I think a jeweler would hand out quite a few jingling coins to you for this bauble."

"Now I'm going to make my long-time dream come true," admitted Charlie the Sailor. "I'm going to buy myself a schooner and go visit my old friends on Kuru-Kusu. I swear by the hurricane, they're capital fellows! I'm only sorry that I'll have to say goodbye to Ellie. For some strange reason, it's not acceptable for little girls to work on board ships, or else I'd take her with me."

Ellie's eyes were already beginning to sparkle with tears, but Mrs. Anna angrily assailed her brother. "Don't you even *say* what you've been thinking about!"

"All right, all right, Sis, don't get excited. I'll stay with you for another week and then I'll be off."

But many weeks went by before Charlie Black succeeded in tearing himself away from the Smiths. His niece simply would not let him go, such close friends had they become in the course of their perilous trip to Magic Land. The day came at last, though, when they had to part, and Ellie tearfully accompanied her uncle to the stagecoach stop.

Ellie attended school for several months, tackling all the intricacies of arithmetic and grammar. Then came summer vacation, and at that time, a letter arrived at the farm.

People rarely wrote to the Smiths, and whenever the Smiths did receive a letter, it was a big event. John turned the envelope over and over in his hands for a long time before breaking the seal. And when he looked at the signature, he exclaimed rapturously: "It's from Bill Canning! It's really been ages since my cousin has brought himself to drop me a line!"

"Read it! Read it, quick!" Mrs. Anna urged her husband.

The letter told of the Canning family's long migrations around the country. Bill had worked as a miner, a fruit-picker in California, a road-builder, and now he had gotten himself hired as a shepherd on a farm in the state of Iowa. Ellie had no reason to pay attention to these details, but the end of the letter forced her to prick up her ears.

"Let your daughter Ellie come and visit us during her vacation," wrote Bill Canning. "I dare say she hasn't forgotten her old playmate, my tall, lanky Freddy. The country around us is very picturesque, and the kids can have a great time..."

Ellie did indeed remember Fred. She had gotten to know him about five years before, when the Cannings were staying over with them during one of their moves. Ellie's memory retained the image of a blue-eyed boy about two years older than she. He had thought up all sorts of games involving hunters, Indians, and soldiers. These games often ended with Ellie's nose broken or her dress torn, but she never whimpered, nor did she complain about him to the grownups.

"Mom! Dad!" exclaimed the girl. "Let me go visit the Cannings! Fred is so nice, and he's a lot of fun!..."

"Ah, my child, you just can't stay in one place, can you?" said John.

Her parents grumbled, but they consented to send the little girl to Iowa.

Ellie's preparations did not take her long. In her knapsack — the same one that she had taken with her on her journey to Magic Land — the girl packed two or three dresses, some underclothing, a towel, a bar of soap, and several picture-books.

Her mother prepared some food for her to take along: bread, fried chicken, some pastries, a bottle of sweet iced tea, and, of course, some bones for Totoshka. How could the little dog possibly stay at home when his mistress was setting out on a long journey?

John Smith drove Ellie and Totoshka to the stagecoach stop, and he turned them over to the care of the coachman and said goodbye to them. The girl was to return home in a month.

Chapter 22

HOSPITALITY

The coachman had been kind enough to Ellie to detour three whole miles off the main road and drive the girl all the way to the farm where Bill Canning was employed.

Hearing the clatter of wheels, a boy wearing shorts and a checked shirt came running out of a cottage that had a thatched roof and two little windows that admitted very little light. He was Fred Canning. He dashed over to the carriage and assisted Ellie, who had almost been rocked to sleep after her three-day journey, in stepping down. "Hey, cousin!" cried Freddy joyfully, "how you've grown! So you decided to come here after all? I was so sure that the very idea of leaving home would be unthinkable for you."

The tall, slender boy picked up Ellie's baggage and headed for the cottage. Ellie thanked the coachman from the bottom of her heart for taking such good care of her, and then she followed behind her cousin. Totoshka jumped about playfully.

Fred continued to chatter: "Well, Ellie, you're really remarkable! I mean, you're such an insufferable stay-at-home, and I'm sure you've never been anywhere except the nearby fairs?"

Ellie smiled and said in a ringing voice: "That's where you're wrong, Freddy! I've gone far, far away twice — to Magic Land!"

"What?!"

Chapter 22: HOSPITALITY

The boy stopped short and dropped everything to the ground. His face turned such a deep shade of red that his big freckles became difficult to see. He clenched his fists and approached Ellie in a passion. "You know I don't like made-up stories," he shouted. "I'll beat you up for that, even if you are a girl! Magic Land indeed!"

"But I'm not making it up," Ellie countered quickly. "I've got a letter with me from Dad to Uncle Bill, and he wrote about it there."

Fred looked at her with amazement for a long time, and then he said calmly, "In that case, you're the luckiest girl in the world... Will you tell me all about it?"

"Of course I'll tell you about it. But you realize, Freddy, that I'll need a whole week to do it. There's so much of it, after all... There was a certain Ogre that one would do well to avoid! He would have eaten me up if it hadn't been for Strasheela and the Iron Woodman. And how about the Saber-Toothed Tigers? And the transformations of Goodwin the Great and Terrible? And the Winged Monkeys?..."

Fred stumbled along, red with embarrassment He had thought of himself as a great traveler, but now, compared to Ellie, he was a nonentity...

Bill Canning was out on the plain, but Aunt Kate, a small, thin woman, gave Ellie a very warm welcome. She heated some water in a big tub so that her niece could wash from her journey. And Fred chattered on the other side of the door, tormented by his impatience to hear as quickly as possible the story of his cousin's amazing adventures.

The rays of the sun fell to earth in a thousand little circles as they pierced the foliage of the oak tree. Birds bounded from one branch to another, and a frolicsome squirrel squabbled with them. Totoshka ran after butterflies, while Ellie and Fred sat down on the grass, and the girl related to him her amazing journeys to Magic Land.

Fred listened to it with bated breath, and every once in a while he would repeat with pleasure that he'd never heard anything so remarkable in his entire life. "And all this happened to you!" he exclaimed. "To just an ordinary little girl... I mean, I'm sorry — to a girl! Ah, why don't such things ever befall me?"

"It's very simple," explained Ellie. "Here in Iowa, you don't have tornadoes like the ones we have in Kansas. For that matter, what difference would it make if a storm did come here? It still wouldn't be able to carry your cottage away to Magic Land."

"That's true," agreed the boy with a sigh. "But go on with your story, Ellie. You stopped at the point where you were attacked by Bastinda's magic wolves..."

"The Iron Woodman took them on," said the girl. "There were forty wolves, and the Woodman swung his mighty ax exactly forty times. If you could only see what an ax it was!"

She continued her story, and Fred listened, sighing with envy. He would have given up half the years of his life to experience even a small portion of what had fallen to Ellie's lot.

Ellie continued her account for several days, and then Fred began to show her some of the surrounding area. The farm was situated in a charming spot. There was nothing here to remind one of the scorching sun of the Kansas prairie. It was a picturesque little corner with forest-covered hills, with cheerful valleys that divided them up, and with cool brooks babbling at the bottoms of deep ravines...

Today, Ellie and Fred would catch some fish in the little lake hidden in the middle of a glen behind some willow trees with many branches. Tomorrow they would wander about the slopes of the hills, following paths beaten by sheep, and then set out to follow the course of some unfamiliar stream.

Their days passed in happiness and contentment.

Chapter 23

AN EXCURSION
INTO A CAVE

Ellie began to learn horseback-riding. Fred talked her into it. "Listen, cousin," said the boy, knitting his brows that had faded in the sun, "it would be an absolute disgrace if you went home after staying with us and you weren't an accomplished rider! You of all people, who are such a seasoned traveler!"

It did not take much to convince Ellie. Bill Canning placed a gentle-mannered horse entirely at his niece's disposal. Fred had a good racehorse, for he was already a superb horseman and he had taken his father's place on the job on more than one occasion.

It was difficult for the first few days. In the evenings, Ellie couldn't even sit down; her back ached, all her bones hurt, and she slept badly. But patience overcame everything, and the day came when horseback-riding turned from a torment into a pleasure for Ellie. Now the friends' outings became much more wide-ranging, and they sometimes rode as far as ten miles or so from home.

One day, Fred asked Ellie, "Have you ever heard of Mammoth Cave?"

"Of course," replied Ellie. "We talked about it in school."

"It's the largest cavern in the world."

"You wouldn't say that if you saw the land of the Underground Ore-Diggers," said Ellie as she burst out laughing. "Now *that's* a cavern!"

Fred took an attitude, as he always did whenever Ellie, even inadvertently, flaunted her reminiscences. Of course,

97

he had had adventures of his own. One time, during a snowstorm in the Cordilleras, he had lost his way and almost frozen to death. On another occasion, he had been chased by prairie wolves, and only the fleetness of his horse had saved him from death. Then again, he had once fallen out of a tree and broken his leg. While there*s no denying that these were most worthwhile experiences, and that they placed him head and shoulders above all the other boys, yet what was all of that compared to what Ellie had lived through?...

But Freddy had brought up the subject of caves for a definite reason. He wanted to show that even Iowa could boast of an item or two in this category. About twenty miles from the farm, in a deep gorge, lay the entrance to a little-known cave which tourists still had not penetrated to, where no one yet broke off pieces of stalactites for souvenirs or wrote their names on the walls with soot from their torches.

"Let*s go see it, Ellie," suggested Fred. "It's far away, and that's why I didn't invite you to go there before, but now you're a skilled rider, so making an excursion like this would be nothing for you."

Ellie accepted his invitation. Then the boy continued, "We'll ask for permission to be gone for the whole day. We'll take along everything we need for a lengthy outing, and we'll go exploring."

They set out early the next morning. Ellie carried with her a bag tightly stuffed with foodstuffs — Aunt Kate did not scrimp, and she placed so much of everything in it that it might well last all of three days. Totoshka settled down in front of her. There was a suitcase strapped to Fred's saddle.

"What's that for?" asked the girl.

"There's a boat in it," boasted Fred. "It's made of canvas, and it's collapsible. Dad made it for me. They say there's an underground lake in one of the grottos. Can you imagine how much fun it'll be to take a ride on it in the torchlight?"

The children rode along at a leisurely pace, and the sun had already risen quite high in the sky when they reached the entrance to the cave. The day was bright and warm, but dampness and chill issued from the dark opening. Ellie shivered and threw her warm shawl more tightly over her shoulders.

"You know, Freddy," she said, "I just remembered the time when Uncle Charlie, the Lion, Totoshka, Kaggi-Karr the Crow, and I traveled through the underground passage that the Queen of the Field Mice directed us to..."

The boy was annoyed. "Listen, Ellie," he said in vexation, "it's really outrageous on your part to keep bringing those things up!"

"What do you mean?" asked Ellie innocently, though her eyes were laughing.

"*This* is what I mean: 'When Strasheela and I...' 'When the Ogre...' 'When the Queen of the Mice...' Is it really my fault if I couldn't be there?" Fred was so angry that he was almost in tears.

"I'm sorry, Freddy. I won't do it any more," Ellie promised, and the boy gradually calmed down.

By breaking off some resinous pine-shoots, Fred prepared a batch of torches. He had some matches with him in the breast pocket of his checked shirt, in a little tin box. The boy unwound some fine string from a bulky ball of it and tied the end of the string to a rock. "I've thought of everything," said Fred. "It's easy to get lost in caves like this."

"Not with a dog along," objected Ellie. "Totoshka will always be able to lead us back the way we came. Isn't that right, Totoshka?" The dog barked with determination.

The children entered the cave. Fred walked in first, bearing on his shoulders the suitcase with the boat, which had shoulder-straps sewed on. He carried the torches in his hand. Ellie followed along behind him. In one hand she carried the provisions, and in the other, the ball of string. Totoshka brought up the rear of the procession: he did not care for caves, and he sniffed the air suspiciously and growled.

Chapter 24

CAVE-IN

At nightfall, the children had not returned home. Apprehension settled in at the Canning cottage. Mrs. Kate conjured up all sorts of dreadful imaginings, and her husband reassured her. "They couldn't possibly have gotten lost — the horses know the way back to the farm. And it's been a long time now since wild animals were heard of in our region. The kids merely got caught late where they were, and they're spending the night in the hills. They took enough food along, and Fred has matches with him."

"They could have lost their way in the cave," said Mrs. Kate. "I've heard that it has a lot of intricate passageways."

"I gave the boy a fat ball of string," said Bill Canning. "And I impressed it upon him most stringently that they were to proceed only as far as the string held out."

They passed the night in trepidation — and their trepidation became even greater in the morning, for Fred's racehorse came running back to the farm with its bridle snapped. It was all too clear that some misfortune had occurred. Everyone who had no chores to do and who was able to ride a horse, set out at once for the cave, and were led by Bill Canning. The advance guard of the rescue party rode the twenty miles in an hour and a half, almost driving the horses to exhaustion.

Chapter 24: CAVE-IN

Ellie's horse was standing not far from the cave, tied to a tree. The children themselves were nowhere in evidence. The string, one end of it tied around a rock, led into the cave. The crowd of rescuers made assumptions: "Could they have gotten lost in the passages? Poisoned by gas? Could one of them have been hurt?"

The men dashed into the cave, carrying bright torches and lamps in their hands (They had brought a whole month's supply of fuel with them from the ranch). Bill dashed on ahead of all the others.

At first, the passage was not very tall or wide, but it gradually opened out and led into a huge, oblong grotto. Stalactites hung down from the ceiling, and these glistened in the lamplight.

After traversing this grotto, the men saw three more passages leading off from it. Fred's string led into the middle one. They continued to follow it yet deeper in, walking on all fours now because the passage was narrow and low. Sometimes the adult men had to bend almost in two. Then suddenly Bill, who was still in the lead, cried out indistinctly: "There's been a cave-in!"

The path was blocked by a rough wall of rocks, both small and large, with the whole weight of the mountain, millions of pounds of it, pressing down from above. And the string led right into this mass — the last trace of the children who had passed this way...

Bill Canning began to sob in despair. "Freddy, my son! Ellie, little Ellie! What a dreadful way to end!"

His friends tried tenderly to console him. "Come, Bill, old man, cheer up! All isn't lost yet. They may be on the other side..."

"Yes, yes!" cried Bill. "We've got to excavate! Hurry! Let's get started!"

More and more new volunteers arrived at the cave, and before long, a sizeable camp was spreading out in the ravine. Campfires were lit, and housewives cooked supper for the rescuers. Aunt Kate joined them there, and she had already aged by several whole years.

The men scoured the entire area to collect tools for their excavation — shovels, crowbars, and pickaxes. Others felled trees in the nearby woods and began to fashion beams to shore up the passage.

The work proceeded at a feverish pace. The corridor was narrow, and no more than three of them could work in it at a time, but the men relieved one another every quarter of an hour. Each of them ate away at the rockfall with renewed vigor, and a long human chain transferred from hand to hand the rocks that had been removed.

Other rescuers painstakingly inspected the right- and left-hand passages leading out of the main grotto. For all anyone knew, one of them might lead down into the depths of the earth, past the cave-in, and the children, having survived the catastrophe, might be down there somewhere, waiting to be rescued. Unfortunately for that idea, one of the corridors turned back on itself and became a closed circle, while the other proved to be a dead end.

At Bill's request, John Smith was notified about the misfortune: a telegram went out to him, and Ellie's father and mother arrived at the site of the disaster on the third day. They were in utter despair. Farmer John joined in the efforts at once, but the first doubts had already appeared in the rescuers' minds. Digging was very difficult in the low, narrow passage, and even after eight days, their gallery extended only 150 feet. By using long drills to tap and feel the way, they concluded that the accumulation was very extensive, hundreds of feet, perhaps. More than that, they could hear ominous groaning sounds in the ceiling of the big grotto. Another cave-in could occur, and this time it would bury *many* people.

John Smith and Bill Canning were the first to suggest that the excavations be broken off. "It's clear that our children can't be saved," said Bill dismally. "If they weren't crushed to death, they're probably dead by now of hunger."

After twelve days, the rescue work ceased.

Chapter 25

AFTER THE CAVE-IN

Fred, Ellie, and Totoshka had *not* perished: the cave-in occurred after they had passed far beyond the danger point. But first a dreadful earth tremor threw them to the floor of the cave, and small stones rained down upon them from the ceiling. Then a deafening din reached their ears, and a gust of wind blew out their torches. Totoshka began to howl in desperation, and the stunned Ellie and Fred were unable to utter even a word.

Then the girl spoke up: "Totoshka knew what he was doing when he was acting so stubborn about not coming in here. Totoshka, baby, you're smarter than we are!"

Totoshka was trembling with fright, but the children felt no better than he did. Fred relit his torch. "Let's take a look at what happened..."

They walked back, looking about them carefully, gazing up at the ceiling and the walls. Fortunately, this part of the cave appeared to be exceptionally solid: there were fissures here and there, nothing more. But after the seekers had gone about three hundred paces, they were forced to a halt: there before them, in a jumbled pile, lay the rockfall.

"We would have had ourselves a nice, solid tomb if we hadn't made it through this area," whispered Fred in alarm. Cool as it was in the cave, there was sweat on his face.

"What are we going to do now, Freddy?" asked Ellie, collapsing weakly on the ground.

"What do we do?..." said the boy undecidedly. "I don't know... Try to find another exit, I guess." But a dreadful thought went through his head: "If there *is* another exit..."

Ellie stood up from the cold floor of the cave. "Let's go. But I'm awfully hungry. We haven't had anything to eat since this morning."

"That's a great idea, cousin!" exclaimed Fred with feigned enthusiasm. "We really must build up our strength before undertaking a difficult journey." So they had something to eat, feeding Totoshka as well, and they drank some iced tea from the canteen.

"We won't take the heaviest things with us," said Fred. He laid the bundle of torches down on the suitcase, giving only three or four of them to Ellie to carry. After discussing the situation, they decided to leave Totoshka there with the food: there might be rats prowling about in the cave, and the loss of their provisions would be an out-and-out disaster. The dog growled in a protective manner, but Fred tied him firmly to the suitcase with his belt.

The children began their exploration. Fred unwound his ball of string, trying not to let the cord break. Who knew, but this fine green string, which Aunt Kate had spun with her own hands, might prove their sole means of salvation?

"There were three passages leading out from the big grotto," said Fred, "and we took the middle one. It would be a good thing if we could get into one of the side-passages. Then we'd make it to the surface..." But this would be possible only if the side-passages happened to connect with the middle one by way of transverse corridors. And they found that there were no such corridors. Whether they wanted to or not, the only way for them to go was ahead.

The tunnel through which the children were walking opened out again and became a large, round cavern. Several openings gaped wide in its walls. Which of these might lead to the surface?

Without letting go of his ball of string, Fred walked resolutely to one of the openings and took a piece of chalk from his pocket. "I'm going to mark every passage we go into," said the boy, drawing a cross on the wall.

They began their search anew. But the results of it were not happy ones. The children roamed for several hours through an intricate network of corridors, but it did them no good. Some of the passages were dead ends, while others grew so narrow that it was impossible even to crawl through them; still others sloped downward to undefined depths...

If it hadn't been for their string and their chalk-marks, which they placed liberally on the walls, the children would have lost their way a long time ago in this dark labyrinth. Every time they retraced their steps, they carefully wound the string back up into a ball.

And so, winded and tired, they were on their way back to the corridor where they had left their things. All at once, the sound of urgent barking reached the children's ears.

"Something's happened to Totoshka!" exclaimed Ellie.

The children dashed forward in a headlong rush. A dreadful sight greeted them. Totoshka was doing battle with a dozen rats, defending their food. Three or four of the rats were lying unconscious on the ground, which showed how intense the fight had been. But the moment the rats saw the children with their torches, they scattered in all directions.

"It's a good thing we left the dog behind to watch over our things," said Fred.

"Yes," agreed Ellie with a shudder. "Otherwise — death by starvation." She sat down on the suitcase, and her eyes filled with tears.

"Hey, cousin, are you crying?" exclaimed Fred, taking her tenderly in his arms. "You, who've been in scrapes like this before? Don't be discouraged — we'll get out of this somehow... There's still the main exit from the round cavern. We haven't tried that one yet, and it may be the best one..."

But the girl could not walk any more — her feet simply wouldn't carry her.

"Then we'll put up for the night," said Fred.

He opened the suitcase and took out the sections of the boat, which he fastened together with nuts and bolts. A long canoe with a sail on it was the result. "See, she's unsinkable!" boasted Fred, smacking his hand against bags of air in the boat's bow and stern. "This will be your bed. You hold onto the provisions and your dog. Totoshka will keep you warm, and he'll also guard the food."

"And what about you?"

"My jacket's very closely-woven and warm."

The children did not know whether they slept for a long time or not. They were awakened by Totoshka's barking: rats were again sneaking toward the food.

For breakfast, Fred reduced the rations considerably, and he did not drink anything at all, though he poured out one lidful from the canteen for Ellie and half that amount for Totoshka. He split each of the torches in two with a jackknife and tied the bundle together firmly. "You know, cousin," said Fred in an apologetic tone, "I'm sure they're digging us out, and we should hold tight till that time."

The children spent that day by the rockfall. They listened carefully to hear if any sounds might reach them from the other side, but alas! everything all around them was dead and silent... On several occasions, they began to shout and bang the rocks themselves. No response.

Many hours went by, and then Fred said with determination: "No, Ellie! If we just sit here and wait for help to come — that'll mean death. It's obvious that the cave-in is too extensive, and we won't even hear the sounds of picks and crowbars — though I'm positive that Dad is out there with his friends..." The boy's voice trembled, but he continued bravely: "Granted that we have only one chance in a hundred to find an exit, we mustn't miss that one chance. Let's go on."

"Yes, let's go on," agreed Ellie. "But what should we do with the suitcase? Leave it behind again?"

Fred thought for a long time. "No, we'll have to take it with us," he decided at last. "The burden is heavy, but after all, it is our bed. Without it, we won't be able to sleep in this cave for even an hour. And who knows, we may cover so much distance today that we simply won't be able to make it back here. I'll carry the suitcase and the food, while you unroll the ball of string."

"Why do we need the string when we've got Totoshka with us?"

"Dad told us to travel with the string, and that's that!" said Fred.

So once again the underground captives resumed their journey, and this time they left the round cavern by the main exit. Fred had a faint hope that this passage would turn somewhere and lead them back up to the surface, though it would be in a different spot from where they had entered it. But they put mile after mile behind them, and the tunnel showed no intentions of turning. Sometimes it would grow wider, and at other times it narrowed (at which times the children thought with horror that they might not be able to crawl through it with the bulky suitcase), and it led them through grottos both large and small…

And then came that critical moment when the string ended. It was thin, sturdy twine, a memory of home, and as long as the wanderers were holding it in their hands, they continued to feel some bond with the upper world. But now this last bond had been broken! What were they to do?

"It would be foolish to turn back," said Fred. "And what use will it be to stay in one place? We'll rely on the chalk."

"Do you still have a large piece?" asked the girl.

"I made marks a little too liberally yesterday," admitted Fred. "But we'll have to economize on it now. I'll draw them such that we'll just be able to make them out."

The trek continued. The passage became lower and lower, and led ever downward. It grew much warmer. Ellie no longer bundled herself so tightly with her shawl to protect herself from the chill, and Fred unbuttoned his jacket. Only Totoshka, in his furry coat, felt as he had before. The humidity in the air increased, and there was water flowing down the walls of the passage, while streams babbled along the floor.

Now that the two children were no longer threatened with death by thirst, they drank their fill. The water tasted like mineral water, and it fizzed with little bubbles of gas.

Chapter 26

THE BOAT
COMES IN HANDY

Another three hours or so of walking — always downward and yet further downward — and the travelers found themselves stepping through water that was ankle-deep. The brooks with their merry babbling cheered them up and dispelled all their gloomy thoughts. The water was too deep for Totoshka, so Ellie carried him in her arms. Fred took her bag of food from her.

But the depth of the water increased: it already reached their knees, and it began creeping upward to their waists...

"Stop!" said Fred. Ellie came to a halt. "What an awful dope I am. Here I am carrying the suitcase, when the suitcase should really be carrying all of us."

"Do you want to put the boat together?" asked Ellie joyfully. (She was quite tired out from the long journey, though she would not admit it.)

"You bet!" answered the boy. "You hold the torch."

It was extremely difficult, if not downright precarious, to put the boat together under the present conditions. All Fred would have to do was drop one nut or bolt into the water, and all would be lost. But the children noticed a ledge on the wall, and they placed Totoshka on it and laid down their provisions. Ellie assisted her cousin, and the assembly was successfully completed.

Fred settled himself in the stern compartment with the oar, while Ellie climbed into the middle section with Totoshka and all their things. Her job was to light the way, to the extent that the smoky torchlight permitted.

The trip became more comfortable now. They no longer had to wade through the water, treading the slippery bottom with their feet and risking a fall at any moment. The boat bore the children forward at a good clip, but where was it headed?... Fred and Ellie tried not to think about that.

The stream soon filled the entire corridor, and by now it was more like a small river, with tributary streams flowing into it from side-passages.

The walls of the corridor suddenly opened out, and a cavern loomed before them. It was difficult to ascertain its dimensions in the darkness, which the light from their torches was unable to penetrate, but it appeared to be quite sizeable.

"We won't go any further," said Fred. "We'll have to spend the night here."

They maneuvered the boat to the shore of this underground lake that filled the entire grotto, and they found a level shore and pulled the boat out of the water. After a skimpy supper, which they washed down with all the water they could possibly wish for, they lay down to sleep.

They were nice and warm as they slept, but Fred awoke in the middle of the night and thought for a long time about this situation in which fate had placed them.

What were they to do? There were only two ways out for them. They could return to the site of the cave-in and wait until they were dug out, or they could continue to navigate the underground river. To go back would be admitting defeat — besides which, just sitting there idly with their arms folded would be dreadful. Continuing onward would mean a struggle — but the struggle was clearly the better of the two courses!

With these thoughts in his mind, Fred dropped off into a deep sleep.

The children were awakened, not by the dawn — which that dark cavern had never seen during the millions of years of its existence — nor by the cold, because it was warm there. They were awakened by the mournful yelping of poor, hungry Totoshka.

Fred lit the torch, and shook his head dejectedly: the number of matches remaining was anything but large. This was yet another danger — as if they did not already have enough of those to contend with!...

The food rations were reduced once again, and after having some breakfast, the children set out once again. During this one day, according to Fred's reckoning, they put no fewer than fifty miles behind them. When the river flowed out of the underground lake once more, it was wider and deeper than before. Its turbulent waters moved swiftly along.

A most perilous moment came at midday, when the travelers appeared to be threatened with either destruction on the spot, or a slow, painful trip back to the point where the cave-in had occurred — which itself would mean death.

Several times already, the cavern ceiling had descended so low over the river that Fred and Ellie had to

110

crouch down almost flat. But they generally got past such spots very quickly. Now, however, the roof began once again to drop down lower and lower, and it came so far down, in fact, that only a tiny gap was left between the water and the rocky ceiling. The waters were raging in a torrent, for they were hemmed in by rock on all sides.

Ellie, her face pale, turned to her cousin. "What do we do now?"

The other stopped the boat by grabbing hold of an outcropping of rock, while ideas rushed feverishly through his head. "Break through. We've got to break through," he decided. "The barrier can't possibly stretch very far!..."

Using signs more than words, he proposed that Ellie take Totoshka and their things and secrete herself in the chest in the prow of the boat, pulling the lid tightly over herself. The girl asked him with a gesture, "What about you?"

Fred merely pointed to the stern-chest.

So Ellie and the dog disappeared into their place of refuge. But the stern-chest on the little vessel was too short for Fred, and the boy was well aware of that fact. Wrapping his jacket around his head, he took as deep a breath as he could, and then he lay down in the bottom of the boat, trying to maintain a prone position. The torch was extinguished. Darkness engulfed the boat, and the irresistible force of the current drew it through the rapids. It banged now against the stony stream bottom, and now against the cavern roof, but all this gave solid testimony to the excellence of Bill Canning's handiwork, for the boat stayed in one piece!

When Fred could no longer hold his breath and was about to open his mouth, he suddenly felt the boat moving more calmly, and air reaching him through his jacket. And how refreshing it seemed to him, that damp, musty underground air! "Well, there's no turning back for us now," said Fred to himself.

Though he knew that the course they were taking did not portend anything good for them, it was as if someone had pressed a cold, strong hand against his heart.

Ellie emerged from her nook, and she looked at the terrified Totoshka and sought assurance in her mind that she herself was not the least bit afraid. Her torch began to blaze, and the sight of Fred, drenched from head to toe, and of the boat all full of water, betrayed to the girl the fact that the adventure had not gone at all the way her cousin said it had. Ellie only shook her head. The boy answered by threatening her with his fist, and he set about bailing out the water from the boat.

They continued their journey.

Chapter 27

THE CAVE OF DIAMONDS

Three more days of traveling came and went. The underground realm into which Fred and Ellie had fallen seemed to have no end. Grottos and corridors, corridors and grottos, rivers and underground lakes succeeded one another in an endless chain, and the travelers had long since lost count of them.

The good thing was that they never again had to contend with torrents comparable to the ones that they had overcome. If another bottleneck of that sort should appear in their path, even if it were only slightly longer — they would suffocate in it! They did encounter rapids and a few small waterfalls, but the boat floated right through these like a cork, and if it filled up with water in the process, Ellie bailed it out with a cup.

The bad thing, however, was that their stock of food was running very low. How many times throughout the trip did the children sing their praises of the judicious foresight of Mrs. Kate, who was a firm believer in the old proverb, "Eat your daily bread, and carry enough with you for a week." Also, they had very few matches left. Fred took an extreme measure: he split each of the remaining torches into several pieces, and now the children had nothing but thin slivers that gave out a weak, flickering light. But they simply had to make do with this light. At night-time, they kept the light burning, so that they would not have to waste a match in the morning. Ellie and Fred took turns sitting up, lighting one sliver from another as it burned itself out. Their supply of slivers, fortunately, was quite large.

On one of the nights, Ellie dozed off, and she awoke in total darkness: she had failed to observe the sliver burning to the end and going out. In terror, she awakened her cousin.

"Freddy, what have I done!"

The boy merely said, "Ah, Ellie, Ellie," but he said it in such a way that Ellie burst into scalding tears. "All right," said Fred, more gently now, "you may as well go to sleep. We'll have to waste a match anyway when we get up." And so they slept for a long time.

It was now the sixth or seventh day since their arrival in the underground world: the children did not know exactly, because neither of them had a watch, and for them, it was nightfall whenever they happened to grow tired.

They had just left behind them a long, wide corridor and were sailing across another lake. Something struck them now about the appearance of the walls. Its rocks were asparkle in a most singular way. The children were no longer astonished by the splendor of the stalactites: during the course of their long journey, they had encountered their columns many times, some of them straight, some of them with whimsical accretions on them. But something was different in this grotto, and it amazed them.

113

There didn't even seem to be any walls of rock stretching along the sides of the lake — rather, it was a dark sky extending upward, with stars glittering on it. Beams of light from these stars sparkled and flashed in shades of red, green, and blue. "What on earth is that, Freddy?" asked Ellie in a timid voice.

"I haven't the faintest idea," answered the boy in an equally low voice. "Precious stones, perhaps?"

The wall rose up steeply from the water at this point, and the travelers were able to navigate their boat right up to it. What appeared to be enormous sequins, scattered about on the rock, were glittering brightly in the light of their slivers.

Ellie, who was the more experienced of the two (having been in Goodwin's magnificent palace), figured out the truth at once. "Freddy, they're diamonds!"

"Are you making that up? More of your gags, no doubt!"

"I'm *not*, I assure you!"

"It would be better if they were pieces of cheese," remarked the boy despondently.

"But you realize, Freddy, they're very precious... not to mention beautiful," the girl added.

"So what if they're beautiful. Are they really any use to us?"

"Don't you understand, Fred? Be nice, pry a few specimens out. If we ever get out of here... I mean, *when* we get out of here," Ellie corrected herself, "a jeweler will make me a lovely brooch and bracelet."

Fred reluctantly set about removing diamonds. Everything went well with the first few of them, but then he nearly dropped his knife into the water. This aggravated him so much that he was minded to throw into the lake all the stones that he had succeeded in obtaining. But the boy carelessly threw his haul over to Ellie and began to row on.

When the Cave of Diamonds was behind them, the girl said meditatively, "You know, Freddy, marvels are about to begin now."

"What are you talking about?" retorted Fred ungraciously. "Now you'll be thinking you see marvels everywhere."

"All the same, I think this route is taking us to Magic Land."

Fred did not say a word — but from the look on his face, his cousin could see that such an ending to their adventure would represent the very apex of his wishes.

Chapter 28

CATCHING FISH

On the ninth day of their journey, their provisions finally gave out. Ellie grew weak from hunger, and Totoshka was also in a bad way; only Fred was able to hold up. As they sailed over a long, narrow lake, keeping to the vertical walls, Fred saw something on them that was not unlike enormous moving globs. "Slugs!" exclaimed the boy. "That means food!"

But he remembered well the words of his father, who had repeated them many times during their excursions over the prairies: "Never eat any unknown food in large quantity straightaway, my boy! Who knows, but it may be something harmful."

Fred decided now to sample these snails himself first. With difficulty he swallowed that loathsome portion, so pungent to the taste. "No, this isn't for Ellie," he decided, and he spat out the underchewed snail.

115

It was well that he did so, because he suddenly felt a burning sensation in his stomach; his head began to spin, and he lost consciousness.

Ellie, panic-stricken, rushed to her cousin's aid. She stuck her burning splinter-torch into a slit in the chest on the bow, and then she began to bustle about: she splashed water on Fred's face and held her canteen up so that he could drink from it. After several minutes, the boy revived, but at that same moment, the torch began to crackle and then went out.

"Another match wasted," murmured the boy with a deep sigh. "But our supply of splinter-torches is almost used up anyway..."

So there was no way they could eat the snails, and once again the travelers were assailed by the specter of hunger. They lit a light and sailed on in silence.

Suddenly Fred's eyes lit up with delight. He saw... Yes, indeed he did see a snail lose its footing on the wall and tumble into the water, and at once an enormous fish's head emerged from below and moved its jaws. There was a small eddy, and then it disappeared.

"What a fool I've been!" cried Fred. "How much time it's taken me to mature from a simple kid to a grown man! All our troubles are due to my own stupidity! Why didn't I think of fish?!"

"But Freddy, how are you going to catch them?"

"Ha, ha, ha, my dear little cousin, you just leave that to me!"

Fred drew forth from under the lining of his cap an angler's fishing-line, one with a large hook. He grabbed a snail from the damp wall, cut a piece off of it, stuck it on the hook, and dangled the line over the side of the boat.

They did not have to wait long for a bite. A sharp jerk, a strike, and behold! a short, chubby fish, one with gray scales and pale pink fins, was flopping around in the bottom of the boat. On its head, in place of eyes, they saw two small, round growths: the fish was blind.

"Do you suppose this fish might be poisonous?" asked Fred meditatively.

"Freddy, dear, let me be the one to try it out this time," implored Ellie.

"No," replied Fred resolutely. "We'll give some to Totoshka to sample. But only a little bit."

The boy struck the flopping fish on the head with his oar, and then he scaled it and gave a small piece to the dog. Totoshka gobbled it down, and he licked his chops and gave every appearance of wanting more.

"No, little friend," said Fred tenderly. "Just have a little patience!"

An hour went by. Totoshka still felt great, and he looked ingratiatingly at all the fish that the boy had succeeded in catching during that time.

"Too bad we have no way of cooking the fish," said Ellie in a dismal tone.

"No matter, we'll eat them raw. But we'll likewise do it a small chunk at a time, or else it won't agree with us."

So the children ate, bit by little bit, and after a few hours their hunger was satisfied. But though they were no longer threatened by starvation, still they wished with all their hearts that their involuntary journey would be over as quickly as possible.

Chapter 29

THE MYSTERIOUS CITY

Their bundle of splinter-torches dwindled with alarming rapidity, and the moment finally came when the sputtering flame at the end of the last of them, flickered and went out. A little red spark glowed for a few seconds more, then it, too, expired. Darkness...

Yes, it seemed to Fred and Ellie that they were enveloped in impenetrable, perpetual blackness, because not one ray of light could penetrate the thick stratum of earth which separated them from the sky and the sun. But what miracle was this? As their eyes gradually became used to the dark, the children began to make out something in it...

"Freddy, my cousin, I can see, I can see!" cried Ellie with a thrill. "Ooh, I can see my fingers... I can see Totoshka... And you!..."

"And I can make out your red sweater! I can see you waving your arms. Hurrah!"

This might seem unaccountable, if not downright improbable, but the travelers really could see. At this moment they were cruising along a broad, tranquil river, and before them loomed a cape, which the river flowed around to the right. The rocks on the shore, the cave ceiling that hung over them — all these things were boldly outlined by some sort of weak yet distinct golden-reddish light. Of course, there was no need now for splinter-torches, nor even full-duty ones, because no torch could possibly illuminate the tableau that surrounded them the way this gentle, diffused light did, shining from its unknown source. And the only reason they hadn't noticed it sooner was because their eyes had been blinded by the fire of the splinter-torch...

"Freddy," said Ellie with conviction, "the land of the Underground Ore-Diggers is somewhere nearby, *that* I'm sure of!" Then the girl burst out laughing for the first time since the present catastrophe had begun. "What good fortune! Now I'll see my beloved Strasheela, and the Woodman, and the Lion again!..."

"But couldn't you be mistaken?" Fred responded cautiously. "Suppose we end up in some other underground kingdom?"

118

"Well, how many of those could there possibly be? No, it was in the land of the Ore-Diggers that I saw a golden light just like this, only it was much brighter, bright enough to enable a person to distinguish objects that were far away."

"But if you're right — I've got you!" exclaimed Fred triumphantly.

"What do you mean, you've got me?"

"I mean an end to your boasting," declared the little boy gaily. "And I, too, will be seeing the wonders of Magic Land with my own eyes."

"Aha, you've got nothing on me. I'll be seeing them for the third time, while for you it'll still be only a first."

After two hours, the river carried the boat into an enormous cavern, whose further reaches could not be seen, even in the golden light. The grotto was simply enormous, yet it was still nothing compared to the Land of the Underground Ore-Diggers. There were no forest-covered hills here, no city...

However, there was a city here after all!

Far off from the shore, Ellie and Fred beheld something not unlike a disorderly heap of buildings, clearly erected by human hands. "A city, a city!" cried Ellie. "Oh, dear Freddy, let's go have a look at it!"

Now that the children felt certain that they were not going to perish, that their journey would soon come to a happy conclusion, they were filled with a longing that could scarcely have come about at all a few days ago.

Fred said that it would not be very expedient for them to leave the boat on the shore.

"But what about Totoshka?" exclaimed the girl. "Couldn't he guard it for you?"

Fred let himself be convinced that he wanted very much to get a look at the mysterious city himself. So the children pulled the canoe up onto the shore, filled it with rocks, and tied Totoshka to it. "If anything happens, then bark bloody murder!" Ellie instructed the dog.

It was a distance of almost half a mile to the supposed city. The road passed through flat areas heaped up with rocks, both small and large, and the children were constantly stumbling.

The more closely they approached it, the more obvious it became that it had indeed been fashioned by human hands.

A mass of buildings appeared to be towering from the hilltops, a result of the houses being erected in several tiers. Taken all together, they brought to mind some sort of gigantic nest made up of individual cells. The houses were round in shape and were topped with rounded arches. There were no windows in them, but small, circular openings were visible in the walls, perhaps to let air through. Several buildings were half ruined, and it was evident that the city had been abandoned long, long ago.

As they came up close to it, Fred and Ellie beheld a fortress wall that loomed up approximately four times the height of a person. And what a remarkable wall it was! It was covered all over with unusually brilliant pictures, which not even the age-old dampness of the underground had been able to ravage.

For this, however, the explanation was simple. The pictures were mosaics, formed out of small pieces of colored glass, and time is powerless over such as that.

The contents of the pictures were of the utmost variety. One of them appeared to depict the judgment of a monarch over his subjects. The monarch, in magnificent attire, was seated on a throne, and those who were being judged were kneeling before him, each of them with a rope around his neck. In another picture one could observe a banquet in progress, while a third showed athletic competitions of some kind...

To Ellie, the faces and forms of the people were vaguely familiar. It was as if she had seen somewhere just such small, chubby people with large heads upon stout necks, with enormous, powerful fists...

"They're Leapers!" the little girl exclaimed suddenly,

120

and she cowered in fright, as if expecting a blow. "Remember, Freddy, when I told you about how Goodwin flew away in a balloon? And about how we set out after that to seek guidance from Stella. The Mountain of the Leapers obstructed the road that we had to travel, but the Winged Monkeys carried us across it... Anyway, these are the same Leapers — and if they're still around, then we're in for trouble."

"Can't you see that no one's been living here for hundreds of years? They've moved on."

All at once, Ellie burst out laughing. "Hey, will you get a look at that — it's a Sixpaw hunt. *Now* do you still doubt that the Land of the Underground Ore-Diggers is close at hand?"

The picture clearly and vividly portrayed a band of small, chubby humans attacking a Sixpaw with spears, and the latter, rearing up on its hind legs, was using its front legs to do battle with its foes.

A furious sound of barking reached their ears from the distance. Fred, twisting himself about, exclaimed, "There are some of them now, in person!"

Chapter 30

THE ADVENTURE
WITH THE BOAT

A whole herd of Sixpaws was approaching the shore (which was plainly their watering spot), plodding along clumsily on their short, powerful legs. Totoshka was barking frantically. Fred realized that the creatures' promenade might well spell disaster for them: all the beasts had to do was step on the boat blindly, and nothing would be left of it but splinters.

121

Waving his arms and letting out deafening howls, Fred dashed back toward the shore, leaving Ellie far behind. She, too, ran back with all her strength, uttering piercing shrieks...

The barking of the dog and the shouting of the two humans frightened the slow-witted Sixpaws, and they turned around and jog-trotted into one of the side-caverns, the same one that they had just come out of. But one of them, bearing to the side, managed to step on the stern-chest in the canoe. The boat crunched, and its stern was reduced instantly to a mass of wreckage. Totoshka, fortunately, had been tied to a ring on the bow end, and thus he escaped injury.

The two children looked at one another in dismay when they reached this scene.

"What have I done?" cried Ellie, bursting into tears. "Why did I have to go look at that horrible city?"

Fred reassured his cousin compassionately. "There's every indication that the end of all our misery is near at hand," he said. "Let's continue on foot."

"And suppose this river fills up the whole cave again? Don't forget, I'm not much of a swimmer."

"But I'm a good one, and I'll help you," said Fred, trying not to appear afraid.

The disaster was beyond repair, and the children, after gathering up everything that had survived the wreck, trudged sorrowfully along the shore. The irrepressible Totoshka, who had already forgotten the destruction that had threatened him only moments ago, scampered along the bank, hunting prey but with no idea of what he expected to catch.

They proceeded for about half a mile. Stepping along the rough, slippery stones that littered the shore, and dragging all their things with them, was not the least bit like sitting peacefully in the canoe and gliding noiselessly over the surface of the water. Only now did Ellie fully realize just how much the boat had meant to them...

Totoshka, who had run about two hundred paces away from the water, began to bark loudly His barking now was not one of fear, but of exhilaration. He was announcing some momentous discovery. Ellie and Fred raced to the spot, and they almost went insane from jubilation: on a high platform of rock, turned upside down, lay a boat!

It was made out of Sixpaw hide, and the animal's bones served as the ribs of the boat as well.

"I think I understand," said Fred. "Those Leapers, as you call them, lived here long, long ago, but then they were apparently forced to relocate elsewhere, and they departed for the upper world. Since the only way to leave here is by water, they constructed boats out of Sixpaw hides and ribs. But they must have had one more boat than they needed, so they left it behind here. Yet they may still have thought they'd be coming back for it, so, knowing the habits of those creatures, they hoisted it up onto this platform. And there, to our good fortune, it remained secure."

"Yes, of course," agreed the girl. "I'm sure that's how it happened."

"I'll run and get the oar," shouted Fred.

"But I'm afraid to stay here all by myself," said Ellie. Her cousin boosted her up, seating her on the vessel's protuberant hull.

The boy was back in no time. It was a most difficult task for them to lower the boat from the platform and to drag it down to the shore, for it was considerably larger and heavier than their canoe. One thing was clear, however: the beast's hide was an extraordinary substance, for the boat was in a perfect state of preservation, and it was roomy and stable.

Fred took a seat in the stern and began to paddle with the oar, and once again they were plying the waters, this time in their new-found little vessel.

Chapter 31

IN THE LAND OF THE
UNDERGROUND ORE-DIGGERS

Shortly after their adventure with the Sixpaw, the children, who were all but drained emotionally by their experience, began to feel sleepy. This time, they were determined *not* to spend the night on the shore: what if wild animals should come along and trample them? Fred sought out a secluded inlet, where the shore embankments were steep and where no one could get at them, and he maneuvered the boat into it.

"I hope this is the last night we'll have to camp out," said Ellie, after they had dined on dry fish and lain down to sleep in the bottom of the boat; "and that tomorrow we'll be among the Ore-Diggers."

"Aren't you afraid they might give us a hostile reception?" asked Fred anxiously.

"To tell you the truth, I am," admitted Ellie. "Ramina warned me that they don't like it when outsiders take an interest in their doings. And even now I remember how malevolent the face of that sentry was who shot an arrow at me... I've got just one hope now: I don't think they'll do us any harm when they see that we're only kids, and learn that we wound up in their country by accident rather than by design..."

"Fine, if that's the way it turns out," said Fred, ending the conversation as he instinctively curled himself up.

In the morning, the river bore them ever onward. It would be unthinkable now even to attempt to postpone facing the inevitable.

They continued along for several hours; the light grew brighter, the arches of the cavern spread further and further apart and rose higher and higher — until at last the Land of the Underground Ore-Diggers unfolded before the travelers, in all its grandeur.

This was an extraordinary sight even for Ellie, though she was seeing it for the second time. And what can be said about Fred? The boy was overwhelmed and astonished. Those boundless heights, where golden-pink clouds swirled about, that gloomy autumn-like expanse with its wooded hills and the little villages scattered among them, that city indistinctly visible in the distance...

All this was spectacular and one-of-a-kind, and it was well worth undertaking a long and perilous journey just to behold it... but would the masters of this wondrous land let them remain alive?...

Then a new marvel caught the children by surprise: Totoshka began to talk.

To be truthful, this came as little surprise to Ellie: after all, the Cavern was part of Magic Land, which is a place where all animals and birds can talk. But Fred was so astounded that he almost passed out. "Totoshka! Are you really talking like a human being?"

"What's so special about that — *arf! arf!?*" responded the dog. "Magic Land is a novel place for our brother here, and there's nowhere else where we can display our capabilities to the fullest..."

Fred burst into uncontrollable laughter. "Not only do you talk, you talk so eloquently. If only our teacher, Miss Brown, could hear you! I guarantee you anything, she'd give you a high grade!"

"I wouldn't be a worse student than *you* are, kid!" said Toto with self-assurance.

At this time, the river, which had been dwindling as they proceeded, abruptly ended altogether. They could see the water bubble and gush along, and then sink into the soil among the stones: it drained into the lake under the ground.

They were obliged to leave their boat behind and continue on foot. The burden that the children carried was light now, because most of their effects were gone. They proceeded for several miles in silence, depressed by the extraordinary nature of their surroundings. Only Totoshka mumbled things to himself, no doubt to exercise his new-found faculty.

Only a short distance now remained between them and the city. All at once, Ellie, looking upward, screamed, "Something's flying! Something's flying!"

Totoshka began to howl plaintively and menacingly, forgetting at once all about his ability to talk, and Fred raised his head. A dark spot was swooping swiftly down upon them from out of the clouds, and it grew and grew. One could already make it out as a monstrous dragon with a rider on its back.

The reptile plummeted to a low altitude and described several circles around the travelers, its yellow-white underbelly gleaming and its leathery wings making a loud noise. The sentinel seated on its back, a bow in his hand and a quiver of arrows on his back, stared fixedly at the children, without uttering a single word. His pallid face with its hooked nose was totally impassive. Then he turned the dragon about and headed toward the city.

"He passing us by," said Fred, taking heart. "The first meeting is always the most important. He's flown away to deliver a report about us. Ellie, do tidy up your hair — you've gotten all disheveled..."

After they had gone another few hundred paces, Fred and Ellie beheld a vast crowd of people, dressed in apparel of all different colors, pouring forth from the city gates. Ellie's heart skipped a beat, yet she stepped straight over to them and boldly addressed several people whose air of importance made them stand out from the others: "We convey to you our most respectful salutations, O overlords of the Undergrounders."

The newcomers bowed low, and Totoshka gave out a bark, which caused no small stir in the front rows of the spectators.

Ellie continued: "We are not enemies, and we're not spies. My cousin Fred here and I have ended up in your country entirely by chance. We were exploring a certain cave back in our own country, and then..." Ellie's voice began to tremble. "Then there was a cave-in, and our escape was cut off. We started off in search of a way out, first on foot, and then in a boat, and we've been traveling many, many days, so many that we've even lost count of them..."

At this point, another mounted guard descended to the ground not far from the crowd. He leaped nimbly from the dragon's back and approached an individual who was standing there with a haughty bearing at the front. He bowed low and communicated something to him, and the individual — who was none other than King Mentaho — said: "Little girl, you're lying. It's just been reported to me that you traveled here in a boat made from the hide and ribs of a Sixpaw. Such boats can't exist on the surface in your country — they're only made here, underground."

"Excuse me, sir," responded Ellie boldly (at which point one of the courtiers corrected her: "You must say 'Your Majesty.'") "I beg forgiveness, your Majesty. We did have a boat made of wood and canvas. That's the one we sailed here in, but it was damaged by a Sixpaw near the ruined city of the Leapers. Then, on the shore, we came upon that skin-boat, which dates from the ancient times."

The simplicity and clearness of Ellie's explanation impressed the listeners in a favorable manner, and their faces became more amicable. King Mentaho said, "You appear to be telling the truth. But tell us, what's your name, what kind of person are you, who is this boy, and what is that remarkable animal you're holding in your arms?"

Ellie began to answer these questions in reverse order. "This animal," she said, "is my little dog..."

"I have the honor of introducing myself: Toto!" the dog cut in. "If we get to know each other better, then you can call me Totoshka."

"Totoshka, you shameless creature, do be quiet!" exclaimed Ellie, jerking the dog's ear. "As you can see, he's a very intelligent and devoted dog, though sometimes he's a little talkative and boastful. As for this boy you've asked me about — he's my second cousin, Fred Canning, from Iowa. He's both brave and smart, he's a fine horseback rider, and he's just been promoted to fourth grade. Now, what can I say about myself? My name is Ellie Smith, and I'm about the most ordinary little girl anyone will ever find on the Kansas prairies..."

A voice filled with spite rang out from among the throng: "Don't believe a word she says! This 'most ordinary little girl' destroyed two powerful witches, Gingema and Bastinda, and she smashed the power of Urfin Jus and his fierce wooden soldiers. I beg your Majesties' pardon for speaking out without permission, but I just couldn't keep silent."

"Who is that?" exclaimed short, stout King Barbedo. "Oh, it's Ruf Bilan! Well, come on out, don't hide on us. You're saying some very interesting things."

The ranks of spectators parted, and a stocky little man in the livery of a lackey stepped forward. His bloated little eyes gazed upon Ellie with unconcealed hostility. Totoshka barked defiantly at Bilan, and the little girl broke into a smile.

"Ah, can this be none other than Ruf Bilan the traitor, former Prime Minister to his Majesty Urfin Jus? So you're still alive, are you, my lord? Up on the surface, we were sure you must have been gobbled up by Sixpaws after you fled underground to escape the people's wrath. But now it seems you're not exactly thriving down here!"

The crowd burst into a roar of laughter, and even the seven kings smiled. The blow had been well-aimed, and Ruf Bilan's fat face turned crimson in embarrassment.

King Mentaho grunted in admiration. "You really know how to handle yourself. How cleverly you told this idler off. You know, Ellie, from the way you conduct yourself, it's indeed difficult to believe that you're an ordinary little girl."

"But she's not, she's not, your Majesty!" interjected Ruf Bilan. "She's a fairy, and she must have some reason for coming to our country a third time. She babbled something about a cave-in, but could anything like a cave-in have enough power to entomb a fairy?"

"If you'd seen it, you wouldn't be talking like that," retorted Ellie indignantly. "It's true that when I last came to Magic Land with my Uncle Charlie, it was at the summons of Strasheela and the Iron Woodman, but this time around, it happened to us against our wills. Fred and I have only one earnest desire now, and that is to return home as quickly as possible, to our parents, who are now mourning us for dead. Isn't that right, Freddy?"

"It certainly is," asserted the boy with effort. These were the first words that he uttered in the presence of the Undergrounders.

"Let us go back up to the surface, your Majesties," begged Ellie. "We'll go see our friends, and, of course, we'll find some way of leaving Magic Land."

"Let you go?" said Mentaho. "That's something we'll have to think about."

"No, your Majesties, don't let her go!" Ruf Bilan cried out frantically. "It's true that — with no evil intention — I deprived your land of its Soporific Water, but — begging your forgiveness for reminding you of it — let me now be the one to point out to you a means of getting it back. Ellie is a powerful fairy, as she's proved on more than one occasion, and her magic art can accomplish many things..."

The hint was all too obvious, and expressions of keen interest appeared in the faces of the seven kings.

"Ah, I see what you're driving at!" exclaimed King Barbedo. "Restoring the Sacred Spring would be a mighty accomplishment indeed!"

"You must be making all this up!" cried Ellie, almost in tears. "What Sacred Spring? What magic art? I don't know what you're talking about..."

"You'll know all about it soon enough," said King Mentaho with an exquisite politeness. "In our present unfortunate position, we mustn't let even the smallest hope of deliverance slip by. We won't harm you or your companions, and we'll treat you with the utmost respect — but as for letting you go up to the surface, that's out of the question at this time..."

They took the travelers away to the Rainbow Palace.

Chapter 32

PERSUASION

Fred, Ellie, and Totoshka were each put up in a splendid room in the Orange Wing of the palace, and given all they wanted to eat, in spite of the general food shortages in the land. The captives were even allowed to go out and take walks, but only under the escort of two spies.

Once or twice, the children went out sailing in a sailboat. A light breeze propelled the little craft along on the lake, which was slightly turbulent, and they could at least pretend that they were free... but the sail was controlled by one taciturn, gloomy-faced spy, while another one sat by the rudder. The kings were afraid that Ellie and her cousin might slip away from Underground Land by the same route through which they had entered it.

The second day after their arrival in the City of the Seven Kings, the reluctant travelers learned the whole story about the Soporific Water. The one who told it to them was Arrigo the Chronicler, a short, lean, middle-aged man with an intelligent face and gray eyes with a thoughtful expression.

From his account, Fred and Ellie became aware of how, several centuries before, the royal hunter Ortega had accidentally stumbled upon a spring of magic water in the labyrinth, and how Bellino the Time Keeper had come up with the idea of putting the kings and their retinues to sleep during the periods between their reigns.

"That was a very good thing to do," said Arrigo in a soft, pleasant voice. "The people would only have to support one royal court at a time, while the other six reposed peacefully in secluded storehouses. The only thing anyone had to worry about was protecting them from the ravenous mice, and their clothes from the moths..."

"And what if the mice ate them all up?" asked Ellie gaily.

"Come now, come now!" answered the chronicler in horror. "Living people? They *were* still alive, after all, even if they were submerged in a magic sleep."

Ellie thought for a few minutes, and then she came out with this question: "Tell me, illustrious Arrigo, have your people ever thought of the possibility of abolishing the office of king and living without them?"

Again Arrigo was horrified. "Live without kings?! Why, the royal authority was established by our forefathers! And besides that, we swore an oath of loyalty!"

Ellie and Fred looked at one another. Yes, the respect that these Undergrounders felt for their kings was still just too great, and it would be difficult for them to overcome it.

In the evening (time of day in the Cavern was determined by sand-clocks), the children were summoned to the Orange Room, to King Barbedo. The king was seated on his throne, with his large, bald head shining feebly in the light of the phosphorescent globes.

"How are your accommodations, Fairy Ellie?" asked Barbedo. "And how is the food? Do you have any further wishes?"

"We have only one wish," said Ellie. "Let us go up to the surface."

"But that's impossible," said Barbedo, "at least until you restore the Soporific Water for us."

"Then, if nothing else, send a messenger to the surface to tell Strasheela we're down here."

"No, that we can't do," said the king with a smile. "If they find out up there that we're holding you here with us, they'll try to free you, and that can lead to all kinds of great unpleasantness."

Ellie and Fred had no response but dejected silence.

Barbedo continued, in an entreating tone: "Truly, esteemed Fairy, what effort could it possibly cost you to put such teeny-weeny little magic into effect, when you've already accomplished such mighty deeds? You flew in from the outer world in your Death-Dealing House and — *crash! crash!* — you landed right on the head of that wicked witch, Gingema. You melted the powerful sorceress Bastinda, who was the mistress of magic wolves and Winged Monkeys..." (Of course, it was that nasty Ruf Bilan who had made all these things known to the Underground Kings. Thus ran Ellie's thoughts.) "And you still want to convince us that restoring the Soporific Water is not within your power?"

All further attempts at persuasion proved fruitless, however, and Barbedo dismissed the two children in exasperation.

When she found herself alone in her room, Ellie decided: "I'll summon Ramina. The Queen of the Mice is a wise fairy, and she'll be able to advise me well."

The girl blew Ramina's silver whistle once, twice, three times. It had no effect. She blew it again and again. Nothing!

And Ellie understood: the whistle's magic did not extend to Underground Land, and the little fairy in the mouse's skin could not appear there before her more sizable friend.

From then on, the children were summoned almost every day by one king, and then another. Sometimes the kings pounced upon the poor girl two, three, or even four at a time. Finally, one morning, Ellie received notification that she was being summoned to appear before the Supreme Council. This announcement threw her into a panic, and she burst into tears.

"Listen, cousin," said Fred. "Why don't you try duping them? Pretend that you're willing at least to try, though you can't guarantee success. That'll make them happy. Of course, you'll have to go take a look at the spring, and you'll take me and Totoshka along and then maybe we'll be able to make a getaway."

"Freddy's come up with a very good idea," said Totoshka, "and I'm firmly in support of his plan."

Ellie wiped away her tears and admitted that the plan was not half bad.

Chapter 33

TOTOSHKA ESCAPES

Standing there before the magnificent assemblage of kings and courtiers, Ellie stated with some diffidence that she would make an attempt to do what they were asking of her, but she was afraid that she might not succeed. Ellie's words stirred up a pandemonium of jubilation.

"At long last!" their cries resounded. "It's about time!" "Such a powerful fairy is bound to succeed!" When Ellie and Fred withdrew from the assemblage, they were utterly deafened.

The next day, a large expedition set out for the defunct fountain. It was led by King Mentaho. They brought a litter along with them, in case Ellie should grow tired. The shining globes on the caps of the Cavern-Dwellers lit the way for them. Fred Canning, too, was given one of these globes to put on his beret. From time to time, he removed his beret from his head and gazed in admiration at this amazing little lamp. Arrigo the Chronicler, who had come along on the expedition (it was his job to write an account of it in his book) walked along beside Fred, and he related to the boy how they came by the phosphorescent globes.

"The glowing substance is obtained from the fur of Sixpaws," said Arrigo. "A regular bunch of them get sheared, though the beasts don't like it and roar something awful during the shearing. The sheared fur is steeped in water in a huge vat. When sample clumps taken from the vat no longer glow in the dark, that indicates that all the glowing substance is now dissolved in the water."

"And then the water is boiled away. Right?" guessed Fred.

"Absolutely right. A crystalline powder something like fine salt is left behind on the bottom and the sides of the vat. It glows so brightly that hands that are rubbed with it seem to be on fire. The powder is mixed with isinglass and smeared onto balls fashioned out of hard wood. The balls retain their glow for centuries on end, and the state keeps a strict count of them."

"That's all most ingenious," said Fred. "Your land has a lot that's singular and good — but it's all of no use as long as you have kings over you."

Arrigo took a look around, to be sure that there were no spies in his immediate vicinity, and then he whispered in Fred's ear, "You know, I've been thinking over Mistress Ellie's words, and I've come to the conclusion now that there's a great deal of truth in them..."

"We've got ourselves an ally now," the boy thought happily to himself.

Ellie made part of the long excursion on the litter. The aftermath of much concerted labor was clearly visible in the Sacred Cavern itself: the whole place had been dug up and excavated.

Ellie stood at what was left of the basin and bade all those who were present, except Fred and Totoshka, to withdraw a little distance away, warning them that the incantations that she was about to recite could be harmful to ordinary mortals. Everyone hustled back in alarm.

Ellie began to speak, all the while making strange gestures in the air with her arms: "Flight from here is impossible when we're so closely watched, my friends, but at least we have an opportunity now to talk privately."

Indeed, during the day, the captives were surrounded continually by spies, and at night, the three were lodged in separate rooms.

"One of us will have to escape to the upper world," Ellie continued. "But who? Totoshka, of course. Their surveillance over him is less intense than it is over us. And I've thought of a way. By using an excuse that I needed to clear up some details regarding the Soporific Water, I managed to talk to Arrigo without any witnesses present. He informed me that the day after tomorrow is the next Market Day: the Ore-Diggers will then be doing business with the Munchkins. Three hundred workers will be carrying to the Market Gate all the goods that have been designated for bartering. Three scribes will go with them to make a list of the purchases, and Arrigo will be one of them. He's on our side..."

"I know, I know," Fred was about to get started, but Ellie quickly interrupted him, waving her arm imperiously.

"Silence, do not interrupt my incantations! *Turabo, furabo, botalo, motalo!...*" She uttered this in such a loud voice that the words reached King Mentaho and his entourage, and the latter drew back in terror.

"Totoshka, Arrigo is going to carry you under his clothing in an inconspicuous way, and he'll be taking advantage of the hustle and bustle of the trading to release you to the surface. Once you're there... Well, you'll know what to do."

"Don't you worry about a thing," answered the dog pretentiously. "Toto has never yet let anyone down."

"I know, I know," said Ellie with a smile. "You're bragging again. Now, once you're among the Munchkins, they'll convey you to the Emerald City. There, Strasheela, with his clever brains, will come up with some way of rescuing us." Ellie concluded in a loud voice:

> "*Bumbara, chufara, skoricky, moricky,*
> *Pickapoo, trickapoo, loricky, yoricky!...*"

She whispered quietly to Fred, "Those are Villina's magic words, but I doubt very much if they'll have any effect, coming from me..."

Ellie waved her arms around her head several times in a circular motion, and stamped her foot three times, then she headed resolutely toward the cowed multitude of spectators. "Your Majesty," she addressed King Mentaho in a solemn manner. "I've done all that I could. No result will be apparent until a week has passed. And there may well not be any," she added cautiously, "if a certain powerful underground Spirit, in his anger at Ruf Bilan's senseless acts, should rise up and counter my magic charms." Ellie observed with vindictive pleasure how the face of the traitor, who was standing there in Mentaho's suite, turned pale when she uttered these words.

Chapter 33: TOTOSHKA ESCAPES

"If that should happen," concluded Ellie, "I'd be obliged to come up with some new, more effective incantations."

The plan for Totoshka's escape succeeded brilliantly. No one noticed Arrigo conceal the dog under his jacket prior to the departure of the merchandise caravan, and Totoshka hid himself there, barely even breathing. Then, when Arrigo and his fellow scribes went out at night through the gate to count up and make a list of the products received from the Munchkins, the Chronicler walked off to the side and released the dog.

Part III

THE END OF THE UNDERGROUND KINGDOM

Chapter 34

STRASHEELA AND THE WOODMAN GO INTO ACTION

The Munchkins were utterly astounded when they saw Totoshka. They burst into merry laughter, and the little bells on their blue hats tinkled in concert.

"The amazing little beast, who is Ellie's companion, has come back to us!" they cried. "But where is Ellie herself, our fairy? And where's the Giant From Beyond the Mountains?"

"I'm sorry, but I don't have time right now to talk with you people at length," replied the dog with an air of self-importance. "I *will* tell you one thing, though: Ellie and her cousin have fallen into captivity in Underground Land, and it's up to me to come to their aid."

This sad news so stunned the Munchkins that they began to sob, and the little bells on their hats tinkled gaily. The Munchkins indignantly pulled off their hats so that the sound they made would not disturb their weeping, and they laid them on the ground. "Good gracious, what are we going to do?" sobbed the Munchkins inconsolably.

"You're going to stop all that useless howling and take me to Prem Cocus just as fast as you can!" ordered Totoshka.

Prem Cocus was the ruler of Blue Land, and his estate was located not too far from there. Several fleet-footed young Munchkins raced toward the ruler's house, transferring Totoshka from one hand to another. By daybreak, they had reached the spot.

"I've got to get to the Emerald City as quickly as possible to see Strasheela the Wise," explained the dog, after giving Cocus a brief account of the events in the Land of the Underground Ore-Diggers.

The ruler well understood the full gravity of the matter. One of the swift-footed wooden couriers had arrived at his place the night before to relay some orders from Strasheela the Wise regarding the administration of Blue Land. Cocus commanded this courier to carry the little dog with him back to the Emerald City.

This mission was accomplished with unheard-of speed: the wooden runner didn't grow tired the way living beings do, and he could run both day and night, since he could see in the dark as well as in daylight.

Ten hours later, the courier was already sounding the bell at the gate of the Emerald City. The door opened after the third ring, and there on the threshold of a vaulted room adorned with an uncounted quantity of emeralds, stood a little man in green spectacles. This was Faramant, Guardian of the Gates. At his side hung a pouch containing green spectacles of every possible size.

"Ah, there you are!" said Faramant calmly. "I was expecting you. But where*s your mistress, Ellie the Fairy?"

When he learned about Ellie's captivity, Faramant stood there in stunned surprise, and then he said: "I'll take you to the monarch of the City, Strasheela the Wise, and he'll be genuinely perturbed, just as I am now. But you must put on some green spectacles. Such was the behest of Goodwin the Great and Terrible. For a time we disregarded it, and in consequence we were hit with great misfortunes." He drew a pair of spectacles from the pouch and, as he placed them on the dog's head and snapped them shut at the rear with a little lock, he said: "These are yours, for here's the little mark on them." At once, every object before Totoshka's eyes assumed one of innumerable shades of green.

It's not known how it happened, but no sooner had Totoshka and his escort taken their first few steps down the street — where the tall buildings almost touched one another up above and cast cool shadows — than the whole City knew about Ellie's sorry fate. Townspeople leaned out of their windows, expressing their sympathy to the dog, and many of them came out of their houses and walked along behind Totoshka and Faramant.

It was a sizable crowd of excited people that approached the palace, but they had to shout and bang their sticks against the fence railings for a long time before finally attracting the attention of the Long-Bearded Soldier. The latter, as always when on duty, was standing inside a certain small turret, looking at himself in a hand-mirror and combing his magnificent beard, which flowed all the way down to the ground. But at length he heard the noise and the shouting, and he lowered the drawbridge and embraced Totoshka, of whom he was very fond.

There are no words that can describe the sorrow felt by Strasheela and Kaggi-Karr, who was his guest at that moment, when they learned that their beloved Ellie had fallen captive among the Undergrounders, and that she had no hope of escaping from them.

Strasheela began to think. He thought for so long that the needles and pins that Goodwin had mixed in with his brains, stuck right out of his head. Then he said: "We'll have to send for the Iron Woodman. Clever brains, of course, are the most important thing in the world, but a loving heart also counts for a lot. Together, the two of us will come up with something more quickly."

Kaggi-Karr flew at once to the Woodman. The Woodman made an appearance there four days later, accompanied by a little old man named Lestar, who was the finest craftsman in all Winkie Land. The Woodman reported that the Crow, after conveying the sad news to him, had flown onward to the Courageous Lion's kingdom to apprize him, too, of what had happened.

When the Woodman talked about the misfortune that had befallen Ellie, he became so upset that tears flowed from his eyes, his jaws rusted and, since he could no longer utter a word, he could do nothing but gesticulate with his hands.

"You've gone dumb again!" exclaimed Strasheela as he untied an oil-can from the Woodman's belt and oiled his friend. "You know you mustn't cry."

"I — I can't help it," said the Woodman with effort. "It — it makes me s-so s-s-sad..."

"You've begun to stutter," said Strasheela with exasperation. "That never happened to you before."

"Wh-what can you do? I'm getting old, m-my friend," the Woodman confessed. "All I have to do is be deeply touched by something, and I-I can't speak. I'll have to see a doctor..."

Totoshka was obliged to repeat in detail, for the Woodman and Lestar, his account of their adventures underground. Ellie and Fred were given, in absentia, a great deal of praise for their brave conduct. And the dog really pulled out all the stops. As Lestar learned about the disappearance of the Soporific Water, he let out a meaningful grunt.

"Did you want to say something?" inquired Strasheela.

"No — or, rather, an idea has came into my head, but no doubt it's preposterous..."

Fleet-winged in spite of her years, Kaggi-Karr did not keep the others waiting for her long. She visited the Lion's domain, and came back with news of a most serious nature.

"The Lion is preparing to go to war against the Underground Kings," said Kaggi-Karr. "When he learned that the kings are keeping Ellie captive and won't let her go, his fury was something I can't even describe. If they had fallen into his hands — or, I should say, into his paws — at that moment, I don*t know what he would have done to them!... Boy, I'm afraid Goodwin may have given him too large a dose of courage," the Crow added anxiously.

"What's he doing?" asked Strasheela.

144

"At the time I flew away, he was preparing to send emissaries to the various parts of his kingdom, to announce a general mobilization of his whole militia."

"Can we do any less?" exclaimed Strasheela, his straw breast filling with martial fire. "We can likewise assemble our army, can't we, Woodman?"

"If it's for Ellie, I'll go through any danger," asserted the Iron Woodman.

"And so will we, the Winkies," Lestar added in a show of support.

Faramant now jumped into the discussion. "We're making a very important decision," he said, "and I feel it's necessary that Ellie be informed about it."

"That's true, but how can we go about it?" asked Din Gior.

"Write her a letter, and I'll deliver it," volunteered Totoshka.

"We thank you in advance for this good deed, dearest Totoshka — but how will you do it?" inquired Faramant.

"Just anyone couldn't have found his way from Underground Land to the upper world, but *I* did it," boasted the dog. "It'll be the merest child's play for me to get back down there!"

Faramant and Din Gior sat down to write their letter.

Chapter 35

TOTOSHKA DELIVERS A LETTER

About two weeks passed after Totoshka's disappearance. The kings did not suspect anything on Ellie's part, because she behaved discreetly. In fact, rather than wait until they started asking her questions about what had happened, she went to Mentaho herself and accused his spies of having done a poor job of keeping an eye on the dog.

"My poor, dear, foolish little Totoshka," wailed Ellie, wiping away her tears. "He's probably been eaten up by one of those horrible Sixpaws, and all because your men didn't take care of my dog!" It ended with Mentaho going so far as to offer Ellie an apology for his spies' carelessness.

Ellie and Fred were living now in a perpetual state of anxiety. Arrigo managed to whisper to them that everything had gone successfully, and that Totoshka had made contact with the Munchkins. All anyone could do now was wait for action of some kind on the part of Strasheela and the Iron Woodman — but how tediously their days of waiting dragged on!

On the fifteenth day after Totoshka's disappearance, Fred and Ellie were taking a walk along the shore of Central Lake, looking dejectedly at its leaden waters, illuminated by the goldenish glow from the clouds. A little ways away strolled two escorts, who never once let the captives out of their sight.

The cousins had received permission to spend time together without the bothersome spies breathing down their necks, and here is how they managed it. A week passed after Ellie had performed her magic over the dried-up spring, and, as one can well imagine, no water appeared. The kings reproached Ellie because her spells were ineffectual, and she returned, quite reasonably: "I anticipated this! The Underground Spirit that controls water is inordinately powerful. Now I'll have to come up with some new incantations — but I can't do it, because conditions aren't right."

"And what conditions do you need?" asked the kings.

"I have to confer with my cousin. He's my assistant, and he knows many occult things. But our consultations

146

must not be heard by any other person's ears, or the charms will lose their potency." Ever since that day, their escorts had remained at a distance.

Ellie said sadly as she looked at the lake, "Where on earth is my beloved Totoshka now, and what ever is he doing?"

All at once, a thin, high-pitched voice sounded from below: "Here I am!" and a small, silky ball pressed against Ellie's legs.

"Totoshka!" exclaimed the girl ecstatically as she clasped him in her arms. "My darling, you're back, you're back!"

When Ellie looked Totoshka over, she came upon a tightly-rolled-up piece of paper under his collar. The girl guessed correctly that this was a letter from the upper world, but there was no way she could take it out now. The spies could not hear their conversations, but they still commanded a superb view of her every action. The children had to wait until they found themselves alone in Ellie's room — a privilege that the supposed fairy insisted on for herself.

Ellie unrolled the paper with great excitement, and here is what was written on it:

Esteemed Ellie, Fairy with the Death-Dealing House, Fairy of the Water of Deliverance —

Greetings!
We — which is to say, Strasheela the Wise, the Iron Woodman, Kaggi-Karr, Din Gior, Faramant, and Lestar — have learned about your lamentable predicament, and our sorrow is infinite. But we will do everything possible, or even impossible, to rescue you. Inform the Seven Underground Kings that if they do not release you and your cousin voluntarily, we will wage war upon them. The Lion is already mo-

147

*bilizing an army of beasts in his own kingdom,
and we ourselves are mustering an army of Winkies and citizens of the Emerald Land.*

*With the greatest impatience we await your
arrival on the surface, and send you a big hug.*

Speaking for all the others,

FARAMANT

When Ellie had finished reading the letter aloud, she wept a few tears, and then she smiled and said, "How kind they all are! How deeply they love me... But war... No, no, I don't want any dreadful war to break out because of us!"

"Well, then," answered Fred, "are we going to sit here until we die? You've consorted so much with wizards and fairies, but it doesn't make a bit of difference, because you don't have even a penny's worth of magic of your own, and you can't restore the Sacred Spring."

"I'm hoping that when the kings realize I'm not a fairy and that there's nothing I can do, they'll let us go."

"And you really think they will!" retorted Fred scornfully. "Those kings are dense and have no sense, like blocks of oak."

"Be that as it may, I won't allow a war!" cried Ellie with conviction. "Still, I will tell the kings that the surface-dwellers demand my release and are preparing to fight. Perhaps that'll frighten them."

"It's worth a try!" agreed Fred.

Totoshka's unexpected reappearance, after having vanished so mysteriously, produced a very strong impression on the Undergrounders. The matter was explained quite simply: the Munchkins took the dog back to the Market Gate and shoved him in through a small hole in the lower part of it, which no one ever took the trouble to guard. And sneaking about unseen along the outskirts of the city would have been of little use to Totoshka.

148

Ellie was summoned to King Mentaho's presence. Looking at the girl probingly, he said: "You were complaining that our people did not take sufficient care of the little animal. And now he's back again. How do you explain that?"

"Perhaps it was through my magic art!" responded Ellie boldly.

Mentaho was embarrassed. "I beg your forgiveness," he mumbled. "Obviously, it's not a good idea for us, who are mere mortals, to interfere in matters of magic. But I'm very happy that you've finally stopped pretending. You'll restore the Soporific Waters for us *now*, whether it wants to flow or not."

It was Ellie's turn to blush this time. "But don't you see, your Majesty, that's something else entirely," she began to equivocate. "We'll talk about that another time. But at this moment I must tell you that I have a most urgent communication for you from the upper world."

"Is it for me personally?"

"It's for all seven of the Underground Kings."

"Then we'll all consider it together at the Supreme Council."

Chapter 36

WAR!

Ellie appeared before the Supreme Council a second time, and she was considerably bolder now than the first time around. She was no longer disconcerted unduly by the rows of courtiers in clothing of all different hues, nor by the majestic bearing of the kings.

It was with assurance in her voice that Ellie set forth Strasheela's ultimatum. But to the children's great disappointment, it did not produce the effect that they would have desired. And the explanation is very simple: the kings and their courtiers, having spent several centuries in sleep, had never actually gone to war, and so they were utterly incapable of imagining what war is like, and how terrible it is.

The first to take the floor was Captain Gaert. He knew about war from the ancient chronicles, written a thousand years back. "War, ho! ho!" he bellowed from the rostrum in an ear-splitting voice. "War — what a jolly undertaking! War — we march out, we beat the drums, *rum-tum-tum!* We smash the enemy, we gather up the spoils: barns filled with wheat, barrels of wine, livestock, fowl! What a feast we'll have after our victory, ho! ho!"

This enumeration of the trophies of war made an enormous impression on the members of the Council: their eyes began to sparkle with greed.

At this point, Ellie jumped in. Unable to restrain herself, she shouted out right from her spot: "You people don't know a thing about war! It's blood, and suffering, and death!... And why are you so firmly convinced that you're going to win?"

"Of that there's not the slightest doubt," answered Gaert. "We have dragons, and we have beasts. All we'll need to do is let a hundred Sixpaws loose against the surface army, after letting them go unfed for two days, and they'll tear everyone into little pieces!..."

Gaert stepped down triumphantly from the rostrum. Ellie was crestfallen: she realized that the Underground Kings had some remarkably powerful facilities at their disposal, that they could apply to warfare.

Mentaho came forward now. Of all the kings, he was the most intelligent. Mentaho did not burst out into martial cheers. He simply said: "Of course, war is not the delightful picnic that Captain Gaert is trying to portray. I'm aware of our weaknesses: if we go up onto the surface, we'll be unable to see anything, and the enemy will capture us with their bare hands. Our dragons and

Sixpaws will likewise be blind in the upper world. But our plan of action does not call for us to go up onto the surface, and why should it? After all, we're not the ones undertaking this war — it's the monarch of the Emerald City who's threatening *us*. So what does that mean? It means, let them come here! We have the wherewithal to engage our enemies, and as long as we're here on our own ground, Gaert is right."

Ellie realized with horror that Mentaho spoke the absolute truth: destruction awaited the surface armies if they should venture down into this alien world that was so utterly unknown to them...

All the speakers who took the floor after that supported Mentaho. The resolution was as follows: *Nothing to be feared from invasion from above, but in event of one, preparations to be made to repulse it. Fairy Ellie not to be released until such time as she has reenchanted the Sacred Spring. No credence to be placed in Ellie's excuses: by clandestinely entering into communication with the surface, she has proved that she commands magical powers.*

At that time, up above, preparations for the great war were proceeding apace.

No sooner had Kaggi-Karr brought the Courageous Lion the news that Ellie was in dire straits, than rabbit heralds began to scurry to all parts of the forest, proclaiming at every woodland junction that their king, the Lion, was calling for a general mobilization. To assure that these cross-eyed messengers would not be devoured by the tigers and leopards, a General Truce was announced. Thenceforth, the beasts of prey no longer dared to molest their smaller brethren, and if it reached the point where one of them simply could not hold out any longer, he could chew on grass, or appease his hunger by eating fruit.

A major obstacle on the road to Blue Land was the Great River, the same one which had occasioned Ellie and her friends such hardship when they crossed it on previous occasions.

The tigers, the leopards, the panthers, and the lynxes did not like water, and the Lion himself would not take to the water except when there was absolutely no avoiding it. But the forest also had smaller streams, and in these streams lived beavers, who were great dam-builders. That very evening, all the beavers were mobilized, and from their number was formed a Construction Brigade under the command of their Chief Engineer, Sharptooth.

The Brigade set out, after receiving a commission to construct in one day a floating bridge across the Great River. A Battalion of monkeys — chimpanzees, macaques, and baboons — was assigned to work with the beavers, and they pulled out large bundles of lianas to be used to tie the logs together.

Feverish work began the moment the builders reached the river. The beavers gnawed down trees growing on the river bank and dragged them into the water, where they placed one log next to another; then the chimpanzees and macaques fastened them together with ropes — or, rather, lianas. The bridge was ready by the appointed deadline, and parrots in the Signal Corps flew off to report it to the Commander-in-Chief.

At noon, a mighty procession set out on its march from the forest. In order of rank strode battalion after battalion of jaguars, cougars, and bears, followed by companies of pumas, lynxes, and panthers. A special detachment of troops was made up of howler monkeys. They were not expected to participate directly in the fighting, but their ear-splitting howls were certain to throw the ranks of their enemies into panic.

One column was made up of rugged buffaloes, aurochs, and bisons: on their backs they carried bunches of bananas and other fruit, which constituted the army's provisions — admittedly not very tempting for the beasts of prey, but useful all the same in satisfying their pangs of hunger.

After saying goodbye to his mate and his cubs, the Lion set out at the head of the company of tigers: they were his personal guard. The military leaders were accompanied by adjutant storks and secretary birds. The adjutants would have the duty of communicating the directive of the Commander-in-Chief, while the secretary birds would keep a chronicle of the campaign and take charge of the distribution of the rations.

The Lion was exceedingly proud of the perfect discipline that he had instilled in his army. He closed his eyes tight and purred contentedly, just like an overgrown house-cat.

Preparations for a campaign were also under way in Violet Land. The Winkies already had some military experience: they had marched against Urfin Jus's wooden army and smashed it. They had one major weapon: the celebrated cannon that had burst after firing its first shot. They had been able to repair the cannon, and there was a supply of gunpowder, which the Giant from Beyond the Mountains had made during his last visit. Aside from the cannon, they had pikes and iron mallets with spikes set into long handles.

The companies of Winkies, who had learned military science under the leadership of Field Marshal Din Gior, were soon marching down the roads.

The inhabitants of Emerald Land were not at all noted for military prowess, but they, too, prepared to undertake a campaign, arming themselves with sickles, scythes, spades, and pitchforks.

It was Strasheela who would be giving the signal to set forth, but he was awaiting the approach of the army of beasts.

Chapter 37

AN UNEXPLAINABLE
DISAPPEARANCE

Ellie was in despair. The kings had rejected Strasheela's ultimatum, and that meant that the monarch of the Emerald City would now be initiating a war, and hundreds, maybe even thousands, of lives would be lost, merely for the sake of freeing two kids from captivity. No matter what else might happen, it was essential that Strasheela be dissuaded from his foolhardy decision.

But how were they to do it? There was no question of sending Totoshka out again: ever since his return, he had been confined in an iron cage, by King Mentaho's orders, and a sentry was on constant vigil beside it. The children thought for a long time about the situation that had developed, and they finally decided on the following.

Fred would have to be the one to escape. Totoshka had been caged, and surveillance over Ellie had increased to an extraordinary degree, but Fred was under virtually no scrutiny. If Arrigo would give him some of his own clothing, Fred could get to the Market Gate and somehow make his way out of Underground Land. Then he would tell the surface-dwellers about the danger that they were heading into.

Several days went by before Ellie was able to talk to Arrigo alone. After some hesitation, the chronicler agreed to the undertaking, though the gravest peril threatened him if the secret should ever become known.

Wine had become a rarity in the Cavern during the last few months, but Arrigo had a bottle at his house that he had keeping for use in just such an emergency. During the night, the Chronicler went to the palace and offered a drink to the sentry guarding Fred's chamber. Arrigo had mixed sleeping powder in the wine.

Fred dressed himself in the Undergrounder's costume, which fitted him perfectly. Arrigo applied make-up to his face, and on the boy's head lay a tall, pointed cap topped by a phosphorescent ball...

Fred's escape caused a great commotion, but it was never solved. The sentry, when he awoke in the morning, was fearful that he would be severely punished, so he swore that he had not closed his eyes once the whole night through nor had he budged from the captive's door.

Fred fooled the guards at the Market Gate by claiming that King Mentaho had sent him to Munchkin Land on an important errand. They let him through, taking him for one of their own kind. When the affair was subsequently investigated, the sentinels were likewise fearful of punishment, and they kept the truth of the matter hidden.

Fred's disappearance was attributed to Ellie's magic spells, and the people's awe of her became even greater. But the watch that they kept over her became utterly unendurable. Two ladies of the court, who were the king's aunts, did not leave the girl's side day or night, and about a dozen spies crowded about her as well.

"Let them do what they want!" Ellie smiled to herself. "At least Freddy is above ground now."

Fred emerged from Underground Land. He could not believe it was true. After so many weeks of monotonous captivity, was he really free, and in Magic Land to boot?

As in the Cavern, a vault spread out above him; but unlike the one down below, this vault was not concealed by goldenish clouds. The dark blue dome of the sky drew back into an immeasurable infinity, and on that infinity shone myriads of bright spots — the stars. Fred's head began to spin, and he could barely stand on his feet. The sweet smells and sounds of this unknown world overwhelmed him completely.

The road to the Munchkins' communities led through the forest. Along the sides grew phenomenally tall trees with enormous whitish-purple flowers exuding a pungent aroma. Little parrots colored in shades of green, red, and blue were flying up from the branches, sleepily chattering all kinds of nonsense. From the depths of the forest came mysterious rustlings and noises.

The very air, breathing the coolness of the night and suffused with the fragrances of flowers, intoxicated the traveler, who had for so long been breathing the stagnant, stuffy rankness of the Cavern. Fred's breast swelled, and he was filled to overflowing with a feeling of vigor and strength. "The Undergrounders are insane, if they deliberately deny themselves the delights of the upper world," chattered the boy as he marched down the road. "If they only knew how nice it is here..."

The newcomer's path brought him at last to a village. Fred liked the Munchkins' round houses peaked with conical roofs, but he had no time to admire their architecture now. He stepped onto the porch of the first house he came to and began to drum on the door. The master of the house, still half-asleep, appeared on the threshold — and he recoiled when he beheld an individual wearing a motley-colored outfit, with a globe on his head that gave out a brilliant light.

"Who on earth are you?" asked the terrified Munchkin. "What do you want?"

"My name is Fred Canning, and I've come straight from Underground Land..."

"But it was only a short time ago that we bartered our goods with the Underground Ore-Diggers, and the next Market Day is still quite a ways off."

"This has nothing to do with the bartering!" exclaimed Fred. "I've just escaped from captivity, but my cousin Ellie is still down there!..."

"What? Ellie? You mean the Fairy With the Death-Dealing House?"

Everything changed when the owner of the house realized who it was before him. He began to shower the boy with expressions of hospitality, but after all the excitement, Fred suddenly felt weak. Added to that, the fugitive had had nothing to eat for over twenty-four hours. He answered the master's questions in a voice that was barely audible, and then he collapsed right there on the porch, totally exhausted.

The confused Munchkin left their guest in his wife's care while he ran out to rouse his fellow villagers. Within a quarter-hour, Fred was ringed by a throng of little men and women wearing pointed hats with bells on them. When he had fortified himself with some milk and fruit, Fred told them that he had to get to the Emerald City as quickly as possible. "I must talk Strasheela and the Iron Woodman out of going through with the war they're undertaking."

The moment they heard that dreadful word "war," the faint-hearted Munchkins burst into tears. "We don't know how to fight, and we don't want to," they said, weeping. "We'll all perish if a war comes..."

"Now cut it out!" cried Fred. "I escaped from the Cavern for the express purpose of assuring peace." The Munchkins calmed down, and they said that peace was a good thing.

"Then take me to the Emerald City," requested the boy.

"The Yellow Brick Road leads there," replied the Munchkins. "But it's a very long journey. Don't you think it would be better for you if you rested for a few hours?"

Fred realized that this would indeed be the best thing for him, for he could barely keep his eyes open, and his feet simply would not walk. His hosts put him in a soft bed, and the boy was soon sound asleep.

Chapter 38

AN ENVOY OF PEACE

Strasheela and all the others welcomed Fred with open arms when they learned who he was. The boy, for his part, gazed with extreme amazement at Strasheela and the Iron Woodman: nowhere else but in Magic Land could such remarkable beings even exist.

Barely two months ago, when he was listening to Ellie's story back in Iowa, he had been unable to shake off his disbelief in it all — yet look at him now! He was actually clasping Strasheela's soft, limp hand and the Woodman's hard iron one. Strasheela was nodding his head imperiously as he talked with him, that head so filled with thoughts and stuffed with bran, while the Woodman's rag-made heart was beating inside his iron breast... And Kaggi-Karr the Crow, perched on the back of the throne, was flashing her intelligent black eyes and asking him about Ellie's well-being in a voice that was perfectly clear (though with a slight burr)...

To the boy, it all seemed as if he were dreaming, and that he would wake up from it at any moment. But every bit of it was real: he was actually standing in the Throne Room of the palace that was built by Goodwin and adorned with an unmeasurable abundance of emeralds, and there were green spectacles over his eyes.

But Fred Canning had not forgotten the mission that Ellie had entrusted him with. "You have no idea of the grave danger you're heading into," said Fred excitedly. "If you could only see the Sixpaws! Just one of those beasts could tear twenty men to pieces — and they've got hundreds of them down there! And those dragons, whose enormous mouths contain rows of sharp teeth, and their

158

clawed feet! How will anyone fight off a monster like that when it swoops down with a hiss, its yellow underbelly flashing? Not to mention that men with spears and bows ride on their backs!..."

Fred spoke long and eloquently, and he was gratified to observe that his listeners were beginning to understand the folly of their undertaking.

"If the Underground Kings were to bring their army above-ground," continued the boy, "it would be another matter — but they're not about to do that. And down below, in the eternal half-light that the eyes of surface people aren't accustomed to, the Cavern-Dwellers have every advantage."

"Then it's decided!" said Strasheela with a shake of his head. "There's to be no war!" All the others agreed with his decision.

"But how are we going to rescue Ellie?" asked the Iron Woodman in a downcast voice. He almost began to weep, but he caught himself just in time.

At this point, soft-spoken little Lestar, the distinguished mechanical engineer from Winkie Land, spoke up. "As far as I can tell, the Underground Kings would let Ellie go if she were to restore their Sacred Spring. Isn't that true?" he asked.

"Absolutely so," asserted Fred. "But Ellie can't do it, because she's really no worker of magic! Things would have gone far better if she hadn't put on airs the way she did!"

"Well, it may turn out that magic isn't even needed," said Lestar with a sly grin. "Tell me, young man, do you know what a water-pump is?"

Fred's face turned crimson with outrage. "On our farm, every boy uses one ten times in a day," he muttered indignantly.

But Lestar, unruffled, continued his questioning: "And did you see any pumps down there in the Cavern?"

Fred pondered about this. "No, I don't think so. What they do have are water-wheels. They're set vertically in the lake, and Sixpaws are cooped up inside them; when they run around inside the wheels and make them turn, water is picked up in scoops and poured out into chutes, which carry it into the city."

"Well, well, how splendid!" beamed the mechanical wizard.

"But what are all these questions leading up to, friend Lestar?" asked Din Gior curiously.

"You see, I've got an idea," said the little old man, "I have the feeling that we'll be able to liberate Mistress Ellie without any bloodshed. But for that to happen, we'll have to restore the Magic Water to the kings, so that's what we're going to try to do."

Cries of acclamation reverberated in the throne room. Everyone sang the praises of Lestar, and he smiled modestly.

"We mustn't rejoice too soon," said the craftsman. "If this water of theirs originates in a spot that's not too far down, then we can pump it out. But I'll have to fashion some long drills to bore through the rock, and, of course, a water-pump with good suction."

Lestar set out for Winkie Land, because only there would he be able to produce those things. Kaggi-Karr flew off to inform the Lion that the war had been called off, and that he was to disband his hordes.

Chapter 39

A STRANGE EMBASSY

The sentinels who guarded the Market Gate heard a loud knocking sound. The Captain of the Guards took a look out the little window. It was a strange sight that met his eyes. Before the gates stood a circle of about ten wooden men, and they were gleefully banging each other on the backs with their enormous fists. The racket they were making was enough to wake the dead!

"Why are you doing that?" asked the startled trooper.

"In order that you'll hear us!"

"Well, you could have knocked on the gate."

"Your gates are still standing," remarked the wooden man scornfully. "You would have cursed us out if they'd tumbled down!"

"Who exactly are you, and what do you want here?"

"We are Deadwood Oaks, and we bear a message to your kings from the Monarch of the Emerald City, Strasheela the Wise."

After conferring with one another, the soldiers decided that there was surely no duplicity here: it was highly unlikely that ten wooden men alone could seize control of an entire kingdom. And if they had come to reconnoiter, then by all means, let them take a look! One view of the Sixpaws and the dragons down there would surely be enough to make them change their minds about unleashing a war.

So they admitted the ambassadors and provided them with an escort, and the Deadwood Oaks began to tramp in a body down the hard-paved road.

The wooden men were received in the throne room, after all the kings and their ministers had assembled there. Ellie was likewise brought in. Since Mentaho happened to be back on the throne that month, it was he who took the letter and began to read it.

> We — Strasheela the Wise, Monarch of the
> Emerald City — the Iron Woodman, Monarch
> of Violet Land — and the Courageous Lion, King
> of the Beasts — convey our heartfelt greetings
> to our brother monarchs, the Underground
> Kings...

Mentaho interrupted his reading and said: "We thank our fellow monarchs of the upper world for their greeting, and we answer them with the same. Please convey it for us!" The Deadwood Oaks grinned stupidly.

Mentaho continued his reading:

> *We are deeply distressed because you are holding captive in your kingdom, without any right to do so, one whom Fate dropped among you by chance and who is very dear to our hearts: the fairy Ellie.*
>
> *However, taking into consideration the fact that you are guided by the most vital of motivations, to wit, your desire to restore the Soporific Waters and to reestablish the system that has obtained for centuries in your kingdom, we renounce any intentions of declaring war against you, and propose settling the matter peaceably...* ("A very discreet proposal," remarked Mentaho on the side.) *We, the residents of the upper world, are the successors of the Mighty Goodwin, and much of his arcane knowledge has been passed on to us. It occurs to us that if Ellie is unable to reenchant the Magic Spring by herself, then she may succeed in doing so with our collaboration.*

The reading was interrupted by a deafening applause. But Ellie felt apprehensive and embarrassed. "What do they count on doing?" she thought. "It's a tremendous miscalculation on Strasheela's part. They won't be able to accomplish anything either, and then we'll *all* be prisoners down here."

When the hall had quieted down, Mentaho finished his reading of the letter. Its contents reassured Ellie.

> *But if the hostile powers turn out to be more than we can handle, and we fail to restore the*

Soporific Water, you will not place any obstacles in our way to returning to the surface. Concerning the fate of Ellie, we will decide that in Joint Council. To assure you of the goodness of our intentions, we are sending you some gifts. At the moment you read this letter, a caravan of five hundred workers will be approaching the entrance of the Cavern, bearing you flour, meat, cheese, fruit, honey, wine...

The thunderous ovation this time outdid anything that had ever previously been heard there in that hall. Such an ovation was quite understandable. The stock of provisions on hand in the Cavern, even counting the ones that had just been purchased this last time, was nearing its end, and famine would be threatening not only the commoners, but the royal courts as well, within three or four days' time.

It was with feeling that Mentaho read the signature: *"Strasheela the Wise. The Iron Woodman. The Courageous Lion. On their behalf, as they are unable to write for themselves, Faramant has fixed his hand."*

The Guardian of the Gates really knew the art of letter-writing!

Tears of joy glistened in Ellie's eyes. "How kind and generous my friends are," she thought. "And even if they fail in their bold undertaking, and they're unable to rescue me from Underground Land, at least I'll get to see them..."

The kings and the aristocrats surrounded the Deadwood Oaks, and they looked them over, feeling them and slapping them on their shoulders and backs. "Yes," said King Elyana contemplatively, "that Urfin Jus was indeed a mighty sorcerer. He was able to bring blockheads like these to life!"

"But Ellie defeated him," commented King Mentaho. "That makes her an even more powerful fairy. The only unfortunate thing is that, owing to some caprice or other, she refuses to reenchant the Sacred Spring!"

The Deadwood Oaks were handed a safe-conduct pass, affixed with the signatures of all seven kings. It was for Strasheela, the Woodman, the Lion, and all their followers, and it promised them safety for the duration of their sojourn in the Cavern, and liberty to return to the upper world unhindered.

The Ministers of Stores had already left the hall: they were running around assembling bearers so that they could go and pick up the cargo of foodstuffs, that generous gift from the surface world.

There is no need to tell that the moment this council adjourned, Totoshka was released.

Chapter 40

ELLIE IS REUNITED WITH HER FRIENDS

About twelve days went by, and then a soldier, flying in from the Market Gate on dragon-back, announced that the Monarch of Magic Land was entering the Cavern with a large entourage.

At once, messengers ran and flew to every part of the country, with the following edict:

> *Entire populace to take part in the solemn reception of guests from above. All work in fields and factories to cease, with exception of the smelting of metals in metallurgists' foundries. Residents to wear holiday attire, to gather along*

*the side of road leading to city from Market Gate.
Sixpaws to be herded into stalls and firmly teth-
ered so that none of them can break free and
cause commotion. Dragon-mounted guards to
fly in circles above procession in manner showing respect, but not to swoop down too low.*

A delighted hubbub arose everywhere. The people
donned their best clothes and their cleanest caps, and then
they ran with light hearts to meet the munificent newcomers from the world above.

The City of the Seven Monarchs was soon empty. Not
one person was left there, other than cripples and decrepit
old men. Kings, ministers, and courtiers, magnificently
dressed in all colors of the rainbow, marched out in an
even column to meet their guests, to the sounds of a band
and the beating of drums. At the head of this column
walked Ellie, carrying Totoshka in her arms. Thousands
of spectators lined both sides of the road for miles on end.
They waved their arms and their caps, and shouted out
joyous words of welcome...

The guests finally appeared. They were headed by six
Deadwood Oaks (soldiers to the last!) marching in step.
The first of these held a bouquet of flowers. The next four
carried a litter, on which Strasheela sat regally, bowing
graciously to the right and left. The litter was followed
by thirty attractive young lads and lasses — pupils of the
Dancing School — carrying enormous bouquets of flowers in their arms. They were under the tutelage of Dance
Instructor Lan Pirot, the former General. Lan Pirot assumed irresistibly elegant poses, and from time to time
he would break out into a dance — to the spectators' great
delight.

Behind them marched the Lion majestically, with Fred
Canning on his back. The boy was exceptionally proud
now, and not for all the riches in the world would he have
given up his present situation. Who among the kids he

knew had ever had occasion to take part in such a re-markable procession, and ride on a lion's back? What sto-ries he'd have to tell back in Iowa! Most likely, no one would believe them, any more than he himself had be-lieved those told by Ellie.

The Iron Woodman, freshly polished and oiled, with a shining golden oil-can swinging from his belt, was car-rying a gleaming golden ax over his shoulder. On the Woodman's head sat Kaggi-Karr the Crow, with beauti-ful gold bracelets on her legs. Not to exaggerate, every one of our heroes had adorned himself to the utmost of his ability for his visit underground.

Din Gior, Faramant, and Lestar came forward behind the others, arm in arm and side by side. Din Gior's beard, which was plaited in strands and reached all the way down to the ground, made an enormous impression on the Cavern-Dwellers.

Several dozen Munchkins were carrying some addi-tional gifts: bundles of clothing and footwear, baskets of toys, and baby-carriages that they rolled along. Their sharp-pointed blue hats swayed rhythmically as they walked, and the little bells suspended beneath the hats tinkled melodiously.

The rear of the procession was taken up by Deadwood Oaks loaded down with levers, wheels, drills, pipes... In their midst, behind the formation, came the craftsmen of Violet Land.

On the whole, this cavalcade made an indelible im-pression on the Cavern-Dwellers: it was some sort of bright, shining apparition from the upper world, one that had brought with it down to Underground Land the ra-diance of the sunlight, the transparency of the air, the blue of the sky...

When the two solemn processions had made contact, and as tall, stately King Mentaho lifted his arm and pre-pared to deliver a solemn speech, Ellie dispensed with all ceremony. Squealing with delight, she ran from the ranks and charged at breakneck speed toward Strasheela's litter. In an instant, the Deadwood Oaks had formed themselves into a staircase, and the girl was in the arms of her lovable old friend. She stroked his kindly, painted-on face and kissed him on the cheeks, and Strasheela exclaimed happily: "Eh-hey-hey-ho! Ellie and I are together — we're together — we're together again! Eh-hey-hey-hey-ho!..."

However, he quickly remembered himself, and he fearfully closed his mouth with his hand: it was not fitting for a personage of his eminence to behave in such a flighty manner.

By this time, the Iron Woodman, Fred Canning, the Courageous Lion, Din Gior, Faramant were also speeding toward the litter... Before long, everything was in a merry commotion. Ellie and Totoshka passed from arm to arm, and King Mentaho realized with bitterness that he would have no opportunity to display his oratorical skill that day. He had to content himself with merely uttering a few polite phrases, and with accepting in return the greetings of Strasheela, the Woodman, and the Lion — sovereigns of their respective realms.

Then all the people mingled together, and the happy crowd thronged into the City of the Seven Monarchs.

Ellie rode on the Lion's back, and by her side walked Fred, who related to her the adventures he had had after leaving the sleeping palace in disguise by night. But he was interrupted in short order by the Iron Woodman, who asked Ellie to listen to how hard his heart had been beating ever since the moment when he had seen her again.

At times, the Lion, too, turned his head and interjected a few words about the mighty fighting force that he had assembled and then discharged, while Kaggi-Karr got into an argument with Totoshka about who would get to sit in Ellie's arms. The pandemonium was enormous, and everyone was extremely happy...

Chapter 41

MECHANICAL WIZARDRY

To honor their eminent guests, the Seven Underground Kings gave a sumptuous banquet. A ballet was performed at this banquet, and the young lads and lasses from Lan Pirot's Academy of Dance displayed their amazing artistry, to everyone's delight. Incidentally, the youthful artists returned home the very next day: a sojourn in the Cavern would be too likely to undermine their precarious health. And with them went the Munchkins who had carried the gifts to the Undergrounders. The little people spent only one day in the Cavern, but for the rest of their lives, they retained in their minds a dread of its gloomy but majestic wonders.

Both hosts and guests slept for a long time after the banquet was done — with the exception, of course, of the Iron Woodman and Strasheela, who never slept at all.

Early the next morning, Lestar rose by himself and set right to work. He had made the acquaintance of Rujero the Time Keeper the night before and had a long conversation with him. Lestar and Rujero took a liking to one another, and a friendship developed between them at once. And so, that morning after the banquet, Lestar sought out Rujero, and he asked him to take him to the Sacred Cavern.

The two new friends walked along and chatted, while the Deadwood Oaks, under the supervision of the craftsmen, dragged pipes, levers, and pulley blocks behind them. From their conversation, Lestar perceived that the Time Keeper was not inclined to the opinion that any wizardry could restore the Soporific Waters. The master

observed Rujero looking slyly over all the complicated
equipment that the wooden men were carrying, and then
grin and say: "The matter can only turn out better with
all these devices here, and the Underground Spirit will
back down. All poor little Ellie had to work with were
incantations. And what are incantations? Nothing more
than words."

"My esteemed Rujero," said Lestar, "I see that you're
a most astute individual. But I don't think it would be a
good thing to express ideas like these to the Seven Kings."

"I'm of the same opinion, my honored Lestar," the
Time Keeper agreed. "Not everything uttered between
two friends is suitable for the ears of their Majesties." The
two old man, quite happy with one another, continued
their trek.

Lestar undertook an in-depth investigation of the Sacred Cavern itself. Bidding the Deadwood Oaks to remain
silent, he placed his ear to the ground in various spots,
trying to detect the sound of water coursing underground.
He held a small mirror over cracks in the rock, looking
for traces of evaporation in them.

He continued his work for a long time, and while he
was thus engaged, Rujero sat down on a rock and rested
from the long journey. Then Lestar walked up to him.

"Well, what is it, my dear friend?" asked Rujero.

"It's hopeful," replied the master cautiously, "but the
wizardry will be long and difficult."

For a start, the Deadwood Oaks, under the guidance
of Lestar and the other Winkies, leveled a square area next
to the basin and set up the support for the drilling apparatus. The work was soon in full swing in their powerful
hands, as they moved enormous rocks around without
the least strain.

"Urfin Jus left you people a good heritage," said Rujero
with a laugh.

"Yes, we definitely mustn't complain," replied Lestar in agreement. "But keep in mind that these men didn't become obedient workers until after new faces had been carved for them. And that was done in accordance with Strasheela's theory."

Not until evening did the company return to the city. Another banquet was already in progress there. This time Strasheela, following the rules of diplomatic etiquette, was giving a diversion for the kings in return, using the products that his own people had brought along.

Several days went by. There was ongoing contact between the City of the Seven Monarchs and the Sacred Cavern as Deadwood Oaks, Winkies and Underground metallurgists trotted continually back and forth, carrying machine parts and other essential materials. But the entrance to the Sacred Cavern was off-limits to the kings, the courtiers, and their spies. At Lestar's insistence, Ellie told the Seven Kings that a dreadful spirit named the Great Mechanic Master lived there, and that this spirit could be conquered only by means of mechanical wizardry. And when mechanical wizardry was being applied, it was exceedingly dangerous for outsiders to be present, for it might have an effect on their reason.

However, it was declared that Ellie's presence at the preparations for the mechanical wizardry was absolutely essential, and she spent her entire days there. The Sacred Cavern itself could not be desecrated by people exercising such normal human needs as eating and sleeping, so a camp for the workers was set up in one of the neighboring caverns. Beds were transported into it, and open hearths were set up for cooking food.

But for Ellie, as a fairy, an exception was made. The Deadwood Oaks built her a cozy little hut right inside the Sacred Cavern, and she was given everything she needed: a bed, a little dining table, a small cupboard for dishes (of which Strasheela had brought her a whole dozen!), and everything else. There, Ellie, weary of all the noise of the workers, spent her hours of rest with Totoshka.

The labors proceeded apace. Augers whirred as they cut into the solid rock. Winkie craftsmen screwed lengths of pipe together for the water pumps and fitted valves to them. The inquisitive Fred was everywhere: sometimes he'd relay one or another of Lestar's directions, at other times he'd haul over to the metalsmith some part that the latter needed, and at still other times he'd oversee the work of the drillers. The boy was utterly thrilled: how could he have expected, before this, that he'd ever have such an opportunity to experience these remarkable adventures?...

Strasheela, the Iron Woodman, and the Lion, however, did not show their faces in the labyrinth: the damp climate of the Cavern did not suit them.

After a sojourn of several days in Underground Land, Strasheela felt very poorly. He could move only with effort because his straw had grown heavy from the dampness, and there was no place where it could be dried out. Cooking in the Cavern was done on small portable stoves whose fires were prevented from penetrating outward and thereby hurting the Undergrounders' weak eyes. Those little stoves did not warm the air around them the least little bit.

Matters were worse with Strasheela's amazing brains. The bran with which his head was stuffed likewise grew damp, and the needles and pins mixed in with them rusted. This caused Strasheela to suffer headaches, and he began to forget the simplest words.

Even Strasheela's facial features began to change, because the watercolors that had been used to paint them dissolved and ran together.

The distraught Faramant summoned a doctor for his monarch. The one who came was Boril, descendant of the same Boril in whose time the first Sleep had been accomplished. Chubby and self-satisfied, just like his ancestor, the doctor examined his distinguished patient. "Hmmmm, hmmmm, it's bad," he mumbled. "Your Excellency has the beginnings of a very dangerous malady — dropsy. The best remedy for that is the warmth and light of the sun."

"I can't play — I mean, stay — here, Ellie," said Strasheela in a muffled voice.

"Then again..." said the doctor reflectively, "then again, the metal-workers' foundry might serve as a good clinic for your Excellency. I submit that in the hot, dry air there, you'd become well again."

They bore Strasheela away to the foundry and set him down in a secluded corner where he would bother no one and would not be in the way of the workers. Faramant, who remained by the monarch's side in the capacity of nurse, made certain that no sparks from the furnace would fall upon Strasheela. If that happened, the patient, far from being cured, would perish.

Dense clouds of steam poured forth from Strasheela during the first day or two in the hot, dry air of the plant, and then he began to return to health with remarkable speed. His arms and legs filled again with vitality, and his brains became clear once more.

The Iron Woodman had it far worse. The humidity penetrated his iron joints, and they began to rust. This rust that formed in the Cavern was particularly corrosive, and even frequent oilings were not proof against it. The Woodman's golden oil-can was soon empty, and every one of his limbs squeaked whenever he moved. His jaws would not move at all, and the poor fellow tried in vain to open his mouth. The Woodman had become mute, and he had turned into an invalid.

Din Gior summoned Doctor Robil to examine him. The physician said: "In order to prevent his Resplendency — or, perhaps I should say, his *former* Resplendency? — from

172

crumbling away to nothing in a mere matter of days, it'll be necessary to immerse him in a barrel of oil. That's the only way he can be saved."

Fortunately, the last transport of provisions had included a quantity of vegetable oil that more than sufficed, and they submerged the Iron Woodman in it so deeply that nothing could be seen above the surface except the funnel that served him as a hat.

To keep the Woodman from becoming bored, the Long-Bearded Soldier sat beside him on a stool and told him various stirring tales of his own past, when he still served as doorkeeper under Goodwin.

When the Woodman felt like taking a walk, he sometimes climbed out of the barrel for an hour or two and went to pay a call on Strasheela or the Lion. The Mighty Lion, the free son of the forests, was likewise doing badly in the Cavern: the King of the Beasts had come down with bronchitis! Boril wrote him a prescription for some medicinal powder, and before long, every apothecary had exhausted his supply: one can readily imagine the size of the doses of medicine that the Lion would need! And when the Lion had swallowed all the powders, he started in on the pieces of paper in which they had been wrapped.

Thus, all was not going too well for Ellie's friends, and this obliged Lestar to make as much haste as he could in the preparations for his mechanical wizardry.

Chapter 42

A NEW USE FOR DIAMONDS

The monarchs of Magic Land and the King of the Beasts were not the only ones who were having a hard time of it in the Cavern. Those who had accompanied

173

them down were also going through trying days. Underground Land's perpetual gloom, the autumnal colors of nature there, and the humid atmosphere made the people feel depressed. They missed their own country, with its blue sky and its sunshine, the cheerful singing of the birds on the boughs of the trees, the rustling of the wind in the groves.

Even the Deadwood Oaks, those powerful and rugged wooden creations, felt their arms and legs, which had become swollen from the dampness, no longer obeying them as well as they had before.

Lestar speeded up his work. During their short periods of rest, the Head Craftsman changed assistants, and then drills bored, pulleys squeaked, and hammers pounded as before. It became evident that the source from which the Magic Water welled up was at considerably deeper down than the Head Craftsman had supposed, but he finally detected its presence in the bowels of the earth. The worn-out drills, which had to be replaced periodically with new ones, came up from the lower depths wet.

Lestar gave his men strict orders not to touch this water, but one day, when they returned to the Sacred Cavern after a lunch break, they saw about two dozen mice next to the drill that had most recently been drawn up. The mice were lying there legs-up, sleeping the magic sleep! They had licked a few drops of Soporific Water off the drill.

The mice slept for several hours, and precautionary measures at the work site were redoubled.

And then came that happy moment when the Magic Water gushed out in a mighty torrent into the basin that had been prepared for it beforehand. Lestar and his assistants, Ellie, and Fred Canning gathered around, and they watched for a long time with a respectful curiosity as the Soporific Water flowed out, seething and sparkling with a bluish color and giving off fizzy little bubbles.

Chapter 42: A NEW USE FOR DIAMONDS

Then everyone set to work. Ellie sat down next to her hut and began to play with one of her diamonds. These little stones, which glittered in every color of the rainbow — the same ones that she and Fred had obtained in one of the grottos — fascinated the little girl in the worst possible way. She admired the diamond's sparkle, and she put it up to her eyes, then moved it further away and tossed it around in the palm of her hand... Engrossed as she was in this guileless occupation, Ellie did not observe what was happening in the cavern. All at once, Totoshka, who was lying in her lap, turned over, yawned deeply, and... went to sleep!

Surprised, Ellie took a look around her. What she saw astonished her. Fred Canning was sleeping in a most uncomfortable position among the rocks. Lestar and his helpers, overcome by irresistible sleep, had sunk down onto the floor of the cave wherever they happened to be standing.

In the wink of an eye, Ellie understood: "Danger! The Magic Water can put people to sleep with its vapor alone!"

She ran over to the Deadwood Oaks, who were grinning stupidly and gawking in silence at what had been happening, and commanded them: "Hurry! Hurry! Pick up the people and carry them out of here!"

All the sleepers were carried at once to the workers' campsite and laid down on beds. Ellie, with intense anxiety, sat there by Fred's side until she, too, was overcome by sleep — but sleep of the normal variety, fortunately.

The sleepers did not awaken for a full twenty-four hours, and they displayed all the innocence of new-born babes. Ellie was dismayed: "What are we going to do with them?"

Then the girl sent the wooden brigadier Arum back to the Cavern to fetch Din Gior and Faramant, instructing him to summon them there in secrecy and not to tell anyone else about it.

175

She took care of Fred herself: she fed him pap with a little spoon and began to instruct him in how to talk. The Magic Water Vapor could not have had too strong an effect on Fred's brain, because in an hour's time he had already begun to smile and say "Mama," and then he grabbed the diamond from the bedside table and stuck it in his mouth.

"Uh-uh, you'll hurt yourself!" Ellie exclaimed, and she took the hazardous plaything away from him.

Faramant and Din Gior arrived several hours later, alarmed by this unexpected summons. When the friends heard the little girl's account of what had happened, they could not understand why everyone else had fallen asleep, but not Ellie. Faramant began to question Ellie rather aggressively about what she had been doing while the others were working, and when it came out at last that the girl had been playing with a diamond, the Guardian of the Gates gave a sigh of relief. "Well," he said, "it looks like the diamond was the talisman that protected you."

"What's a talisman?" asked Ellie.

"It's an object that shields people from misfortune," explained Faramant.

All three of them rejoiced that the girl decided to occupy herself with the diamond at the particular moment she did. What if she had fallen asleep along with the others? All of them might have lain there in the enchanted sleep for the longest time before it would occur to the brainless Deadwood Oaks to take any kind of action.

Faramant and Din Gior began the reeducation of Lestar and the other Winkies, while Ellie spent her time with Fred and Totoshka.

They were able to keep these events secret from the families of the kings. When Lestar regained his memory, he sent the Deadwood Oaks to let the Magic Water out of the basin through a special tap, and then he left the area to report to Strasheela.

176

Chapter 42: A NEW USE FOR DIAMONDS

In the dry air of the foundry, the monarch of the Emerald City felt splendid, and his head virtually swam with brilliant ideas. He did not bother to tell anyone about some of them, as he alone would be able to understand them. But when Lestar made his report, Strasheela was struck by such an idea in his brilliant head that it made him jump up and down with delight. He ordered the Craftsman to summon Rujero the Time Keeper to his presence at once.

After saluting Rujero, Strasheela asked him: "Tell me, my friend, do you have any really compelling need for seven kings and all the riffraff that hang around them, all of whom it's necessary for you people to feed?"

After thinking it over, Rujero answered: "Truthfully speaking, we have no special need of them. But the people are used to it... And then again, each king and his entire retinue are asleep for six months out of seven."

"But during the seventh month they hold banquets, at the common people's expense!"

"That's true," admitted Rujero, somewhat embarrassed.

"Then why not simply put the entire company of them to sleep at one time?" asked Strasheela.

"All seven kings?!" exclaimed Rujero. "Why, that's a *great* idea! But... but here's the problem. They're sure to guess that there's some ulterior motive behind it all, and they won't go along with it."

"But suppose we put them to sleep in such a way that they don't suspect anything?"

"That'll be difficult," said Rujero. "Mentaho is ruling at this moment, and he's very intelligent and astute."

"We'll put him to sleep too, and his wit won't be of any help to him. Lestar, my friend, tell him what happened to you people in the cavern."

When Rujero had heard the account of how people had fallen asleep merely from the vapor of the Magic Water, he exclaimed: "That changes matters completely!

We'll have the whole horde of them assemble there and let the magic sleep overcome them unawares. But there's still one difficulty: those of us who are carrying out this scheme will go to sleep along with them. And if we're not there with them, it'll look very suspicious."

"Don't worry," said Lestar. "We have a talisman for that very emergency." And he told the Time Keeper about the effect that diamonds had.

Rujero was ecstatic. "Then it's settled! We'll put all those spongers to sleep, and the country will breathe freely again."

"What then?" asked Strasheela.

"What do you mean by 'then?'"

"When they wake up."

"If we just keep them in the vicinity of the spring, they won't wake up," countered Rujero.

"I beg pardon, my friend," said Strasheela in a meaningful tone, "but that will be the same thing as murdering them."

"Excuse me, your Excellency. I hadn't thought of that. We'll have to bring them to the Rainbow Palace, and let them sleep in their storage chambers."

"And what then?" persisted Strasheela.

"What do you mean, 'What then?!'" retorted Rujero with vexation.

"Well, they'll eventually awaken some time!"

"We could give them more of the water to drink," replied the Time Keeper, uncertain.

"It would be better to leave them to die in the Sacred Cavern!" exclaimed Strasheela derisively. "It would be quicker, and cost you less trouble."

"Your Excellency, *please* explain yourself — I simply don't follow you," Rujero implored him. "Your ideas are too deep for me, and it's not for nothing that the residents of the Emerald City call you the Triply Wise!"

"You've heard about that?" said Strasheela, smiling graciously. "Very well, I'll explain my idea to you. After their magic sleep, the people reawaken in a state like that of newborn babies. Isn't that so?"

"Right!"

"Over the course of several days, they have to be reared again, and reminded of all the things they once knew but forgot?"

"Right!"

"Then who would stop you from instilling in the mind of that same King Mentaho, when he reawakened, the idea that, before his enchanted sleep, he wasn't a king, but, rather, a smith, or a metallurgist, or a plowman, and from teaching him the fundamentals of a new trade?"

If lightning had struck Rujero in the foot, he could not have been more overwhelmed. The Time Keeper's face lit up in a radiant smile. "Your Excellency," he cried, "you are positively the greatest thinker in the world!"

"Oh, that's been known to everyone for a long time," answered Strasheela modestly.

Chapter 43

SEVEN SHIFTY SCHEMES

Rujero's joy was short-lived. One of the courtiers delivered a message to the Time Keeper that King Mentaho wanted to see him. Rujero reported to him at the designated time. The king led him into a small room and closed the door firmly behind them. From this precaution, Rujero realized that the discussion was to be secret.

Mentaho seated the newcomer in a soft armchair, and then he took a seat facing him. "How are you, my dear friend?" asked the king in a kind voice. "You seem to be have a lot of concerns lately."

"Quite a lot," affirmed Rujero.

"You should take care of your precious health and delegate part of your concerns to others," continued Mentaho in a tone that was unusually obliging. This put the Time Keeper on his guard at once. At no time had Mentaho ever talked to him in this manner before. "Careful, Rujero!" the old man said to himself. "The king wants something out of you, something very important."

"By the way," said Mentaho, as if bringing up the matter casually, "I've heard that the reenchantment of the Sacred Spring is nearing completion?"

"You're not mistaken in that, your Majesty!"

"Well, a delightful idea has come into my head in connection with that," Mentaho giggled nervously. "I don't know if it will meet with your approval or not, my dear friend?"

"Speak, your Majesty!"

"The first who's due to be put to sleep is myself," continued the king. "But, to speak truthfully, I've come to the conclusion over the past few months that the magical sleep is not such a good thing, and that life itself is far more interesting — especially when you're a king!"

"Then continue to be king," said Rujero with restraint.

"Yes, but the king who's ruling and the king who's waiting his turn to rule — they're two completely different things."

"I don't understand your idea. Please explain it more fully."

So Mentaho began to tell him point-blank: "I'll give a banquet for my fellow kings and their courtiers. The wine that we serve them will have Soporific Water added to it (as much of it as possible, hopefully!), and so the whole company will fall into the enchanted sleep!"

When he noticed the stupefaction in the face of the man he was addressing, he asked him dryly, "Don't you like my idea? Perhaps you think that one of the other kings is more capable of governing the kingdom than I am?"

180

Rujero thought for a moment. "If I don't go along with him, Mentaho will find himself others to help him, and danger will be threatening all of us." So he expressed total agreement with the king's plan.

The king's face lit up, and he began to promise Rujero all kinds of benefits: "You'll become the highest-ranking individual after myself, and I'll build you a house no less fine than the Rainbow Palace!..."

"I don't need any reward, your Majesty," said Rujero. "Count on me, all will be done."

"But not a word to anyone, especially Ellie and all the other surface people!"

"My lips are sealed!" averred Rujero. "But don't you take any action on your own, for that might spoil everything. When the time comes to act, you'll be alerted."

He took leave of King Mentaho, and the next day, he was summoned by King Barbedo. Fat, bald-headed Barbedo looked nothing like the graceful Mentaho, with the handsome face and gracious smile. But when he took the Time Keeper into his private office and carefully closed the door with a bang, something in Barbedo's manner was strikingly similar to that of Mentaho. This caught the perceptive Rujero's eye immediately. "Well, it looks like something devious is afoot here as well," he thought.

The king began the conversation with topics wide of the mark, but Rujero understood his intent at once. And it came as no surprise to him when Barbedo, after much beating around the bush, proposed to him that they put all his rivals to sleep in order that he, Barbedo, could rule alone for as much time as destiny had allotted him to live, and then let his eldest son ascend the throne. And the others? Well, let them just continue to sleep in peace, for when they were asleep, they'd have no cares, no worries...

"I'm sure you agree with me, my dear friend," Barbedo intoned sweetly, "that the constant change of kings is an utter disaster for our country. It's caused our good people so much suffering..." (The plump man even began to weep.) "And of course, the one who was first to come up with the happy idea of putting an end to all this squabbling, that person has earned the right to take advantage of its fruits..." ("If you really *had* been the first!" thought Rujero contemptuously.) "And you, my dear Time Keeper — I'll shower you with diamonds and emeralds, and you'll become the wealthiest man in all the land."

Of course, Rujero gave his promise to him as well that he would see his underhanded scheme through to a successful conclusion, and he asked the king not to undertake anything without his knowledge. When he had returned to his senses, he thought, "I wonder if it'll go any further. Are there only two double-dealers among the Underground Kings? Will this business end with them?"

Alas, the business was *not* over. The Time Keeper was summoned to secret meetings with Kings Elyana, Caroto, Lamente... The feeble Arbusto had likewise gotten it in mind to eliminate his rivals and rule strictly in his own right. "I don't have much longer to live," mumbled the ninety-year-old Arbusto, "and I can't waste all my time sleeping. Even if it's only for two or three years, I must remain king of our land..."

And Bubala, who was sixteen, repeated words that his tutor had prepared for him: "I'm the youngest of them all, which means that I'll be ruling the kingdom for a long time, and I'll accomplish many glorious deeds during my reign."

Even the widowed queen Raffida, mother of the infant Tevalto, came to see Rujero to make an effort on behalf of her son (which proves, among other things, that the woman's mind is in no way inferior to the man's when it comes to concocting new forms of guile).

Rujero promised his aid to all the double-crossers, and each of them was very happy with his talk with him, promising him every possible benefit.

Chapter 43: SEVEN SHIFTY SCHEMES

Needless to say, Strasheela and Ellie *were* informed of these shifty schemes. (The Woodman, seated in his barrel of oil, was not quite up to foiling other people's plots, while life itself had become positively abhorrent to the ailing Lion — though, because of his fondness for Ellie, he had not returned to the surface.)

Rujero had run to see the monarch of the Emerald City directly after his meeting with King Mentaho. Strasheela approved of the way in which Rujero had pretended to agree, and he urged him to try to hold out until the labors at the Sacred Cavern were terminated completely. The wise man of straw found Rujero's second visit less surprising, and after that, he ceased to be surprised at all.

"All kings — both below ground and above — are crafty and cruel in equal measure," said Strasheela. "Just think, every one of them, from the suckling Bubala to the ancient Arbusto, every one of them came up with the self-same idea — to get his rival cousins out of the way so that he could assume all the power himself. And you know, my esteemed Rujero, I haven't the slightest doubt that each and every one of them would be glad to bring about the deaths of his relatives through the enchanted sleep."

"I'm dead certain of that," agreed Rujero.

"But why do they all have such similar ideas?" Strasheela went on. "They're simply blinded by the grandeur of the royal authority, and they don't want to share it with anyone else. I'm really happy that I've come up with the idea of reeducating them. And I'm sure that after that's been done, they won't be such bad people after all..."

Chapter 44

THE GREAT "SLEEPENING"

The news was spreading all over the Cavern: the sorcery of Ellie and her friends was nearing completion, and the Great Mechanic Master would soon be vanquished. This report aroused feelings of exultation among the kings: let's not forget that each of them counted on eliminating all his rivals and becoming sole ruler in his own right.

A date and an hour were soon designated for the consummation of the miracle. Rujero the Time Keeper and Arrigo the Chronicler, who were in charge of the festivities, announced that anyone who so wished might be present, but attendance would be limited to those who had had occasion to be put to sleep at one time or other. It was imperative that this condition be strictly adhered to, for to violate it might cause the whole enterprise to fail.

It was also announced that latecomers would not be admitted to the Sacred Cavern. So, as one can well understand after such an advance warning, all the eager spectators were in their places long before the affair started. The kings arrived with their wives and children, their ministers and counselors, their administrators-in-chief and just plain administrators, their lackeys of every rank, their royal guardsmen and spies...

The Deadwood Oaks had set up stone benches around the basin, arranging them in the manner of a huge amphitheater. In the first row, the place of honor, were seated the various kings and their families, while the ministers and counselors sat further back. The commoners stood on their feet as close as they could to the rear.

Hundreds of phosphorescent lamps on the guests' headwear illuminated the cavern with a soft light that cast no shadows; everything was clearly visible, even in the remotest corners.

A rostrum had been set up in the vicinity of the basin itself, for the orators who would be speaking.

Never before had the bowels of the earth witnessed such an awe-inspiring sight. The royal courts were seated by sections, just as they normally were at the Supreme Council. It was as if the seven-colored rainbow itself, aglow with the purest of hues, had come down from the skies to play with all the shades of color it had at its disposal...

Around the basin, at even distances, stood the Deadwood Oaks, who had received fresh coats of paint for this festive occasion.

Ellie stepped up onto the rostrum with a bleached wand in her hands. This time, Totoshka was not with her: the dog had stayed at the campsite, watched over by one of the Winkies. Behind Ellie stood Fred Canning, Lestar the Craftsman, Arrigo the Chronicler, and Rujero the Time Keeper. All of them, Ellie included, were clutching something in their fists. Ellie began to speak, in a clear, ringing voice that could be easily heard throughout the whole cavern:

"Your Majesties, and Citizens of Underground Land! For the purpose of restoring to you the Soporific Waters that have dried up, we have had to undertake a long, difficult, and dangerous task... Yes, it was dangerous, because if we made the slightest blunder, then the Cave Spirit, who was already incensed because of Ruf Bilan's headlong acts, might finish us off without mercy." (A murmur of horror arose among the listeners.) "But we acted discreetly, and in accordance with the system..."

Whatever that system was, not one of the participants knew. Not even Ellie herself. But Lestar had instructed the girl to use that word, and it greatly elevated the speaker's standing in the eyes of the audience.

Ellie continued: "And now we stand at the brink of success." She waved her wand and began to recite an incantation:

> "Barramba, marramba, taricky, varicky,
> Cuporos, shaforos, baricky, sharicky!

Loathsome Spirit, Great Mechanic Master, retire to the deepest bowels of the earth and give us back our treasure — the Soporific Water!"

Ellie stamped her foot on the ground three times, and after the third stomp, a muffled noise and roaring sound were heard somewhere in the depths of the cave. (It was Lestar's skill that had simulated this theatrical effect.) The spectators' faces turned pale with terror, and the people almost fainted, but at that moment, a deafening torrent of water poured forth into the basin through a huge pipe!

A wild outburst by hundreds of voices filled the cavern. "That's it! That's it!" cried the people, almost delirious with ecstasy. "I recognize it by its bluish sparkle!" "I know it by the little bubbles fizzing out from it!" "I know it from its smell!"...

When the excitement had died down, Rujero stepped up onto the rostrum. His speech went on for about half an hour. He retold the ancient story about how the Magic Water was first discovered, how Bellino the Time Keeper had come up with the plan of putting the kings to sleep during the periods between their reigns, and how this arrangement had continued peacefully through the centuries. The speech was a thoroughly dull one, and several listeners began to snore. But the end of the speech really roused them. Rujero said:

"Formerly, the Soporific Water appeared only once a month from the depths underground, and it returned there after a very short time: such was the Great Mechanic Master's will. But the magic art of Ellie the Fairy and her friends has proven stronger: now this magical draft is available to us the whole year round, and those who so wish can be put to sleep at any time, and for any duration."

Each of the kings assumed that this remark was directed personally at him, and referred to the imminent realization of his underhanded scheme, and so every one of them assumed a dignified air.

Rujero stepped down from the rostrum, still clutching his little object, as before. The Time Keeper was followed by the next speaker, King Mentaho. The audience felt disheartened: Mentaho loved to talk at dreadful length.

And in fact, he did come to the point slowly. After giving his eminent guests the respect that was their due, the king began by telling the story of Strasheela, which he had heard from the straw man himself. Then he went on to the Iron Woodman's story, and he was about to speak of the Lion, when all at once he began to yawn. He had just enough time to amble back to his seat, and he fell at once into magical sleep. Almost simultaneously, everyone who was present there in the cave likewise went to sleep — everyone, that is, except Ellie, Fred, Lestar, Rujero, and Arrigo.

They were clutching diamonds in their fists, and that is what saved them from the vapors of the Soporific Waters. Of course, the Deadwood Oaks didn't go to sleep: they merely stared stupidly with their button eyes and had no idea of what was going on.

Thus did the six kings and one queen fall into the very snare that they had set for one another.

The spectators who were seated on the amphitheater benches went to sleep in comfort, leaning on one another's shoulders or breasts. However, the lackeys, the soldiers, and the spies, who had all been standing at the rear, sank to the ground wherever they stood, and the overall picture reminded one of a battlefield strewn with the bodies of fallen warriors.

Ellie and the others with the diamonds in their fists hastened to exit the Sacred Cavern. Diamonds were diamonds, but all five of them were already beginning to feel the languor that was preliminary to sleep. However, everything had gone exactly as they wanted it.

The Deadwood Oaks remained behind in the cavern, for the Soporific Waters had no effect on them. Their brigadiers, Arum and Befar, had been directed to attend to the transfer of the sleepers to the Rainbow Palace.

In the opinion of Strasheela and Lestar, not all the sleepers should be removed from the cavern at one time; rather, they should be taken out in small batches, one after the other, over a period of days. In that way, they would likewise reawaken in small batches, in the course of a week or two, and those entrusted with their reeducation would be able to handle the job more easily.

And that's how it happened that the Land of the Underground Ore-Diggers saw the greatest upheaval in all its history.

Chapter 45

REEDUCATION

In Munchkin Land, not far from the entrance to the Cavern, in a beautiful glade by a silvery brook, several large tents had been pitched. Ellie and her friends had been living in them since their return from Underground Land.

Or, rather, they spent only their nights in these tents; during the day, they lounged around on the soft grass in the shade of fruit-trees.

"It was pleasant, warm, and dry in the metal foundry," Strasheela expounded at some length as he let the sun shine successively on each of his straw sides, "but in one's homeland it's always better. The farm where I was made isn't too far from here. It didn't happen all that long ago, but it seems to me as if whole centuries have passed since then."

"It's almost as nice here as it is in my home forest," said the Lion, who had recovered from his bronchitis up here on the surface. "All the same, though, something's missing here..."

"I know what you miss," laughed Ellie, playing with his stiff whiskers and blowing on his nose, causing the Lion to close his eyes tight and sneeze. "You're bored without all the deference you're entitled to as king — you ambitious creature, you!"

Fred Canning was helping the Winkies get the Iron Woodman back into shape. After the Woodman's prolonged sojourn in the barrel, the oil had coagulated, and his limbs had lost their suppleness. Lestar and his assistants took their monarch apart screw by screw, and they wiped the oil off every one of his parts, cleaned them, and laid them out to dry in the air — placing Fred on guard lest some mischievous magpie should grab some important part or other of him.

Totoshka was running up and down the bank of the stream, barking at the bright little fishes that darted about in the water.

The only friends missing from this group were Kaggi-Karr, Faramant, and Din Gior. The Crow had flown to the Emerald City to notify the residents that their beloved monarch would soon be returning to them, and that he had accomplished some thrilling new exploits in the Underground world. The Long-Bearded Soldier and the Guardian of the Gates had departed right after her, to prepare the triumphal reception.

Everyone felt light-hearted and free. It goes without saying that the guests from the upper world had left the

Cavern the moment they put the Seven Kings and their entourages to sleep, and they had taken Ellie with them. When departing, they did not even ask for any safe-conduct pass, for it was no longer needed.

In some fashion, without even bothering to hold an election, the Undergrounders designated Rujero the Time Keeper as their new monarch, and Arrigo became his closest aide. The two men wasted no time: they assembled the populace and announced to them the fate that awaited the kings, their courtiers, and their servants. The people went wild with delight when they learned that this remarkable inspiration had originated with Strasheela, and they praised him to the skies.

Everyone promised to say nothing to the sleepers about their pasts when they awoke, so that their reeducation might proceed without any snags. The people kept this promise religiously, because the one traitor who might have tried to frustrate the plan — Ruf Bilan — had, by common agreement, been put to sleep and borne away to the Sacred Cavern for a period of ten years. To prevent anyone from entering there by chance and drinking the Soporific Waters, the cave was walled off.

The first group of sleepers to awaken, the one headed by King Mentaho, did so one week after the Day of the Great Sleepening. Rujero, keeping a promise that he had made, sent a messenger to Ellie to notify her of this, and she and her cousin returned to the City of the Seven Monarchs to see how the reeducation would proceed.

When the children entered the Cavern (the Market Gate having in the meantime been demolished, by Rujero's order, and the sentinels removed from the area), they screamed in terror. On the road before them, stretched out to its full monstrous length, lay a dragon with gaping yellow eyes, drumming its jagged tail against the ground.

"What's this monster doing here?" exclaimed Ellie, all set to turn around and flee.

Chapter 45: REEDUCATION

"This is Oyho," said the messenger who accompanied them. "He's the most intelligent and obedient of all our dragons. Oyho, bow to our guests!"

The dragon bowed its hideously ugly head three times to Ellie and Fred. The children burst out laughing in spite of themselves.

"You can pet him," said the messenger. "He'll like that."

Ellie put her hand on the reptile's pleated neck, and the beast began to thump its tail with pleasure.

"Now take a seat," said Rujero's envoy, pointing to something resembling a palanquin fastened to the dragon's back.

"What for?" protested Ellie. "We can get there more easily on foot."

But the messenger was adamant. "King Rujero's orders... and besides, you'll have to do it later anyway."

Though they caught nothing of the import of these last words, the children nevertheless seated themselves in the palanquin; the messenger sat down in the front part of it and grasped the bridle, and Oyho took off. Ellie's and Fred's hearts froze, and they clutched one another as the ground sped by beneath them. But after a few minutes, they began to find themselves enjoying the swiftness of their flight, and it was with sorrow that they eventually stepped out of their cockpit: their aerial journey was over much too quickly.

The moments of reeducation brought a great deal of amusement to those who were present during it, but, in obedience to Rujero's strict orders, it was necessary to keep this amusement under control.

Mentaho, the first of the kings to awaken, was also the most conceited of them all. He was inordinately proud his descent from the legendary Bofaro, and to him, the common people were as nothing. But Rujero instilled in this vain man's mind the idea that he was really — a weaver! — and an actual weaver taught him the rudiments of the trade. The ex-king sat down at the loom and began to manipulate the shuttle briskly, saying: "What a bore this job is!" Ellie and Fred could barely restrain their laughter and, accompanied by a dirty look from Rujero, they dashed from the room.

And so it went. King, ministers, and counselors became miners, smelters, metal-workers, tailors, cooks... Lackeys, soldiers, and spies became plowmen, farmers, hunters, fishermen...

The specter of famine was gone forever from Underground Land.

Chapter 46

TO THE SURFACE!

But the very existence of Underground Land itself was drawing to a close. King Rujero and the newly-constituted Council of Elders (which included two of the former kings in its membership) made the following announcement: "Anyone who wishes to leave the Cavern and resettle on the surface may do so unhindered. The Council of Elders has already made an agreement with the Munchkins. There is enough room for everyone among them, in Blue Land, and on the surface, our people will receive plots of land for cultivation."

To decide on this most important question properly, a meeting of all the people in the Cavern was called. The first to speak at it was Arrigo.

"A thousand years ago," he said, "our forefathers were exiled from the upper world because of a crime committed by Prince Bofaro. It would serve no useful purpose now for us to decide on whether or not that verdict was just. The important thing is that the people have continued living in the Cavern. And how suitable is it for living in? Just look at how pale our faces are, how gaunt our chests, how thin our arms and legs! How sickly and weak our children are, and how many of them die in child-hood!"

"That's right!" cries resounded. "Arrigo is speaking the truth!"

"Of course, life in the Cavern is possible," continued Arrigo, "and we ourselves are living proof of it. But no one is likely to argue that its climate is detrimental. Doc-tors Boril and Robil have observed that life-spans among us are considerably shorter than those on the surface..."

"It's true, it's true!" shouted Boril and Robil.

"Even magical beings like Strasheela and the Iron Woodman almost succumbed when they were with us, and the King of Beasts cleaned out every apothecary's shop — he even came within inches of devouring the apothecary himself to boot, because the fellow smelled like medicine..."

The throng burst into laughter.

"As you see, my friends," Arrigo concluded, "now that no one's compelling us any longer to live in the Cavern, it's time that we put an end to our thousand-year exile and resettled once more on the surface."

"One question!" Tall, thin Doctor Robil stepped onto the rostrum. "Our esteemed Arrigo speaks very well, but let him answer me this: how are we going to live in the upper world, given our weak eyes?"

"Allow me, allow me!" Plump Doctor Boril rolled out of the crowd like a ball. "By asking such a question, our esteemed Doctor Robil has displayed his extreme igno-rance in questions of medicine."

Robil snorted angrily. The rivalry that had existed be-tween the doctors' ancestors centuries before was still in evidence now between the descendants. "Ignorance?" thundered Robil. "Prove it!"

"Yes, ignorance!" declared Boril boldly. "Just as our ancestors' eyes became accustomed to the gloom of the

Cavern, so will our eyes become accustomed to the bright light of the surface world. And I have proof. Citizen Venyeno, would you step up here?"

A middle-aged man in a plowman's attire came forward.

"You see this citizen," Doctor Boril went on. "He's been living on the surface for two weeks now. By day, he remains concealed in a dark tent, but he goes outside at night, and when daylight comes, he remains there in the open, for longer and longer stretches each time. It's all part of an experiment I've conceived. Now, friend Venyeno, how do you feel?"

"Well, I'm getting used to it little by little," replied Venyeno, slightly flustered. "Yesterday, I stayed in the full light of day almost till sundown... and nothing happened!"

The thunder of applause was its own reward for the intrepid plowman, and Robil hid himself among the crowd in disgrace.

One other important question was decided at that meeting. The Cavern had its rich metal deposits, but no such wealth was to be found on the surface. What should they do?

One of the Ore-Diggers took the floor. "Eh, my friends, what is there to talk about? Won't we all be working for ourselves? We won't be breaking our backs now the way we were when under the kings..." At this point, the speaker was shushed from all sides, and he bit his tongue, realizing suddenly that he had blurted out a mite too much. "What I mean is, we can arrange to dig in shifts. Each person can work in the mines for two months of the year, and after that, the time he spends on the surface resting will be all that much sweeter."

"That's right! Very true!" cried the smelters. "And we'll work in shifts as well!"

In that way, the people themselves resolved all the important problems, and the Cavern began to empty. The

former laborers and tillers of the soil yearned for the sunshine, the blue sky, and the clear air, and they blessed
these events that had brought them liberation from their
dreary existence in the earth's subterranean abysses. The
people who had undergone reeducation had admittedly
never seen any real hardship in their lives, so they did
not fully understand why the others were so happy. Yet
they, too, preferred to live above-ground rather than below.

Chapter 47

HOMEWARD BOUND

Of course, Ellie and Fred could not wait around for all
the sleepers to be reeducated, and for the general migration to be completed. It was time for them to return home,
to their families who were in mourning for them.

Ellie was determined to have a visit with Ramina,
Queen of the Field Mice, prior to their departure: the girl
did miss the kind little fairy. But before all else, she asked
her cousin to tie Totoshka as firmly as possible to a tree.

This time, the whistle worked perfectly: the grass began to rustle with the sound of dainty feet, and there before Ellie stood Ramina, her golden crown on her head,
her ladies-in-waiting accompanying her.

Totoshka began to bark and to chafe at the leash that
was holding him fast — but Fred Canning stared, and his
eyes popped right out of his head: the boy realized that
he was beholding a marvel, the latest in a whole series of
marvels in this strange world into which Fate had
dropped him. The Mouse began to talk in a thin, comical
voice: "You summoned me, dear sister?"

"Yes, your Majesty! I've truly missed you, and I wanted to see you again before I left Magic Land."

"I'm very grateful that you remembered," said the Queen, "the more so since this will be the last time we meet."

"Won't I ever be coming here again?"

"Our race is gifted with the ability to foresee the future, and this prescience tells me that a long and brilliant life is awaiting you in your own country. But you'll never see your friends here again."

Ellie burst into tears. "I'm going to miss them so much."

"Human memory is merciful," said Ramina. "You'll be sad and bitter at first, but then oblivion will come to your aid. The past will be covered by a cloud of mist, and you'll remember it only as a vague dream, like a wonderful tale of old."

"Do I have to tell Strasheela, the Woodman, and the Lion that I'm leaving them for good?" asked the girl.

"No," replied the fairy. "They're such good and tender-hearted creatures that there's no point in making them sad. Leave them with hope. Hope is a great solace in times of sorrow..."

The wise Mouse might possibly have given Ellie much more of her sage counsel, but at that moment, Totoshka broke loose from his leash, and Ramina vanished with a peep.

Fred stood there for a long time in utter stupefaction. "You know, cousin," he said, "of all the impossible wonders in this impossible realm, the one I just saw is, in my opinion, the most impossible of all." He added, in an embarrassed tone, "You'll have to forgive me for laughing at you a little..."

Ellie declined to make another journey to the Emerald City, saying that she had already admired all its wonders more than once, while Fred had been there on his own and so he already knew what it was like. "It's a shorter distance from here, from Blue Land, to the Valley of the Magic Grapes," said the girl. "The Munchkins will take us there and help Fred build another land-boat, and we'll get across the desert in some way or other."

"I've sailed on yachts before," Fred echoed to his cousin, "and I know how to handle a sail."

Present at one of these conversations, however, was Rujero, who had become a good friend to the children. The old man frowned when he learned of Ellie's plans. "What you have in mind is something entirely unnecessary, not to mention dangerous," he said. "The Great Desert rarely allows people to leave it, once they've entered it. It was a matter of great luck that Charlie the Sailor was able to cross it twice. But it would be utter madness to rely on the skill of Fred (who is, after all, only a boy!), and we, being your friends, will not allow you to go off to certain death."

"But how are we going to get home?" asked Ellie.

"I have just the means for it," smiled Rujero cannily as he stroked his long gray beard. "Just settle on a day, and everything will be ready."

Strasheela, the Woodman, and the Lion would rather that Ellie had remained there with them for a long, long time, but the girl would not agree to spend more than one additional week in Magic Land — even though she knew that when she said goodbye to her beloved friends this time, it would be forever.

When news of Ellie's imminent departure was relayed to the Emerald City via the avian network. The first to fly in from there was Kaggi-Karr the Crow, and she was followed quickly by Din Gior, the Long-Bearded Soldier; by Faramant, Guardian of the Gates; and by Lestar, the skilled craftsman. Even a number of residents of the Emerald City made the long (and now safe) journey along the Yellow Brick Road, so that they might look once more on their beloved little Fairy who had done them all so much good.

The entire population of Blue Land, headed by Prem Cocus, their leader, assembled to see Ellie off. So, of course, did the former Cavern-Dwellers, who had now completed their migration to the surface. Many of them still walked around wearing black bandages over their eyes, to protect them from the sunlight.

No one knew by what means Ellie was going to depart from Magic Land, but every one of them believed in her powers — it was an article of faith. If Ellie got it in mind to do something, so they said, then it would be done.

A bustling camp spread out around the glade where Ellie's tent stood. The tender-hearted little Munchkins would weep at one moment because the Fairy with the Death-Dealing House was leaving them, and then laugh with joy because she had succeeded in escaping so many perils in Underground Land. They shifted from one mood to another with amazing rapidity, but regardless of whether they were weeping or laughing, the little bells on their hats responded with the same merry tinkling.

Fred Canning was touched to the bottom of his heart when he saw the homage that was being rendered to his cousin, that ordinary little girl from Kansas who, regardless of that fact, thanks to her kind heart, had done so much for the people of Magic Land. Even he, Fred, a little boy from the United States, was being honored as if *he* had also done something great and wonderful. But Ellie...

"You know, cousin," he said, "I've read in newspapers about the send-offs they give crowned people, such as sultans, pashas, and emperors. But, to be honest, none of them ever saw such sincere ecstasy and words of praise as this..."

At last the departure day arrived. Ellie, her eyes flooding with tears, kissed Strasheela's beloved painted face, and she hugged the Iron Woodman and spent a long time running her fingers through the Lion's stiff, tangled mane.

She clasped the distraught Kaggi-Karr to her breast, and said farewell to Din Gior, Faramant, Lestar, and Prem Cocus. "We *will* see each other again, my dear, wonderful, and extraordinary friends," babbled the little girl.

Then Rujero appeared in the glade and stepped through the crowd of well-wishers, who moved aside to make way for him. Ellie, upset as she was at having to leave them, looked at the old man in bewilderment: where was the means he proposed using to send them home?

Rujero looked upward. A black dot appeared in the blue of the sky. It approached closer and closer to the ground, growing larger and larger as it did so, and before they knew it, a huge dragon, with a man guiding it, touched down in the glade.

The dragon looked amiably at Ellie with huge eyes like the saucers that go with teacups. The panic-stricken Munchkins scattered in all directions: they had never seen a dragon before.

"It's Oyho!" exclaimed Fred and Ellie.

The reptile smacked its tail against the ground.

"It'll be nothing at all for Oyho to carry you easily across the World-Encompassing Mountains and the Great Desert," said Rujero. "He's unusually hardy, and we've gotten him used to daylight. Our driver, Rakhis, will go with you only as far as the World-Encompassing Mountains. After that, you'll be flying him on your own."

Now the children understood why Rujero had compelled them to ride dragon-back beneath the roof of the Cavern, amid the goldenish clouds. The wise old man had so insisted in order that Fred would learn how to guide the dragon.

"What do we do with him then?" asked Ellie.

"Unless you want to keep the dragon with you on your farm," said Rujero with a laugh, "just turn him loose, and I guarantee you he'll find his way home."

And so came the sad moment of parting. Once more, Ellie hugged and kissed her friends, and Fred, too, said goodbye to everyone. Totoshka passed from arm to arm for the longest time: Strasheela and the Woodman caressed him, while the Lion extended him his paw affectionately.

The driver seated himself on the reptile's neck. The passengers climbed up a flight of steps into a sort of cockpit, and they waved their hands to the crowd of well-wishers, who numbered in the thousands.

"Goodbye, Ellie," shouted the Woodman, unable to keep back his tears, "goodbye! My heart tells me that you're leaving us for good!"

The Iron Woodman's loving heart had indeed suggested the bitter truth to him. But the Lion and Strasheela would not go along with that. "No," said Strasheela, "our Ellie will return to Magic Land again!" And the Lion nodded his big, shaggy head in agreement.

The enormous dragon flapped its wings and rose into the air, stirring up a whirlwind all around, and it had soon vanished into the blue reaches of the sky.

THE END

THE
FIERY GOD
OF THE
MARRANS

Chapter 1

THE OUTCAST

Give me your hand, my young friend, and together we will fly far, far away, to Magic Land, a land that is cut off from the rest of the world by a Great Desert and by a range of enormous mountains. There, under an eternally warm sun, dwell some adorable and comical little peoples — the Munchkins, the Winkies, the Quadlings, and many other different tribes as well.

It was to Munchkin Land that the tornado conjured up by the witch Gingema bore a little house from Kansas, with a girl named Ellie and her dog Totoshka inside it. Gingema perished, and a series of remarkable adventures began for Ellie and Totoshka.

In those days, the mighty wizard Goodwin lived in the center of the country, in the magnificent Emerald City. Ellie set out to see him, in the hope that Goodwin would help her to return home.

Along the way, Ellie picked up a live scarecrow of straw, named Strasheela, a Woodman made entirely of iron, and a Cowardly Lion. Each of them had his own fondest wish. Strasheela wanted some brains to place inside his straw head; the Woodman yearned for a loving heart; and the Lion needed courage. And though, as a wizard, Goodwin turned out to be a humbug, he did grant all their wishes. He gave Strasheela some clever brains made of bran, with needles and pins mixed in; to the Iron Woodman he gave a fine silk heart stuffed with sawdust; and to the Cowardly Lion, courage, which fizzed and foamed in a golden saucer.

203

Goodwin was bored with his life in Magic Land, and he departed from it in a balloon. As he flew off, he designated Strasheela to be his successor, and the latter became the ruler of the Emerald City. The Winkies, the inhabitants of Violet Land, elected the Woodman as their ruler, while the Courageous Lion became the King of the Beasts.

Ellie herself returned home to her Mom and Dad when the fondest wishes of her three friends had been granted. She and Totoshka were transported there by Gingema's magical Silver Shoes, which the dog had found in the witch's cave.[1]

Strasheela did not enjoy his high position as monarch of the Emerald City for long. A powder that brought things to life fell by chance into the hands of a malicious and wily joiner named Urfin Jus, who lived in Munchkin Land. The joiner manufactured some wooden soldiers and brought them to life, and with this mighty army's help, he seized control of the Emerald City. Strasheela and the Iron Woodman, who had come there to rescue him, became Jus's captives. The latter put them behind bars, at the top of a lofty tower.

Strasheela and the Woodman wrote a letter to Ellie in an appeal to her for assistance, and their good friend Kaggi-Karr the Crow delivered it to her in Kansas. The little girl did not just leave her friends in their predicament — she set out for Magic Land a second time. She was accompanied by her uncle, the one-legged Sailor Charlie Black, who was a great master at inventing anything imaginable. He built a land-boat, and in this boat he and Ellie crossed the desert.

The struggle with Urfin Jus and his mighty wooden soldiers was not an easy one, but Ellie and her friends were finally victorious.[2]

---

[1]All these events are described in detail in the book *The Wizard of the Emerald City*.

Chapter 1: THE OUTCAST

Urfin was brought to trial. He deserved a severe punishment for all his crimes, but Charlie Black, the one-legged Sailor, turned and said to his fellow judges: "My friends, wouldn't it be better simply to leave this man alone with himself?" Ellie concurred: "That's right. That would be the most severe punishment possible for him."

Strasheela, the Iron Woodman, and the Courageous Lion agreed with the Sailor and the girl, and the ex-king of the Emerald City was escorted to the City gates, to the hoots and jeers of the townspeople and the farmers. Along the way, someone, in an effort to "rub it in," thrust at him the wooden Clown that he had once brought to life, his pet and informer, and Urfin Jus mechanically clutched him in his hand.

"You may go wherever you please," said his escort, Faramant, Guardian of the Gates, to Urfin, "and do try to become a good man. You yourself will be the first one to benefit if you do."

Jus made no answer to these kind words. He threw Faramant a baleful look from under his shaggy eyebrows, and then he trudged quickly away from the City, along the Yellow Brick Road.

"Everyone's deserted me," reflected the former king of the Emerald City bitterly. "Everyone who sought to flatter me during the days of my supremacy, who feasted at my banquet table, who praised me to the skies — now they're all glorifying little Ellie and the Giant from Beyond the Mountains..." (That's what people in Magic Land called Charlie Black.)

But when Urfin turned around, he saw that he had been mistaken. One creature had remained faithful to him after all, for there was Topotun the Bear, plodding along behind his master at a distance. No, Topotun would never leave him, no matter what misfortune Urfin Jus fell into.

---

[2]These events are described in the book *Urfin Jus and his Wooden Soldiers.*

Urfin was the one who had brought the bearskin to life, using the mysterious virtue of the Magic Powder, when it was lying on the floor as a pitiful, dusty rug, and the Bear was bound to him by everlasting gratitude for this...

Softening his voice, Urfin called out: "Topotun, come here!"

The stuffed Bear trotted joyfully up to his master. "I'm here, Monarch! What is your command?"

"Monarch..."

That one word soothed the wound in Urfin's heart. Yes, he was still a monarch, even if it was only over one lowly servant and one insignificant Clown. But what if...? Vague hopes flashed through Urfin's mind. Could his enemies be celebrating their victory over him a little too soon?

He, Urfin Jus, was still young, he was free, and no one could take his indomitable will away from him, or his ability to make use of his shrewd, resourceful mind and his skilled hands when circumstances were favorable.

Urfin's hunched posture straightened up, and a weak smile lit up his swarthy face, with its shaggy eyebrows and its rapacious mouth with teeth bared. Turning and facing the direction of the Emerald City, Urfin threatened with his fist: "You'll be sorry yet, you miserable simpletons, for letting me go free!..."

"Yes, they'll be sorry," peeped the clown.

Jus seated himself on the Bear's back. "Carry me back to my homeland, my glorious Topotun, to Munchkin Land. There, you and I have a house. I hope no one's disturbed it. We won't find any shelter till we've reached it."

"We've got a garden there, monarch," Topotun joined in, "and plump rabbits are found in abundance in the forest nearby. I don't need food myself, but I'll catch them for you."

The Bear's good-natured face positively lit up from the pleasure of knowing that he would again be living

206

with his adored master, in peace and contentment, far away from everything.

But such were not Urfin's thoughts. "The house will serve as a temporary refuge for me," pondered Jus, "and I'll lie low there till everyone's forgotten about me. And then... then we'll see!..."

Urfin Jus's journey to Munchkin Land was an arduous one. He had hoped to return there unnoticed, but Kaggi-Karr thwarted him in that. With the help of her numerous relatives, the Crow tracked the outcast, no matter what direction he took. Everyone living near the Yellow Brick Road was informed by Kaggi-Karr's emissaries, at the appropriate times, of Urfin's approach.

Men and women, old and young, emerged from their houses and lined up alongside the road. They did not utter a single word, but their eyes, filled with contempt, followed Urfin as he moved along. It would have been easier for Jus if they had cursed him out, or thrown sticks and stones at him. But the deathly silence, the hate written on every face, the icy stares... All these things were many times worse.

The vindictive Crow had calculated correctly. Urfin Jus's homeward journey was reminiscent of a prolonged procession to an execution.

How Jus would have enjoyed hurling himself upon every one of his enemies, grabbing hold of his throat, listening to his death rattle... But that was impossible. So he rode along on the Bear, with his head bowed down low, and he gnashed his teeth in rage.

Eot Ling the Clown, after seating himself on his shoulders, whispered in his ear: "Don't worry, master, don't worry — all this will pass! We'll have the last laugh on them yet!"

Urfin spent the night in the forest under the trees, for not one resident of Emerald Land or Blue Land would offer him his bed for the night. The outcast fed on fruit that he picked from the trees. He grew very thin, and when he approached the Forest of the Saber-Toothed Tigers, he almost wished for an encounter with those savage beasts so that his suffering would be ended. But his craving for life and his desire for revenge against those who had offended him — these things had the upper hand, and Urfin slipped through the dangerous stretch unnoticed.

There, at last, was his own house. The outcast was relieved to see that the Munchkins had not touched any of his possessions, and that all his property had been preserved intact. He removed the key from its hiding place, opened the locks, and stepped into the rooms, which were gloomy and full of the dust that had accumulated during their owner's long absence.

Part I

THE GIANT BIRD

Chapter 2

THE AERIAL COMBAT

Seven years passed after Urfin Jus's removal from power in the Emerald City. Many things in the world changed. Ellie Smith, who had left Magic Land for good, graduated from high school and enrolled in the College of Education in a nearby city: she had selected for herself the humble role of public-school teacher. Her younger sister Annie (who had been born during Ellie's sojourn in the Underground Kingdom) entered first grade and began to learn the mysteries of the three R's.

Charlie Black, the one-legged Sailor, bought a ship and made several cruises to the isle of Kuru-Kusu, and its inhabitants gave him a warm welcome every time.

And what happened in Magic Land? The Winkies and the Munchkins continued to live as before, but life changed completely for the Underground Ore-Diggers, the people among whom Ellie had stayed during her third and final journey to wonderland.

Ellie and her second cousin Fred Canning had many strange, remarkable adventures there, in the colossal Cavern. They succeeded in restoring the dried-up Spring of the Soporific Water, and they used that water to put to sleep the seven kings who took turns ruling the Ore-Diggers. The most comical and curious thing of all was the way the kings, when they awakened, forgot all about their royal standing and became smiths, tillers of the soil, and weavers. They labored diligently, side by side with their former subjects, making livings for themselves and their families.

211

After abolishing the royal authority, the Cavern-Dwellers resettled in the upper world and took up residence in a stretch of vacant territory that bordered on Munchkin Land. There, they sowed wheat and flax, they cultivated gardens, they fattened up livestock, and they refined metals. It was some time before they were able to give up wearing dark glasses, because their eyes, which had been accustomed to the semidarkness, were long unable to tolerate sunlight.[1]

Urfin Jus's life alone proceeded without change through his long years of solitude. He spaded his garden and began to cultivate vegetables, and he took in three harvests per year.

How assiduously the ex-king examined the ground of his plot of land as he wielded his spade! How he longed to find even one little seed of that extraordinary plant from which he had extracted the Powder of Life! Oh, if such a seed should come into his hands, he would not use it this time to create more wooden soldiers! No, he'd build an iron-encased monster impervious to arrows and fire, and then he'd make himself monarch of Magic Land once more.

But his searches were fruitless, if not downright misguided — for if even one sprout, one living part of the amazing plant had survived eradication, the plant would have filled up the whole surrounding area again in no time.

Every evening, every morning, Urfin looked up into the sky, hoping that a storm would break out similar to the one that had once dropped the seed of that remarkable plant his way. But the violent tornadoes that did sweep over the land left nothing but devastation in their wake.

So Urfin, after being king and reveling in the awareness of his power over thousands and thousands of people,

---

[3]Ellie's third journey is detailed in the book *The Seven Underground Kings.*

now had to be content with the humble role of market gardener. Of course, he had no need to worry about subsistence beneath the blessed sky of wonderland, the more so since Topotun often brought his master a nice, plump rabbit or hare. But that was not what the exile wanted: he often dreamed during the night that the royal mantle was lying on his shoulders — only to awaken disappointed, with his heart pounding.

During the first months of his life of solitude, Urfin often encountered Munchkins whenever he went out walking, especially if his steps took him in the direction of Cogida, the village where he had been born and raised. But his fellow Munchkins shied away from him as if he were afflicted with the plague, and they avoided eye contact with him as much as possible; even their backs seemed to radiate abhorrence.

But the weeks stretched out into months and the months into years, and the people's hostility toward Urfin began to lessen. Memories of his misdeeds faded away as they became overshadowed by more recent events, by fresher worldly concerns.

After several years, the residents of Cogida began to say hello to him in a friendly manner, and if Urfin had wished to resettle in the village, no one would have stood in his way. But Urfin responded sullenly to their greetings and never entered into conversation, and he made it clear to all by his manner that human company was distasteful to him... The Munchkins merely shrugged their shoulders and walked away from the unpopular joiner. Urfin continued as before to give himself over to gloomy thoughts about the revenge he would exact against the people if there were any way for him to do so.

Then Fate stepped in.

One day, around noontime, Urfin was digging in his vegetable garden, when all of a sudden, his attention was caught by an ear-splitting screech coming from above. The

213

outcast raised his head. High up in the blue vault of the sky, three eagles were fighting. The battle was a savage one, and two of the birds were attacking the third, trying to pummel it with their beaks and with blows of their wings. The victim of the attack was fighting back desperately and trying to slip away from its enemies, but it was unable to do so. The eagles did not at first appear to Urfin to be particularly large, but as they flew lower, Jus could see that their size was enormous.

The horrendous battle went on, and the screeching of the giant eagles grew in intensity as the birds moved closer to the ground. The wounded bird was weakening under the blows of its enemies, and its movements became more and more erratic. Suddenly, folding its wings, it plummeted downward in somersaults.

The eagle hit the ground in the glade in front of Urfin's house, making a dull thud. The gardener approached it timorously. The bird might be mortally wounded, but it could still injure a human being with an impulsive smack of its wing.

As Urfin approached the bird, he verified how truly colossal its dimensions were: its outspread wings occupied the entire plot from one edge to the other — a distance of about thirty paces. Then Urfin noticed with amazement that the bird was still alive. Its body was trembling, though this was barely noticeable, and there was a strange mixture of arrogance and entreaty in its eyes. The other two eagles swooped down now: they clearly intended to finish their enemy off.

"Protect me," mumbled the enormous bird hoarsely.

Jus picked up a robust stake that stood leaning against the fence, and he raised it in a determined manner. The attackers soared upward again, but they continued to circle around Urfin's grounds.

"They're going to deliver me the death blow," said the wounded eagle. "Dig a pit next to me, human, and pretend you're preparing to bury me. My enemies won't leave this area until they're sure I've been entombed. When it gets dark, I'll hide in the bushes, and you can throw the dirt back into the empty pit."

The shrewd deception was carried out that night, and in the morning, the monstrous eagles, after circling around over the empty tomb, flew away to the north.

Chapter 3

CARFAX'S STORY

The marvels of Magic Land are beyond count, and an entire human lifetime would not be sufficient for a person to learn about all of them. Though its size may not have been all that large, how remarkable it was for the variety of its natural wonders, and for the number of tribes of people, of amazing animals and birds that dwelt there.

In a secluded valley of the World-Encompassing Mountains, in the northern part of it, there lived a race of giant eagles. It was there that Carfax, Urfin Jus's unexpected guest, had originated.

Here is the story that Carfax related to the outcast, after he had recovered from his wounds:

"Our race has dwelt in the World-Encompassing Mountains for a long time," said the Eagle, "and its population is very small. And the reason for this is as follows. Our food consists of the aurochs and mountain goats that inhabit the mountain slopes and the bottomless ravines. The goat tribe might multiply and live without a care in the world, but we eagles, by hunting them, make that impossible.

"With out keen eyesight, our strength, and our speed in flight, we could exterminate all the goat and aurochs, but that we don't do: the disappearance of the animals

215

would signify our own end as well, for we would die of starvation. For this reason, since ancient times, the number of members of our tribe has not been allowed to exceed one hundred."

"How have you managed that?" asked Urfin, who was now quite interested.

"Our laws regarding this are very strict," answered Carfax. "An eagle family has the right to hatch a nestling only at such time as one of the full-grown members of the tribe dies of old age or is killed in an accident, for instance, in crashing against the side of a cliff during a careless attack on his prey."

"But who is granted the right to provide the replacement for the deceased?"

"That right is given in turn, in accordance with the strictest priority, to all the families that inhabit Eagle Valley. This custom has been rigorously adhered to throughout the centuries, but lately, it was violated, and this has brought great misfortune down upon our people's heads. We live for a very long time," continued Carfax, "150 — two hundred years, and for this reason, it's far from every year that a little one arrives in our valley. If you could only see how the she-eagles look after it, how they fight over who will feed the chick or shelter it under her wings! Often, the little one's natural mother is shoved aside... But what can you do?" sighed Carfax. "The maternal instinct among out womenfolk is very strong, and the opportunity of hatching a chick comes to each of them only once or twice in her long lifetime."

"How much simpler this business is among us humans," thought Urfin. "We can have as many children as we want, even though they can be a regular burden."

"I'm eighty years old," Carfax continued, "and among us giant Eagles, that's just when we're in the prime of vitality and health. This year, for the first time, it came the turn of me and my mate, Araminta, to hatch a nestling. How happily we awaited that blessed day when my wife would be granted permission to lay an egg. What a cozy little nest we constructed out of thin twigs and leaves in a depression in the cliff!... Then everything collapsed. Our despicable leader Arrahes, in violation of the ancient law, announced that *his* family would be the one to hatch the chick! He needed a successor, since his only son had recently been killed while hunting an aurochs..." Carfax quivered with indignation as he told about his leader's ignominious actions, and the gardener thought with disdain about how he, Urfin, would never get so excited over such a trifling thing.

"Tell me, human, was Arrahes really worthy of continuing to be our leader after violating our forefathers' customs so disgracefully? I, for one, felt that it would be a disgrace in itself to defer to him. I found myself some supporters. We plotted an uprising, to depose Arrahes. Unfortunately, our ranks had been infiltrated by a miserable traitor, and he told the leader about everything, even giving the names of the conspirators. Arrahes and his followers attacked us unexpectedly. Each of my allies was confronted with two or three adversaries. Araminta died within minutes after the fight began. I was attacked by Arrahes himself and the eagle who had given the conspiracy away. Seeking salvation in flight, I cut across the World-Encompassing Mountains and penetrated deeply into Magic Land. My enemies were right behind me... The rest you know," concluded Carfax wearily.

There was a long silence. Then the Eagle said: "My life is in your hands. I can't possibly return to the mountains. If I took up residence in even the remotest part of them, Arrahes and his spies would hunt me down and kill me. And I can't hunt in your forests. You've been feeding me little animals that you call rabbits and hares. They taste very good, but would I ever be able to spot them in the dense thickets, much less succeed in grasping them in my claws?..."

After doing some thinking, Urfin said: "Topotun has been catching game for you, and he'll continue to do so until you're recovered. After that, we'll see — for maybe I can come up with a way to feed you."

THE FIERY GOD OF THE MARRANS

In Urfin's dark mind, the idea was now born that this enormous bird might be useful to him for his own purposes. Here was his long-awaited means of rising again from obscurity and "taking fate by the horns," as he liked to express it.

"But I'll have to be very careful," reflected Urfin. "This bird, with his strange ideas of fairness, won't help me if he thinks that my actions are in even the slightest way dishonorable... But I won't rush myself, for I have plenty of time to think it all out."

Chapter 4

URFIN JUS'S THOUGHTS

By plying his guest with subtle questions, Urfin Jus ascertained that in Eagle Valley, nothing was known about the affairs of humans. Carfax proved to be ignorant both of Urfin's swift rise, and of his ignominious fall. The exile forbade Topotun from breathing even a word about the past, and he ordered the Clown to keep his eyes open and make sure that the bird and the Bear, who loved to gab, were never alone together. He himself began to act more boldly. He had long conversations with the Eagle, who was well on the way to recovery, and he confessed, in a manner made to appear casual, that he had only one desire in his mind — to do good for humanity.

"If that's the case, then why do you live in the woods, so far away from the rest of the pack?" asked Carfax with surprise.

"Don't you see," answered the wily Urfin, "helping out only one village is too trivial for me. But if I were able to gain dominion over the entire nation, then I'd show myself and prove my worth."

"Who would prevent you from becoming leader?" asked the simple-minded Eagle, puzzled.

"My fellow countrymen don't understand me," was Urfin's deceptive answer. "They think my striving for power is motivated by plain ambition, whereas in fact I have far higher goals before me."

They had many other conversations along similar lines, and the Eagle ended by being convinced of Urfin's nobility of purpose. Carfax agreed to assist his friend in attaining a high position among men, that he might then accomplish all the good works he had in mind.

That was exactly what Urfin Jus wanted. It remained for him to think up the exact way he would make use of the giant bird's assistance in regaining his earlier power. "But there can't be any war..." Urfin pondered. "If, for the sake of coming up in the world, I should ask Carfax to kill even one human being, he'll guess my true intentions right away. He might tear me to pieces for deceiving him..." Urfin pictured with horror the monstrous bird attacking him. "No, a more subtle procedure is called for. With the Eagle's help, I'll have to make myself monarch of some backward nation. When I've taken over that nation, I'll have both an army and a weapon... After that, watch out, Strasheela and Woodman!"

Urfin began to throw ideas around in his mind as to which part of the country would be easiest for him to take over as monarch. Then he remembered the Leapers.

The Leapers were a warlike tribe that inhabited the mountains between the Great River and Stella's dominion. No one had ever yet succeeded in crossing the territory of the Leapers, for they allowed no one to enter their area.

Ellie Smith, during her first sojourn in Magic Land, made a journey to see Stella the Good Fairy, accompanied by her friends Strasheela, the Iron Woodman, and the Courageous Lion. The domain of the Leapers, surrounded by mountains, placed an insurmountable barrier in their path. Strasheela attempted to climb up the mountain, with the Lion behind him, but they were beaten back by the Leapers' powerful fists. Ellie and her companions would never have made it to Stella's Rose Palace if Ellie had not been mistress at that time of the Golden Cap, which gave her power over the Winged Monkeys. The girl summoned the Winged Monkeys, and they transported the travelers to Stella's palace by air.[3]

Many centuries ago, the Marrans (for such was the name the Leapers called themselves) had lived in Underground Land, on the bank of the river that flowed into Central Lake. According to legend, they went underground to hide out from powerful enemies that harried them from all sides. There, among the rocks, the Marrans constructed a city, whose ruins Ellie Smith and Fred Canning had seen during the latter stages of their long, hazardous journey through the depths of the earth.

During that bygone period, the Marrans knew how to make fire, and they made iron weapons, caught fish, and hunted Sixpaws (which lived in abundance in the surrounding area). But in the course of time, the Marrans had become too numerous; they did not have enough fish and animal meat, and agriculture was out of the question in their territory's stony soil.

So the Marrans, under the leadership of Prince Gron, left their gloomy abode. They tried to take over part of the extensive flatlands belonging to the Underground Ore-Diggers, but the warriors of the Seven Kings fought off their attacks and drove the Leapers up to the surface.

The Marrans had a very hard time of it in the upper world. Their eyes, which were accustomed to the never-ending murk of the Cavern, could not, even after many months, adapt to the brilliant light of day. The migrants could move only by night. Half-blind, they roamed about

[3]This episode is described in detail in the book *The Wizard of the Emerald City.*

Magic Land for a long time; they perished in battles with the indigenous inhabitants, they suffered enormous losses to predatory beasts, they died of starvation, they drowned while trying to cross rivers... And several years went by in this way.

During the period of their wanderings, the Marrans became wild; they misplaced their tools here and there, and they lost the ability to make use of fire. Finally, Gron led a much-reduced group of fugitives to an isolated valley that no one else was living in, and this was to be their place of refuge for centuries. Here, they became numerous once more, but they remained at a very low level of development.

In the beginning, the Marrans passed on from father to son their recollections that their ancestors had lived in some sort of strange, gloomy world, but then the recollections became legends, and eventually, even the legends were completely forgotten. The Marrans lived in isolation for such a long time that people living in other parts of Magic Land knew very little about them.

Urfin Jus likewise had only a scant knowledge of the Marrans. What were their dwellings like? What did they eat? Was there anything that they were enthusiastic about? What sort of thing would fire their imaginations? Urfin did not have the answers to any of these questions. And going calling on a powerful, independent tribe, not knowing what awaited him there, was simply too dangerous.

"I'll have to carry out a preliminary reconnaissance," thought Urfin. But who would make such a reconnaissance? There was no way for him to go and do it in person: when the time came, he would have to make his first appearance before the Leapers *as ruler*, without being anticipated beforehand. Should he send Topotun? No, the bear was heavy and clumsy, and he did not have sufficient intelligence to hide and act under cover, as befitted a good scout. Then Urfin's eyes fell on the wooden Clown, who was puttering about in one corner of the room.

"There's the one I need!" exclaimed Jus joyfully. "Eot Ling, come here!" commanded Urfin, and the Clown, rolling over, toddled toward him.

"Do you need me, Monarch?"

"Yes. I'm thinking of entrusting you with a most important matter."

Urfin Jus disclosed his plans to the Clown and told Eot Ling what it was necessary to do. The Clown heard Urfin Jus out and then remarked: "The Country of the Leapers is very far away, Monarch. A journey there will be long and dangerous."

"Carfax can make the journey in only a few hours. He'll fly you there, and you can observe everything you have to observe."

Urfin Jus and his loyal servant Eot Ling waited with impatience as the Eagle continued to recover. The enormous bird devoured rabbits and hares, which Topotun procured industriously, down to the last bone. Carfax became attached to the good-natured Bear, who, stinting nothing in the way of strength, prowled about the forest in search of game.

At last, the time came when the Eagle, for the first time since his fall, made an initial, though still hesitant, flight. When he flew down low over the forest, the strokes of his mighty wings caused the branches of the trees to sway back and forth, and terrified squirrels plunged headlong to the ground. Each day, Carfax flew a greater distance and higher up in the air than the day before; his strength increased, and finally the day arrived when he asked Urfin Jus to take a seat on his back.

Urfin agreed, though very cautiously: there was no question that it would be a dreadful experience for anyone to find himself high up in the air, feeling no support under himself but the moving back of an eagle. But if he did not steel himself and undertake the flight, then he would never see the country of the Leapers, and that meant that he would never seize power nor exact vengeance against his enemies. So Jus overcame his trepidation.

The first step of anything is always difficult. But before long, Urfin was deriving pleasure from directing his face into the wind, and looking down with pride on the fields and forests slipping past below him.

"Mine!" he mumbled softly so that Carfax would not hear him. "All this will soon be mine once again!"

Urfin told the Eagle about his plans to assume power over the Leaper tribe. "These are primitive, ignorant people," said Jus, "and their life is extremely harsh. I want to bring them every possible happiness that's attainable by any person under the sun in our Land."

Carfax agreed to fly Eot Ling to the Leapers. Urfin sewed an outfit from rabbit-skin for the Clown. When Eot Ling put it on, he was transformed into a small, agile creature. Now, if the eyes of any Leaper should fall upon him, the latter would in no way suspect that this was really a scout who had come there from the outside regions.

So one morning, Carfax took off from the glade in front of Urfin's house and flew eastward, to the Country of the Leapers. From the Eagle's neck hung a bundle of rabbits — his food supply. On the Eagle's back, clinging to his feathers, lay the Clown.

The Eagle returned toward evening on the following day. He told about how he had transported the spy across the mountain during the night, while the Leapers were asleep, and set him down in an isolated area. Eot Ling would be waiting for him ten days later in that same spot.

How long those ten days seemed to Urfin!

But the moment arrived at last when Carfax returned from his second flight and bore with him the Clown, who was safe and sound — and very satisfied. The first thing Eot Ling did was to strip off the rabbit-skin suit, which he had had enough of, and he gave his Master a meaningful look. The latter understood that their conversation would have to be a private one, and he carried the Clown into the house.

"Well, Monarch!" exclaimed Eot Ling happily as soon as the two of them were alone, "what simpletons those people are! Ah, what simpletons!..." Then he added, knowingly, "But even simpletons can be dangerous, and you don't stick your finger into their mouths!"

"So tell me!" Jus ordered him with impatience.

The Clown launched into his account of what he had seen and heard in the Country of the Marrans during his ten-day sojourn among them.

Chapter 5

THE LIFE AND CUSTOMS OF THE LEAPERS

Eot Ling had learned many things. Dressed in a gray outfit that made him resemble a large rat, he lurked about near the settlements, sneaked into habitations, and watched and listened. On only one occasion did he almost get caught. A little boy picked him up (for children are always more observant than adults), but the Clown bit him so hard that the curious little boy screamed out in pain and let his dangerous catch go.

Here is what Eot Ling learned.

The Leaper Tribe is numerous, their adult males alone numbering several thousand. (At this disclosure, Urfin nodded his head approvingly and thought: "I'll get a strong army out of those.")

Leaper Land spreads out within a circular valley surrounded by a range of steep-sloped mountains. The mountains keep the wind out of the valley, and it is always warm there during the day, though the nights are chilly. The inhabitants build no houses, for they lack sufficient know-how to do that. They live in straw huts, or even under open canopies. They dress lightly, the men wearing long trousers and sleeveless jackets, and the women, short dresses. The Marrans barter with the Quadlings, Stella's subjects, for clothing, axes, knives, and shovels. In exchange, they offer them the precious stones that they mine in the mountains.

The Leapers are short in height, but they are thick-set, and have large heads, long, powerful arms with huge fists, and leg-muscles so highly developed that the people are able to make enormous leaps. That is why the inhabitants of the neighboring regions have nicknamed them the Leapers. But the Marrans themselves do not care for this nickname. They are ruled by Prince Torm...

"I suppose he's some venerable old man with a long, gray beard?" said Urfin, interrupting the Clown's account.

"That's where you're wrong, Monarch," Eot Ling contradicted. "Just imagine, they wear no beards or moustaches at all. They consider facial hair to be most uncomfortable, and they have a very curious method of getting rid of it. In their land, there's a certain spring surrounded by acrid brown mud. When a young Marran sees his moustache and beard starting to grow, he heads for this spring and rubs his face with the mud, and then he lets it dry in the sun. After a few hours, the mud crumbles away in pieces, and it carries the hair with it, once and for all. The one who has accomplished this operation is greeted by his kinsmen with singing and dancing, and only then does the Marran receive the right of citizenship and is allowed to marry."

"That's truly amazing," commented Urfin.

Eot Ling continued his lengthy narrative.

In the valley of the Leapers, there are frequent thunderstorms. Eot Ling had spent only ten days there, but even during that time there had been two storms.

225

"Thunderstorms are dreadful in the Land of the Leapers. Lightning flashes continually, thunderclaps merge together into a continual deafening pandemonium as they echo from the mountain slopes, and rain pours down in torrents. Lightning often strikes the Marrans' straw huts and sets them on fire. The dwellers leap away in terror, and they do nothing but stand there and look at the raging flames, not even trying to put them out. To the Marrans, fire is a dreadful punitive deity, and they worship it — but they don't bring themselves to make use of fire in their modest way of living."

"Now that information's a real treasure," thought Urfin. "There's a place where I can truly show myself to great advantage!"

"A vast shallow lake overgrown with reeds lies in the center of the valley. A multitude of ducks make their nests in those reeds. When the young hatch and are still unable to fly well, the Marrans organize hunts and hit the ducklings with slings. Their meat is salted and then preserved in natural storerooms — frigid caverns that lead into the heart of the mountains.

"Fertile fields spread out around the lake. There, the Leapers sow wheat. They don't bake bread, because they're unable to make fire. The grains of wheat are ground between millstones, and they use the resulting flour to make *turia* with cold water."

"I've got them!" exclaimed Urfin. "When I teach them to cook their ducks and to bake bread, they'll gladly follow me wherever I want them to. In their eyes, I'll be a great miracle-worker."

"In spite of this meager diet, the Marrans are a very healthy and strong people. They have plenty of free time, and they give it over to sports — leaping, foot racing, and, most of all, fisticuffs.

"Boxing competitions are the Marrans' favorite pastime. The violent blows that they deal each other could knock a bull off its feet, but they don't even faze the fighters. They have an amusing way of giving recognition to the winner. He has the right to put make-up (in the form of dark clay) over his bruises and put them on display, as a badge of distinction. The loser, on the other hand, must cover up his own injuries and get them to heal as quickly as possible. It's considered a brazen act for the loser to boast of wounds inflicted upon him in a bout.

"The Marrans are ardent sports fans, and they make bets on boxers and racers. But money is unknown among them, and they use their own freedom to settle their accounts. The loser labors for the more fortunate fan for a period of one month, two months, or even longer: he builds him a new hut, he works in his field, he grinds his grain, he catches ducks and salts them for him.

"Those who have thus fallen into temporary servitude are distinguished by a special mark: acidic Euphorbia juice is employed to draw a vertical stripe on his forehead, and this stripe lasts a long time. If it fades away before the term of servitude is over, a new one is drawn. Sometimes, a poor fellow who goes overboard in his betting does not finish his bondage for years on end, and his mark of servitude eats indelibly into his skin."

Even the dour Urfin became cheerful as he listened to these engrossing details about life among the Leapers. He became more and more firmly convinced that subordinating these simple-minded people to his power would be a simple matter.

As Eot Ling finished his narrative, he cautioned his master: "The Marrans are a dangerous people, Monarch! They're hot-tempered and quick to make reprisals. The moment one of them feels that he has been deceived or offended, he spoils at once for a fight, and there will be no mercy in it either for himself or for his adversary."

"Fine, fine, my faithful servant, you've obtained some very valuable facts. I can see that the Marrans will make good soldiers, but it's not by strength that we'll win them over. A sly stratagem is called for here, and I already know what action I'm going to take."

Urfin walked out to the back yard and began to boil water in a cauldron, and he dyed his best suit red by using the juice of the madder root. Thus began his preparations for his risky undertaking.

Chapter 6

AN AMAZING MANIFESTATION

Urfin Jus was totally convinced that Carfax's coming was a new gift to him from Fate, after having apparently forgotten about him for years on end. It remained only for him to make use of this gift. But Urfin really did not have a thing to learn in this regard. He had decided to appear before the Marrans as a terrifying embodiment of a master of Fire. The Leapers would be spellbound by his might, and they would recognize Urfin at once as their leader.

It was nine days to the next new moon. On that moonless night, the Marrans would see Urfin in a flash of fire against the dark sky, and he would descend to them on the back of a prodigious bird. Who wouldn't shudder when he beheld wonders like those?...

The outcast prepared to forsake this precinct that had now become hateful to him. The tireless Carfax made several trips to the Land of the Marrans, accompanied by the Clown. There, under the cover of night, Eot Ling concealed Urfin's joiner's tools and the most essential household items. Toward the end, the Eagle transported Topotun. The devoted beast would be an invaluable guardian to his master in the midst of his strong and dangerous subjects-to-be, being invulnerable to arrows and spears, not knowing sleep, and needing nothing to eat. Another important fact was that no bears roamed the Land of the Leapers, and in their eyes, Topotun would be a sensational creature.

And so the appointed day arrived, and Urfin set out on his long journey. This time around, he did not lock up his house, as he had done previously — no, he dragged brushwood inside and set fire to it! Whether he succeeded in gaining power over the Leapers or not, there was no way that he would return here, to the humdrum, monotonous existence of a humble gardener. "Come what may, I shall meet Fate head-on!" resolved Urfin.

He would begin his new life in a blaze of fire, and it was in a blaze of fire that he left his old one behind.

Urfin's house flared up like a huge bonfire. The people living in Cogida could see the glow from afar, and in its faint illumination, an enormous shadow floated over the village.

Centuries had passed in the Land of the Marrans since their migration from Underground, and these centuries had seen their share of natural disasters: fires, floods, and avalanches. But never before had the Marrans experienced events so disturbing and shocking as those that occurred on that memorable evening. First of all, after the onset of twilight, an extraordinary brown animal appeared in the streets of the settlement where Prince Torm resided, and it began to cry out in a thunderous voice: "Get ready, Marrans, get ready! This very evening, your mighty ruler-to-be will appear before you in the sky — he's Urfin Jus, the Fiery God!"

This was echoed by the thin, penetrating voice of a little wooden man seated on the animal's back: "People of Marran Land! Be happy and rejoice, for Urfin Jus, the Fiery God, is coming down to you from the skies!"

The half-dressed Marrans ran out of their huts and from under their canopies and, trembling with bewilderment and fear, they asked Prince Torm what all this meant. But Torm could give them no answer. The strange heralds continued to shout their messages.

Then an enormous shadow materialized over the village, and a fiery glow was visible on top of it. "It's lightning flashes..." whispered the stunned Marrans. The shadow swooped down lower and lower, and a blaring voice boomed down from above: "Greetings to you, my beloved Marrans!"

A colossal bird landed in the clearing before the amazed throng, and a man leaped nimbly from its back, a man dressed in a scarlet cloak and a bright red cap with white feathers on it. In his upraised hand burned a torch that spewed out sparks far and wide. It was as if a living fire had materialized there in the dark of the night.

Yes, Urfin Jus knew how to make this first appearance of his before the Leapers an extraordinarily effective one!

In their confusion and terror, the people fell to their knees, covering their faces with their hands to protect them from the brilliant fire. The newcomer from the heavens began to address them in a reverberant voice:

"Don't be afraid, my children! I come to you not to do evil, but, rather, to do good. And the first thing I'm going do is to make you see for yourselves that fire, which has always brought you death and destruction, will henceforth become your faithful servant. Good Topotun," and Urfin turned to the bear, "get the straw!"

Nearby lay a pile of straw that had been prepared for the construction of a hut. The Bear dragged several arm loads of it toward his master. Jus made it into a neat pile, and then he set it afire. The flames shot up into the air, and the frightened Marrans began to draw back.

Urfin burst out laughing. "There's no need for fear! Illustrious Torm and Princess Yuma! And you, esteemed elders Crem, Lax, and Venk! Approach!"

Excited voices could be heard in the crowd: "He knows all of us by name! Oh, wonder! Oh, wonder! He's not a man, he's a god!..."

Eot Ling proclaimed in a brassy tone: "To the Mighty Urfin, everything is subservient — both earth and heaven!"

Then simple-hearted Carfax added in his low, hoarse voice: "Urfin Jus is nobly-born, and he wishes good for everyone."

The flames began to die out, and the Marrans, bolder now, approached the bonfire. The night was cool, as it always was in the valley, and the people were chilled to the bone. But as they drew near the fire, they felt a pleasant warmth. Torm and the elders placed first one side toward the fire and then the other, and they got it into their heads that this heavenly newcomer had brought the warmth and light of the sun with him.

They accepted Urfin's magical powers without challenge: he did not become a mere king over the Marrans — he made himself their divinity.

Chapter 7

CHARLIE BLACK'S CIGARETTE-LIGHTER

There was one object that Urfin Jus valued more highly than any other among all his possessions. That object was worth very little in the outside world beyond the mountains, but in Magic Land, it was a real sensation.

It was nothing more than an ordinary cigarette-lighter, an elegant, flat little knickknack whose owner could hide it in the palm of his hand.

This cigarette-lighter had come into Urfin's possession after he had been ousted from the throne and while he was sitting up in the tower awaiting his trial. Charlie Black, the one-legged Sailor, had come to see the ex-king. He talked with Urfin for a long time and tried to make him feel some remorse for the crimes that he had committed; but Jus did not display even a trace of remorse.

The exasperated Sailor turned to leave, and as he did so, a shining object slipped from his pocket and fell down into the straw that covered the floor. Before Black had gotten past the door, the prisoner had made a dive for the fallen object. It was a cigarette-lighter, and Urfin was well aware of how valuable it was.

Footsteps were again heard outside: the Sailor had noticed his loss. Urfin quickly slipped the lighter under the straw mattress and sat down on the edge of the bed. Charlie Black left the place empty-handed, but this caused him no grief — he had a spare lighter in his knapsack.

Urfin concealed his find in his clothing and took it with him when he went into exile. The lighter gave off an aroma that Urfin found pleasing: it was the aroma of benzine — though the outcast did not have the slightest idea what benzine was. In the course of time, the benzine evaporated away, and this worried Jus; but he managed to get hold of a small bottle of light, clear petroleum, and that took the place of the benzine.

Urfin Jus kept the lighter for years and years, as a pretty trinket that could be taken out from time to time and admired. But now, when he resolved to assume the role of Fiery God to the Marrans, it stood Urfin in good stead indeed. For it was with its aid that Jus demonstrated to the Leapers that fire was subservient to him, that it would flare up in an instant at his command.

It was one thing to strike steel against flint, to wait for the spark to hit the tinder, and then to fan it to produce a flame. All that takes a great deal of time, and it's not very impressive to watch. But it was something else altogether for fire to leap in an instant from the master's outstretched hand and ignite a tuft of straw, causing it to erupt in a dazzling and intensely hot blaze.

Of course, he could just as easily have obtained some matches from the village store, but the lighter filled the bill much better for someone who wanted to pass for a god of fire!

Urfin struck the Marrans' imagination the very first evening he arrived among them: he produced fire again and again in his outstretched hand, eliciting enthusiastic shouts among the onlookers.

Chapter 8

HOW GODS LIVE

So completely was Urfin Jus possessed by his desire to make himself monarch of Magic Land once more, that he didn't want to waste even a single day unnecessarily.

He spent his first night in Torm's hut, in the latter's own bed. The next morning, he announced to the Prince that construction of a palace for him, the Fiery God, must be undertaken at once. Most sumptuous were the manors that he, the God, had left behind him in his heavenly domain.

Thousands of men set about carrying stones from the slopes of the mountains to the hilltop that Urfin had selected. Other workers scooped up gummy silt from the bottom of the lake, to serve as cement.

Urfin showed the Marrans the way to lay the foundations of a building by fitting one stone against another and binding them fast with cement. The Marrans proved to be quite imitative, and the job proceeded quickly with them. Jus appointed the most skilled of their number as masters and foremen. During a storm, while thunder was booming and lightning was flashing without letup, and the terrified Marrans were lying in their huts, shutting their eyes tightly and covering their heads with their arms, Urfin retrieved his tools from their hiding place.

Eot Ling the herald announced to the Leapers that the objects that their monarch would be working with were sacred. The Sun, Ruler of the Heavens, had sent them to the Mighty Urfin, and even touching them without the God's permission would be an enormous sin.

Urfin began by making jambs for the doors and windows; he hewed beams for the ceilings and rafters for the roof, and he constructed window frames. In his accomplished hands, the work proceeded apace. He derived much pleasure from this labor — it had been many years since he had last taken up an ax and chisel. Urfin might gladly have dispensed now with all his ambitious designs. But he remembered the disgrace in which he had been escorted out of the Emerald City, and how contemptuously everyone had treated him when they felt that he was no longer capable of doing them any harm. "No mercy to my foes! Revenge, revenge!..." Urfin whispered darkly through his clenched teeth.

Respectful onlookers thronged about Urfin, admiring his handiwork. Everything connected with the joiner's work — the screech of the plane along the board, the banging of the chisel, the buzzing of the saw — to the Leapers, all this had the appearance of some sort of miracle which only gods had the power to accomplish.

Prince Torm was delighted beyond measure when the Fiery God gave him permission to plane the wood a few times himself. He gathered up the shavings that fell to the ground and carried them triumphantly into his hut, a sign of divine favor.

The walls of the palace rose higher and higher with each passing day, and the building became more and more impressive. The Marrans gazed upon it with reverent awe.

There was one curious trait in the Leapers' makeup: after running and leaping to their hearts' content during the day, they dropped off into a death-like sleep at night, one from which it was impossible to awaken them, even if someone were to shoot off a cannon right next to their ears. Urfin Jus took advantage of this in a clever way.

Through Eot Ling, he announced to the natives that every family would have to bring forward a precious stone as a gift for their God, or else some misfortune would strike them in the very near future. The frightened Marrans hauled their finest valuables to Urfin. Then one night, when the inhabitants of the valley were submerged in their deep slumber, he flew on the Eagle's back to Quadling Land. He found a merchant there in Rose City, and he gave him two dozen precious stones. The merchant undertook to buy Urfin beautiful furniture, rugs, curtains, kitchen utensils, glass for the windows, and many other things.

During the nights that followed, all the items that he had purchased were transported to Marran Valley and hidden in an isolated cave. Carfax did not care for all this secrecy. "Why don't you make your purchases openly, in the full light of day?" asked the virtuous Eagle.

Urfin dissembled and resorted to trickery. "My dear friend Carfax," he said, "you've got to understand that while I may be deluding the Marrans, I'm doing it with a noble purpose in mind. When they see for themselves that I do indeed possess the gift of magic, they'll be more willing to follow behind me to the good life."

The construction of the palace was presently complete. It was covered by tiles made by the womenfolk out of clay, and fired by Urfin himself. But there was nothing inside the house, and the windows were merely empty frames.

That evening, Urfin said to Torm: "Illustrious Prince, I hereby invite you, your wife, and your counselors to come to my palace for a housewarming tomorrow."

"But there's nothing in your palace, Mighty Urfin," replied Torm, surprised.

"Don't let that perturb you," said Urfin with a super-
cilious smile. "A divinity is capable of things that you
simple mortals don't have the slightest conception of."

Urfin and the Bear toiled all night, not resting for even
a minute. In the morning, when Torm and the elders approached the palace, they let out cries of astonishment.

The palace was asparkle with the freshly-washed glass
in the windows. Inside, unprecedented luxury greeted the
visitors: sumptuous carpets covered the floors, and
brightly-colored curtains graced the windows. The rooms
were filled with elegant furniture, and delightful aromas
of food wafted from the dining room.

"This is a miracle!" cried the Marrans, and they fell to
their knees.

The Prince, the Princess, and their grandees took exceptional delight in this fire-cooked food. The table was
laid with fresh bread, roast duck, baked fruits, and various other delicacies whose taste had hitherto been totally
unknown to the Leapers.

"So this is how gods live!" said Torm, enraptured, as
he leaned against the back of his chair and rubbed his
stuffed belly.

"Yes, this is how gods live," concurred Urfin. "And
you Marrans can live like this too from now on, if you'll
carry out my commands obediently."

"We're ready to do so, Mighty God!" cried the Leapers.

"First of all, you'll have to build houses," said Jus.

"Houses for us? For us?" exclaimed the Marrans in
holy dread. "Ones like yours?"

"Well, not *exactly* like mine," remarked Urfin casually.
"Of course, they'll be a little smaller and a little less elabo-
rate, but you will be living in houses, at any rate. Moreover, you'll be obliged to cook food with fire. You've seen
for yourselves how much better this food tastes than the
other kind."

The fear that the Marrans had held for so long of fire,
that dreadful, punitive divinity, was clearly evident in
their faces.

"Follow me!" ordered Urfin.

He led his guests into the kitchen and showed them the flame, burning tranquilly in the stove. "You can see how I've tamed fire," said Jus. "It will make just as peaceful an appearance on your own hearths; it'll heat your cottages, and your womenfolk will cook soup and bake rolls over it."

"The Fiery God of the Marrans is truly great and good!" said Torm and his counselors in Urfin's praise.

That very day, in the secluded valley of the Marrans, a great building program was launched. The whole brunt of the labor fell on the commoners. The nobles did no work themselves: they merely bossed the bricklayers and carpenters that Urfin had trained, and the latter toiled from sunrise to sunset, with short breaks for meals. The workers recalled sadly their merry boxing, running, and leaping competitions, and they began to think that perhaps the appearance of the Fiery God among them was not really such a great benefit after all. But their religious awe did not permit them to dwell on such thoughts.

It was with great pomp that Torm, Venk, Grem, and the other notables later accomplished their moves into their new houses. The people, thronging outside windows covered with mica, strained themselves to catch sight of the silhouettes of banqueters and to make out the sounds of drunken voices — for Urfin had also taught the Marrans how to prepare intoxicating beverages from grains of wheat.

The Marran notables were now solidly behind Urfin. Even if they had guessed that Urfin was nothing more than an ordinary human who had taken the title of god upon himself, they would still have followed him to the ends of the earth. They felt only horror now as they recalled their former existence, when they had dwelt in huts like scum of the earth and had fed on such things as turia and salted duck...

The Marran aristocrats, since the olden days, had been amassing a large store of precious stones — amethysts, rubies, and emeralds. They, too, had done some bartering with the Quadlings on previous occasions, exchanging the gems for items of foremost importance. This trading was now greatly expanded.

The Marrans stepped out onto the slopes of the mountains facing Stella's dominions, and they waved their arms and shouted, thereby attracting the Quadlings' attention. The Quadlings approached them, admiring the glitter of the precious stones.

Before long, a regular bazaar had materialized at the foot of the mountains. The Quadlings brought chickens and rams, milk and meat, fruit, fabrics, and fine furniture to sell. And when Torm acquired for himself a little carved table and set of accompanying chairs exactly like those in the God's palace, conjectures about the true state of affairs crept into his head — though he kept them all to himself.

The commoners, of course, did not build themselves any stone houses. They could hardly be up to it, with the tribal leaders harnessing them to do other heavy labor! When the leaders were finished with the building of their houses, their next step was to expand their crops: the baking of bread and the rapidly developing wine-distilling enterprise all required considerably more grain than before. And firewood was needed to heat the stoves in the aristocrats' houses — for which purpose a column of woodcutters filed into the forest every morning, to return in the evening loaded down with heavy bundles. For the ordinary people, at least, life had been much easier before.

Two or three months went by, and more new burdens were imposed upon Prince Torm's subjects.

The nobles, competing with one another to see who could furnish his house most lavishly, squandered away all the valuables that their ancestors had accumulated, and they no longer had anything to use for purchasing beautiful carpets and costly furniture and clothing. So the aristocrats forced the poor devils to obtain more emeralds and diamonds for them.

Since all the precious gems had already been removed from the surface, it was necessary to dig mines. To prevent the walls of the mines from caving in, they had to strengthen them with props, and to obtain the props, they had to travel far into the forest.

Fearful that the miners might begin to secrete the precious stones that they found, the rich placed overseers to watch them; and to assure that the overseers themselves would be honest in the performance of their duties, they paid them quite handsomely. This resulted in yet more suffering for the poor.

The wise Carfax observed these melancholy scenes, and they disturbed him very much. The Eagle himself was not doing badly at all in Marran Valley. Goats roamed about the mountains, and they were caught up in the giant bird's claws. There were hordes of ducks on the lake, and Carfax had no qualms about eating such prey.

But his heart grew heavier with each passing day. In the evenings, the Eagle would talk with Urfin: "Where's the happiness you promised these poor people?"

Urfin would exclaim with mock enthusiasm: "Why, just look at how Prince Torm lives! And Venk, and Grem, and the others!"

"But there are only a few like them," protested Carfax. "The overwhelming majority are now much *worse* off."

"You can't have everything at once!" Urfin retorted. "The others, too, will have their turn."

"I believe you less and less," remarked the kind-hearted bird sadly. "The Prince and his counselors are rolling in luxury because thousands of other people are toiling for them."

To avoid an out-and-out argument with the Eagle, Urfin tried to stay out of his sight as much as he could. And everything in the valley of the Marrans continued to go according to that shrewd and ambitious character's plans.

Part II

TOWARD SEIZURE
OF POWER

Chapter 9

STRASHEELA — ENGINEER

After his third parting with Ellie, Strasheela returned to the Emerald City in a very melancholy spirit. He no longer derived any pleasure from the title "The Triply Wise," which had previously been such a source of pride; he was no longer overjoyed by reports of good grain and fruit harvests; he was no longer entertained by the dances arranged in his honor by Lan Pirot, former General of the Wooden Army and now dance instructor at the Choreographic Institute.

When Strasheela said goodbye to Ellie, he expressed a firm conviction that the girl would return to Magic Land. But he had a feeling that this time, their separation would be for good, and that fact depressed him. As if that were not enough, the Iron Woodman was in a hurry to return to his own home in Violet Land, and at such an inopportune time.

"Stay with me for a month, at least!" entreated Strasheela. "We can talk about the old days, and recall how we battled the Ogre, and how we pulled the Lion and Ellie out of the Deadly Poppy Field..."

"I can't, my friend, I can't!" The Iron Woodman was full of excuses as he stepped back and forth in a steady rhythm and listened anxiously to hear if his heart were beating within his breast or not. "As you know, I haven't been well, and life in Underground Land has had a terrible effect on my health. On the whole, you and I are getting old, my dear friend, we're getting old! Once again I've got to consult my doctors."

The Woodman's treatment consisted of having a skilled craftsman remove the patch on the monarch's iron breast, add fresh sawdust to his cloth heart, and solder the patch back on — and the heart began to beat again with all its former vigor. Then they oiled the Iron Woodman's joints and polished him all over.

The Iron Woodman departed, but the Courageous Lion and Kaggi-Karr the Crow stayed on for a while in the Emerald City. The three friends talked to their hearts' content: they recalled old times, denounced the malicious Urfin Jus's actions, and expressed their happiness about the Underground Kings, whom the ingenuity of Strasheela the Wise had transformed into industrious artisans.

Then the Lion, too, went home, for he missed his Lioness and their cubs. Only Kaggi-Karr stayed with Strasheela, and the poor devil became dreadfully bored. He would have liked to spend more time with Faramant, the Guardian of the Gates, and with Din Gior, the Long-Bearded Soldier, but they, too, returned to performing their own duties.

Faramant settled once again in his little sentry-box by the City gates, and whenever anyone arrived, he would put green spectacles on him so that the latter would not be dazzled by the splendor of the Emerald City. "I'm complying with the directive of the Mighty Goodwin," said the amiable man, "and I'll continue to comply with it until I'm buried in the ground. And my successor will likewise continue the same way..."

Din Gior, ex-Field Marshal, resumed his post on a high tower, and, looking into a hand-mirror, he combed his remarkable beard with a golden comb. And whenever he was occupied with this pleasant task, visitors might have to whistle and shout to him for an entire hour to get him to lower the drawbridge, for the Long-Bearded Soldier could see and hear nothing else.

So Strasheela decided to undertake a major project of some sort in order to drive away his devastating boredom. Locking himself in his Throne Room, he began to think. His thoughts were so intense that his head swelled to phenomenal dimensions. The needles and pins (which Goodwin had mixed in with the bran to make his brains sharper) stuck right out, and they made Strasheela's head look like an enormous hedgehog.

At last, an amazing plan was born within Strasheela's thought-filled head: he made up his mind to convert the Emerald City into an island!

When he confided his thoughts to Din Gior and Faramant, they were convinced that the monarch had taken leave of his senses.

"No such thing!" countered Strasheela. "I don't know if you're aware of it, but an island is what they call a piece of dry land that's surrounded on all sides by water. Ellie told me about them when she was teaching me ge-o-gra-phy. Our City can't travel to the river for the water to surround it, because cities don't walk. However, a river can come to the City, for it's in motion. I'll order that a channel be dug around our City, and the little Affira River, which supplies us with our water, will fill it up."

Strasheela stopped to catch his breath after his long speech, and his listeners looked at him with amazement. Faramant asked him: "Why should it be necessary for the Emerald City to be converted into an island?"

"In the event of an enemy attack, it'll strengthen our de-fens-ive ca-pa-ci-ty," Strasheela clarified. Din Gior, Faramant, and Kaggi-Karr looked at the straw man with respect: where did he come up with such long and learned words, anyway?

"But who's going to dig the channel?" asked Din Gior. "A vast amount of earth will have to be removed, and the work could drag out for years on end."

"It'll be fine if it does take years," said the monarch gaily. "At least I'll be occupied, and I won't be bored. I'll have the Deadwood Oaks dig the channel, since they have nothing better to do either."

Strasheela and his aides took a walk around the City. A large number of stakes were driven into the ground to mark off the edges of the future man-made lake, and then the grandiose construction project began. The lake would measure four miles in length and five hundred feet in width. If an enemy should ever get it in mind to attack the Emerald Island, such an imposing watery barrier would be most difficult for him to cross.

Day and night, the tireless Deadwood Oaks toiled. Day and night, shovels bit into the ground, and wheelbarrows creaked as they carried away the soil that had been removed. This soil was used to fertilize stony areas and to transform them into productive fields.

Strasheela forgot all about being bored, for he was up to his neck now in work. He spent all his time on the building-site from morning till night (and sometimes even during the night, if the moon happened to be shining), checking things out, measuring, and issuing commands to correct any mistakes he saw. The Chief Engineer (for such he now was) was accompanied by a retinue of wooden couriers, fleet-footed runners who dashed about at his command, filling the area around them with a merry clatter.

While work was proceeding on the channel, a large park was being roughed out along the City walls. Along the edges of broad walks were planted the finest trees to be found in the country's vast forests. Given the favorable climate, transplanted trees could adjust to their new environment at any time of the year. Beautiful pavilions and summerhouses were built in the open glades in the park, while the places where the walks intersected were adorned with fountains.

All the citizens assisted in the construction of the park, for they realized that it would be a splendid recreational spot for them.

The months and years went by, and the gigantic pit grew ever wider and deeper. At last came the moment of triumph, when all that was needed was to let the water into it. A canal was dug leading from the Affira River, and nothing but a thin bulkhead prevented the water from pouring into the bed that had been prepared for it.

The honor of striking the first blow went to Strasheela. He took a pickax in his limp hands and struck at the little barrier with it, and then the powerful Deadwood Oaks ran forward and finished the job. The waters of the Affira surged into the basin.

The crowds of people who had gathered on the banks of the reservoir broke out into cries of jubilation. Some prominent citizens lifted Strasheela onto their arms and carried him all the way around the City. From time to time as they were making this honorary round, the monarch ordered them to stop, and he would take off his hat, with its little golden bells hanging down from the brim, and make a speech about the importance of the lake to their defense.

Strasheela's speeches were listened to with great attention, and they drew forth thunderous applause. The residents of the City had been proud enough before, because their monarch was the only one in the world who was stuffed with straw and who had brains made of bran with needles and pins mixed in. But now that he had displayed such exceptional engineering talents in addition to everything else, their adoration knew no bounds.

An outdoor party for everyone in the whole land was held in the park, and the people who attended it ate mountains of cakes and pies and drank 140 huge barrels of lemonade.

It goes without saying that the Iron Woodman; Lestar the engineer; the Courageous Lion; Prem Cocus, monarch of Blue Land; Rujero, monarch of the Ore-Diggers, and Kaggi-Karr the Crow were special guests at the festivities. They were shown all the respect befitting their high ranks. In charge of all the ceremonies were Din Gior, the Long-Bearded Soldier, and Faramant, Guardian of the Gates — who for this occasion had prepared a supply of green spectacles for all the guests.

A detailed account of this holiday was entered in the chronicles of Emerald Island — for that was what the capital of Emerald Land now began to be called. Those who are interested may read this account in the City Library, Section 7, Shelf 4, no. 1542.

In a few weeks, the little Affira River, whose waters were swift-flowing and deep, had filled the gulf to its very edges. Stylish boats owned by the wealthier citizens began to appear on its mirror-like surface. The custom soon arose of holding rowboat races, as well as regattas of yachts equipped with sails. At Strasheela's command, a lifeguard station was opened, for little children swam in the lake from morning till night, and unfortunate accidents could easily occur.

To communicate with the mainland opposite the City gates, a round-the-clock ferry was established. It was manned by the sleepless Deadwood Oaks. They towed the ferry along a sturdy cable that stretched across the water, carrying upon request anyone who wished to cross over to the island or to leave it. However, if enemies should ever appear at the landing, the ferrymen were to bring the ferry back to the island at once and to raise an alarm.

Chapter 10

THE MAGIC TELEVISION

Work is a glorious and sacred thing! The person who spends his time in intelligent, productive labor will have a full and happy life, whereas the idler will grow bored, for he will not know how to pass his hours.

Strasheela could sense the undeniable truth of this when the prodigious labors on the lake and the park were complete. Once again, he did not know what to do to occupy his long days and his no less long nights. Of course, he could always do calculations in his head, but it was impossible to keep on calculating for twenty-four hours a day!

Then about that time, that time that was so difficult for Strasheela, something unexpected occurred which threw many of the townspeople into consternation: a flock of Winged Monkeys appeared high in the air, to the South of the Emerald Island.

The residents of the City had long been acquainted with those powerful beasts. Goodwin the Great and Terrible had contended with them at one time, and he had lost out in the conflict. Ellie had summoned them to the palace while in possession of the Golden Cap that gave a person power over the Monkeys. The girl wanted the Monkeys to fly her home to Kansas, but the Winged Monkeys were unable to leave the confines of Magic Land.

Right now, the Winged Monkeys were in a peaceful frame of mind. They landed on the square before the palace, and their Leader, who was carrying a package of some kind in his hands, asked for admittance to see the mon-

249

arch of the City. One of the courtiers ran in with the message, and Strasheela ordered that the visitor be admitted at once.

The Leader of the Winged Monkeys and the Straw Man knew each other from way back. It was this Leader who had once taken Strasheela apart, at Bastinda's command, scattered his straw to the wind, and thrown his head and his suit down onto the peak of a lofty mountain. But why dwell on the past? There was no cause for any hostility between them now, especially since the errand on which the Leader had come to see Strasheela was a pleasant one.

The old acquaintances bowed courteously to one another, and the Leader said: "Your Excellency, the Triply-Wise Monarch of the Emerald Island! I have the great honor of presenting you with a gift from our kind mutual associate, the mighty Fairy Stella, monarch of Rose Land. Having learned about your unhappy frame of mind, the Fairy is sending you this object, which is calculated to cheer you up."

With these words, the Leader carefully unwrapped the package — and in it was a splendidly-crafted rosewood box with a front side made of thick frosted glass.

"How did Lady Stella find out about my unhappy mood?" asked Strasheela in surprise.

"With the help of this very box," explained the Leader. He leaned toward Strasheela's ear and whispered so that the courtiers would not overhear him: "You must recite the following magic words: *Birelya-turelya, buridakl-furidakl, The edge of the sky is red, The grass is green instead. Little box, little box, be obliging, Show me so-and-so...* And the box will show you whatever you want to see. But if you transpose any words of this incantation or say it wrong by even one letter, it won't work. After you've seen everything you want to see, you must say: *Little box, this session I would end. My deepest thanks to you I extend.*"

The Leader of the Monkeys made Strasheela repeat the incantation until he knew it by heart. Then Strasheela whispered the magic words and made this request: "*Little box, little box, be obliging, show me the Fairy Ellie!*"

But the frosted glass remained dark.

"No, no," said the Leader of the Monkeys, bursting into laughter. "I'd like very much to see the Fairy Ellie myself, but the box works only within our country's boundaries."

Then Strasheela made a wish to see the Iron Woodman — and wonder of wonders! the screen brightened, and the Woodman became visible on it. The good soul was undergoing his latest course of treatment: he was standing there with his arms raised above his head, and Lestar the craftsman was soldering a patch onto his breast. When the artisan finished his work, the Woodman took a walk about the room. The figures were tiny, but they were very clear. And more than that: the sound of the Woodman's voice could be heard from the box, faint, yet perfectly distinct. The Woodman said: "Thank you, my friend Lestar. My heart is beating in my breast as it did before, and it's as full of love and tenderness as it used to be!"

Strasheela was thrown into utter ecstasy. "This is truly a magical remedy to drive away boredom!" he exclaimed, and then he expressed a wish to see the Lion.

His wish was instantly granted. The Lion, who looked as if he had just put away a substantial breakfast, was lying in his deep, cozy den, surrounded by the members of his family.

"It's a miracle, a miracle!" repeated the delighted Strasheela, and he presented Stella's emissaries with a generous gift of the finest fruits from his garden. He asked the Leader of the Monkeys to convey his most heartfelt thanks to Lady Stella.

As he was leaving, the Leader of the Winged Monkeys said quietly to Strasheela: "Lady Stella has ordered me to warn you to keep your eyes on Urfin Jus."

All this was still during the period when Urfin was spending his unhappy years in exile, but the Fairy Stella possessed the gift of prophecy, and she had the good sense to know that all kinds of unpleasant surprises could be expected from Urfin.

Strasheela was disturbed when he heard the Good Fairy's warning. As soon as the Monkeys were gone from the Emerald Island, the monarch pronounced the incantation and made this wish: *"Little box, little box, be obliging, show me Urfin Jus!"*

Strasheela instantly saw the far-off land to the West, and Urfin's cheerless house, and the man himself with a disgruntled look, digging up a bed in his garden. Topotun the bear was seated on the porch, having an argument with the wooden Clown. There was nothing suspicious about this scene, and Strasheela went on to other scenes with his box.

For a while, it was impossible to tear him away from his Magic Television for days on end. Keeping Stella's counsel in mind, Strasheela checked from time to time on what Urfin was up to. But he never saw anything that could be cause for alarm. Urfin weeded the beds of his garden, he ate roasted rabbits, and he went out for walks. "I can't understand what possible threat that sulky outcast can pose to me," grumbled Strasheela.

After the first few months, Strasheela's fascination with the Magic Box gave way to disillusionment, and he turned the Television on more and more infrequently. Kaggi-Karr the Crow was very much of the same opinion about it. "What use is that thing, really?" she said. "It lets you *look* at the Iron Woodman or the Lion! So what? Can you embrace them? Can you talk to them? There you are! Let's plan something better, let's go visit the Violet Palace in person!"

About twice every year, Strasheela and the Woodman each paid the other a visit, and the one would stay with the other for a long time. The Courageous Lion came to see them as well, though he was getting on in years and had less "get-up-and-go."

When the party was assembled, the friends would hold endless debates about which was better: brains, a heart, or courage, and they recalled the happy times when their beloved Ellie had visited Magic Land, and all of them had gone through so many perilous adventures together.

It was during reunions like these that Strasheela forgot completely about how essential it was to keep his eyes on the malevolent Urfin Jus. Would that he hadn't! After seven years of forced inactivity, Urfin was beginning once again to put some ambitious plans into action.

Chapter 11

HAPPINESS LIES BEYOND THE MOUNTAINS

Several months went by after Urfin Jus's appearance in the Valley of the Marrans and his proclamation of himself as their Fiery God.

Discontent among the commoners increased every day. The residents recalled sorrowfully that happy time when they may have been ignorant of fire, yet they had not had to exhaust themselves under the burdens of labor that their ruling class had imposed upon them since then.

But the Marrans did not dare grumble, even within their immediate family circles. It had happened more than once that verbal abuse directed against the Fiery God, uttered in the presence of no one but one's wife and children, had become known to the authorities, and the culprit had been severely punished. After being thrown into the newly-built prison, the poor devil would think, as he scratched his battered flanks: "Who could possibly have overheard my disrespectful remarks? Surely it couldn't have been that rat that was digging through scraps at the entrance to my hut, that repeated them to the Mighty Urfin?"

In fact, it was not a rat: it was the elusive spy Eot Ling who sneaked about the community, dressed in rabbit-skins.

All the same, Urfin Jus could feel that an explosion of popular indignation was imminent. It would be a violent and uncontrollable explosion, and the three dozen police-men, whom Prince Torm had selected from among his loyal followers, would be unable to put it down.

"The time has come!" Urfin decided. "The time to cast this miserable, long-suffering horde onto the prosperous regions of the Winkies and the Munchkins. Being starv-ing and angry, the Marrans will sweep through Magic Land like a whirlwind and demolish everything in their path!"

Eot Ling the wooden Clown approved of his monarch's decision. "There may well be an uprising if we delay any longer," said the Clown. "I've already seen clubs hidden under the straw in many of the huts."

"We'll redirect those clubs against the subjects of Strasheela and the Iron Woodman," said Urfin sullenly.

The next day, at the Fiery God's bidding, the entire population of Marran Valley assembled in the broad clear area by the lake. In the front stood the strong, thickset men; further back flocked the old people of both sexes, and the women and children. Urfin Jus towered over the throng. He was standing on a large rock that Topotun had dragged forward. Dressed in his scarlet cloak and his red hat, its feathers glowing blindingly in the rays of the sun, Urfin looked like a real God of Fire.

Jus raised his hand, and everyone fell silent.

"My beloved Marrans!" he began in a strong, hollow voice. "I know that many of you are living in a wretched state, and that you see me as the cause of it..." Men lowered their heads, and Urfin went on: "Your hearts are open to me, just as if they were the palms of your hands. Now you, Boice, and you, Hart, and you, Clem — tell me, for whom have you prepared the clubs that are hidden in your huts?"

Vertical stripes indicating former servitude glowed a bright crimson on the foreheads of the Marrans that Jus had named. Policemen hurried forward to arrest the conspirators and take them away to prison, but Urfin stopped them with a stately gesture.

"No need for that! I pardon them, for they did what they did without thinking. O my children, O Marrans! Yes, things are difficult and strenuous for you, and who's at fault for this? Not your good Prince Torm and his noble counselors, of course. They would like to offer the good things of life to each and every one of you, but they're unable to, and it's all the fault of — Destiny! Yes, Destiny!" Urfin repeated reverberantly. "Take a look around you!"

He indicated the surrounding area with a sweeping gesture, and the Marrans looked at their valley as if they were seeing it for the first time.

"In this poor, cramped spot, there are a lot of rocks and very little fertile soil! Even the splendid fruit-trees that one finds in such abundance in other parts of the country, do not grow here. There are no pastures here where one can breed fat sheep and milk-cows. But just turn your eyes to the north and the west!..."

The heads of all the listeners turned as if one.

"If the mountains were not in the way, you'd be seeing fertile plains with fruit orchards and flourishing fields of grain, and a multitude of warm, comfortable homes. It is there — *there* — that I shall lead you, my children, and it is there that you will find the good things of life in great profusion! Your happiness lies beyond the mountains!"

The orator was interrupted by a wild roar from the crowd. "Lead us there, Father!" cried the aroused Marrans, and those who were marked with the badge of servitude shouted loudest of all. "Lead us, mighty God!"

Urfin restored silence with a wave of his hand. "Those regions are inhabited by weak, delicate creatures who are not accustomed to fighting and combat..."

"*We're* not afraid of combat!" screamed the stalwart Boice, one of those who had hidden a club in his hut. "We'll show them, those weaklings, ho, ho, ho!" A chorus of militant voices lent support.

Thus did Urfin cunningly direct the people's anger against the totally blameless Winkies and Munchkins.

The meeting was adjourned.

Urfin began to issue some practical directives. As squadron commanders he designated Boice, Clem, Hart, and others who loved to fight, all of them sturdy, spirited fellows. "Choose only healthy young men for your squadrons. We don't need any antiques! Let the antiques stay home and prepare to receive the spoils of war."

A coarse laughter was his answer. The future soldiers venerated their leader already.

Carfax had flown off that morning to the distant mountains on a hunting expedition. When he returned, he found an unusual amount of activity going on in the valley. Detachments of men were marching along the roads, under the leadership of commanders. Young Marrans were fencing with clubs in areas that had been beaten smooth. War-cries filled the air.

"What's happening here?" the surprised Eagle asked Urfin.

"The Marrans are preparing for war against the Winkies and the Munchkins," replied Urfin bitterly, "and I, in all conscience, can not hold them back from it. These poor people have such a hard life here in their sparse valley."

"You vile person!" thundered Carfax. "You clearly put them up to it yourself, and now you want to enjoy the fruits of a war of conquest!"

The giant Eagle moved toward the man in a threatening manner, opening wide his powerful beak. Urfin bared his chest. "Go ahead, strike me!" he said in a quiet voice. "Hit me, but just kill me with a single blow."

Carfax drew back. "You're despicable!" said the Eagle softly. "You know I can't inflict the slightest injury on a person who saved my life. You knew it all along, you scoundrel! You plotted your machinations behind my back — and with my assistance, at that... Woe is me, hapless being that I am who became a tool in the hands of a rogue. I'll atone for my sin now with my death, but remember, Urfin! You won't come to any good end, and I say this at a moment of precognition, which we giant Eagles sometimes have."

Having uttered this ominous prophecy, Carfax rose into the air and headed for Eagle Valley to meet his fate. He knew that death awaited him there in the person of Arrahes, his sworn enemy, but he had no intention of staying here any longer with Urfin and showing, by his mere presence, that he approved of and supported his plans.

Chapter 12

ON THE MARCH

Urfin's army consisted of twenty companies, with a hundred men in each company: Jus estimated that two thousand warriors would be sufficient to conquer Violet Land, Blue Land, and the Emerald Island. The army began its march at noon, and the entire population of the valley accompanied the army as far as the mountains. Every soldier carried with him a slingshot, a supply of stones, a sturdy club, and a sack containing provisions for the first part of the campaign.

When the Marrans were down the mountain, the leader found it extremely difficult to keep the army marching properly, with one company following behind the other at the established intervals. Files were continually breaking up as one warrior and then another ran off to the side to look at a butterfly or a bird or a flower — all of which were nonexistent in the valley.

Urfin rode along on the Bear, and he recalled bitterly his obedient, perfectly-disciplined Deadwood Oaks. With the Marrans, in contrast, it was a case of their still being flowers that would not ripen into fruit till a later stage.

As soon as evening twilight had descended over the earth, the files of Leapers mingled with one another, and the soldiers began to succumb to sleep. Urfin barely had time to hurry and post sentries before the whole army was deep in slumber. A half hour later, he went out to check on the posts — and every one of the sentries was asleep, despite his strict order to guard the camp. Some were curled up into balls on the ground, while others were snoring in a sitting position, and a few had even contrived to go to sleep while standing, by wrapping their arms around trees. Urfin, in his outrage, ordered the Bear to turn them upside down and to lean them against the treetrunks. But they continued to sleep as peacefully as ever!

Every one of these defenseless warriors could have been cut to pieces like baby chicks if an enemy had attacked them during the night. But there were no enemies of any kind in the vicinity, and Urfin, giving up on military regulations, went off to sleep himself, in a tent that had been purchased from the Quadlings. The sleepless Topotun guarded his repose.

Chapter 12: ON THE MARCH

A cold pre-dawn wind roused the Marrans. Shivering and stretching, they ran to wash themselves in a nearby stream. The host resumed its march after a scanty breakfast.

A few hours later, they were stopped short by the Great River. It was on this river that Ellie and her friends had once been caught by a deluge. The river bore Strasheela away, and Ellie and the Lion came near to perishing in its waves. The Marrans gazed with amazement and fear upon the river. They had never seen such a quantity of flowing water in their valley: all they had were streams that originated up on the mountain slopes and emptied quickly into the central lake.

The river held the army up for a long time, since the Marrans did not know how to swim. It was necessary to construct rafts, and the leader himself was kept busy as a ferryman. At last this formidable barrier was behind them, and the disorderly columns continued on. The soldiers were feeling hungry, because they had already eaten all their provisions on this second day of their campaign.

The road led them to a grove of fruit-trees, and then the fun began!

Amid laughter and shouting, the soldiers dashed toward the trees, knocked fruit down from them — both ripe and unripe — and they began a gargantuan feast. Their faces deadened with delight, the Marrans gobbled down these novel delicacies, and it did Urfin no good to dash about among them ordering them to show restraint: no one even listened to him.

The lesson was a harsh one. By nightfall, everyone in the army had a stomach-ache. Even Krag the high priest, who had accompanied the army, and the company commanders were not to escape the general misfortune.

They remained in this one spot for three days. Fortunately, they came through without a single fatality, for the Marrans had strong stomachs. As the soldiers began to recover, Urfin Jus spent long hours hardening them to the strictest discipline, and drilling into their heads the notion that it was necessary to obey his commands. But it was a difficult thing to reeducate these people in such a short time, simple-minded as they were, quick to grasp things and just as quick to forget them.

When they had been on the march for ten days, a Winkie village appeared to the side of the road. With great difficulty, Urfin was able to convince his warriors that it would be senseless for the entire army to attack such a tiny hamlet. They sent Boice's company to capture the village.

Of course, no battle ensued. The moment the Winkies saw that horde of savage, big-headed men rushing upon their village with their clubs upraised and shrieking at the top of their lungs, they surrendered instantly, and they were driven from their houses.

The pillaging began at once. There were twenty-three houses in the village, and fierce fighting broke out in every one of the twenty-three. "This is mine!" screamed the enraged Marrans as they pounded one another with their powerful fists and grabbed some ordinary household item back and forth from each other's hands — a chair, a towel, a pillow.

From time to time, one of the plunderers himself would fly out through an open window or door, and those who were left inside would continue their brawl — to the amazement of the Winkies, who had congregated a little ways away. Finally, only one, the most battle-hardened, would be left in the room. He looked over the conquered premises triumphantly and proclaimed: "This will be my home! I'll go back for my family this very day and fetch them, and then we can live here."

When Boice's company rejoined the main forces, it was found to be one commander and twenty-two warriors short. "Where are the others?" asked Urfin, surprised. "Did they fall in battle?"

"No, monarch," replied one of the soldiers. "They stayed in the village."

"What do you mean, they stayed in the village?" Urfin's black eyebrows frowned in vexation.

"You did say we'd be living in warm, comfortable houses when we'd conquered them," the soldier explained. "Well, they conquered them, so they're going to live there."

"I'll be confounded!" Urfin almost blurted out aloud. "So my entire army unravels into the conquered villages, and Topotun and I arrive at the Violet Castle all by ourselves. No, that's not how it's going to be done!"

Urfin was obliged to enter the village himself and drag Boice and his soldiers out of the houses that they had seized. For a whole hour the leader demonstrated to the simple-minded fellows that uncounted riches lay before them, and he described the splendors of the Emerald City. But all this was too much for such poor, undeveloped minds to take in, and the houses of the Winkies, so pretty and cozy, were lying right there before them.

Urfin finally succeeded in leading the soldiers away, and the Winkies set about restoring order in their ravaged houses.

And what did Boice's company look like after their first military "operation?" One of the men was walking along wearing a saucepan on his head. Another had his arms loaded with knives and forks, while a third had tied an enormous wooden washtub to his back. And two strapping young men were dragging a bed along, complete with mattress, pillows, and blankets. Urfin, normally so sullen, laughed to the point of tears when he beheld this scene.

However, the possessors of these trophies did not amuse themselves with them for long. The first item to be discarded was the bed; the washtub flew after it, and all the remaining items followed behind them in their turn. In the same way, children part quickly with toys that they have grown tired of.

Chapter 13

THE CAPTURE OF THE
IRON WOODMAN

Urfin's army moved rapidly forward. The Winkies, being peaceable craftsmen and tillers of the soil, could offer no resistance to the hordes of powerful, fleet-footed youths that pounced upon them so suddenly.

Jus's lessons paid off now. No longer did the Marrans stay behind to settle in houses that they had seized, nor did they touch any dishes or furniture, taking away only clothing and blankets. And they emptied out the stores of food: milk, butter, cheese, flour. They seized chickens and geese, and they slaughtered cows and sheep. After their departure, so it was said, it was as if a ball had rolled over the villages.

There was no way that any of the Winkies could warn the Iron Woodman of the danger that was approaching. Urfin adhered to all the dictates of the art of war. A series of patrols marched ahead of the army, and they intercepted all those who tried to steal to the northeast. In this way, the monarch of Violet Land would be taken unawares.

Only a few miles remained now to the Iron Woodman's castle. Urfin commanded his main forces to remain where they were, while he himself went on ahead with two dozen scouts. Topotun and Eot Ling the Clown were also with him.

The scouts stole forward cautiously, almost on all fours, keeping their ears open all the while. Before long, they heard a sound. Urfin lay down on the ground, setting an example for his soldiers and for Topotun. Eot Ling

262

moved on ahead, his rabbit-skin apparel making him indistinguishable from the gray earth.

A few minutes later, the Clown returned and reported quietly: "The Iron Woodman is over there. He's uprooting tree-stumps."

Uprooting tree-stumps just happened to be the Woodman's favorite pastime. It reminded him of the old days, when he was like other men and worked in the forest, and planned to accumulate a good savings, set up a household, and marry the pretty girl he loved. But the girl had a wicked aunt, and the aunt put the witch Gingema up to enchanting the Woodman's ax. The ax chopped off first his legs, then his arms, and finally even his head. An accomplished blacksmith forged all new parts for him out of iron, but he had not been able to manufacture a heart. The Woodman had received a heart from the Wizard Goodwin, however, and he was very happy with it.

Uprooting the stumps resulted in great benefits, for the Woodman presented the cleared fields to the Winkies, and they planted them with wheat. It was not for nothing that the Winkies took pride in the Woodman and loved him as if he were their own father: he was, after all, the only monarch in the world who worked for his subjects!

Urfin continued to question the Clown. "Is he alone?"

"He's alone."

"And where's that dreadful ax of his?"

"It's lying twenty paces away from him."

A plan of attack was worked out. Urfin ordered the Marrans to surround the Woodman and to charge at him from every direction at once. Topotun, for his part, was to run over to the ax and rest his massive bulk over it — for if the Woodman should succeed in gaining possession of his ax, the battle could have only one outcome: the iron powerhouse would be able to fight off any number of assailants.

Not suspecting a thing, the Iron Woodman leaned on the stout stake that he had placed as a lever under the

root, and his thoughts could not have been more pleasant. He had recently received the news that Strasheela
and Kaggi-Karr would soon be coming to pay him a visit,
and that meant that they would once again be reminisc-
ing about the past.

This peaceful scene changed in the twinkling of an
eye. Fierce, half-naked figures burst out from behind
nearby tree-stumps and mounds, and with a howl they
charged at the Woodman. So disconcerted was he by the
unexpectedness of the attack that he did not even think
of grabbing the stake, which might have become a good
weapon in his hands.

"Get your ax!" he thought. "Quick, get your ax!"

Shaking off his attackers, the Woodman ran over to
where his ax was lying. But the ax was already hidden
beneath the Bear's ponderous frame, and it would not be
easy to dislodge him from the spot.

The Marrans hung from the Woodman's back, and they
clung tightly to his arms and legs. Urfin had chosen the
strongest and most nimble men in all his army to be his
scouts. The struggle did not last long. The Iron Woodman
was soon lying on the ground, with ropes around him.
Tears of helpless rage were about to start flowing down
his cheeks, but fortunately, the Woodman remembered:
"I'll rust! And there'll be no one to oil me..."

By sheer will-power, the Iron Woodman got control
of himself and lifted his eyes: before him, a crooked smile
on his face, stood Urfin Jus.

"You!... It's you!..." exclaimed the defeated hero in
amazement. "But Strasheela told me you were living quietly in your house in Blue Land..."

"And just how did he know that?" asked Urfin suspiciously.

The Woodman almost blurted out the existence of the
Magic Box, and he caught himself in the nick of time: he
absolutely could not betray this important secret to the
enemy. But Urfin himself freed him from his dilemma.

"Ah, I understand!" he said. "It was the Munchkins who reported it to him, of course! Yes, I did live there for many years, but as you can see, I'm here now, and I have, not two hundred clumsy wooden soldiers, but thousands of strong, spirited Leapers at my disposal!"

"How ever were you able to gain power over them?" asked the Woodman in amazement. "They never let anyone into their domain."

"For me they made an exception," gloated Urfin in a mocking tone. "They understand just who I am. But let's get to the point. Once again I make you an offer: will you become my deputy in Violet Land and rule the Winkies in my name?"

Jus could have designated another deputy, but he flattered himself to think that such an illustrious personage as the Iron Woodman would bow down to him and heed his commands. The Woodman, for that matter, could have pretended to give his assent and then betrayed Urfin, but he was much too honest. Therefore, he answered proudly: "No, never!"

"Mark my words, you'll be sorry!" threatened Jus maliciously. "This time around, I won't imprison you up in a tower — it'll be in a deep, gloomy underground cell, where the dampness will finish you off in no time!"

The Woodman shuddered at the mere thought of such a dreadful fate, but he repeated firmly, in spite of that: "No, a thousand times, no!" He thought to himself: "Ah, if only Strasheela has the good sense to look in the Magic Box! It won't do *me* any good, but at least he'll escape these woes!"

As luck would have it, a little titmouse was flying by. When she saw that something unpleasant was happening to the monarch of their country, she swooped downward and began to fly in circles over the captive Woodman's head. The latter cried out: "Relay the message to Strasheela in the Emerald City that he must take a look in the Box!"

"What box is that?" thought Urfin. "He's delirious from terror."

The titmouse continued to circle around above the Woodman, and the Woodman cried out to her again and again that Strasheela absolutely had to look in the Box, that his very fate depended upon it. Urfin hurled a stone at the bird in annoyance, but the titmouse dodged it, and as she flew away, she cheeped: "I understand! Strasheela must look at the Box! It's vitally important!" The Woodman felt relieved, and he rested more comfortably and calmed down.

Urfin's main army soon reached the spot, and the Woodman realized what a terrible force it constituted. No, *these* were no brainless Deadwood Oaks who could easily be frightened by a single solitary shot from a wooden cannon.

The Iron Woodman was extremely heavy, and Urfin constructed a sturdy litter to carry him on. Four Leapers bore the defeated monarch away, and the troops marched triumphantly on the Violet Castle. It is difficult to expect that the Winkies, once deprived of their leader, would be able to defend the castle. Urfin occupied it without the least resistance.

Urfin did not allow his boisterous army into the castle, lest it damage the furnishings inside it. He stationed his commanders in the outbuildings, and Crag the High Priest received the iron cage in which Bastinda the Witch had once confined the captive Lion. Crag found these quarters very comfortable, though a little confining. The rank and file camped out in the open air, and at night they covered themselves with blankets that they had seized from the Winkies.

The Iron Woodman was taken to a deep dungeon. The captive hero lay in a damp corner and thought woefully: "What's going to happen now? Will Strasheela successfully defend the Emerald Island, or will he, like me, become the cruel invader's prisoner?"

266

Chapter 14

THE SERVICES
OF THE MAGIC BOX

Strasheela was preparing for his departure for the Winkie Country. He normally traveled in a palanquin borne by Deadwood Oaks, who were now the nicest and most dedicated workers in all of Emerald Land. The Long-Bearded Soldier was standing before the monarch as Strasheela gave him some last-minute instructions regarding the time when he would be absent.

Just then, Kaggi-Karr the shaggy Crow burst through the open window of the Throne Room. Kaggi-Karr had the privilege of appearing before the monarch at any time without being announced, for she was Strasheela's oldest friend. It was to her that Strasheela owed his present high position, for Kaggi-Karr had been the one who advised him, when he was still hanging from a pole in the middle of a wheat-field, to acquire brains.

"D-a-a-anger!" shrieked Kaggi-Karr. "A very serious report has come in through the avian network!"

"What sort of report?" asked Strasheela. "From whom?"

"A report from our friend the Iron Woodman," answered the Crow. "He directs you to look at once at the Magic Box and see for yourself how very serious it is!"

"Where is the Magic Box?" asked Strasheela nervously.

The Magic Box, it turned out, was not in its customary spot. The cleaning-lady had grown tired of dusting it off, so she had placed it in a closet. But the Box was soon there before Strasheela. He worriedly pronounced the magic words: "*Birelya-tirelya, buridakl-furidakl, The edge of*

267

the sky is red, the grass is green instead. Box, Box, be obliging, show me the Iron Woodman!"

As the frosted surface of the glass turned light inside, Strasheela and Din Gior clutched their heads, and the Crow cawed wildly with alarm. The Television showed the interior hall of the Violet Castle — and there on the throne sat Urfin Jus! Before him stood the Iron Woodman, bound hand and foot.

"Oh, woe!..." groaned Strasheela. "The Woodman is a prisoner... So *that's* why Stella mandated me to keep my eyes on that cunning Urfin Jus! But ssshh... Let's listen to what they're saying."

Urfin's words came through loud and clear over the Television: "So, for the fifth time you refuse to be my vassal in Violet Land?"

"For the fifth time I tell you 'no,' you contemptible usurper, and I'll tell you the same thing the tenth time, and the hundredth!"

Strasheela welled up with pride in his undaunted friend, and the Crow shrieked: "Ur-r-fin is a cr-r-r-eeep!" Unfortunately, Urfin Jus did not hear her outburst. He ordered the guards: "Take the captive away and put him in the deepest and dampest dungeon!"

Strasheela trembled with fury, and he felt a passionate longing to be there at his friend's side: if he could not help him, then at least he would share his fate. Kaggi-Karr, in her anger, attacked the screen with her beak, aiming at Urfin's hateful face. But fortunately, the glass held firm: it had apparently been conceived with such eventualities in mind. "Hey, there, take it easy!" Strasheela cautioned the Crow.

They watched dejectedly as some Marrans led the Woodman along a half-lit corridor, until the monarch of Violet Land had been dropped off in a dark underground dungeon. Then the screen went dark, for it could not pick up even one ray of light.

"What are we going to do now?" asked Kaggi-Karr, upset.

"I'm going to think," replied the monarch of the Emerald Island, and he became submerged in his thoughts. As always in such cases, his head began to puff up and swell, and needles and pins stuck right out from it. The Crow looked at her friend with compassion. "Isn't that painful?" she asked him quietly.

"Lay off me, please," mumbled Strasheela, "don't disturb my concentration."

He thought for an entire hour, and then at last he looked at Kaggi-Karr triumphantly. "I've got it!" he said. "You'll have to fly to where Urfin's forces are."

"What for?" asked the Crow, surprised. "Could I really hold back that entire army if it should advance upon us?"

"It never entered my mind that you do *that*," retorted Strasheela. "You'll be my in-form-ant in the enemy camp," he uttered pompously.

"And what does that mean?" inquired Kaggi-Karr.

"Don't you see, the Box isn't much use to us as long as the Woodman is sitting in a dark underground cell. So you'll fly out to Violet Land, where you'll observe everything, you'll keep your ears open, and stay abreast of all that's going on there. Every day, precisely at noon by the sundial, I'll ask the Box to show you to me, and you'll relay everything to me that you've learned."

The Crow was delighted. "Oh, so I'll be a scout in Urfin's camp?"

"That's right," affirmed Strasheela.

"That's how I would have expressed it. But you said 'in-form-ant,' 'abreast'… Where do you come up with all those learned words?"

"Here, ma'am, here," said Strasheela, slapping himself on his bran-stuffed head — whose needles and pins were now slowly sinking back into it.

"Yes," said the Crow respectfully, "they knew what they were saying when they gave you the title 'Triply Wise.'"

"Well, what did you expect?" replied the monarch.

269

Since Violet Land was a whole day's journey away as the Crow flies, there was clearly no time to lose, so Kaggi-Karr departed at once. "If I learn anything of particular importance," said Kaggi-Karr, "I'll send it to you via the avian network. Keep the Throne Room window open day and night."

The Court Clockmaker was ordered to alert the monarch every day a few minutes before the hour of noon. Strasheela would then sit down in front of the Television.

The Crow, as was to be expected, had not yet reached her goal the first day: she was still approaching Violet Land. But the communiqué session on the following day was most successful. Kaggi-Karr had evidently learned the exact time, for Strasheela saw her on the palace roof at noon.

The Crow was looking in the direction of the Emerald Island, and she said slowly and distinctly: "My friend, the situation is worse than we thought. Urfin Jus has managed in some way or other to make himself overlord of the Leapers, and he's put together a sizable army of them. I wasn't able to count how many soldiers he has, because they don't stay put for even a minute: they're constantly running and jumping. But there are considerably more than a thousand of them. All of Violet Land is under their sway. They've been robbing the Winkies and taking away all their food stores. The residents are going hungry, and they're digging up roots and eating whatever grains they're able to pick up from the fields. In the days to come, Urfin is planning to march on the Emerald City, and at the moment he's drilling the soldiers — who are, I must tell you, a most ignorant lot. I tried to see the Iron Woodman, but I couldn't get through to his dungeon. I'm fearful that the poor man will rust. That's all for now. Tomorrow's session — same time, same place!"

The Crow made a bow to her unseen listener and then flew off to a nearby grove of fruit-trees to have her lunch.

Strasheela marveled at how briefly and succinctly Kaggi-Karr had reported on everything that was happening in the enemy's territory. He wanted to extend some praise to the Crow, but alas! the Television did not provide for that possibility.

Chapter 15

THE ASSAULT ON THE EMERALD ISLAND

Communiqué sessions were held every day at noon. There was nothing new to report. According to the scout's report, the Woodman was still sitting in the dungeon, as before, but she, Kaggi-Karr, did see him every day. The prisoner was led daily before Urfin, who endeavored to persuade him to submit to the conqueror. But the Woodman remained steadfast. His spirit had grown stronger since he had caught sight of Kaggi-Karr at the castle window and thus realized that Strasheela was aware of the danger. This had made it easier for the Iron Woodman to bear his monotonous captivity.

The drilling of the Marrans continued, and the recruits mastered the intricacies of marching in a column, attacking in all directions, turning around, and suchlike things. Urfin stinted no effort, and he spent all his time with the soldiers, from morning till night.

Of all the personnel who were employed as servants in the Violet Castle, Urfin kept only Fregosa the Cook — for her cuisine was exceptional. Fregosa had been in service in the castle for many years. She remembered Bastinda, and how she had loved to eat well. Of course, Bastinda could not tolerate anything that was liquid, such as kissel or stewed fruit, and she had good reason to be afraid of liquids — for Ellie melted the witch by pouring a bucketful of water on her.

Of all the masters she had served, Fregosa loved the Woodman most of all: he was so unpretentious! But now the cruel Urfin Jus had come and replaced the gentle Woodman. More than once, Fregosa planned to mix poison in the soup and thereby put an end to Urfin's grandiose schemes. But she quickly realized she would not eliminate the usurper in *this* way, for he seated Crag the High Priest at the table and made him taste first every dish that was served.

Fregosa's worries were soon over, however, for Urfin's army set out on its march against the Emerald Island. Urfin left Boice as viceroy over the conquered Violet Land, for the man appeared to him to be the brightest of all his lieutenants. He gave Boice half a company of Marrans to serve as a garrison. In Jus's estimation, such a number was quite sufficient to keep the meek Winkies in subjection.

Things became difficult for Kaggi-Karr the Crow when they marched away. Communication had to be maintained no matter what happened, yet how could she tell the exact time without a sundial?

When noontime approached, the scout looked continually at the sun and the shadows of the trees. Her reports were very brief, and the Crow repeated them several times each in the hope that at least one of them would reach Strasheela. And in fact, they did, because the ruler of the Emerald Island could never tear himself away from the Television for long at a time. Strasheela knew, from his informant's daily communiques, that Kaggi-Karr held long conversations with the Woodman during the night, when the Marrans were submerged in their deathlike sleep, and she bolstered his morale. The Crow even suggested to the Woodman that she free him by breaking his bonds with her strong beak. But the Woodman refused, saying that he would not get very far at nighttime, for the fleet-footed Marrans would quickly overtake him. However, Kaggi-Karr did get hold of some oil from the army stores, and she oiled the Woodman's rusted joints.

Strasheela did not limit his television communication to the Crow alone. His field of vision sometimes caught the sullen Urfin at the head of his army, sometimes one of his companies marching slowly across a rocky plateau, and sometimes the litter on which the Marrans were lugging the captive Woodman.

The Emerald Island prepared urgently for defense. These preparations were led by Strasheela, Din Gior, and Faramant.

The Long-Bearded Soldier, whom Strasheela had promoted once again to his old rank of Field Marshal, forgot all about his beard, and Faramant hid his pouch of green spectacles in a far-away place. The three of them, along with Strasheela, constituted the General Staff. The Staff members understood that the lake would hold back the attacking army for a little while, and all the citizens glorified Strasheela's foresight in converting the Emerald City into an island. "Our monarch can see many years into the future!" the people said proudly.

All the same, it was clear that enemies could eventually find one means or other to cross over the lake. This meant that the main line of defense would have to be the City walls.

Under the Field Marshal's leadership, the townspeople carried piles of stones up onto the walls, they heaped up arm loads of straw, and they prepared copper vats filled with water, which they would heat to boiling before the assault began and then pour down on the attackers' heads. The weaponers got only two or three hours of sleep a day: they worked hard constructing tight-fitting bows and fashioning arrows, while the blacksmiths forged iron tips for them. Carts drawn by tiny horses, and wheelbarrows as well, creaked along the roads leading to the City. The people laid in a stock of provisions for a long siege. The residents of the Emerald City well remembered what it meant to be under Urfin Jus's rule, and they did not want to go through it a second time.

When Urfin's army had reached a point three days' march away from the capital of Emerald Land, an important piece of news was conveyed to Strasheela via the avian network. It was delivered by a Blue Jay.

"In accordance with the directive of Kaggi-Karr the Crow," shouted the Jay, out of breath, "I hereby report to you, our Triply Wise Monarch, the following! Urfin Jus's troops are now gathering planks and logs from the farmsteads. They are very heavy to carry, and Urfin's soldiers are exhausting themselves, yet they are dragging these cumbersome objects all the same. Lady Kaggi-Karr does not understand the purpose of such an action, and she is therefore alerting you to it."

Strasheela summoned a war council immediately.

Field Marshal Din Gior suggested that the logs were to be used as battering rams, to knock down the City gates. But as to what Urfin needed the planks for, he could offer no explanation. Faramant, Chief of Requisition, thought that they were dragging the planks and the logs with them to use to build fires, to warm themselves with at night and to cook food. The prominent townsmen had nothing to say.

Then Strasheela took the floor. "Some strat-e-gists *you* are!" he said with disdain. "Isn't it obvious to you that Urfin knows about our lake? Since there's no way for people to travel over water by foot, it's necessary to construct a bridge over the water. *That's* why our foes are bringing those materials with them." The embarrassed council members remained silent.

On the third day after the council meeting, Urfin's hordes were pouring across the plains near the Emerald

274

Island. The Marrans had been robbing the populace during the course of their march, and so they strutted about now both in the violet outfits of the Winkies and in the green tunics worn by the farmers of Emerald Land. They were armed with slingshots and clubs. The appearance of the army was most alarming.

A broad expanse of water shone before Urfin Jus's eyes. He had been aware that a lake had been constructed around the Emerald City: tidings of it had spread everywhere, and even the Winkies knew about the lake. But the conqueror had not imagined the lake's extent, and so he had not thought that it would pose such a serious obstacle. In his mind, he congratulated himself for providing himself with building materials.

The ferry men had propelled the ferry to the City side at the very first appearance of the foe at the far-off approaches to the lake. Now, in obedience to Faramant's command, they loaded it with straw, and the Guardian of the Gates set the straw on fire. The ferry burned within minutes, leaving nothing but the charred shell of a vessel, and even this was sent to the bottom. All the pleasure-yachts and crafts were likewise destroyed following the ferry.

Urfin reacted calmly to the destruction of the ferryboat: he had foreseen that the City's defenders would do that very thing. The construction of a bridge was a must. It would be a difficult job, but Jus was not one to turn back when faced with adversities. So the Marrans became porters, carpenters, and sappers.

There was feverish work activity during the day, but at night, the army plunged into its deep slumber. If only the General Staff of the besieged City had known about this weak point! For some reason, though, Kaggi-Karr had said nothing about it. No doubt she had thought that the Marrans, when sleeping that way, were in a normal sleep. And even if they had known, the lake itself would have prevented the townsmen from making any sorties.

With dismay, the defenders of the City observed the narrow length of the bridge growing longer and longer with each passing day, but there was nothing they could do to hinder the Marrans. The park spread out in a wide belt between the City walls and the lake. The arrows that the besieged shot out over it would not even reach the foe...

A month went by. A sturdy bridge now stretched from one shore of the lake to the other. The first company of Marrans proceeded across it single-file, and the others followed behind. Soldiers armed with slingshots were carrying long planks and sawed-off sections of logs. The besiegers flooded over the park. Hiding themselves behind treetrunks, they made their way to the City walls. This venture was anything but safe. The Emerald City defended itself gallantly. Arrows whistled down from above, and wounded Marrans crawled back amid groans. The buglers in Urfin's army sounded retreat. The soldiers took cover in places where the arrows could not reach.

Jus sent several hundred Marrans into the woods to cut down supple branches. Then the soldiers began to weave these branches into shields. This work was still unfinished when evening came, and sleep, as always, overcame Urfin's troops. The Commander was deeply alarmed: the whole fate of the siege hung in the balance. Calling on Topotun for help, Urfin set to work himself...

Din Gior and Faramant were not sleeping that night either: they had their own bold plan. When the world was totally enveloped in heavy darkness, they stole noiselessly out through the City gates. With loads of straw and burning torches in their arms, the two heroes ran toward the bridge, intending to set it on fire. But when they reached it, they stopped short, powerless: they saw only the flames of their torches reflected in the dark water. Urfin and the Bear had removed the nearest link of the bridge!

Yes, the antagonists were worthy of one another!

In the morning, everything began all over again. But this time, the attackers were invulnerable. Covering themselves with their sturdy shields, they crawled right up to the walls.

There was a lively exchange of missile-fire between the adversaries. Sling shooters hurled volleys of stones up onto the walls, and the townsmen had to take cover behind the brick abutments. The City's defenders, in their turn, shot arrows from their bows, and they flung down chunks of granite and masses of burning straw.

Hiding behind their shields, the Marrans were carrying out some mysterious task. They rolled stumps of logs over to the walls and laid long, flexible planks across them. Strasheela and his Staff watched this strange activity, with no idea at all of what was going on.

When about a hundred such planks were arrayed along the walls, a signal sounded on the bugle, and warriors with clubs stepped onto the ends of them. The free ends stuck up into the air... Field Marshal Din Gior turned pale and began to mumble: "We're lost... Those are projectile devices! I've read about such things in the ancient Chronicles — but where did Urfin ever find out about them?"

The Marrans did their work efficiently and quickly. Two or three soldiers leaped simultaneously onto the free end of each plank, and the opposite ends sprang upward and hurled the men high into the air.

Several dozen Marrans hit their targets. They grasped the edges of the wall with their tenacious hands and assailed the defenders of the City.

The townsmen panicked. Abandoning the wall, they raced for their houses, in the forlorn hope of sitting it all out there. Faramant and Din Gior stood their ground gallantly, and even Strasheela tried to lift up a heavy stone in his straw arms.

But the forces were just too unequal. The Commander-in-Chief and his Staff were captured, and Strasheela found himself Urfin Jus's prisoner once again.

The new ruler at once offered him the opportunity to declare his submission and become the conqueror's viceroy in Emerald Land. Like the Woodman, Strasheela refused point-blank. Urfin commanded, "Take this stubborn person and his iron friend to the tower where they were confined once before. But don't put them at the top of it — put them in the damp basement beneath the tower. Let's see how long they'll last *there.*"

In spite of this misfortune that had befallen him, Strasheela was happy to see his friend again. The Woodman nodded his head silently as a token of greeting, for he did not have the strength to speak.

Strasheela walked along behind the ponderously-tramping Iron Woodman, and he thought sadly about the Magic Box, which Jus would now be taking possession of. It would be a disaster if he should guess its secret, for then Urfin's power would become even greater. But then Strasheela recalled that no one knew the magic words but himself, and without those words, the Box was nothing but a pretty knickknack. And Urfin would never get those words out of him, no matter what means he applied.

The captives were taken to the same dungeon where Strasheela had once been suspended from a hook as a consequence of his rebellion against Urfin. The familiar hook still stuck out from the wall, but it had rusted during the passing years.

"I was here before and escaped, and I'll escape this time as well," declared Strasheela jauntily. The Iron Woodman shook his head.

After his conquest of the Emerald City, Urfin Jus resolved to take the Deadwood Oaks back into his own service once again. These wooden men, being invulnerable and untiring, would be able to render him great assistance. But Kaggi-Karr dashed all hope of that. Immediately after the fall of the City, she assembled the Deadwood Oaks in a glade in the forest and organized a meeting. Taking up a position on the head of a strapping Deadwood Oak, which took the place of a rostrum, Kaggi-Karr called the meeting to order.

"Listen to me, wooden men!" she began to address them loudly. "Let it be known to you that the reins of government in Emerald Land have been taken up by me, Kaggi-Karr, who am acting in the place of our good monarch, Strasheela the Wise. Will you swear obedience to me, as your rightful ruler?"

"We swear!" answered the Deadwood Oaks in a dissonant chorus.

"Then pay attention to what I say! When merry, smiling faces were carved on you to replace your savage mugs, your natures changed. Since that time, you've been unable to harm people, and everyone came to esteem you as good, conscientious workers. But the vicious Urfin Jus intends to take up his chisel once more and turn you back into monsters and evildoers. Is that what you want?"

"No, no, we don't want that! It's better to do good!"

"Well, then, there's only one thing you can do: flee to the Tiger Forest and hide there in its deep ravines while waiting for Urfin's power to be nullified. And I promise you, as regent of this country, that you won't have long to wait."

So the Deadwood Oaks tramped in a body to the Tiger Forest, and Urfin Jus's hopes were blasted. Only among his former policemen did he find a few who did not care who their master was, and they reentered Urfin's service.

Chapter 16

THE NUTS OF THE
NUKH-NUKH TREE

Once the City was in their hands, the Leapers poured through houses and shops, and they took over the palace. Everything in the Emerald City amazed and delighted them. Amid laughter, the soldiers pulled the green spectacles off the eyes of the townspeople and put them on themselves. And they could not get over their surprise at the way everything around them appeared to be green.

The Marrans took no particular interest in the emeralds between the stones of the pavement and on the roofs and walls of the houses, for these stones were found in abundance among them in the mountains. But the height of the buildings, which seemed almost to touch one another overhead, and the luxury of the rooms, which were overlaid with carpets and filled with beautiful furniture — those things were a source of utter astonishment to a people who had been living in straw huts.

And now the Fiery God's generous promises were realized! Urfin's soldiers would ensconce themselves in the home of a well-to-do craftsmen or merchant and drive the owners right out, amid a deafening shriek: "This is mine!" The evicted residents left the island with tears in their eyes. Now they even missed the days when Urfin Jus had come among them with the Deadwood Oaks. The latter, at least, were not after the good things that others had, and they did not need shelter, or food, or clothing. And while Jus exacted a heavy tribute from the citizens at that time, he did not drive them out of their homes.

Urfin began his restoration of order in the City by ex-
pelling the soldiers from the palace. "The palace is for
your god to live in!" it was announced to them. "No one
can be in here except the Mighty Urfin's bodyguards,
whom he will select from among his most worthy warriors. And visitors are not to be admitted until they have
been announced to the Monarch."

Alas! the bodyguards did not live up to the faith that
had been placed in them. They slept, as usual, like dead
men that very first night. And if Din Gior and Faramant
had not been in captivity, Urfin himself would have been
taken prisoner that same night. But those two bold ones
were languishing in prison, and the conqueror greeted
the morning light with relief after a sleepless night.

To Urfin's great surprise, who should fly in through
the open window of the Throne Room but his former faithful assistant in matters of sorcery — Guamokolatokint,
the Great Horned Owl.

"Guam!" cried Urfin in amazement.

"Guamoko!" the Owl corrected him severely. "I hereby
remind you that you and I agreed that I would settle for
nothing less."

Urfin, in spite of himself, had to admire the persis-
tence of the bird, who had not forgotten his presumptu-
ousness even after ten years.

"Guamoko it is, Guamoko," conceded Urfin. "But in
any case, I'm glad to see you alive and well, old friend!"

"You know, king, news of your arrival in our region
reached me the same day your army laid siege to the Island."

"Then why didn't you come and visit me at once?"
inquired Urfin.

"I've grown old, and I've gotten sluggish. I planned
to every day, but each time, I put it off."

The truth of the matter was that the cunning old creature had been waiting out the siege to see how it would

turn out. If Urfin had been beaten back and gone away empty-handed, Guamoko would not even have considered going to see him. Now, however… Now it was different, and with the victor he could be friends again.

"I've brought you a nice gift," continued the Great Horned Owl. "Are you aware that I'm now the ruler of all the local tribes of the great horned and other owls? Out of respect for my knowledge and experience, they feed me mice and little birds…"

"All that is pretty much beside the point," Urfin interrupted impatiently.

"Just listen further. One day, my subjects were unable to catch me my usual allotment of mice, and they offered me some sweet nuts of the nukh-nukh tree in their place. Nuts are no food for the likes of us, but I had to agree anyway. I did not peck at too many of them, but what do you think happened? I was afflicted with such an insomnia that I didn't close my eyes for a whole twenty-four hours."

Urfin quickened at once with elation. "What's that you say? Nukh-nukh nuts…"

"That's what your guards need. I've been in the City since yesterday night; I checked on the vigilance of your sentinels more than once, and — I'll say it in all honesty — I've never seen a sleep like that in all my life. Even if you cut them to pieces, they wouldn't wake up."

"Nuts that produce insomnia — that's a miracle!" agreed Urfin. "I'll send a dozen people into the woods with baskets, and you, dearest Guamokolatokint, you can point out the nukh-nukh tree. I never knew of anything like that existing in Munchkin Land."

"It grows only in the vicinity of the Emerald Island," explained the Owl, flattered that Urfin had called him by his full name.

"If the nukh-nukh nuts prove themselves," said Urfin, in a display of generosity, "I'll order three hunters to catch you fresh game every day."

A precious cargo had been delivered to the palace within a few hours. Urfin ordered that a strong extract be made from the meat of the nuts and mixed with vanilla and other spices, and when night came, he commanded each of his guardsmen to drink a mug of this beverage. From that time on, the patrols did not fall asleep during the night, and the self-styled king felt calm under their protection.

Of course, as it turned out, nukh-nukh nuts were not entirely harmless. The person who drank the decoction saw various apparitions while he was awake. His eyes wandered, and he was tormented by a baffling feeling of sadness. His pleasant frame of mind did not return to him until he drank another serving of the potion.

No dispatches of any kind were received from Violet Land, and Urfin assumed that his power was firmly established there. So he turned his sights to the West. Jus sent out three select companies of troops to conquer the Munchkins and the Ore-Diggers; they were under the leadership of Hart, whom he had promoted to the rank of Colonel. "Blue Land must be conquered within three weeks," commanded the king.

There were no bounds to Urfin Jus's happiness: it seemed to him that he was achieving all his aims with amazing precision, even in spite of his being abandoned by the Giant Eagle. "It's just as well that Carfax left me," Urfin reflected aloud as his eyes followed Hart's columns marching down the Yellow Brick Road. "It's hard to deal with a bird who's a nut about integrity. Can you imagine, he won't even admit that there *is* such a thing as duplicity, ha-ha-ha! And yet, without duplicity, could I ever have become a king and a god? The future promises me nothing but victory and glory..."

Part III

THE
AMAZING
MULES

Chapter 17

THE DAYDREAMS OF
ANNIE AND TIM

When Ellie returned to Kansas after her third trip to Magic Land, she found that she now had a little sister at home there. The little one had been christened Anna, in honor of her mother, but everyone called her by the nickname "Annie." The presence of this little living miracle — the baby — caused Ellie's recollections of her remarkable adventures to fade a little.

The first stories that Annie heard from her older sister were fabulous tales about the Emerald City and Goodwin the humbug Wizard, about Strasheela and the Iron Woodman, about the Cowardly Lion and Kaggi-Karr the Crow, about Urfin Jus and his Wooden Soldiers, about the Seven Underground Kings, and about all the happenings, both gruesome and pleasant, that Ellie had lived through in that amazing region cut off from the rest of the world by a sandy desert and by mountains.

The one who became little Annie's best friend was Tim O'Kelly, who lived on a neighboring farm located only about a quarter of a mile away from Farmer John's house.

Tim was a year and a half older than Annie, and his friendship assumed the nature of protectorate. It was both funny and moving to watch this chubby little boy, himself still not all too steady on his feet, protecting his little girlfriend from angry turkeys and calves that wanted to butt her.

The children were inseparable, and no one could begin to count how many times a day they rushed back and forth from one farm to the other.

Each of the farm wives, Mrs. Anna Smith and Mrs. Margaret O'Kelly, looked upon both little ones as their own, and they caressed each of them with equal affection, and spanked each of them with equal impartiality.

Tim O'Kelly, too, was a constant listener to Ellie's marvelous stories, just as much as her little sister was. It is no wonder, therefore, that as Tim and Annie grew older, it became their most fervent aspiration to visit the Land of Wonders and to meet the engaging and happy people who lived there.

Annie and Tim well remembered that Ellie's second trip began when Kaggi-Karr the Crow came to her to deliver a call for help from Strasheela and the Iron Woodman. Ellie's friends had been imprisoned by the malevolent Urfin Jus, and they were appealing to their loyal friend, the Fairy with the Death-Dealing House, to come to their rescue. So Ellie, accompanied by one-legged Sailor Charlie Black, had set out on the perilous journey, and she triumphed over the wicked Urfin and his mighty Wooden Soldiers.

And so, the ingenuous children were eager to see Kaggi-Karr in every crow that happened to appear anywhere in the immediate vicinity. Ah, just let one little piece of news reach them from that mysterious land of Ellie's childhood, and how boldly they'd rush into battle with evil magicians and wicked sorcerers! But the trouble was, all the crows that they attempted to make friends with turned out to be just ordinary birds, and not messengers from Strasheela at all!

The crows were glad to accept the food that Annie and Tim gave them, and they spread the word about these good-hearted children all over Kansas. Before long, un-counted flocks of black crows were clustering on the roofs of the houses and barns, fighting with one another for every vacant branch on every tree. And all of them awaited handouts from Tim and Annie...

The result of all this was that the indignant farmers, fearful of losing their harvest, organized a large-scale hunting party to go after the venturesome birds. Sticks and stones flew through the air, rifle and pistol shots reverberated, and Grandpa Ralph unearthed in his shed an old, old cannon left over from the period of the Civil War. He filled it with powder and buckshot, and boomed it at the largest of the flocks.

The effect was most striking. The cannon burst, and it was only by a miracle that Grandpa Ralph survived — but the host of crows was so terrified that they dispersed and flew away in every direction. "And to think that Kaggi-Karr might have been there among them!" the children sighed.

On the day when Annie turned seven, her big sister gave her the whistle that she had received from Ramina, Queen of the Field Mice. Ellie parted with this souvenir without any regrets because, as she put it, Kansas was no place for marvels. But Annie did not share that opinion at all, and that very evening, she and Tim hid behind the hen-house, and the girl blew the whistle three times. And what do you think happened? A marvel did occur after all!

A multitude of mice appeared there before the de-lighted children. Now any other girl, seeing all these little gray creatures, would have let out a scream that could be heard all the way to heaven and then run away, but Annie Smith was not such a girl. She stood there calmly and gazed curiously at her tiny guests.

The mice liked Annie's fearlessness, and a large mouse that appeared to be the Queen of the tribe stepped out from the quivering gray carpet that covered the ground. She stood up on her hind legs and pointed her intelligent black eyes at the little girl's face. She peeped something, but alas! only in the Land of Wonders do humans and animals share a common language. Annie said sorrowfully to Tim: "Maybe the Queen of the Mice is telling us the latest news of Magic Land or even giving us advice on how to get there, but her speech is impossible to understand."

After waving her front paws three times as a sign of farewell, the Queen led her subjects away, and nothing was left there in the dust but their tiny footprints.

Annie and Tim continued to have meetings with the mice, for the children never lost hope that the Mouse Queen would finally speak to them in a human voice. But this did not happen, and it all came to an unfortunate end.

One day, Mrs. Anna came out to the far end of the yard, where Annie was in the process of trying to understand what the Mouse Queen was saying. She did not possess the same lack of fear that her daughter did, and, letting out a piercing scream, she was almost ready to faint — but the mice disappeared in the twinkling of an eye, as if they had vanished right into the ground. Mrs. Anna lashed out at the children with a frightful scolding.

"You naughty children!" screamed the furious woman. "You're simply driving me crazy with all the things you come up with! First flocks of vile crows swarm to the farm, then you bring in millions of mice... Just wait till they feed on the eggs in the hen-house and gobble up the grain in the bins."

"There are far less than a million of them, Mom," said Annie with a smile. "They're very nice, and completely harmless. They only come when I blow this whistle, and they don't bother anything on the farm."

"I won't hear another word!" shouted Mrs. Anna angrily. "Give me that whistle!"

And so, to Annie's great sorrow, the whistle was taken away from her, and the meetings with the mouse tribe ceased.

There was nothing they could do, and they had to abandon hope both that Kaggi-Karr would come, and that the Mouse Queen would help them. Then Annie and Tim recalled the underground river that had led Ellie and her second cousin Fred Canning to the realm of the Seven Underground Kings. To the children, an underground journey seemed like something that could be easily accomplished.

"Really, all we have to do is get hold of a good boat," they reasoned, "and we'll stock it with as many provisions as we can: candles, torches, matches... After cruising along for a few days, we'll be in Underground Land. From there, it'll be the simplest thing to reach the surface, in Magic Land."

The children gave much thought about whether or not they should take Totoshka along on their journey. There was no denying that the dog was a great expert on Magic Land and would be very useful there. But dogs have short life-spans, and Totoshka had already grown old; he had lost his old energy and drive, and he had grandpuppies. Annie and Tim decided to make one of these grandpuppies, a dog named Arto, their traveling companion.

Arto was very much like what Totoshka had been in the days of his youth. He had the same silky black fur, the same intelligent eyes beneath shaggy brows, and the same devotion to his masters and readiness to sacrifice his life at any time for their sake.

Annie informed Artoshka of her decision. Did the little dog understand? Most likely he did, because he began to wag his tail most ingratiatingly.

In the fall, Annie Smith and Tim O'Kelly went away to school. Tim's time to enroll had actually come a year

earlier, but how could he really go away to school without his Annie? By resorting to screams and tears, the little
boy had obtained his parents' consent to remain at home
for one more year.

Now he was a whole head taller than Annie and the
other boys and girls in their first-grade class. Red-faced,
fair-haired, broad-shouldered, and with strong fists, he
was Annie's faithful protector against anyone who tried
to pick on her.

Of course, Tim and Annie sat at the same desk and
did their lessons together. "What an inseparable pair!"
said the grownups with a smile.

During their first vacation from school, Annie and Tim
asked their parents' permission and then traveled to the
state of Iowa to see Fred Canning. As John Smith saw his
little daughter off on her long journey, it was obvious from
his sly smile that he understood why Annie and Tim were
undertaking the trip. But he made no outward sign of
this to them, and merely wished them a pleasant time.

Alfred Canning, who was now a student at the Institute of Technology, gave a warm welcome to his little
cousin Annie and her friend. But when Annie timidly
asked him to take her, Tim, and Artoshka into the cave
where the underground river began, the young man burst
out laughing. "Didn't Ellie tell you, little one, that the
entrance to that cave collapsed? It was for that very reason, in fact, that we were obliged to embark on our amazing journey..."

"I know that," objected Annie, "but I thought that the
passage to the underground river must surely have been
dug out."

"Why?" asked the student.

The girl was genuinely surprised. "Very simple — so
that everyone can travel to Magic Land!"

Alfred laughed until he almost fell over. "Ah, you're
something else, little one! Would you like it, perhaps, if a

travel agency opened here and hordes of tourists flocked to the Enchanted Country?"

"Well, what would be wrong with that?" inquired Tim O'Kelly.

"That would be dreadful," explained the young man in a serious tone. "Magic Land is such a good place for the very reason that it's cut off from the rest of the world, and that's why the good witches Villina and Stella live there, and animals and birds can talk, and a continual summer reigns. If loud-talking, unmannerly gentlemen and ladies from the States were to descend on the place, it would mean the end for those gentle, simple-hearted creatures — the Winkies and the Munchkins! As a matter of fact, a certain enterprising speculator who was on the make did come to our area and offer me a heap of dollars to show him where to dig a passage into the cave. But I didn't accept any money, and the place I indicated to him was the wrong one. He and a dozen workers probed there for about two weeks and eventually they drove away empty-handed."

"So that means there's no point in even dreaming about going there," said Annie sadly.

"With you, it's different," Alfred consoled her. "You're Ellie's sister, and in Magic Land, Ellie is honored as a powerful fairy who's done a great deal for the people who live there. I think that Strasheela and the others would be very happy if you, Annie, and your friend Tim were able to cross the Great Desert and the World-Encompassing Mountains and end up in their blissful realm."

"Yes, but how are we going to accomplish that?" sighed Annie.

"Where there's a will, there's always a way," said Alfred. "Just keep thinking about it, and you'll find a way to reach the land of your dreams. I'll be thinking about it too, and something is sure to come up quickly."

Their conversation with Alfred gave the children hope, and they returned home relieved.

Chapter 18

A SHIPMENT FROM FRED

Vacation time was nearly over when a postal truck delivered to John Smith's farm two enormous boxes lashed to the roof of the truck. It was with great difficulty that the postman and the driver got the boxes down and dragged them to the house; after receiving a tip, they drove away. John Smith's address was written in large letters on the lids of the boxes, and the name of the sender was given as Alfred Canning, town of Neville, state of Iowa.

"It's from our nephew Freddy," said Mrs. Anna. "I wonder what it is, coming in such huge boxes. Perhaps it's fruit. But why so much of it?"

"Mommy," said Annie, who had placed her ear against the side of one of the boxes. "There's something moving about inside."

"Oh, come now!"

But her daughter's words made the farm wife nervous, and she gave these unusual cartons a wide berth. They decided that they would not open them until Mr. John came in from the field.

The day dragged on endlessly for Annie, Tim, and all the other neighborhood boys and girls who had learned about this occurrence. The children confirmed that a rustling and knocking sound was indeed coming from the boxes. Interest in the strange packages had reached an unusually high pitch when Mr. John returned from the field. The farmer armed himself with a chisel and tongs and began to unpack one of the boxes. He had hardly lifted the lid slightly, when a vibrant bray was heard inside. John drew back, Mrs. Anna crossed herself, and the boys and girls squealed with delight.

"It's a horsie!" cried three-year-old Bob.

"That can't be," replied Farmer John. "What horse could ever last for three days shut up in a coffin like this with no air and no food?"

However, when the lid fell away, a sturdy bay mule did clamber out of the box, and it struck the ground with its hoof and neighed again.

"Saint John and all the saints in heaven!" exclaimed the flabbergasted farmer, and he seized the mule by the bridle so that it would not run away. "Does this animal come from Magic Land? I would have sworn it did if Fred Canning's address hadn't been on the lid."

Her father's words made an extraordinary impression on Annie. She felt at once that if it were her destiny to go to that Wonderland, the means of doing so was right here before her eyes.

Farmer John looked for a letter from Fred among the packing material, but he did not find one. What he did find was a splendid saddle with a soft pillow and silver-plated stirrups. The letter was found in the other box, which contained a gray mule slightly smaller than the first one. A second saddle was there as well.

Here is what Alfred Canning wrote:

> "Dear Cousin Annie! Your desire to go to Magic Land was so great that I had to rack my brains and accommodate you. I worked all summer constructing these mechanical mules, and I am now sending them to you and your friend Tim O'Kelly..."

Farmer John had to interrupt his reading of the letter, because Tim began to yell at the top of his lungs, and he performed a flying leap which would hardly be possible otherwise for a boy of his years. When they had calmed Tim down, the farmer began to read further in the letter.

> *"These mules,"* wrote Alfred, *"need neither food nor water, and they get their energy from solar batteries that I have mounted inside them under their skin... The sun in the Great Desert will be more than enough, and that means you'll never need worry about the mules coming to a stop at the halfway point through lack of food."*

Further down in the letter came instructions on how to operate the mules. A peg was hidden in each mule's mane, one that could be moved backward and forward. If one moved it as far back as it would go, it meant "stop." In the middle position, the mule would travel at a moderate trot, and if the peg were pushed as far forward as it would go, the mule would break forth into a gallop. Making the animals turn right and left was even simpler: all one had to do was pull on the bridle.

Alfred wrote that keeping the mules in the sun for two to three hours a day would be enough. If they were in motion on a clear day, the batteries would recharge automatically. The inventor stated that, to avoid possible trouble, he had shipped the mules with the batteries uncharged.

"Then why did they neigh and climb out of the boxes by themselves?" asked Tim O'Kelly, who had rather a good grasp of things mechanical for someone his age.

Farmer John thought for a moment, and soon he came up with the explanation: "At the time they were shipped, the sun apparently warmed the sides of the boxes so much that it was enough to charge the batteries," he said decisively. "But the devil take me, if the lad hasn't come up with a remarkable invention!... Yes, it looks like these mules can be depended upon!"

"And they'll see Tim and me boldly to Magic Land!" exclaimed Annie gaily.

"Well, we'll have to see about that," replied her father with feigned severity.

Alfred concluded the letter by giving Annie and Tim a warning that was of no small importance. He advised them that when they went on their trip, they were to reveal to no one — and that meant *no one* — the secret of the amazing beasts. Let everyone think that they were merely ordinary beasts, which they resembled completely to the sight. In this way, there would be less danger of anyone taking them away from the children.

"Fred seems to be dead certain that Tim and Ellie will be setting out on their journey today or tomorrow," mumbled the farmer. "Yet the school term will be starting soon."

At this point, strangely enough, Mrs. Anna stood up for the children. "Ellie missed more than just a single year," she said, "but God teaches everyone in His own way. The things she saw and lived through were the equivalent of years and years of study for our little girl..."

"Aren't you afraid to let them go to Magic Land alone?" asked John, surprised.

But his wife believed that every person's destiny was ordained for him at the time he was born, and that there was no escaping one's fate. "It's just as possible for a person to fall off a porch and break his bones,' said Mrs. Smith, "while someone else, like our Ellie, can come home safe and sound from three incredible journeys."

As luck would have it, Ellie herself came home the next day, and she proved to be Tim's and Annie's most enthusiastic intercessor. By dint of such vigorous solidarity, the children won out. Even Timothy O'Kelly's parents agreed to let the boy go.

It was decided that Annie and Tim would start out on their trip the following Sunday, when Farmer John, who would not be working, would be able to escort them for a distance of perhaps twenty miles from their house.

Ellie was delighted with the mules. "If only Totoshka and I had had steeds like these when we were wending our way down the Yellow Brick Road!" she exclaimed. "Remember that, Totoshka?"

Totoshka did remember. He realized that he was not going to be taken along on this new journey to Magic Land, but he accepted the fact. "What can you do?" thought the dog. "Old age, you know! Let Artoshka go. The old must give way to the young."

Ellie gave the mules names. She had taken a course in Ancient History the previous semester, so she named the gray mule Caesar and the bay mule Hannibal. The children liked these reverberant names very much.

Chapter 19

THE JOURNEY BEGINS

It was early on an August morning that Annie and Tim O'Kelly said goodbye to their families and set out on their journey. Their gear had been thought out down to the smallest detail, and Ellie, the seasoned traveler, had been especially helpful in this.

Their store of provisions was placed in double leather bags, which were slung over the backs of the mules. The children carried knapsacks containing everything most essential for the road: they were loaded with spare underclothing, soap, toothbrushes and tooth powder, knives, spoons, and other small items for traveling. Over her shoulder, Annie hung the spyglass that Charlie Black the one-legged Sailor had given Ellie. [Around her neck hung

Ramina's whistle, which her mother had finally restored to her.] Each of the kids held a compass on the left wrist and a watch on the right. In Tim's bag was a deflated volleyball. The reason for this was that Tim had decided to teach the Munchkins and the Winkies the worthy game of volleyball. Tim was an accomplished player, and even the older boys accepted him on their team. In addition to all this, Tim was armed: a strong bludgeon with a bulge at one end hung down from his belt.

A small bag was strapped to Annie's saddle, and out of it peered the little face of Artoshka. The dog's black eyes sparkled merrily, for he was very happy to be along on the journey. When he had had enough of sitting in the bag, he gave out with disjointed yelps, and they put him on the ground, where he ran along behind the mules.

John Smith accompanied the children on his chestnut filly, Mary. Hannibal and Caesar were set at their slowest speed, but even so, the farmer's mare had a hard time keeping up with the vigorous mules that were powered by solar energy.

"Nice little beasts, there's no denying that!" mumbled John contentedly. "If I could attach the likes of them to the plow, God alone knows how many acres I could till per day..." The mules wiggled their long ears with vexation, as if they understood what the farmer had said.

Presently it came time for them to part company. John hugged Annie and Tim tenderly and wished them a pleasant trip, and he bade them be careful and not to linger too long in Magic Land, because their parents would be thinking about them day and night and waiting for them.

Tim and Annie moved the pegs forward to the fast speed. The mules kicked loudly with their hooves, the dust flew up from beneath their feet, and by the time five minutes had passed, the farmer could barely make out two vague spots in the distance. "God strike me dead!" whispered the astounded John Smith, "look at that gallop! You and I are as far behind them, Mary, as a tortoise is behind a hare. Well, it's unlikely that any foe will be able to catch *them* on the road..."

The farmer turned his mare around and began to trot homeward, meditating on all the strange events that his family had been involved in ever since that memorable day when the tornado conjured up by the wicked witch Gingema had descended upon Kansas.

Annie and Tim took pleasure in their speedy race. Fields and rivers flashed past them, and appeared to be driven along by a head-wind. The occasional pedestrians they encountered looked after them in amazement, and the carts loaded with sheaves whizzed by like mileposts.

By evening, the travelers had put many miles behind them. They stopped to pass the night in a secluded stand of woods far from any habitation. Ellie took from her pack some of the "all-purposeful" material that Uncle Charlie Black had prepared long ago. In accordance with its owner's wishes, it could be an inflatable boat, a sail, or a spacious tent. On this occasion, they made it into a comfortable tent, and the children spent the night peacefully in it, guarded by the faithful Artoshka.

The days followed behind one another, just like our traveler's fleet-footed mules. Annie and Tim maintained a course to the northeast, avoiding settled areas whenever possible. When they came to streams, they filled their sizable canteens with water, but their steeds did not need to be watered. The weather remained clear and sunny, and it was not necessary to charge the beasts: they accumulated energy as they ran.

The first wide river that the travelers encountered on their journey brought them to a halt. Annie was already preparing to inflate the all-purposeful material with air, to make a raft out of it. But Tim remarked that it would not be easy to transfer the mules on a slippery raft without some sort of railing or guard. "Come on, Annie," the boy suggested, "let's try to swim across the river without dismounting from our saddles."

Setting their controls for the slow speed, the children guided their animals boldly into the water. And then, o wonder! the mules swam as if they had done this very thing many times. There was plenty of empty space inside them, and they remained afloat extremely well in the water. Their powerful legs flailed the water to such good purpose that in an instant they found themselves on the opposite bank.

"Hurrah! Hurrah!" cried Tim. "With mounts as good as our Caesar and Hannibal, we could cross the ocean!"

The children could not avoid an encounter with great peril on a vast prairie, which was the haunt of wolves. Prairie wolves, which had gathered in an enormous pack, barred the travelers' path, and when the latter wanted to turn back, they found foes waiting behind them as well.

"Ahead!" commanded Tim. "Full speed ahead!"

The mules dashed forward like a whirlwind. Several wolves rolled to the side with their heads broken and their ribs fractured. One large beast, apparently the leader of the pack, made a leap, endeavoring to drag Tim from his saddle, but the fearless boy struck the wolf on the forehead with his bludgeon, for all he was worth. The stunned predator rolled over sideways; the pack opened up before them, and in a minute it had been left far behind.

Tim was pleased with himself in the extreme, and he sang his own praises to the sky. "Did you see how I got him right between the eyes?!" exclaimed the boy. "I killed him for sure with my bludgeon!"

Annie expressed doubt on that score, and Tim suggested that they go back and take a look. But Annie had no desire to contend with the wolves again, so she made haste to agree with her companion. Tim whistled a military march.

Only then did Artoshka dare stick his head out of the bag. He had hidden it there when he spotted the pack of ferocious wolves. The dog was bold by nature, but at the same time discreet. He realized that a contest with the wolves would be unequal: one predator could break his back with a single blow of its paw, or bite him in two in its enormous mouth filled with sharp teeth.

When he saw that their enemies were far behind, Artoshka barked after them contemptuously, and Annie burst out laughing. "Be quiet, will you, hero!"

Chapter 20

THE GREAT DESERT

The compasses assisted the travelers in maintaining their proper course, but even without them, the children knew that they were traveling in the right direction. So many times had Annie's big sister told her about her journey with the one-legged Sailor, that it seemed to the girl that she had already been here. It was as if she herself had felt the sultry breath of the wind blowing in from the desert that previous time, and seen the hideous heads of the lizards that hid in the dunes.

And there was the woods beyond which the Great Desert began.

"Hi, old friend!" cried Annie joyfully. "It was from your trees that Uncle Charlie built the Land-Boat. It should be standing somewhere right now at the edge of the forest, but we won't bother looking for it. Will we, Tim?"

"What do we need a boat for?" retorted the boy in a firm tone. "Our Caesar and Hannibal are neater than any boat, on land *or* in water!"

Tim and Annie prepared themselves carefully for the risky crossing of the Desert. They decided that they would set out at daybreak, while it was still cool. The children filled their canteens with water from a spring located in the forest, and they drank so much of it that their stomachs almost burst. Before departing, they poured water over each other and the dog, from head to toe.

The travelers put on dark glasses with screens to protect their eyes from the fine sand and dust. Artoshka, catching the unusual scent, jumped into the bag to hide, and his young mistress approved of this action on his part. Needless to say, the dog, too, had drunk his fill of water.

The children were in a sober mood. They ceased to banter with one another as usual when they talked, and their hearts were beating faster. The days that they had spent on their journey up to now seemed like child's play compared with what yet awaited them.

The Great Desert spread out, majestic and gloomy, before them, and its age-old silence seemed to harbor menace. But the children shook off their languor at last.

"Well, what are we waiting for?" said Tim. "We've got to get going." He thought to himself that he would give up his life for Annie without the least regret if need be.

"Yes," the girl concurred. "If we stay in one place, we won't make any progress, as Strasheela the Wise would say." Annie knew many of the sayings of Strasheela the Triply Wise, Monarch of the Emerald City, from her sister's stories.

The children rode at the middle speed. Traveling at a gallop would not be to their advantage: the mules' hooves would stir up thick clouds of dust, and the mounts themselves would bog down too deeply in the sand. The beasts trotted along at a moderate pace, but when Annie looked about her a half hour later, the edge of the forest was barely visible on the horizon. The mules, charging their batteries as they went, put mile after mile behind them, and Annie's head was now occupied with one major thought: how to avoid Gingema's dreadful Black Rocks.

Annie had learned from her sister about how the wicked fairy Gingema, long before her death, had surrounded Magic Land with huge chunks of rock and endowed them with the mysterious power of attracting to themselves anything that moved. Ellie and Charlie Black had almost been forced to remain forever at one such Rock, because the Rock captured the Land-Boat and would not allow the travelers to go more than a hundred paces or so from it. The Sailor and the girl would have perished in the desert if Kaggi-Karr the Crow had not saved them. It was she who, after being set free, returned with a cluster of Magic Grapes, which nullified the power of the rock.

Of course, the magic of the rocks might have ceased or grown weaker with the passing years, but it would be better not to risk it.

Following her big sister's instructions, Annie stopped Caesar every half hour and looked at the far-off horizon through the telescope. Then, after several hours of traveling, at a time when the sun was high in the sky and the children's clothes had dried completely, and when each of them had managed to drink his fill of water about three times — Annie observed a little black spot in the distance.

"I see Gingema's Black Rock!" exclaimed the girl, quite excited.

"Where?" replied Tim. "Where is it?"

Taking a look through the glass himself, the boy confirmed that the enchanted Rock did indeed loom black among the sands.

They had worked out a plan at home to help them in outwitting Gingema's evil spell, and Ellie was the one who had thought it up. The plan was clever, yet simple. If two people of equal strength should pull some object — for example, a table — in opposite directions, it would not move from its spot. Ellie instructed the children to ride exactly in the middle between two of Gingema's Black Rocks . One Rock would pull the travelers to the right while the other pulled them to the left, and the forces of the two Rocks would cancel each other out.

After spotting the first magic Rock, Annie and Tim turned to the side and rode along silently until they observed another. It did not seem too difficult to calculate a path that would lead exactly through the middle. Our riders set the mules at the top speed. The beasts, knowing no fatigue, took off in a gallop, raising clouds of sand.

But when the travelers were actually between the Rocks, they felt a mysterious force drawing both their mounts and themselves to the left. Perhaps they had miscalculated the center and were closer to the Rock on the left, or perhaps its magic power was stronger than that of the other — Annie and Tim didn't know. Whatever the cause may have been, they sensed with horror that Gingema's evil spell was trying to pull them from their saddles.

Annie, growing weaker and weaker, suddenly felt that she could no longer keep her place in the saddle, and with a weak cry she slipped down onto the sand... Unfortunately, she did not fall, but landed right on her feet, and the hostile force compelled her to run, swaying as she did so, straight to her doom.

Tim's mule was stronger and had already nearly broken free of the danger zone, but then the boy heard Annie's cry and saw Caesar speeding along behind him with an unoccupied saddle.

Tim could have saved himself in a matter of a few seconds, but he did not hesitate even for a moment. "Annie's in trouble! Annie will die!"

With an effort, Tim turned Hannibal around and galloped after Annie. He leaned down and, with a mighty jerk, he pulled the girl up onto his saddle.

The children were unable to recall later on all the details of these dreadful minutes, which seemed to them to last a century. They were aware only of the mule laboring under a double load, kicking up sand with its hooves, draining itself of energy in its struggle against the witchcraft. But it was winning, inch by inch, foot by foot...

Closer, closer to freedom... At last, with a whinny of triumph, the marvelous steed was speeding along once more without any restraint!

They caught Caesar, but Annie, in her weakened state, continued for a long time to ride on Hannibal, with her comrade supporting her.

When the girl was herself once more, she thanked Tim with tears in her eyes, and the boy, embarrassed and blushing, resisted: "All right, all right, that's enough! It was all Hannibal's doing..."

And so Gingema's Black Rocks were left far behind them. The mules rode with spirit across the crumbly sand. At a time when real animals would have been exhausted, the mechanical mules seemed just as fresh as they had been during the first minute of the journey.

When the children lifted their heads, they could clearly make out the snowy peaks of the World-Encompassing Mountains looming on the distant horizon. Half of their journey had been accomplished, and what a half!

There was no longer any need to hurry, so the travelers stopped to take a rest. Tim and Ellie had to force themselves to eat, for they still had not collected themselves after the peril that they had lived through. They did, however, drink a great deal of water.

Chapter 21

OVER THE MOUNTAINS

What the travelers aimed to do was to reach the Valley of the Magic Grapes, where Ellie and Charlie Black had made a stopover after *their* crossing of the Desert. But Tim and Annie had altered their course while contending with the Black Rocks, and thus they approached the mountains at a different spot. It is true that here, too, flowed streams bordered with fruit trees, but there were no grapevines anywhere in evidence.

The wonders began the moment Annie and Tim pitched camp in a certain comfortable glade. Artoshka was the first to surprise the children. When Annie pulled him out of his bag, the dog yawned, sighed, and spoke out in a clear, resonant voice: "F-foo... I was getting so tired of sitting in that dark, stuffy hole. At last I can stretch my legs!..."

Annie and Tim had known for a long time that animals and birds can talk in Magic Land, yet it was still with astonishment that they looked now at their hitherto silent traveling companion. But a moment later, they were astounded even more. The dog dashed gleefully around the mules, trying to grab them by the feet, and Caesar spoke up in a pleasant baritone voice: "Hey, there, friend, you'd better watch out! Otherwise, I'll give you a kick with my hoof, and you'll be gone in a flash!"

Hannibal added his support in a hollow bass tone: "Yes, these dogs are truly dreadfully bothersome creatures..."

"What!" exclaimed Ellie. "Did you just start to talk, my friends?"

"And why shouldn't we?" responded Caesar calmly.

Indeed, why *shouldn't* mechanical mules come to life and begin to talk in the Land of Wonders, if a straw figure and an iron woodman could be alive and talk there? It was totally within the natural order of things, and the children were most happy to accept this natural order.

Caesar was clearly more inquisitive than his companion, for he asked the following question: "Tell me, please, Annie, what do our designations mean? Why are we called Caesar and Hannibal, and not something else?"

Annie and Tim were in a quandary. They *had* finished only the first grade, and history is not one of the things that is studied there. However, when Ellie had given the beasts their names, she had explained to her little sister what they meant, and Annie remembered bits and pieces of this.

"Well, you see," said the little girl, knitting her brows, "Hannibal and Caesar were celebrities of some kind back in ancient times. They were either presidents or generals — *something* along those lines..."

The emulous beasts graciously consented to answer to their names. After having some supper, Annie, Tim, and Artoshka went to sleep, and the mules stood calmly by the trees, awaiting the sunrise: they would then be charged with energy once again, and that took the place of both food and drink for them.

When it was morning, Tim got to work on an important matter. He drew from his pack some horseshoes with sharp spikes and screwed them onto Caesar's and Hannibal's hooves. Such horseshoes would only have held the animals back while traveling across the sands, but they were absolutely essential for the stony mountain paths.

That same morning, the travelers ate the last of the provisions that they had brought with them from home, and they marveled at the exactness with which Ellie had calculated how large a supply of food they would need. The children filled their bags with superb fruit that they picked from the trees and put water in their canteens, and then they took to the road.

Oh, how arduous that road turned out to be! Steep ascents and perilous descents, narrow ledges that overhung chasms, shaky screes ready at any time to disintegrate into full-scale avalanches of rock, deep ravines, obstructions in their path...

At times, they had to spend whole hours conquering one small section of path only a few hundred feet long. It was at times like these that Annie and Tim fully appreciated the merits of Caesar and Hannibal. Though far from being able to match themselves with the mountain goats that our travelers saw on the summits of far-off crags, the mechanical mules displayed miraculous agility all the same.

Untiring and fearless, and nimble as cats, they clambered along the steep slopes, warning their riders as they did so to cling tightly to their saddles. When they were coming down a mountain, they tucked in their hind legs and almost crawled on their bellies, and when they ascended, they clutched the rocks with their front hooves.

The mules jumped over narrow crevasses, straightening their bent hind legs like springs, and at these points, the riders clung to the necks of the noble beasts and tried only to keep from flying right out of their saddles!

But presently they came to a gulf so wide that it would have stopped the finest steed in the world. A mist rose up from the bottom of the gulf, and from somewhere down below came the dull roar of unseen torrents.

What were they to do? Could they ride around the obstacle? Cliffs towered up to their right and their left, cliffs that were beyond the power of even Caesar and Hannibal to climb.

Tim and Annie turned pale, and then they looked at one another dismally. They had ended up in a trap, and the only way out for them was to turn around and look for a new path among the maze of mountain ridges...

But at that moment, the sound of gigantic wings was heard above them, and a colossal shadow of something fell across the path. The children lifted their eyes and beheld an enormous Eagle swooping down toward them from high above. Annie screamed in terror and covered her head with her arms, and Tim, with a menacing look on his face, raised his bludgeon to strike — though he realized how absurd it would be to combat such a monstrous bird with a weapon like that.

But Carfax (for it was none other) landed in a clear area not far from the travelers, and he said in a pleasant voice: "Don't be afraid, children. I never harm the weak and helpless!"

Tim found these words insulting and frowned, but Annie summoned up the courage to remove her hands from in front of her face and look at the giant bird. There was such nobility in Carfax's bearing that the girl felt better at once.

"I see, children," continued the Eagle, "that you're headed for Magic Land from the outside world. You've traversed a long and dangerous path, but this obstacle is too much for you to overcome."

"That's right, sir," replied Annie. "There's no way that our mules can leap across this gulf..." Then she took the liberty to add, "But if *you* were to carry us across, it would be very nice."

"That wouldn't be at all difficult," agreed the Eagle good-naturedly. "Bend down onto your saddle, little girl..."

No sooner did Annie do as Carfax had advised, than his powerful claws grabbed hold of Caesar carefully under his belly. The girl did not even have time to be frightened as she saw the chasm beneath her with the mist swirling at the bottom; the wind whistled in her ears, and in about a minute the mule was already standing on the other side of the abyss, neighing happily. Before long, Hannibal and Tim were there by Annie's side.

"The road from here on is safe, so you won't be needing my services any more," said the Eagle, and he soared into the air.

"Thank you, kind friend, thank you!" was all that the children managed to shout after him, and the giant bird quickly vanished behind a nearby cloud.

But how was it that Carfax was still alive? After all, when he left Urfin Jus, he had been heading for his homeland, where death awaited him from Arrahes the leader and his aides.

Chapter 21: OVER THE MOUNTAINS

Well, here's what happened. Only three days before Carfax's return to Eagle Valley, his sworn enemy Arrahes had perished in a skirmish with the King of the Serpents, whom he had challenged to single combat because of his inordinate vanity. The eagles had not yet had time to elect a new leader, so Carfax assumed that title himself. He found himself a new mate and settled down to a peaceful and contented life.

Ah, if only Tim and Annie had known about the events that had been occurring recently in Magic Land! If only they had been aware of how this very Eagle had unintentionally aided wicked Urfin Jus in gaining power over the Leapers! Then they would not have let Carfax leave them so easily: they would have entreated the noble bird to rectify the evil that he had done to so many people.

But Annie and Tim had no evil presentiments, and Carfax tried to hold himself as aloof as possible from human affairs, especially after Fate had brought him and the shifty Urfin together. Without suspecting what a powerful ally they had lost for the coming fight, the children gazed for a long time at the cloud behind which Carfax had disappeared. Then Tim exclaimed gaily: "What an adventure that was! Even Ellie never had one like that!"

"That's true," replied Annie. "She never even heard that such eagles exist in Magic Land."

"You and I were really lucky," said the boy. "If it hadn't been for that bird, think of how much time we would have wasted in the mountains..."

The children set their mules in motion and continued on their way.

The most difficult part of the journey was over. Artoshka had had the easiest time of it. He sat there in his hiding place with only his nose and his eyes sticking out, and at the most precarious moments, he hid himself in it altogether and even began to shut his eyes tight. His reasoning was that the danger wouldn't be so terrible if he didn't see it.

They were obliged to spend the night on the very top of the ridge, on a glacier. There was no way for them to pitch their tent, and the cold pierced the travelers to the bones! But Caesar put forward a practical idea. Acting on his suggestion, they folded the material over several times and spread it out on the ice, and Annie and Tim lay down in the middle with the mules on either side. The mules' bodies radiated the heat out that they had accumulated during the day, and the children, with Artoshka snuggled between them, passed the night without any discomfort.

The next day, the road became more congenial; the ascents and descents were less steep, and first grass, and then bushes and trees, began to appear on the slopes.

The World-Encompassing Mountains were now behind them, and Annie announced triumphantly to her fellow-travelers: "We're in Munchkin Land!"

Chapter 22

HIS FOXINESS, KING KEENSNIFFER XVI

Annie was mistaken. Since they had deviated from the route that Ellie and the one-legged Sailor had taken over the Great Desert, our travelers had crossed the World-Encompassing Mountains in a different place, and Munchkin Land was situated off to their right. But where had Annie and Tim actually ended up?

The children observed that the path that they were riding along through the forest had not been trampled down by human feet. Most likely, it was wild beasts that had worn it down.

The lane gradually widened, but our wayfarers encountered no one, and only some jaunty magpies up in the trees commented loudly about the children's dress and their appearance.

Annie and Tim felt utterly exhausted after their difficult two-day journey through the mountains. Since the weather was splendid, they did not bother to spread out the tent, but lay down right on the soft grass under a bush. Tim went to sleep in an instant. Annie's eyes were just closing, when all at once she heard a far-off wailing of many voices, and someone's plaintive cry: "Help! Ah, help me!... I'm dying!..."

The cry was coming from a nearby clearing. The girl tried to awaken Tim, but that was not such an easy thing to do. So Annie walked alone through the bushes. And what a sight greeted her! In the middle of the clearing lay a large red Fox, his front leg caught in a trap, and he was crying out pitifully. Several slightly smaller she-foxes were clustered around him, and they were likewise howling and wailing in sympathy with the captive.

But the moment they beheld Annie, this animal concert came to an abrupt end, and the she-foxes took shelter in the bushes. The Fox that was caught in the trap looked at the girl with forlorn eyes that positively begged for help.

Now Annie loved animals, especially those that were hurt and suffering. She felt sorry for the unfortunate Fox, so she was determined to help him. The girl walked a little closer to the captive. "How ever did you manage to fall into a trap like this, you poor thing?" she asked tenderly.

But before the red Fox could give her an answer, a blackish-brown vixen leaped from a thicket and angrily attacked Annie: "How can you dare, you brat, to talk so impertinently to the ruler of this land? I'll have you know that before you is his Foxiness Keensniffer XVI, monarch of the Fox Kingdom!"

"Ah, I beg your pardon, your Foxiness," Annie addressed the King with a smile. "I'm from a foreign country, and I didn't suspect your exalted rank."

King Keensniffer XVI graciously accepted Annie's apology, and he explained how he had fallen into misfortune. He had been so engrossed in his pursuit of a fat hare, that he had not noticed the trap, which some hunter from neighboring Munchkin Land had placed here long, long ago. The steel blades had caught his leg.

This had happened a week ago, and not a single person had appeared in the glade during all that time. And if it hadn't been for her Foxiness Queen Fleetfoot and the lords and ladies of his court, who had located the ensnared king, he would have perished of hunger and thirst.

Keensniffer told her that he had already seriously considered escaping his captivity by biting his paw clean off, but such an action would be tantamount to forsaking his throne. According to the laws of the Fox Kingdom, no cripple could be ruler. The little girl from the foreign country had arrived there just in time: she was saving more than just Keensniffer's life, she was perpetuating his royal authority.

When Annie had heard the king's agitated account to the end, she set about trying to free him, but unfortunately, she did not have strength enough to pull the trap open and free his paw. The girl began to head resolutely back to get Tim, but the vixens gave out with such an anguished wailing that she stopped in spite of herself.

"How helpless I am," she thought with exasperation. "If Ellie had been in my place, she'd certainly have already found a way out of this predicament." Annie looked about her in every direction, and she saw not far away a sturdy branch that had been broken from a tree during a storm. "Ah, there's the very thing I need!" she exclaimed joyfully.

After placing the branch between the teeth of the trap like a lever, Annie leaned on it with all her strength; the teeth moved apart, and the overjoyed king pulled his paw out. A loud chorus of foxy voices rang out in praise of the liberator.

Keensniffer's paw was in a sorry state: the wound was bleeding and inflamed, and it would have to be attended to at once. With some difficulty, Annie lifted up the Fox and carried him back to her campsite. The foxy retinue followed respectfully behind her.

When Artoshka, peeking out of the bag, caught sight of this pack of foxes, he gave out with such a deafening bark that even Tim woke up. He was most surprised to see Annie in such unusual company. After hearing her story, the boy approved wholeheartedly of his resourceful friend's action.

Annie took a first-aid kit from her knapsack, and she rubbed the wound with iodine and bandaged it. The King felt better at once, but he was still unable to walk.

"Where does your Foxiness command us to take him?" asked the girl politely.

"To my palace, in Foxburg," replied the Fox King in a weak voice.

When Annie and Tim lifted the Fox King up onto Caesar's back, Artoshka stuck his head out of his hiding-place and yelped in outrage. But when the dog received a healthy whack on the nose from Tim, he realized that it was not always appropriate for him to express his feelings so loudly. Hiding himself in his bag, he grumbled quietly: "Why are they treating that swell-headed one that way? Even if he *is* a mighty ruler, it's the duty of any upstanding dog to chase him away, without sparing any strength..."

The mules set out at a leisurely trot, and the king's retinue ran along behind. The obliging Tim set the Queen on Hannibal's back. Keensniffer XVI showed Annie the way among the dense network of paths that cut through the forest, and the girl and the king talked.

315

"Tell me, your Foxiness," asked Annie, "how many subjects do you have?"

"Oh, many thousands. The last time we took a census of them was about five years ago, so I don't know the exact number of residents of the Fox Kingdom right now."

"But where do you get food from?" asked Annie in surprise. "You'd need an awful lot of rabbits and hares to feed such a mass of mouths."

"Nature has taken care of that," explained the Fox King. "We cultivate rabbit trees, on which grow fruits the size of a full-grown rabbit. Their pulp isn't the least bit inferior to real rabbit-meat in appearance and taste..."

"How many wonders there are in Magic Land," thought Annie in spite of herself. "Even Ellie never heard of the giant Eagles, the Fox Kingdom, and rabbit trees, though she was here three whole times..."

"And why do you bother hunting if such remarkable trees grow in your land?" inquired the girl.

"Their fruits taste good," answered Keensniffer, "but we leave them to the commoners. To eat the same food as farmers and laborers — *fie!*" The King winced squeamishly. "Then again, what a pleasure it is to pursue a hare and to feel your teeth penetrating its living flesh!" Keensniffer's eyes sparkled in a bloodthirsty manner. "It's not for nothing that among us, hunting is allowed only to the royal family and the princes. And if any commoner should venture to do so, the death penalty awaits him."

Ellie was sorry now that she had saved the King from the trap. But then again, she thought, if he *had* died, a successor would have taken over the rulership of the land. And the state of affairs in the Fox Kingdom would have remained as it was.

The King changed Annie's train of thought by asking the question: "What kind of animals are these that we're riding on? I've visited many a region of our land, but I've never seen anything like them."

"You won't see anything like them even beyond the mountains," said Annie. She attempted to explain to his

Foxiness how the mechanical mules operated, but she understood so little about it herself that nothing came of her explanation. The King fathomed only one thing: these animals, which were called mules, fed on sunshine. That did not surprise him in the least.

"To each his own," he reasoned. "Our commoners feed on the fruit of the rabbit tree, our aristocrats eat live rabbits and hares, and your mules feed on sunshine. But a nice big hare is the best of them all!"

Chapter 23

A PRICELESS TALISMAN

The Fox Kingdom was of considerable size: the mules had to spend about two hours on the road to the capital.

At last there appeared the low mounds which made up Foxburg; they were arrayed in two rows along the sides of a broad avenue. It was easy to guess that they were artificial, but who had built them — the she-foxes of olden times or someone else — was something that Keensniffer XVI was unable to explain.

There were countless openings that gaped black in each mound, and these were the entrances to the fox burrows. Red and blackish-brown fox cubs were playing at the bases of the mounds.

King Keensniffer explained to Annie: "Our nation is divided up into two tribes: the Red, and the Blackish-brown. At one time, these tribes lived separately and were at odds with one another, but a hundred years ago they united and resettled in this spot that had mounds suitable for foxholes. There's one practice that has remained with us from the olden days: if the King is from the Red tribe, then it is imperative that his wife be from the Blackish-brown. If the King is Blackish-brown, then his wife must be Red."

Annie was not listening very attentively to the King: she and Tim were far more absorbed in the picture of life among the Fox Nation. And there was truly a great deal to marvel at in Foxburg.

Beyond the mounds spread plantations where grew the very trees that Keensniffer had been talking about earlier. Large oblong fruits covered with leathery shells hung from their branches. Every so often one of the fruits, evidently ripe, broke off and tumbled to the ground. The shell broke on impact, and the luscious pink pulp could be seen through the crack.

A she-fox, walking on her hind legs, approached the fallen fruit and grabbed it in her forepaws, and she bore it away somewhere, no doubt to a storehouse.

All the plantation workers who were occupied in this business walked on two legs. Some of them were using sharp twigs to loosen the earth between the trees, while others were carrying water in the shells of huge nuts and watering the plants; still others were snapping up harmful insects and maggots from among the slits in the bark. The only ones to run on all fours were the young vixens who were sent on errands.

Our travelers encountered a strange procession. Four bearers were carrying a lavish palanquin, and an elderly Blackish-brown she-fox was sprawled out pompously on a silken couch inside it. The she-fox and the King exchanged bows. "My aunt, Princess Sharpears, is going out to pay some calls," the Queen explained to Tim.

Annie asked the King: "Can your craftsmen really make such amazing things?"

"Unfortunately, no," remarked Keensniffer. "Our forefathers bartered with humans for luxury items, and they gave them fruits from the rabbit tree in exchange."

"And do you still carry on trade?"

"Ah, no, no." The King waved his good front paw in vexation. "And please don't bother asking what their reason was for stopping. We'll talk about it later, much later..." Annie fell silent, bewildered.

In addition, she saw a red vixen wheeling three cubs along the walk in a baby-carriage. The little ones were frolicking happily, but the red nanny was coaxing them to lie down quietly and was smacking them gently on their sides.

The palace of King Keensniffer XVI was a mound just like all the others, but there was only one entrance to it. It was so high that Tim and Annie were able to walk through it without bending down, and they found themselves in a large cave.

To the children's surprise, the cave was brightly lit by self-luminous globes hanging down from the ceiling. Annie recalled her sister's story about her trip to Underground Land and guessed that these lamps, saturated with a substance from the fur of Sixpaws, had come from there. It was apparent that the foxes had traded with humans for these as well, but the girl had no intention of questioning the King about it. She still had in mind his annoyance at her last question.

There were two thrones at the rear wall of the cave, one situated a little higher, and the other a little lower. With great dignity, the King and Queen took their seats on these, while the courtiers, standing on their hind legs, lined up along the wall. "Everything's just as it is with people..." thought Annie with a smile.

King Keensniffer made a speech. He recounted briefly the misfortune that had befallen him, and he expressed his most heartfelt thankfulness to Annie for rescuing him from certain death. "But don't think for a moment that I'm going to limit my gratitude to mere words — I'm going to do more. You're going to receive a gift that will be very useful to you in our country. Prime Minister Longtail, come forward!"

A stately Blackish-brown Fox with a remarkably long, bushy tail approached the throne. The Minister was clearly very proud of this tail: it was combed strand by strand and perfumed.

Longtail stopped before the throne and said: "I await your Foxiness's command."

"Go to our royal treasury and bring me the Silver Circlet!" ordered the king.

A commotion arose among the courtiers. Some of them groaned softly, while others extended their front paws toward the king in an entreating manner. It was evident that the Circlet in question was an item of exceptional value. But no one dared voice a word of dissent to the monarch: his Foxiness Keensniffer XVI was not one to be trifled with.

Longtail reappeared in the hall a few minutes later, carrying in his front paws a broad silver circlet adorned with rubies. The Circlet was extraordinarily beautiful, and Annie's heart began to beat joyfully at the very thought that it would soon be hers. But she was a modest little girl, and receiving such a valuable gift for merely doing a good deed — saving another person's life — seemed to her a most uncommendable act.

"Your Foxiness," said Annie, "you exaggerate the part I played in rescuing you."

"Exaggerate?!" answered the king in surprise. "Why, you helped me keep my throne!"

"But you could have managed it without my help."

"How?"

"You needed only send messengers over to Munchkin Land, and men from there would have come to your aid, as your royal dignity demands."

The King began to laugh bitterly. "You greatly underestimate our faculties, little girl! Let me inform you that we did send three messengers to the Munchkins, one after the other, and they all perished for their monarch's sake!"

"Perished? But why?"

"A ferocious Saber-toothed Tiger, one that's perpetually hungry, took up residence along the only road leading from our country to Munchkin Land. It need only get its claws on a fox, and it tears him to pieces and devours him. And *that's* the reason why commerce between us and the humans came to an end eight years ago."

Annie exclaimed in surprise: "A Saber-toothed Tiger settled among you?! But didn't the Deadwood Oaks wipe them out, at the command of Strasheela the Wise?"

Now it was Keensniffer's turn to be amazed. Rising from his throne, he said solemnly: "You know Strasheela, the Deadwood Oaks, and the Saber-toothed Tigers?! And you come from beyond the mountains? Then let me tell you who *you* are, your Grace! You're Ellie, the Fairy with the Death-Dealing House! I welcome you to Foxburg!"

He seated the embarrassed little girl on his own throne and bowed deeply before her, and the Queen and all the courtiers did the same. Only Tim remained standing upright, unable to understand why they were rendering such homage to his little friend, while Artoshka growled angrily in his arms at the sight of so many foxes before him and what a splendid hunt he could have had.

Stepping down from the throne, Annie said: "You're mistaken, your Foxiness! Resume the seat that's yours by right and listen to me. Ellie is my older sister. She's indeed been to Magic Land more than once and accomplished many glorious exploits here. But me, I'm only little Annie Smith, I've been in your remarkable country only two days, and I've done nothing to earn such acclaim."

The King disagreed. "Your services have been enormous. You've saved the country from a change of dynasty and, possibly, civil war. Your services have earned you this Silver Circlet, whose magical properties you will now learn."

King Keensniffer sat down on the throne and put on the Circlet. Annie began to admire its loveliness, but at that moment the Fox touched a little ruby star that glittered on the front edge of the Circlet... and vanished! Yes, he vanished, and so did the massive throne on which he was seated. Annie and Tim stood there, gaping in amazement, and Artoshka began to bark in a deafening voice that made the foxes tremble.

A minute went by, and then the throne, with the king still seated on it, reappeared as if out of nowhere. Keensniffer, delighted, burst out laughing when he saw Annie's surprise. "As you can see, your Grace, this Circlet makes its wearer invisible. All you need do is touch this little star." The king indicated it with his paw. "And it also renders invisible all the things that the wearer of the Circlet is touching at the time. And it has one other amazing property: this Circlet will fit any head, and it expands and contracts depending on the size of the head."

Annie still felt uncomfortable at accepting such a priceless gift, but the King forcibly thrust it into her hands, not even listening to the girl's ardent expressions of gratitude. "Take it, take it," said the King encouragingly to Annie. "I have no need for it. If I make myself invisible too often, my subjects might forget what I look like, and that's not too good a thing to happen to a king, ha-ha-ha!"

Annie timidly tried on the Circlet, and it fitted itself at once to her head, as if a skilled craftsman had adjusted it to her size. "Oh, how nice, Annie!" exclaimed Tim, captivated. "It fits you! That's a marvel in itself! Now disappear!"

The girl's finger touched the little star, and Annie vanished from sight! Tim could see everything right through the spot where she was standing.

Artoshka pleaded resentfully: "Lay off with those tricks, Annie! Don't frighten decent dogs like me!"

A ringing laugh was heard from the empty space, and then the words: "Hey, Tim, catch me!"

Tim raced to where the sound of the voice was coming from, and no sooner did he touch Annie's hand than the girl slipped away, and her call came from a different corner of the cave. After several unsuccessful attempts to catch her, the exasperated boy stopped. "All right, you!" he cried. "This is ten times worse than when you play blindman's bluff!"

At this point, Annie reappeared out of thin air, after touching the little star once more.

King Keensniffer said: "It is only fitting that the Silver Circlet should go to your Grace. You are the sister of the fairy Ellie, who destroyed Bastinda, and it just happens that this magical talisman belonged to Bastinda in the olden days. The wicked Gingema pulled me out of my mother's burrow when I was still a little baby fox and sent me as a gift to her sister at the Violet Castle. There are no foxes at all in Winkie Land, so I was quite a sensation there. Bastinda kept me captive for several years. You know, of course, from your sister's stories how difficult it was to break out of the Wicked Witch's castle. But I succeeded in doing so!" — The king swelled with pride. — "I observed how the Witch made use of the circlet, and I was able to pull it out of her treasury, so — bye-bye, captivity! This talisman saved me a lot of misfortune when I was making my way home, and it helped me in seizing power in the Fox Kingdom. But I part with it now without the least regret, because..." He came closer to Annie and whispered to her: "I'm afraid that my rival, the Blackish-brown Prince Knockknee, might capture it in the course of our struggle over the throne..."

When Annie heard this admission, she decided that she was doing a good turn after all in relieving Keensniffer of the dangerous talisman, and she left Foxburg with a clear conscience, to head first for Munchkin Land, and from there to the Emerald City.

But before Annie, Tim, and Artoshka could depart, they were obliged to attend the banquet that his Foxiness King Keensniffer XVI arranged in his guests' honor. The rabbit-tree fruits that were served to them proved to be excellent, and the children were given several of these fruits to take with them on the road. In exchange, Annie gave Keensniffer her blue cape. The Red Fox donned it with great pride, and announced that it would henceforth serve as the royal mantle in Foxland.

Chapter 24

MUNCHKIN LAND

King Keensniffer's envoys accompanied Tim and Annie as far as the border of the Fox Kingdom, to the place where the path began that led to the Munchkins. They also told them where the last Saber-toothed Tiger in Magic Land usually lay in ambush.

The path was not one of the best, for it twisted and turned and was overgrown with grass, and the children maintained their mules at a running pace. Caesar and Hannibal snorted in spite of themselves: during their sojourn in Foxburg, they had become charged to the brim with energy, and all they could think of now was how to expend it.

But the riders gave the mules free rein when their eyes caught sight of a tiger's striped coat beyond a bend in the path. It was the beast of prey, under cover, lying in wait for unwary foxes.

When the Tiger heard the clattering of hooves (Tim had removed the iron horseshoes from them once the mountains were behind them), it went on the alert. But the children set the pegs at full speed, and the mules flashed by it like the gust of a windstorm.

The bewildered Tiger mumbled: "Eh-he-he, I'm getting old and sluggish. I didn't even get a look at what passed by so briskly. But they definitely weren't foxes..." It hid itself once again in the thicket.

Annie and Tim rode on for a few hours more, and then, at last, Blue Land spread out before them in all its splendor, a land the little girl knew well from her big sister's stories. Once again, Annie was overcome by a strange feeling: it was as if she had already seen those marvels, that emerald-green grass, those trees with their amazing fruit, and those babbling brooks with gold and silver fishes splashing about in them.

And of course, the girl did not feel the least bit surprised when some droll and engaging Munchkins, wearing their wide-brimmed hats with little silver bells, came out from behind the trees.

These diminutive people, who were dressed in blue tunics and tight-fitting trousers and whose jaws were continually in motion as if they were munching on something, stopped at the edge of the glade. It was with astonishment that they looked at the boy and the girl, who towered over them on full-sized mules with shining coats of fur. The look on the Munchkins' faces was clearly one of fear.

Annie was the first to break the silence. "Hello, my dear friends, the Munchkins!" exclaimed the little girl in her clear child's voice, and she dismounted from her mule and took a few steps forward. Tim, who was on his guard, remained in the saddle.

"Hello, mighty Fairy!" responded the bravest of the Munchkins. He bowed to the newcomers. The remaining Munchkins followed his example, and the bells on their hats tinkled melodiously.

"Why do you think I'm a fairy?" asked Annie with a smile.

"Because only a fairy could be wearing such a gorgeous silver circlet on her head. And you look very much like the Fairy with the Death-Dealing House, who freed us from the wicked Gingema, and then defeated the malicious Urfin Jus and his wooden soldiers."

At this point, the Munchkins burst into sobs, and in order that the tinkling of the bells would not interfere

325

with their weeping, they removed their hats and placed them on the ground.

"Why are you crying, my dear friends?" asked Annie in surprise.

One of the Munchkins answered: "We're crying because the wicked Urfin has again enslaved Magic Land and put Strasheela the Wise into prison…"

Annie's and Tim's eyes grew positively round with amazement. "But how could that have happened?" asked the girl.

"*I'll* tell you about it!" sounded a voice out of nowhere, and there, directly in front of Annie, appeared a little old woman dressed in a white cloak decorated with sparkling little stars.

Annie was not frightened. After all, she had been hearing stories of wizards and fairies ever since her first awareness of the world around her, and the most amazing phenomena were everyday occurrences to her: that was how her big sister had educated her.

"Hello, Lady Villina!" the girl greeted her boldly. "Have you flown here from Yellow Land?"

"Yes, of course, my dear child," replied the good Fairy tenderly, and she gave Annie a hug and a kiss. "I've already been following your adventures for several days, and I'm most happy that you aren't wasting any time." With these words, Villina touched the Magic Circlet lightly.

"That's a gift from the King of the Foxes," said Annie, embarrassed.

"I know, dear, and I congratulate you. This talisman will stand you and your friend in very good stead in your struggle with Urfin Jus."

"What's that, ma'am?" exclaimed Annie in terror. "Will we really have to fight that nasty old Urfin too?"

"Yes, my child, you'll have to," the Sorceress asserted calmly. "Your sister Ellie and her friends dealt too leniently with that vicious individual, and now you see the result. He's regained his strength, created an army out of the Leapers, and put Strasheela and the Iron Woodman into prison."

"What? The Woodman too?"

"That's right. Your friends-to-be are now in the enemy's power, and only the Courageous Lion is in safety, in his distant forest. You understand, my dear girl, I don't have the freedom to leave the confines of my own dominions for long at a time, so the only way I can help you is by advising you. But I'll do everything within my power..."

"Thank you, ma'am," said Annie. "If Fate brought Tim and me here to deliver Strasheela and the Iron Woodman from their misfortunes, we'll do our duty."

"I feel exactly the same way as Annie," added Tim in support.

"Now I'll consult my Magic Book," said Villina, and from the folds of her cloak she drew forth a tiny book the size of a thimble. She placed it on a rock, blew on it, uttered some magic words, and the book expanded into an enormous tome. Villina began to flip through its pages, mumbling in a pattering voice: "Crows... grapes... monkeys... mules, mechanical... nukh-nukh tree... Ah, here it is: PRISONERS!"

The old lady began to recite her incantation:

Bambara-chufara, skoricky-moricky,
Turabo-furabo, loricky-yoricky...

The Munchkins, closing their eyes tight, repeated after her in alarm: "*Bambara-chufara, loricky-yoricky...*"

Words appeared on the blank page of the book, and Villina solemnly read them aloud:

"Let the little girl Annie and her companion, who have reached our land on extraordinary mounts that feed on the rays of the sun, set out for the Emerald City along the Yellow Brick Road..."

"How strange," said the Sorceress, interrupting her perusal. "Ten years ago, this book sent your sister Ellie off along the Yellow Brick Road, and now your turn has come too, my child... But let us continue.

> ...In the palace formerly belonging to Good-win, Annie and her friend must get hold of Strasheela's Magic Box, which Urfin has wrongfully appropriated. The Silver Circlet will aid her in this. The Magic Box will take care of the remaining..."

"Hmmmm..." persisted the Sorceress, "the end isn't completely intelligible, and the book won't tell us any more. It is evident that the matter will be made clear on the spot when the time comes. Well, my children, set out on your journey, and I wish you all success! Goodbye!..."

The book shrank again and disappeared into the folds of her cloak, and in another second, the Sorceress herself disappeared. A vortex began to whirl around in the place where she had been standing, and then it blew away, leaving a trail in the thick verdure of the glade.

The Munchkins gazed in awe at the patch of ground where they had just seen Villina, and then Annie got a mischievous idea into her head. She decided to demonstrate to these guileless creatures that she was no less capable of performing miracles than the elderly Sorceress of Yellow Land. She touched the ruby star on the Circlet adorning her head - and she, too, vanished to the sight.

Two disappearances, one after the other - that was too much for the timid Munchkins. With cries of terror they bolted for the nearest bushes and hid in them. Annie, reappearing after a few seconds, and Tim, who was not happy with her little prank, spent a long time in reassuring the little people who had gone into hiding, before the latter dared come out and talk with them again.

Once the Munchkins were satisfied that it was the Silver Circlet that had been the cause of Annie's disappearance and reappearance, they acknowledged without hesitation that the girl was a fairy even more powerful than her sister.

The Munchkins earnestly entreated Annie to oust the cruel Urfin and his Leapers and return the good Strasheela to power. They brought forward a multitude of provisions for the travelers to take with them on their journey, and Annie gave the Munchkins the fruit of the rabbit tree. The little people were delighted, and they said: "We haven't tasted these extraordinary fruits since the time when that bloodthirsty Tiger settled by the road to the Fox Kingdom."

"Why don't you kill it?" asked Tim.

The Munchkins were so astounded that the little bells on their hats did not stop jingling. "Us?!" they cried out. "Small and weak as we are?!"

Tim smiled condescendingly. "If I had time, I'd direct the work myself, but I'm sure you'll manage even without me. Here's what you do. Dig a deep, wide pit with perpendicular walls right on the path about three hundred feet from the beast's den. Camouflage the pit with branches and leaves. Take a couple of rams to the spot, and have them bleat at the top of their lungs. The Tiger won't waste any time charging his prey, and that'll be the end of him!" The Munchkins broke out into a vigorous dance, and they jumped about until they all but collapsed from exhaustion.

A few days later, the residents of Blue Land carried out Tim's plan, and the Tiger met its death in the trap that had been laid there for it. The Munchkins drove a stake into the ground near the pit, and on the stake they fastened a sign with the following inscription on it:

HERE LIE THE REMAINS
OF THE LAST TIGER IN MAGIC LAND.
WE WERE TAUGHT HOW TO DESTROY THE ROGUE
BY A BOY FROM BEYOND THE MOUNTAINS,
THE MOST GLORIOUS TIM.

GLORY TO HIM, GLORY, GLORY!

The Munchkins informed the travelers that when they headed for the Emerald City, they would have to pass through the sizable community of the Underground Ore-Diggers. Many years had passed since the Ore-Diggers left the Cavern and resettled in the surface world, but people still referred to them as Underground, from force of habit.

"They won't hurt us, will they?" asked Artoshka nervously.

"Come now, they're fine people," the Munchkins assured them. "They do have one habit that not everyone cares for: when they talk, they look, not at the person they're talking to, but at the ground. But the explanation for that lies in the fact that they're still not used to the bright light of day."

Saying a friendly goodbye to the Munchkins, Tim and Annie promised to return to see them again on their way back home. After all, the road over the World-Encompassing Mountains began here. Caesar and Hannibal took to the road gaily: more than anyone in the world, they loved to be in motion, for such was their nature.

That day, the children passed several villages inhabited by the Munchkins. Everything in them was blue: blue houses with blue roofs coming to a point, blue gates in blue fences, blue barriers around the gardens and fields, blue clothing worn by the residents... The Munchkins greeted the travelers cordially. By some mysterious means, they had learned already that the younger sister of the Fairy with the Death-Dealing House had arrived in their land, and that she intended to meet the vicious Urfin Jus in combat.

In the last of the blue communities, Tim and Annie were shown the way to reach the Yellow Brick Road.

After parting company with the Munchkins and wishing them success in the coming struggle with their merciless foe, our travelers soon rode out into the clearing where John Smith's house-trailer had landed after its amazing journey through the air. The trailer was still there even now, a bit darker due to bad weather, but still livable. On the door could be seen the half-effaced message "Not at home," written in the young Ellie's clumsy, childish scrawl.

Needless to say, the children did not pass up this opportunity of going inside the trailer. Everything was in total disarray. Chairs were lying overturned on the floor, and a portion of the dishes had smashed to pieces when they fell out of the kitchen cupboard. As a keepsake, Annie took a little plate painted in all different colors, that her sister had once eaten off of. Tim arranged the chairs around the table and wiped the dust off them.

Silently, the children left the house, which no human had set foot in for ten years. "Gingema's cave is somewhere nearby," whispered Annie. "I'm terrified..."

"Don't be afraid," Tim reassured the girl. "With our mules and the Silver Circlet, no enemy is going to terrify us... And don't forget, *I'm* with you!" The boy straightened in the saddle and made a wild face.

"Ah, you little braggart!" said Annie with a smile. "Anyway, you and I are still awfully small, Timothy, my friend!..."

Part IV

THE
SILVER
CIRCLET

Chapter 25

GUESTS OF THE
ORE-DIGGERS

After leaving the old trailer, the travelers quickly spotted a crossroads with three roads leading away from it. The signpost had three markers on it: the first one read "THE ROAD THERE," the second, "THE ROAD HERE," and the third had the sign "Y.B. ROAD."

"Here's the very thing we need!" exclaimed Annie joyfully.

"But what does it mean?" asked Tim in bewilderment.

"You mean you really don't understand?" The girl explained, "It's the Yellow Brick Road, and it's exactly the way I pictured it from Ellie's stories. I can almost see Ellie walking down it, wearing her magic Silver Shoes, with faithful old Totoshka trudging along behind her..."

"Funny that you should mention that," remarked Artoshka from his bag. "I wouldn't mind running down that glorious, smooth road myself, and if I don't, my legs will go completely numb."

Tim and Annie dismounted from their mules, and they let the dog run free. The children began to stroll at a leisurely pace along the yellow bricks, to which time had added a luster. The mules followed along behind them. Artoshka poked about the bushes blithely and barked at the squirrels, which chattered tirades back at him from the upper branches.

Annie found it inexpressibly strange when she thought of how she was walking down the selfsame fabulous road

335

that she had dreamed about so much during the earliest years of her life, the road on which Ellie had once met Strasheela, the Iron Woodman, and the Cowardly Lion... The girl began to tremble with fear: she imagined that the dreadful Ogre was hidden in the bushes, and that he was about to grab her, just as he had grabbed Ellie so long ago. But the Ogre had been away from the land of the living for ten years, for the Iron Woodman had slain him.

The travelers passed the night in the forest, and by noon of the next day, they observed that they were beginning to near the Ore-Diggers' community. The path broadened into a wide road, with wheat-fields rustling in the wind and gardens blooming along its edges. At one spot, a farmer was ploughing a field, using a Sixpaw whose eyes were tightly bound. It was apparent that the eyes of these subterranean monsters were still not accustomed to bright sunlight.

Tim and Annie gazed curiously at this strange beast, with its thick white fur, its enormous round head and round body, and its six stout, round legs. The Sixpaw was so strong that it pulled the heavy plow along effortlessly, turning over extensive layers of black earth.

The plowman, in his turn, stared back, with his eyes agog, at the strangers passing by him on remarkable animals never seen before in Magic Land.

Before they reached the village, the children observed a small factory by the roadside, and the noise of machinery and the sounds of hammers pounding against anvils issued from within it. The Ore-Diggers had continued to process metals that they mined in the Cavern, even after resettling on the surface.

The arrival of Tim and Annie in the village was an occasion for great excitement. Grownups and children alike came running out of their beautiful, tall, red-roofed houses, and our travelers soon found themselves ringed by curious onlookers. The Ore-Diggers had long, pallid faces, and they lifted their eyes for a mere instant toward the travelers and then lowered them again to the ground.

A tall, thin elderly man with a long white beard introduced himself to the children: "I am Rujero, leader of the Land of the Ore-Diggers!"

"Oh, I've heard so much about you from my sister!" exclaimed Annie excitedly. "Weren't you the last Time Keeper in Underground Land?"

Rujero smiled. "I little thought that people still remembered me there beyond the mountains. It's all due to Ellie's efforts, of course?"

"Who ever else?" exclaimed Tim. "All the kids on our farms are well acquainted with the names of the Underground Kings." Then he added politely, "Not to mention your own!"

The monarch invited Annie and Tim to the table. The mules were placed in a sunny spot to recharge, and Artoshka was left to guard them.

Rujero's house had several beautifully furnished rooms, and some small globes hung down from the ceiling in each of them. The leader explained that these illuminated the house during the night. Bright shades predominated in the coloration of the walls and the furniture: green, light blue, orange. It was evident that, in the course of centuries of underground captivity, the Ore-Diggers had grown weary of the faded, gloomy colors of the Cavern.

To celebrate the arrival of his eminent guests, Rujero held a banquet. He cautioned Annie and Tim: "The things that some of my fellow-tribesmen say may seem strange to you. But I implore you to maintain your composure, even if it should be difficult to do so."

Several dozen people were seated at long tables in a large hall. The Ore-Diggers felt at ease in the semidarkness and coolness of the room, and Annie observed that they had bold, piercing eyes and faces filled with dignity.

The host seated the girl between two individuals who were getting on in years. Her neighbor to the left, who was stocky and redheaded, introduced himself: "Barbedo!" The other, seated to her right, who had thick eyebrows and a mop of black hair that hung down over his forehead, likewise told her his name: "Mentaho!"

So Annie's table-companions were two of the last of the Underground Kings! Annie almost started to giggle, but then Rujero's caution had its effect, and she controlled herself.

The tables were loaded with every possible kind of delicious food: cakes on huge platters, pastries in various shapes, pies, turtle soup, bowls of superb fruit, pancakes with honey. They washed the food down with sparkling lemonade.

Annie's neighbors sought to strike up conversation with the girl. Former King Mentaho sang ardent praises of his present trade: weaving. "How proud I am that I'm a weaver, dearest Annie," said Mentaho, "and that all my forefathers were weavers. I believe that weaving is the most important occupation in the whole world. Just imagine if there were no weavers: people would have to dress themselves in animal skins, as they did thousands of years ago. And their intellect would be reduced to the level of beasts."

"Come, now, Mentaho, don't get carried away!" shouted one of the guests gaily. "Don't forget about the people who cultivate the flax!"

Another added: "Tell me, friend, what good would your material be without us, the tailors?" The dinner became merry and noisy.

It was Barbedo who held Annie's attention. The fat old man proved to be a confirmed revolutionary. He said excitedly: "I can't understand why our fathers and grandfathers put up with royal authority for such a long time! I wish I'd been alive during that period — I would have been the first to revolt against the tyrants!"

338

The animated discourses of Mentaho and Barbedo seemed downright laughable to Tim and Annie, and they understood now why the host who was giving the banquet had asked them to maintain their composure. But here's what was *really* surprising! Several dozen people listened to the demoted kings, but not even the shadow of a smile glimmered in anyone's eyes. On the contrary, the guests at the table nodded their heads sympathetically and put in remarks indicating their approval. Yes, there was a lofty and pure spirit in these people, who after long centuries had become inured to the harsh conditions of life underground. Now that they had re-educated their ex-kings and changed them from parasites and oppressors into hard-working craftsmen, the tactful fellow-citizens had no intention of reminding them of the past, neither by word nor tone, lest they debase their present virtues. They understood everything and they forgave everything.

Tim and Annie, all but staggered by the nobility of the Ore-Diggers, fell silent and sat calmly until the banquet was over. It ended in the evening. Tim waited until the host had seen his other guests to the door, and then he shared with him the sad news about how Urfin had once again taken over the Emerald City.

"I've long known about that, from the Munchkins," declared Rujero. "We've concluded a pact with them, and we're going to assist one another in the event of an enemy attack."

"But what steps are you thinking of taking?" asked Annie anxiously. "My sister has told me that the Leapers are a very strong and very warlike people."

"We've prepared a few surprises for them," said Rujero with a smile, "but we can't breathe a word about them to anyone!"

After several hours of riding, Annie and Tim heard a clattering sound, and a strange creature ran out from around a bend in the road. It was a wooden man, but not at all like the Deadwood Oaks, as Annie imagined them. He had long, slender arms with many fingers, long legs that were well adapted for running, and a long, sharp nose which, it appeared, could sniff out everything all around him.

Annie realized that she was looking at one of the former policemen who, after Urfin's overthrow, had become couriers and postilions. "Stop!" cried Annie in a commanding tone, and she blocked the wooden man's path. He stopped at once.

"Who are you?" asked the girl.

"I'm Rellem, courier to the monarch of the Emerald Island, Strasheela the Triply Wise."

"You mean Strasheela's free?" said Annie joyfully. "Is he the one who sent you with a message?"

"Alas, no, dearest lady. The Emerald City has been seized by enemies, our monarch is in prison, and the people have been driven from their homes and wander about the fields, without clothing and without food."

"And where are you speeding to?" asked Tim.

"To the honorable Prem Cocus, ruler of the Munchkins, and to the honorable Rujero, ruler of the Ore-Diggers. I've been sent to them by Lady Kaggi-Karr, acting ruler of the Emerald Island, to warn them of the peril of enemy invasion. Needless to say, the Munchkins and the Ore-Diggers will be no match for the warlike Leapers, but at least they'll be able to hide their property and their food stocks."

"That was good thinking on Kaggi-Karr's part," remarked the boy.

"What do you expect?" said Annie with pride for the Crow. "She's the wisest bird in all Magic Land. I'm sure she'll be a great help to us in the fight with Urfin Jus." Then, turning back to the courier, she said, "Tell me, Rellem, are the Leapers far from here?"

"They're at a distance of one day's traveling for me," said the wooden man. "But that's not very near, because I run very fast, and there are few in this country who can compare with me."

"And what's the news from the Winkie Country?" asked Annie. "The wicked Urfin conquered them too, didn't he?"

"Conquer them he did, but not for long," answered the wooden courier. "Kaggi-Karr disclosed to me the account she heard about what happened there. It was relayed to her by the birds, and it's likely that even Urfin himself suspects nothing of it." And here is what Rellem told them.

After the departure of Urfin Jus's main forces, the Winkies had for a few days hearkened obediently to every directive of Boice, commander of the small garrison of Marrans. But Lestar, who was the Iron Woodman's friend and chief advisor, was a resourceful and ingenious man. He was the one who had constructed the wooden cannon which at the time of the struggle with the Deadwood Oaks, had scattered Urfin's wooden army with but a single shot. Lestar began to observe closely the life and habits of the Marrans, and it was not long before he became aware of their main weakness — their total helplessness while they were sleeping.

Fearing nighttime attacks, the Marrans lay down to sleep in rooms with solid doors fastened shut with sturdy bolts and locks. But what were locks to the skilled craftsmen of Violet Land?

One day, the Leapers awoke to find their arms and legs firmly bound. The rebels took them to the dungeon, where they found plenty of time to regret how reckless they had been to put so much store in the Fiery God's generous promises.

Lestar understood that this one easy victory would not be the end of the matter, that Urfin would send a large detachment of his army, and then the real struggle would begin. So he began preparations for this struggle. Lestar proclaimed a general mobilization of all men between the ages of eighteen and thirty, and this came out to about three thousand. Those who were older than thirty manufactured weapons: they forged swords and daggers, and heads for spears and arrows. Piles of weapons and shields accumulated in the vast front hall of the Castle.

The Winkies who had undergone military training before under the tutelage of Din Gior, were promoted, at the behest of Commander-in-Chief Lestar, to corporals, lieutenants, and captains, and they began to drill the young. The populace was filled with martial spirit. "Victory or death!" cried the Winkies.

Rellem's account made Tim and Annie very happy. It meant that the Leapers were not so terrible as they seemed, and that it was possible to see justice done in their case.

"Thank you for the good news, friend Rellem," said Tim. "Continue on your way, and deliver the instructions to the Munchkins and the Ore-Diggers that they hide their property and their foodstuffs as best they can." The boy continued: "The best thing they can do after that is to go out into the woods and the thickets. Let the conquerors find only empty villages - that'll dishearten them right away! Prem Cocus, of course, has already heard about us. Convey our greetings to him and tell him that we, Annie and Tim, will do everything possible to defeat the malicious Urfin Jus."

Rellem, standing up straight before Tim, reported: "All your directions will be carried out, kind sir. And I have the following to tell you as well: there are enemy squads on the Y. B. Road, but the place where it crosses the Great River is held by a whole detachment of Leapers. And these don't sleep at night, because they drink a potion made from nukh-nukh nuts."

The wooden courier told the children what kind of nuts these were and what they did. After providing the travelers with this valuable information, Kaggi-Karr's herald took off at a full gallop and was quickly lost to view.

Annie's and Tim's spirits were quickly dampened. The road had hitherto seemed friendly and peaceful, but the news that enemies were to be found somewhere down it changed everything. A chill ran through their hearts, their anxiety made their senses keener, and the children peered sharply toward the horizon.

That night, Tim and Annie did not spread their tent. They spent the night in a half-ruined hut, which the girl recognized as the Iron Woodman's old cottage. A dust-covered flask of oil, which the Woodman had once used to lubricate his iron joints, still stood on the shelf.

Chapter 26

THE CIRCLET BEGINS TO WORK

The next day, the children moved forward with extreme caution. They viewed the straight sections of the road ahead through the telescope, but whenever they came to a bend, they stopped and sent Artoshka on ahead as a scout. The little dog would slip noiselessly through the bushes and size up the situation.

After one such excursion, Arto returned in agitation, with his fur in disarray. "Enemies up ahead!" he reported. "No less than a dozen of them are there, and they're lined up along the edge of the road."

A council of war was called at once. Even the mules took part in this, for Hannibal explained: "We don't bear the names of famous generals for nothing, and that qualifies us to discuss military matters."

Tim and Annie agreed with that. The girl asked the dog: "How are the Leapers armed?"

343

"They have slingshots and supplies of stones, and ponderous clubs."

Caesar said: "Hannibal and I can gallop past the squadrons so fast that the men won't even have time to reach for their weapons. Would you care to see it for yourself?"

"And receive a stone in my back?" said Annie, bursting into laughter. "No, thanks! Besides, Urfin mustn't even know that we're in Magic Land at all. Once he learns about it, he'll be on the alert, and it'll be that much more difficult for us to carry out the instruction given by Villina's Magic Book."

"Why don't we sneak through the woods and make a detour around the patrol," suggested Tim.

"That's impossible," objected Artoshka. "The underbrush is too thick."

They lost themselves in thought, and then all at once Annie exclaimed joyfully: "How stupid we are! We completely forgot about the Silver Circlet. We'll pass them by while invisible."

Every step was quickly taken that would throw off the Marrans' sense of hearing. The children took off their shoes, and Tim muffled the mules' hooves with leaves, tying them on with vines.

They performed a test. The children walked along the yellow bricks, holding hands and leading the mules along behind by their bridles. Then Annie touched the little ruby star. Would it succeed or would it fail?

"Invisible and inaudible!" Artoshka the observer reported happily as the procession passed within two dozen paces of him. If the dog, with his sharp eyes and keen ears, could detect nothing, then the Leaper patrol was even less likely to observe the travelers.

And in fact, this means of getting past the enemy squadron succeeded brilliantly. But the travelers had to operate in a different manner when they encountered the large detachment of Marrans that had been sent out against the Munchkins and the Ore-Diggers. These were the ones that Rellem had been sent to warn Cocus and Rujero about.

The tramping of many feet and the drone of voices reached the ears of Annie and Tim while they were still far off. There was no way that they could pass by Urfin's soldiers on the narrow road. Fortunately, there was a path that led a little ways into the forest. After moving about fifty paces to the side, mules and humans alike huddled close together, and Annie pressed the secret star.

A reckless mob — three companies of Urfin's army — passed them by, laughing and chattering, and not one of the fighting-men guessed that there were enemies in concealment nearby.

By evening of the next day, the blue surface of the Great River appeared before them. Since Rellem had alerted them to the fact that the ferry crossing was in enemy hands, our travelers turned off the road ahead of time and walked along the bank. When they found a suitable spot, they forded the river without even dismounting from their mules.

The journey that lay between them and the Emerald Island would take them two days if they were to travel on foot, but only a few hours if they rode the mules. But in this densely-populated area, they would have to proceed most cautiously. Leapers were snooping about everywhere here, and it wouldn't do to catch their eyes prematurely. Even the residents of Emerald Land, if they encountered a little girl looking so much like Ellie, would almost certainly talk with one another about her, and the word could well reach Urfin. The children decided on a bold move: they would go on foot. It would be easier that way for them to make use of the magical Silver Circlet.

Annie and Tim thought about what they should do with the mules. It would be dangerous to leave them in the sunlight: they would become so charged with energy that no tether would be able to hold them. So Tim stationed the mules in a shady thicket, tying their feet firmly just in case, and covering the steeds with branches and foliage. No chance traveler would notice the mules now.

The children placed the most essential items in their knapsacks, and they said goodbye to Caesar and Hannibal, asking the wonderful beasts to summon up all their patience and to await their return — something which might not happen for a while.

Then they stepped back onto the Yellow Brick Road and began to march, in their invisible state, in the direction of the Emerald Island. Everything here was green. Green groves concealed farmhouses with bright green walls and pale green roofs. The fences around the gardens and the wheat-fields were a sea-green color, while the road-markers were painted a dark shade of green.

Annie knew from her sister's accounts that green predominated as well in the outfits that the residents of Emerald Land wore. But the farmers that the children managed to spot in the distance were going about in tatters whose color could not even be made out. The Marrans had robbed them clean.

Chapter 27

OYHO'S MILITARY EXPLOITS

In the meantime, the host of Marrans that Urfin had sent out was marching to conquer Blue Land. The soldiers were led by Colonel Hart, a heavyset, powerful brute with enormous fists. A deep furrow on his forehead indicated that he had spent many years in servitude — he bet far too recklessly on the competitions!

When they were near the Ore-Diggers' community, the soldiers lined up in formation, and the noise and singing in their ranks ceased. Hart sent out scouts, and they returned quickly with the news that they had not encountered anyone, but that their way had been barred by some sort of structure that they couldn't make heads or tails of.

The host took the offensive. But when the Marrans passed a bend in the road, they were stopped by a barricade. Yes, the Ore-Diggers did not just sit there with their arms folded when they were expecting enemies.

A towering mound stretched between the houses at the edge of the village, and in it, in capricious disarray, were mixed tree-stumps, iron plows, harrows with their prongs facing upward, massive cupboards and garden benches... The attackers were prevented from going around the barricade by deep trenches with sharp-pointed stakes pointing upward from the bottoms.

While Hart was thinking about how to deal with this difficult situation, Rujero the leader appeared on the top of the mound. "What do you need here, you men from a far-off land?" he demanded in a loud tone.

Colonel Hart stepped forward. "In the name of his Highness King Urfin the First, I summon you to surrender and to acknowledge his sovereignty."

"And what advantage will that afford us?" inquired Rujero.

"Well, he'll..." Being unskilled in diplomatic negotiations, Hart stumbled. "You'll be paying the Mighty Urfin tribute, and in exchange for that he'll defend your land from enemies..."

Rujero burst out laughing: "We've been living here for eight years already, and this is the first time we've seen any enemies. And those enemies are — *you!* Now, then, are you going to defend us against your own selves?..."

The Colonel sensed that he was losing this verbal duel, and he turned nasty. "Enough of this talking!" he bellowed. "Shoot him, fellows!"

But before the soldiers could pick up their slingshots, Rujero took cover behind the barricade, and from imperceptible holes in it gushed forth powerful streams of cold water, which knocked the stunned Marrans off their feet and soaked them to the skin.

This was the Ore-Diggers' first "surprise." They had hauled their pumps in from their gardens, laid in as large a supply of water as possible, and used this water to cool the Leapers' military ardor.

Slipping in the puddles of water, stumbling, falling down and rising again to their feet, the soldiers retreated in panic. Hart and the company commanders somehow managed to restore order and reassembled the men in ranks. Hart menaced the village's unseen defenders with his fist. "You won't get rid of us with tricks like *that!*" he threatened.

The hot sun of Magic Land quickly dried off the soaked Marrans, and it dried up the puddles in the road as well. Once again the army went on the attack.

The Ore-Diggers' supply of water was now exhausted, and its isolated, feeble remaining spurts no longer daunted the attackers. Clinging to branches of trees, to handles of plows, to anything that happened to be sticking out, the Marrans clambered up onto the barricade, and before long they were near the top of it. Then Rujero's second "surprise" went into action.

An enormous dragon flew out of a nearby grove, swiftly flapping its leathery wings and opening wide its mouth filled with sharp teeth, and it swooped down on the hostile army.

The ancient race of flying dragons had long since died out all over the world, and what remained of it had survived only in the humid semidarkness of Underground Land. The Ore-Diggers had tamed them, back when they were still ruled by kings, and the Royal Guard had used them to carry sentinels on their backs. Of all the dragons, none was tamer and more intelligent than Oyho. It was he, in fact, who had carried Ellie and Fred back to Kansas after Ellie's third visit to Magic Land.

And it was Oyho now whom the Ore-Diggers had summoned from the Cavern and sent into battle. Mentaho sat in a little house on his back, guiding the actions of the flying monster. In his new life, Mentaho was a weaver. But no matter what one might say, he was of royal birth and had received fine military training, and his military skills had resurfaced now in his memory during this time of peril for the Ore-Diggers.

It would have cost the mighty beast no effort whatever to destroy the Marrans by the dozen, but such an order was not even issued. The wise Rujero realized that the real cause of all this misfortune in Magic Land was the ambitious Urfin, and that the Leapers were only poor victims that he had duped. So the ruler of the Ore-Diggers ordered Mentaho and the dragon merely to sow panic in the enemy ranks and to force them to flee.

Mentaho carried out this assignment brilliantly. He understood that the first thing to do was to deprive the attackers of their leaders. With his experienced eye, he picked Colonel Hart out of the swarm of foes as the leader endeavored to restore order among his warriors. At Mentaho's command, the dragon carefully seized Hart in his powerful claws and set him down at the top of a tall palm tree. Then he did the same thing with the captains.

The trunks of the palm trees were completely bare, and the unfortunate commanders had no way of climbing down the trees on their own. While the army was scattering in disarray, the Ore-Diggers would have the chance to get Hart and his aides down.

Oyho, whistling loudly, soared above the road down which the terrified Marrans were running. Swooping down, he made out as if he were going to strike this soldier or that one, and the poor fellow fell to the ground with a scream.

As if that were not enough, Sixpaws, with hoarse, savage roars, came running out of nowhere, with drivers on their backs to control their blind dash. This was the third and last of the leader Rujero's "surprises."

The enemy detachment suffered a crushing defeat. Hundreds of Marrans, throwing their weapons aside, ran in every direction through the woods and fields.

Timid and half-naked figures drifted along the roads of Magic Land for a long time after that. With voices trembling with shame, they asked for food and shelter for the night.

When the battle was over, Rujero sent a messenger to Prem Cocus with news of the victory. The Munchkins, who had already been able to leave their dwellings and hide in the dense thickets, were glad to return home.

The defeated Marrans made their way one by one back to the Yellow Brick Road, and they trudged silently eastward, toward the Emerald Island. They were in no hurry whatsoever: to the defeated warriors, it seemed that it would be a terrible thing when they appeared before the terrible eyes of Urfin Jus, their leader.

Chapter 28

NEW CARES FOR URFIN JUS

When Urfin Jus seized power in the Emerald City the first time around, there were renegades among the residents, and they switched to his side and entered his service. First and foremost of these was Ruf Bilan, whom the king promoted to the rank of Chief Administrator of

Chapter 28: NEW CARES FOR URFIN JUS

State. After Urfin Jus's overthrow, Ruf Bilan fled to Underground Land, and there, after further misdeeds, he was put to sleep by the magic water for a period of ten years.

But living in the city yet were Cabur Gwyn, former viceroy of Blue Land; Enkin Fled, who had governed the Winkies in Urfin's name, and a few other traitors. They had been pardoned and allowed to retain both life and property, and the soft-hearted Strasheela had even given them access to the court. What an enormous mistake this was on the monarch's part!

The moment Urfin Jus was established once again in the Emerald City, every one of his former ministers and counselors came to see him, expressing profound happiness at the occasion of his return. Urfin took them all back into his service and conferred high positions on them. He raised wealthy merchant Cabur Gwyn to the rank of Chief Administrator of State. Enkin Fled became Chief of Police.

When Urfin looked over the property that he had seized from Strasheela, his attention was drawn to a rosewood box of exquisite workmanship with its front side made of frosted glass. The king tried to open it up, but he had no luck. While he was puttering around with the television, Cabur Gwyn came in to him with a report.

"That box doesn't open, your Excellency," stated Gwyn politely. "No one knows what's inside it, but the box is magic."

"Magic?!" Urfin's eyes began to gleam with rapture. Had he indeed come upon some new marvel, one unknown to him as yet, that he could utilize for his own purposes?

"That's right, your Excellency," asserted Gwyn. "I've observed our ex-monarch a number of times, uttering words of some kind to it, and then various moving pictures appeared in the glass. It showed the Iron Woodman, and the Courageous Lion, and sometimes even you…"

"It's a magic mirror!" Urfin realized. "So *that's* how Strasheela knew where I spent the first years of my exile. He saw me in this mirror! I just must learn its secret!" Then Jus asked: "What are the words that Strasheela uttered?"

"No one ever heard them. The monarch always spoke them in a whisper."

"Have Strasheela brought before me!"

Within the hour, the ex-ruler of the Island was there before Urfin. Strasheela had become a pitiful sight: his facial features had begun to run together because of the dampness, and his legs could barely support his now-heavy body. But his spirits were bright as ever. "What do you want of me?" he asked in a hoarse voice.

"I want you to reveal the secret of this rosewood box to me. Tell me the magic words needed to get it started, and you'll go free. Moreover, I'll also liberate your friend the Iron Woodman. I know he's not having an easy time of it in captivity." But Urfin's thoughts were: "I'll free them, all right — but under strict surveillance."

"And what if I refuse?"

"Then I'll burn you and scatter your ashes to the wind."

"Go right ahead and burn me! Perhaps the wind that scatters my ashes about will also tell you the magic words!"

No persuasions and no threats would force Strasheela to disclose the secret, so he was taken back to the dungeon to rejoin the Woodman. There, Strasheela revealed the magic words to his friend. He was afraid that the magic box would become nothing more than a useless trifle if Urfin should really fly into a rage and destroy him, Strasheela.

Urfin needed desperately to learn the secret of the box. His aura as a god of fire had diminished considerably in the Marrans' eyes after they had left their secluded valley. Yes, the Mighty Urfin could still produce fire, as before, with a barely visible motion of his hand. But the

Marrans had observed that the people living in Violet Land and the Emerald Island commanded this magic to almost the same degree. All they had to do was strike the end of a little wooden stick against the black side of a small box, and the end of the stick would burst into flame. The Winkies called these mysterious little sticks "matches." Did that mean that all of the Woodman's and Strasheela's subjects were gods of fire as well? For that matter, even some of the bolder Marrans themselves had learned to produce fire by this miraculous method. Were they gods too?

Though the Marrans had not yet realized that he had made fools of them, they were coming very close to drawing that conclusion. That was the report that Urfin received every evening from his chief spy, Eot Ling the Clown. And if that bold tribe of men should rebel, how could he possibly keep them in subjection?

All that would change if Urfin were to command the secret of the magic box. He would be able to tell every one of his subjects what he had been doing at such-and-such hour of the day, no matter in what place he happened to be. This omniscience would be truly godlike.

Jus came up with the totally absurd idea that he could guess the secret of the box merely by pronouncing a multitude of words in various combinations. So he sat down in front of the television and mumbled:

> *"Shalash-yeralash, zarevo-marevo,*
> *Pooficky-mooficky, chickalo-brickalo…*

Box, be kind to me, show me a picture!

> *Kalamass-palamass, bakhali-trakhali,*
> *Sherity-merity, show me with clarity…*

Box, be my good friend, show me everything around me!…" But the box remained silent and dark.

Urfin did not understand that he could mumble gibberish for a million years and still be just as far from his goal as a traveler who thought that he could reach the edge of the world on foot.

Then Urfin in his rage threw the Magic Box to the floor and began to kick it with his feet. But Stella's marvelous creation was unbreakable. Another time, in vexation, Jus hit the glass with a hammer. The hammer merely bounced back and struck Urfin in the forehead.

"Bring Strasheela to me!" he bellowed, opening the door to the hall. Then he endeavored once again to persuade the former Monarch of the Emerald Island: he flattered him and threatened him — but all for nothing.

Strasheela gallantly safeguarded the secret. Even Urfin's offer to declare the obstinate person his co-ruler, meaning that he would share his power with him as an equal, was turned down. How simple and easy it would be to destroy the straw man! But then the secret of the box would die with him, and so Strasheela continued to live.

And Urfin, pointing his inflamed eyes once again at the frosted glass, began to mumble more meaningless words...

Chapter 29

THEY MEET KAGGI-KARR

Annie and Tim reached the Emerald Island without any mishap. Protected by the Magic Circlet, holding each other by the hand and taking turns carrying Artoshka, they walked along unseen by anyone, yet nothing around them escaped their sharp eyes.

Chapter 29: THEY MEET KAGGI-KARR

The children found shelter in an abandoned farmhouse not far from the Lake. (They were not surprised at the transformation of the Emerald City into an island, for they had heard about it from the Munchkins.) Once inside the cottage, they could take off the Circlet: they would always have time to resort to the magic again if any outsider should be seen approaching.

Tim and Annie were eating the stale bread that the Ore-Diggers had given them, and throwing the crumbs out the window for the birds. All at once, the sound of wings was heard in the air, and a large Crow appeared on the window-sill, with a crafty look in her black eyes.

"You're here at last!" exclaimed the bird joyfully. "How wearisome it's been waiting for you, since that day when you crossed the mountains!"

"Are you Lady Kaggi-Karr?" asked the girl happily. (She had to be particularly respectful to the Crow, since she carried the title of ruler of the Emerald Island, even if it was only temporary.) The Crow nodded her head to answer in the affirmative. "But how did you know about our arrival in Magic Land?"

Kaggi-Karr burst out into raucous laughter. "My dear Annie! You simply can't imagine how effective an avian intelligence service can be! When you and Tim were sitting by the campfire talking about your affairs, a certain commonplace little sparrow was puttering about somewhere to the side, and you couldn't possibly have thought that it was carefully catching every word of your conversation. What happens then? Then it flies to the nearest post and relays exactly everything that it's learned. The news races on and on, conveyed by swift wings, and after a certain number of days it finally reaches me, head of the avian network of Magic Land, and now also holding down the additional job of acting ruler of the Emerald Island."

Annie and Tim stared open-mouthed at the Crow. Then the latter continued: "You mean your sister didn't

tell you about the services that my avian network rendered to her and the Giant from Beyond the Mountains
at the time of the war against Urfin and the Deadwood
Oaks?"

"I do recall something about it," babbled the girl.

"That's human gratitude for you!" said Kaggi-Karr
reproachfully. "But all right, let's not talk about it. I'm
really glad that you, Annie, your friend Tim, and the dog
Artoshka have arrived here. The one thing I can't understand is how you learned in Kansas that we had fallen
once again into misfortune and needed help."

Kaggi-Karr leaped into the girl's lap and snuggled up
against her, expecting to be caressed. Annie was deeply
touched, and as she stroked the Crow's smooth black
feathers, she explained: "You see, it came about entirely
byaccident. We were unaware that Urfin Jus seized power
once again and put Strasheela and the Iron Woodman into
prison."

And Annie began her long narrative. She spoke about
her childhood dreams — her own and Tim's — of visit-
ing Magic Land, something they just *had* to do; about the
mechanical mules that Fred Canning had manufactured,
and about how she and Tim had outwitted Gingema's
Black Rocks… As she concluded her story, she gave Kaggi-
Karr a demonstration of the Silver Circlet's performance.

"As your uncle, the Giant from Beyond the Mountains,
would have said, I swear by the sails!" exclaimed the
Crow when Annie's shining face reappeared beneath the
Circlet. "That's the most amazing story I've ever heard in
the whole world! The birds already informed me about
the Silver Circlet, but it's one thing to receive reports, and
another to see the Circlet with my own eyes! And now
that we have it, we'll win out over the wicked usurper
and liberate our friends. Not far from the city gates stands
the old Tower, and the Iron Woodman and Strasheela are
confined in its dungeon. I don't know where Faramant
and Din Gior are located, but we'll find that out with the

help of the Magic Box." And Kaggi-Karr gave her new friends a brief account of what the Magic Box was and what its properties were.

It was decided that the Crow would go out on reconnaissance and find out where the Television was. The only bad thing was that Urfin knew the Crow, and if he saw her, he would begin to suspect that something was amiss.

"Why, you can fly invisible," said Annie.

Kaggi-Karr felt very proud, and she puffed herself up in her happiness. The girl placed the Magic Circlet around her neck. It shrank at once and fit exactly around Kaggi-Karr's neck. Annie pressed the little star, and the Crow vanished. The only way they could guess that she was flying away was by the sound of her wings.

The hour during which Kaggi-Karr was absent seemed very long to Annie and Tim. But at last, the familiar sound of wings proclaimed the fact that the scout had returned. Once relieved of the Circlet, Kaggi-Karr gave a report on the results of her reconnaissance.

As it turned out, the Box was sitting in a wall niche in the Throne Room; there was nothing to stop anyone from taking it, and if the Crow had had enough strength, she would have carried the Box away in her claws then and there, because the Throne Room had been vacant at the time.

It was too late to go to the palace that same day, for the sun was about to set. Tim announced that he would go there himself the next morning, and Kaggi-Karr would be his guide.

Chapter 30

THE QUEEN OF THE FIELD MICE

Tim set out for the City, with the talisman on his head and the Crow on his shoulder, leaving Annie under Artoshka's protection. If danger should threaten, they would have to take refuge in the cellar.

At one time, every newcomer was struck by the splendor of the Emerald City: its beautiful house-fronts, its fountains, its banners fluttering in the wind, its emeralds glittering everywhere, its crowds of motley, well-dressed residents...

None of that was left, now that Urfin and the Marrans were in control. The banners had been taken down, the fountains were dry, the emeralds had been gouged out from the homes and towers and hidden away in the royal storerooms, the residents had been driven out of the City. Only the strange figures of the Marrans, with their thick-set bodies and their oversized heads, could be seen on the streets.

Tim looked carefully ahead of him, avoiding any undesirable contact. He and the Crow had arranged that whenever he had to walk straight ahead, Kaggi-Karr would sit there quietly, but if it became necessary for him to turn, she would touch the boy's right or left ear with her claw. There was no way she could give signals in her sharp crow voice, and Kaggi-Karr was unable to whisper.

Accompanied by the Crow, Tim reached the Throne Room without any misfortune. What luck! The hall was empty. In an instant, the boy had possessed himself of the Magic Box and was headed for the exit. But at that moment, footsteps were heard.

Tim stood there, rooted to his spot. Urfin Jus walked into the hall. The boy recognized him by his magnificent attire, his thick black eyebrows, his malicious expression. Urfin Jus was alone. And Tim got the audacious idea into his head to put an end to Urfin's dominion over Magic Land at one stroke. "I'll kill the foe!... I'll untie all the knots at once... I don't have any weapon on me, but wouldn't this heavy box itself make a good weapon?..."

Without reasoning the matter out any further, the invisible spy, with all his strength, bashed the king on the head with the Magic Television. Tim was more than strong enough, and Urfin fell crashing to the floor, but as he fell, he let out a wild cry. His skull was much stronger than Tim had thought, and it took even that blow in stride.

In response to his cry, Cabur Gwyn, Enkin Fled, and some guards ran in. "Close all the doors and windows!" screamed the king. "There are enemies in the palace!"

In order to distract the men's attention, Kaggi-Karr flew off from Tim's shoulder and began to scurry all around the room, letting out piercing caws. Gwin and the Marrans raced around trying to catch her, and they raised a frightful commotion. While this was happening, Tim, still invisible, raced for the palace exit, losing his way in the unfamiliar passages and corridors. For about five minutes Kaggi-Karr made fools of the enemies, and then she darted out through a small open window. Ruffled and excited, the Crow sped back to the cottage where Annie was hidden. The girl was terrified.

"What happened to you? Where's Tim? Did he get the Box?" Annie plied the Crow with questions. When she heard the account of what had happened at the palace, she wrung her hands. "Poor Tim! He must be dead!"

"That's very possible," Kaggi-Karr agreed glumly. "I held the men's attention for a long time, but Tim might have gotten lost and fallen into the enemies' hands."

Annie burst into bitter tears, but at that moment, a voice was heard: "Don't cry. Here I am!"

And Tim O'Kelly appeared there before his friends, with the Circlet on his brow and the rosewood Box in his arms. It turned out that he had managed to jump out a first-floor window at the very moment when the pursuers were about to close it.

The girl was extremely happy, but she began to rebuke Tim for his recklessness. "Look what you've done!" she exclaimed. "Now Urfin has found out that Strasheela's followers are on the island, and he'll be taking action."

Tim turned both red and pale, reflecting the contrition he felt, but then he retorted: "The disappearance of the Box would have put Urfin on his guard anyway."

"Well, when that happened... If he merely saw that the Box was missing, he might have thought anything, but now he knows what's going on."

"You find out when you get bopped on the head like that," said the Crow, thus summing up the strange adventure in the palace.

At this point, our friends burst out laughing in spite of themselves as they pictured Urfin's terror and surprise at being knocked down by a blow from nowhere. Then Tim said: "I just didn't think that good-for-nothing had such a thick noggin!"

They laughed again, but then Annie said in a worried tone: "Anyway, we'll have to act, and there's no time to lose. I'm afraid that Urfin will put Strasheela in another prison, and we won't be able to use the Box ourselves because we don't know the magic words."

The acting monarch of the Emerald Island looked at the silver whistle hanging around the girl's neck, and she asked her: "Tell me, Annie, isn't that whistle from Ramina?"

"That's right," answered Annie. "My sister gave it to me."

"Then what are you waiting for?" exclaimed the Crow in exasperation. "Summon the Queen of the Field Mice at once! Ramina is a most powerful fairy, and she'll help us."

Embarrassed at her own absent-mindedness, Annie blew on the whistle three times. There was the pattering of little feet... And Tim barely had time to take hold of the collar of Artoshka, who was about to dash forward. An irresistible hunting instinct to pursue mice impelled the dog to fling himself on his prey.

"Pardon me, your Excellency," said Annie by way of apology for the dog's bad manners. "I summoned you because we're in the direst need of your assistance."

It was difficult to fool the experienced eye of the fairy Ramina. She did not confuse Annie with her older sister. "Hello, my dear," the Queen welcomed the girl. "[I remember you from those times when you summoned me to Kansas, and] I heard a long time ago about your arrival in our land, but to one of my dignity, it is not fitting to appear without being summoned. You must be Ellie's younger sister. What's your name?"

Annie introduced herself, and then she introduced her companions, Tim and Arto. Then, without wasting any time, she stated briefly what service she expected from the Queen of the Field Mice. Ramina began to think, to figure things out. "Strasheela is being confined in the dungeon of the ancient Tower. You need to know the words required to operate Stella's rosewood Box? Well, know them you shall!" And the Queen vanished so suddenly that Artoshka, tearing himself loose from Tim's hands, snapped his teeth at the empty air.

Ramina was a fairy of no small power. And among her talents was the ability to transport herself instantaneously from one place to another. In a certain fraction of a second she reappeared in the dungeon where the Woodman and Strasheela were sitting. They joyfully welcomed their unexpected guest, and they rejoiced even more when they learned who had sent her.

"Annie Smith, sister of our dear little Ellie, is here! She's come from beyond the mountains on some amazing steeds that feed on the rays of the sun? Ey-hey-hey-ho, my bliss knows no bounds!" And the delighted Strasheela sang and danced up and down, though his clumsy legs supported him badly.

The Woodman placed his hand to his breast and said: "Oh, how much love and affection I have here now! And I'll give out all of it now to our new little friend, being that she's our dear Ellie's sister!"

In response to Ramina's request, Strasheela quickly repeated Stella's magic words to her. "You won't forget them now, your Majesty?"

"Oh, my memory is infallible!" said the Queen with a laugh, and she disappeared. And just in time, for a noise was heard on the other side of the door: it was the Marrans, who had come to take the prisoners away to the other dungeon, as commanded by Urfin Jus. But this precaution was useless, now that the deed had been done.

Ramina returned to Annie and Tim. The entire company, including the Crow and the dog, committed the magic words firmly to memory: who knew what might possibly happen to any of them?

Ramina and Annie engaged in a long conversation, and now that they were able to understand one another, the Queen inquired about the fate of all her acquaintances from beyond the mountains. She asked most of all, of course, about Ellie. "I predicted to Ellie that she wouldn't be returning to Magic Land," said Ramina sadly, "and as you can see, I was right. Mighty fairies like us have the ability to predict the future." However, she preferred not to answer the question regarding the outcome of the battle that Annie and her friends were undertaking.

When she learned that Ellie was doing very well in her college studies and would soon be a teacher, the Queen expressed her approval of her choice of a specialty. "Ellie is so gentle, and she loves children so much; she'll make an excellent educator," declared Ramina.

The Queen was also curious to learn what had happened in the outer world to Charlie Black, the one-legged Sailor, and to the bold Fred Canning. "They're both good people and deserving of happiness," said Ramina.

When they told the Queen that it was Fred Canning who had constructed the amazing mules on which Annie and Tim had ridden to Magic Land, Ramina wanted very much to see them in operation. Annie promised to carry out her wish.

They parted with expressions of mutual respect and friendship. The farewell scene was spoiled when Artoshka tore himself loose from the arms of Tim, who had been staring at them.

Chapter 31

IN THE NEW JAIL CELL

After the Queen of the Field Mice disappeared, Annie decided to try out the Television. She was apprehensive of the possibility that the Box might have been damaged when Tim bashed Urfin Jus on the head with it. Placing the Television on a wobbly table, the girl nervously pronounced the magic words: *"Birelya-turelya, buridakl-furidakl, The edge of the sky turns red, The grass turns green instead. Little box, little box, be obliging, Show me Strasheela and the Iron Woodman."*

The frosted glass burst instantly into light, and a road appeared on it. The Woodman and Strasheela were walking down the road, surrounded by guards.

"There you are!" cried Annie. "They're taking them to another jail."

Strasheela could barely even trudge along, and the Woodman was supporting him; his legs were giving way under him, and his head slumped down on his breast. He was clearly at the end of his strength. And the Woodman was not much better off himself. Even over the Television, they could hear the creaking of his joints, which had gone unoiled for a long time.

Annie was seeing Strasheela for the first time, but so well did she know him from her sister's tales that it seemed to the girl that she had sat beside him many, many times, held his soft, clumsy hands, and stroked his keen head that was stuffed with bran... "Poor thing, poor thing," whispered Annie amid tears. "What have they done to you?"

The party heard the Woodman trying to comfort his friend. But this proved to be completely useless. Then the iron man picked up Strasheela in his arms and carried him like a compassionate mother carrying her child.

Ah, Woodman, Woodman! Your tender heart never let you down, even in the most trying moments of your life... If only all people of flesh and blood behaved the same way you do, how much more beautiful life would be on earth!

The acting monarch of the Emerald Island, being the least sentimental of all the viewers, calmly traced the route along which the Marrans were taking the prisoners. From time to time she would mumble: "Two Oak Crossing... 'Strawberry Hill' Farm... Where are they headed now? Ah, yes, of course, the Lovers' Bridge... I know, I know!" she cried out suddenly. "They're taking them to the Oll Birn estate!"

"What are you so happy about?" asked Annie reproachfully.

"Because I'm familiar with every stone in that place, of course," answered the Crow. "And if they put them in the vegetable storehouse... ah-ha-ha, that's where they've taken them, all right!" Kaggi-Karr began to laugh, and she answered her friends' silent question by explaining: "There's a hole in the roof there. And through that hole

I've plucked so many of Birn's apples and pears, ha-ha-ha!"

Annie and Tim felt more cheerful: now the possibility of their communicating with the Woodman and Strasheela, had appeared. Their happiness became even greater when the screen showed them the inside of the shed, and they saw that Din Gior and Faramant were already there. The children recognized them both — the first by his long beard, and the second by the green spectacles that he never removed.

"Hurrah! hurrah! hurrah!" cried Tim, dancing up and down. "Now we can free all four of them at one time!"

The task facing Annie and Tim was indeed considerably easier now. The fate of the Long-Bearded Soldier and of Faramant, Guardian of the Gates, had been worrying the children, and they had had no idea of where to look for them. This new discovery made it most likely that they could accomplish everything at one stroke.

Now that they were reassured on that score, it was possible to go on to view other sights. The children asked to see Urfin Jus. The dictator was seated on the throne, looking very baleful. Tim felt enormous satisfaction when he saw a huge bump on his head, barely concealed by a bandage.

The Chief of Police, the stocky, red-headed Enkin Fled, was standing before Urfin, and the potentate was giving him instructions. Rubbing his bump, he said, "I have the feeling that some of Strasheela's unknown friends have appeared near the Emerald Island. If all this had been happening eight years ago, I'd stake my life that it was all due to that fairy, the little brat Ellie."

Annie giggled, and then she quickly clapped her hand over her mouth, as if afraid that Urfin might hear her. The latter went on: "Get all the policemen on their feet, all the counselors, all my adherents! Make an announcement: whoever locates the enemies will receive ten... no, on second thought, make that five huge emeralds from my treasury."

At the Crow's request, she switched the screen to Violet Land. Kaggi-Karr wanted to see Lestar. The girl was already well acquainted, from Ellie's accounts, with that ingenious little old man, the finest craftsman among all the Winkies.

The viewers saw Lestar standing on a huge mound of earth. On either side of it stretched a deep trench, and along the inner edge of it rose little stone towers with embrasures.

"They're building fortifications!" cried Tim. "Rellem was telling us the truth!"

"How could it possibly have been a lie?" retorted Kaggi-Karr with dignity. "After all, I was the one who dispensed to him the information." (The Crow adopted many of Strasheela's "learned" words, and from time to time she liked to throw them into her own speech.)

Then Annie's heart began to beat with excitement: out from behind a heap of clay, in a majestic manner, walked the Lion. He said to the engineer: "Lestar, old friend, our work is proceeding very well, but are you quite certain that Urfin won't attack us before we finish it?"

"I've taken measures," replied Lestar. "I've established guard posts on all the roads leading to the Emerald Island. Those further away are being manned by birds, while wooden couriers have been stationed at the nearer ones. The moment Urfin's army is on the march, we'll know about it within a few hours' time. For now, though, all is quiet."

"Yes," said the regent of the Emerald Island respectfully, "Field Marshal Din Gior's training is in evidence here. I'm sure I'd be making no mistake if I designated Lestar as acting monarch of Violet Land. I think he'd be just right for such a high position. I'll send the directive to him this very day by the avian network. And it turns out that the Lion has also come to Winkie Land. That's just splendid! And now, what's going on among the Munchkins? What kind of success did Colonel Hart enjoy, and what did he succeed in conquering?"

Once again, the spectators could not help but be amazed. The screen showed them a lively little blue village. Little children, dressed in blue shirts and short pants, were playing in the street beside blue porches. Two women in blue dresses, carrying blue pitchers on their heads, were talking about something or other in a very spirited manner. One of them was continuing a sentence that she had already started: "...can't remember ever being so happy at being able to get out of that hole. My baby girl Rin was coughing so..."

"And all those intrepid Ore-Diggers!" the other joined in. "The way they smashed those presumptuous invaders!..."

"Yes, it was a piece of good fortune for us that they left the Cavern and resettled in the upper world." The first had said all that she had to say, and she walked off, balancing the blue water pitcher on her head.

Annie's and Tim's eyes lit up with joy. "Were the Marrans really defeated there too? Oh, no, that's impossible..."

Annie began to flip the screen to other Munchkin villages - and everywhere she looked, there was felicity, peaceful labor, carefree merriment..."

"The Ore-Diggers' village, please," requested Annie. They saw the familiar village and a crowd of Ore-Diggers dismantling the huge mountain in the middle of their street. And among them were several captured Marrans, who were working diligently alongside the victors.

"Hurrah! hurrah!" shouted Tim jubilantly. "Victory!"

There could be no doubt of it: Urfin Jus's plans of conquest had collapsed in the East as well as in the West. Everyone was extremely happy, and only the Crow complained about communications: the news through this path had reached them late. "I'll have to undertake some reforms," said Kaggi-Karr pompously. "I'll issue a reprimand and establish standards of service."

Yes, this time things were different, unlike nine years ago, when Urfin had dashed about the country like a thunderstorm with his invincible Deadwood Oaks. The experiences of the past had taught the people many things. They now clung firmly to their happiness with their own hands, and they would no longer submit so easily beneath the conqueror's heel. This time, they did not need much help from the outside in their struggles against their enemies.

Annie and her friends now had a task that was much simpler: the first thing they would have to do was liberate the prisoners, and then they would deal Urfin a knockout blow.

It was already evening when the children tore themselves away from the Television. They took one last look at Strasheela and his friends, who were languishing in their captivity. Din Gior and Faramant lay down to sleep, while the Woodman made an attempt to dry Strasheela out by placing him down under the last rays of the setting sun, which filtered in through a tiny window in the wall.

Annie said: *"Little box, this session I would end. My thanks to you I extend."* The Television went dead.

The Crow said: "Tomorrow morning I'll go to the prisoners and comfort the poor devils by telling them about everything I've seen today." Then all at once she bowed down before the rosewood Box: "Forgive me, stupid bird that I am, for the bad things I said about you, in such a disrespectful way. I see now that you're the greatest marvel in our land."

Chapter 32

THE QUEST FOR THE SOPORIFIC WATER

In the morning, Kaggi-Karr flew to Oll Birn's shed and talked with the prisoners. Escape from the shed was impossible: the master had made it very sturdy, with thick walls and a solid door. And behind the door there stood always a guard who was one of the sleepless consumers of nukh-nukh nuts.

When she returned to the farm, the scout related all that she had seen, and concluded her report as follows: "Unless we can put the guards to sleep, we'll never get our friends out of captivity. And the only thing that can help us in that matter is the Sacred Source."

"Are you referring to that magic Spring whose water put the Underground Kings to sleep?"

"Yes, that very one," affirmed Kaggi-Karr. "The journey will be long and difficult, but I see no other way out." They were all in agreement with the regent.

To avoid wasting any time, they resolved to set out that very day. Kaggi-Karr returned once more to the prisoners and urged them to bear with them patiently for a few more days.

Annie wanted to take a look at the land of the Underground Ore-Diggers before they set out, but the Box remained dark and silent. The children realized that it was not able to show the Cavern, which was hidden under a thick stratum of earth. After a conference, they buried the Television by the wall of the house, since it would be inconvenient and difficult to lug it with them.

The mules were still lying calmly in the place where they had left them. After about three hours in the sun,

369

Caesar and Hannibal were so charged with energy that they brayed continually, urging their masters to get moving on their journey.

It was essential that they liberate their friends as quickly as possible, so Tim and Annie, throwing caution to the wind, set out down the Yellow Brick Road at full tilt. And where was the security detachment that could possibly have detained them?! The Marrans barely managed to make out two vague silhouettes of some species of unfamiliar beasts dashing by them like a whirlwind. To this must be added the fact that discipline among the roadside guards had lapsed to a high degree. The blame for this must fall on the scattered fugitives from Hart's army traveling along the road, telling the guards about flying monsters and unknown six-legged beasts, which they expected to appear unexpectedly at any moment in these areas.

Tim was not worried about the possibility that reports of them might reach the Emerald Island. Before any of the couriers, who were not too enthusiastic to begin with, could make it to Urfin, the children would already have reached the Cavern and returned with the Soporific Water.

Three days of furious racing went by, and our friends found themselves at the gates leading down to the Underground Kingdom. Kaggi-Karr stopped at that point. "I had my fill of looking at this Cavern when I was here with Strasheela and the Woodman," said the Crow testily. "Better that I warm myself in the sun."

Annie's heart grew numb with apprehension: she would now be going down into that strange realm where her sister had had such extraordinary adventures during her third trip.

An eternal autumn reigned over the meadows and hills of the enormous grotto that the travelers were now entering. Shades of crimson, red, yellow, and brown predominated everywhere. Goldenish clouds swirled high above them, hiding the Cavern's stony ceiling from view. It was a strange, majestic, and at the same time melancholy world...

Annie shuddered, and she said to Tim in an undertone: "Just think! Entire generations lived out their lives here, without ever once seeing the sunlight... Poor things! I feel so sorry for them!..."

Everywhere, it was deserted and silent, the only sounds coming from distant plants where metals were being processed.

The mules pranced jauntily down the well-trodden path. The children began to look more boldly about them. They gazed with curiosity at the city that was visible in the distance, in whose midst the seven-colored palace of the Underground Kings loomed majestically. The rainbow colors in which the towers of the palace had been painted, had faded to a large degree since the departure of the kings from their royal residence. The bricks of the walls and towers were beginning to crumble and disintegrate. The Underground City was well on its way to desolation...

A loud noise from overhead caught the children's attention. They lifted their eyes and froze: a monster with leathery wings spread out wide was swooping down upon them like an enormous dark cloud.

It was a dragon!

Annie and Tim closed their eyes in horror and clutched their heads with their arms, expecting that enormous mouth, all filled with sharp teeth, to pull one of them right out of the saddle. But instead of that, they heard a harsh bass voice greet them. Then a man scurried out the factory door, and he waved his arms and cried out: "Don't be afraid! He won't hurt you! It's Oyho!"

Indeed it was Oyho, the dauntless warrior, who had smashed the whole Marran army singlehandedly. But here, there was no question of any skirmishing. The

371

mighty beast could see that it was a boy and a girl before him, and moreover, the girl bore a resemblance to Ellie like that of two drops of water — Ellie, whom he had once borne over the mountains on his back.

The children calmed down and began to gaze curiously at the dragon, and the latter circled around above them as a sign of respect. At this point, the riders noticed that their mules were moving more and more slowly. From a trot, they soon slowed down to a saunter, then they began to stumble, and finally, they sank to the ground with a gasp.

The children managed to leap from their saddles, and they stood there in bewilderment beside the inert beasts. Caesar whispered: "All... energy... used up..." And he fell silent, unable even to finish his sentence. These children of the sun, as it were, had grown helpless in no time in the gloomy world of Underground, where not a single life-giving ray of sunlight ever penetrated.

"What are we going to do now?" asked Annie, worried.

Tim shrugged his shoulders. But by that time, the Undergrounder had approached him. The tall man, who had a pale, handsome face, introduced himself: "I'm Elgaro, assistant to our ruler Rujero. I wouldn't be mistaken, would I, if I assumed that you, dear girl, are the sister of Ellie, who was our guest here eight years ago?"

"That's correct," affirmed Annie, telling him her name and that of her companion.

"I'm happy to welcome you and your friend to the Cavern! It looks a great deal less lively than it did at the time when your sister was here. But we live in the upper world now, and we take turns coming down here one month out of every year to work in the foundry or the mine."

"Yes, I heard about that from your ruler, Rujero."

"I see that you're in difficulty. Something's happened to the beasts that were carrying you on their backs. What can I do to help?"

Annie began to tell him the story. Elgaro already knew about the defeat of the Marrans, but he was wholly ignorant of the captivity of Strasheela and the Iron Woodman.

"I'm really sorry to hear about it," said the Ore-Digger. "I saw Strasheela and the Iron Woodman when they were here eight years ago, and I've retained the most pleasant memories of them. They behaved with the utmost dignity, like born rulers of their people."

"You can get them out of their predicament," said Annie. And she proceeded to tell the Ore-Digger her objective in coming down into the Cavern.

"The Soporific Water is normally given out only with our monarch Rujero's written permission," said Elgaro. "But in view of the present extenuating circumstances, you shall have some. But I feel it necessary to warn you, my dear Annie and Tim, that the water doesn't retain its properties for very long. You must cover it very tightly and put it to work as quickly as possible."

"We'll try," asserted Tim.

At Elgaro's bidding, the dragon carefully bore the two mules, one after the other, back to the entrance of the Cavern. Oyho took Tim there as well, for it was up to the boy to recharge the beasts with solar energy. When the dragon had returned, Elgaro attached to his back the pavilion that had once housed Ellie and Fred, and he commanded: "Take us to the water!" And Annie's heart froze when the dragon, flapping his wings loudly, rose into the air.

Two large bottles of Soporific Water were delivered to the conspirators' headquarters — which was the cottage beside which the Television was buried. The whole trip, there and back again, took a week.

Chapter 33

LIBERATION

After they had returned from their expedition, the Crow alerted Din Gior and Faramant that they were not to go to sleep that night. They were strictly forbidden to drink any of the water that their jailers brought them with their meals. There was no need to inform Strasheela and the Woodman about these things, since they never slept, and never ate or drank anything.

Strasheela normally spent the night doing arithmetical calculations. He had become so proficient at it that he could multiply any number up to a thousand in his head. Of course, his mental faculties had grown weaker now, for it had been a while since he had last cleaned his brains. As for the Woodman, he passed the nights mentally composing letters that he would have sent to Ellie if he had been able to. These letters were very moving and eloquent, and it is a shame that Ellie would never receive them.

It was Tim who took upon himself the liberation of the prisoners. First of all, it would be necessary to substitute the Soporific Water for the water that the sentinels were drinking. In one of the abandoned farmhouses he found a pitcher exactly like the one that the guards were using. The boy sneaked up to the guardhouse and switched pitchers.

It was the Marrans' custom to drink liberally after their profuse meals, and this time was no exception. Each of the jailors took his turn with the pitcher. A short time went by, and then the Marrans' heads began to nod, as if some irresistible weight were on top of them. One by one, the guards sank to the floor, and they were overcome by magical sleep — which was difficult to distinguish from death.

"Everything is ready!" exclaimed Tim triumphantly as he watched the Marrans through the little window in the guardhouse. "Now I can really perform some wizardry!"

Tim removed the bolt that fastened the prison door shut from the outside, and stepped onto the threshold. "You're free, my friends!" he cried. "Follow me!"

At this point, Tim experienced the greatest danger of his entire sojourn in Magic Land: the Woodman enfolded him in an embrace of iron. If this had happened at another time, when the ruler of the Winkies was at his full strength, it would have gone badly for the boy. As it happened, he got off now with squeezed ribs.

The liberated captives followed Tim along the road to the conspirators' headquarters, which, fortunately, was not far away. The Iron Woodman bore Strasheela on his shoulders, and he carried in his hand the weightiest club that he was able to find on the persons of the sleeping jailers. Din Gior took big steps, smoothing out his remarkable beard as he walked, while Faramant dashed along behind him, puffing and panting.

Freedom!

And what happened to the Marrans who had drunk the Soporific Water?

They did not sleep for too long, only until morning. This is explained by the fact that they did not drink the magic water until three whole days after it had been taken from the Sacred Spring, and by that time, its effect had greatly weakened.

The reawakening of the guards was unpleasant in the extreme: the door to the shed was wide open, and the prisoners had disappeared. But the Mighty Urfin had ordered them to guard these captives particularly closely, and had threatened them with dire punishment for any carelessness. The jailors were not going to wait around and suffer the consequences - they deserted from the army. It was dangerous to remain there in Emerald Land, so they set out in a body for their homeland, and eventually arrived there safely.

But the most surprising thing in this whole affair was that the fugitives, who were avid consumers of nukh-nukh nuts, were completely cured of their harmful addiction to these nuts. They no longer felt compelled to drink the nut extract every day, their heads no longer spun, the hallucinations that had tormented them vanished, and their pleasant frames of mind returned. In a word, the former "insomniacs" were fully restored to health, and they slept at night the same way as everyone else.

Later, the Soporific Water's curative properties became widely known all over Magic Land, and the other hapless nukh-nukh nut addicts journeyed to the Cavern to be cured of their unwholesome habit.

The Mules, which were now filled with energy and life, were awaiting Tim and the freed captives at the cottage where Annie, Artoshka, and Kaggi-Karr were in hiding. There was no time to lose. Tim seated Strasheela in the saddle with him, and Annie did the same with Faramant. Din Gior, with his long legs, was an excellent walker, but there was no mule — neither live nor mechanical — that could support the Iron Woodman's weight.

The Silver Circlet was placed once again on Annie's head, but it would be awkward to utilize it to conceal an entire party of people, both mounted and on foot, from the eyes of others. For this reason, they relied on their good luck and set out to the southeast, toward Winkie Land. There, the Courageous Lion and Lestar were waiting for them, and it was there that they would measure strength with the audacious Urfin Jus if he should take a notion to pursue them.

By daybreak, they had traveled a considerable distance, and they set up camp in a thick wooded stretch.

It was only here that Strasheela and the Iron Woodman finally got a good look at their liberator, Annie. Their joy when they did so was exceptional. The Iron Woodman's heart beat vigorously within his breast, and Strasheela felt an unprecedented burst of strength. This, of course, can be partly explained by the fact that he had been riding on Hannibal's warm back and thus had largely dried out.

Neither of the friends could get his fill of looking at Annie. They assured the girl that she was the very image of Ellie, and the sight of her brought back fond memories of their happy times of old. When Annie in turn delivered a warm greeting to them from her sister and assured them that Ellie had never, never forgotten them, the Woodman was so transported that his eyes welled with profuse tears. Needless to say, his jaws quickly rusted. It was necessary to lubricate them with oil, which Tim, luckily, happened to have in his knapsack.

Faramant and Din Gior thanked their rescuers from the bottoms of their hearts. The captives had been fed badly while in prison, and their conditions had greatly declined, but they had maintained their good spirits. Their mood was a happy one, and they told jokes and laughed.

Faramant made the whole company laugh. He fastened green spectacles onto Artoshka's eyes, snapping them shut from behind with a tiny lock. The baffled dog looked around himself in perplexity, unable to understand why everything around him had become so green. Then he began to growl at Faramant and tried to bite him. Arto did not calm down until the spectacles had been removed.

"But Totoshka *loved* wearing green spectacles," remarked Faramant to the dog reproachfully.

Din Gior, who had made the entire journey on foot, had gotten his long beard quite dusty, and Annie beat the dust out of it with a branch, after which she combed it and plaited it in three strands. This attention was just what the Field Marshal needed.

After a light breakfast, they lay down to sleep under the spreading bushes.

Tim, Din Gior, and Faramant, after their sleepless night, slept now for a long time, but the Woodman and Strasheela still would not give Annie any peace: they did not cease to ask her about how she was living, how Ellie's studies were coming along, how big she had grown, etcetera, etcetera, etcetera. Then they changed to questions about the kindly Giant from Beyond the Mountains, about Fred...

Finally, when they saw that the girl's eyes were closing and that her tongue could no longer utter another word, the two friends realized that they would have to let Annie get some rest, and she fell sound asleep right in the middle of a sentence.

The Woodman and Strasheela, in their delight, spent the whole day extolling the virtues of the two sisters. Strasheela was obliged to carry on this conversation in a rather uncomfortable position, hanging from Hannibal's back with his head down. The Iron Woodman had placed him there that way in order that he would dry out.

By evening, everyone awoke refreshed and in good spirits. It was still too early to set out again, and Annie recalled her promise to show the mechanical Mules to the Queen of the Field Mice. She blew the whistle, and Ramina appeared in the clearing with several ladies-in-waiting. "Greetings, your Majesty!" said Annie. "I summoned you in order to show you the beasts on which we came to Magic Land. We call them mules. Aren't they truly handsome?"

"They're magnificent!" replied Ramina, admiring the proud, graceful steeds with their smooth, shining coats. "And didn't you say, my child, that they don't require any food except the rays of the sun? That's nothing short of a miracle!"

"But don't you see," Annie objected, "we don't call it a miracle, we call it an invention. The real miracles are

378

here, among you. Gingema's Silver Shoes, Stella's Magic Box, Villina's Magic Book, Bastinda's Silver Circlet... Your own ability to appear anywhere in an instant in response to the sound of the magic whistle — those are the *real* miracles!"

Ramina burst out laughing. "For us, those are the most ordinary things. But the things that you have cited, dearest Annie, are but a small portion of our 'miracles.' Our country was created that way by Hurricap, a mighty wizard of ancient times. It was he who conferred the gift of speech on the animals and birds, caused an eternal summer to flourish here, and shut off this remarkable corner of the world with mountains and a Great Desert. Honor and glory to him for that!"

"Honor and glory!" repeated the whole company.

The Mules began to neigh and to stamp their hooves, calling out to their masters to resume their journey.

"Yes, they're truly miracles," exclaimed Ramina in parting, "even if they do come from beyond the mountains. A pleasant journey to you, my child, a pleasant journey to all of you! And remember, if ever you need me, I'll always be there at your service."

The Queen and her entire retinue disappeared.

The journey to Violet Land was accomplished without any mishap. From time to time, the fugitives did encounter small detachments of Marrans, but the latter did not dare attack a force as impressive as what our friends presented. The Woodman and Din Gior raised their heavy clubs, and the Mules stomped with their hooves and gnashed their teeth in the enemy's face. The Marrans gave the appalling beasts a wide berth and raced to Urfin Jus with a report. But Captain Clem's company, which he sent out in pursuit, was unable to overtake them.

At last there came the moment of the long-awaited meeting.

The Lion, who had become very sentimental in his old age, was phenomenally delighted to see his old friends again — Strasheela, the Iron Woodman, Din Gior, and Faramant. And when Annie walked up to him boldly and slapped him lightly in the face, the Lion all but fainted. "Aren't you ashamed of yourself, picking on those who are smaller than you?!" exclaimed Annie, repeating the words once uttered by her sister, and she took the now fearful Artoshka in her arms.

"Have I perhaps been sleeping for ten years and just reawakened?" said the Lion in amazement as he looked at Annie and the dog. "Ellie? Totoshka? But no, it couldn't be!"

They told him the true story, and he walked over to Annie and began to rub his head against her shoulder like an overgrown contented cat. And when the girl began to play with the tuft of his tail, tears of happiness poured forth from the old Lion's eyes...

And what joy the Winkies felt when their beloved leader appeared before them once again, accompanied by his new friends, who from that moment on became infinitely cherished by his simple-hearted subjects as well.

Winking non-stop, the Winkies broke out into such frolicking that the flashing of their violet clothing dazzled Annie's and Tim's eyes. They snapped their fingers loudly and boasted that if their affairs were going well and all disasters had bypassed them, it was solely because they had never forgotten their promise to wash three times a day, in honor of the Fairy with the Water of Liberation! They promised to charge even their descendants to adhere strictly to this sacred duty...

When the Winkies learned that the girl who had arrived with the Iron Woodman and Strasheela was not the Fairy with the Water of Liberation at all, but, rather, her younger sister, they were not the least bit distressed. They nicknamed Annie the "Fairy of the Victory to Come" and took her to Fregosa the Cook.

The kindly woman ushered Annie straight into the washroom, and she washed her and bade her change into a violet dress, one that the Winkies had tailored for Ellie and which the latter had left behind at the Violet Castle. Then Fregosa took care of Tim and Artoshka.

Strasheela and the Iron Woodman at once underwent major repair work. No one dared remove Strasheela's precious brains from his head, and so his entire head was hung up to dry. The people laundered his suit, pressed it, and stuffed it with fresh straw, and they cleaned his boots. And when Strasheela appeared before Annie fresh and fragrant with the aroma of the field, his facial features were still run together, and so the girl took out her brush and paints and touched up his eyes, nose, and mouth.

Even before she was finished, Strasheela began to sing at the top of his lungs: "Ey-hey-hey-ho! I'm with Annie again, again, again!" The serenely happy Strasheela sang and danced up and down, not the least bit self-conscious because the Winkies, after all, were not his own subjects!

As for the Iron Woodman, the finest craftsmen in the land, headed by Lestar, laid him out on the carpenter's bench and busied themselves with him for a whole day: they took him apart and put him back together again, they unscrewed various small parts and screwed them back in, they oiled and polished — and when they were finished with him, he was good as new, like one just out of the workshop. They stuffed his heart with fresh sawdust, and it became once again the kindest and most loving heart in all of Magic Land.

When the Woodman appeared among his people, he shone so brilliantly that it brought tears to the eyes of all those who looked at him. The artisans had made him a new ax to take the place of the one that he had left behind with Jus, and the Woodman waved it menacingly, making the air whistle all around him. "*Now* let's see who beats whom!" he cried.

Chapter 34

A MONSTROUS DECEPTION

Urfin Jus's fondest dream had come true. He had once again seized power in Magic Land. But the surprising thing was that, as had happened during his first time around as ruler, he did not feel happy. The ambitious dictator yearned for universal admiration; he wanted crowds of people to gather, to throw their hats into the air, to cry out in rapture whenever he made an appearance in the streets or on the squares.

But that did not happen. At banquets, he listened with distaste to what were always the same words of praise delivered by a few bootlickers, headed by the Chief Administrator of State, Cabur Gwyn, and the fat, flabby high priest, Krag. But he had ceased to go out into the streets at all since a time when he had nearly been killed by a stone hurled down upon him from a rooftop. And he suspected that that stone had been launched from a slingshot held in some Marran's hand.

And his power? Where was his power?

From Blue Land, which he had sent Hart's hand-picked troops out to conquer, scattered refugees began to appear. Pitiful, haggard, and in tatters, they painted the king such a picture of their defeat that he was unable to sleep for several nights, and whenever he heard a suspicious sound, he would run to the window to see if it were not Rujero's dragons flying down on the City.

The refugees' accounts weakened the army's martial spirit, and Urfin made haste to get rid of them. He dismissed them from the army, as being unfit to serve a king, and bade them betake themselves homeward.

No better were the reports from the east, from Winkie Land. Worried because he had received no dispatches from Captain Boice for the longest time, Urfin sent a wooden courier out to him. The messenger Veres returned with bad reports. He related that the Winkies had revolted almost at once after the departure of the main body, that they had captured Captain Boice and his army and were holding them even now in captivity. However, he had managed to overhear that the captives were doing very well, how they received three meals a day and were even allowed to go out for walks.

Strasheela and his friends, who had escaped from their prison, had all turned up in Violet Land. And there were also people there from beyond the mountains: a little girl, whom the Winkies had designated as the Fairy of the Victory Yet to Come, and a boy who was about a whole head taller than any of the residents of Magic Land. They had come on some amazing beasts that, so it was said, fed on the rays of the sun.

Urfin was enraged when he heard this report. He ordered Veres not to breathe a word about what he had seen in Winkie Land, and, to be on the safe side, he locked him up.

Urfin's mind was filled with grim thoughts. Both West and East were lost, but things were no better in Emerald Land. Here, of course, the inhabitants would dare put up no resistance. After being driven from the Island, they had settled down as best they could on a few farms that the Marrans had not captured, and there they led a life of privation and poverty. There was no need to expect any danger from them.

But the dictator was worried about his army, which was the sole support that kept him in power. This support was beginning to totter dangerously. Jus knew about this from the one intelligence agent whom he could fully rely on, who was selflessly devoted to him — Eot Ling.

The Wooden Clown prowled about the country day and night, and nothing in it escaped his attention. And thus the Clown reported everything to the ruler.

The army was in a state of ferment. The carefree and flighty Marrans had had their fill of military service. They did not report for drilling and did their best to evade guard duty, while others were already deserting.

A few soldiers had married farmers' daughters and announced that they were leaving the army to settle down to a life of peaceable labor. Many Marrans were envious of them and were prepared to follow their example.

Urfin was deeply worried by the circumstance that his soldiers had developed a passion for consuming nukh-nukh nuts. Urfin preferred that the extract of the nuts be given only to those who absolutely needed it: those who were on nocturnal guard duty or doing reconnaissance at night. But if they gobbled down too many of the nuts, then the supply of nuts in the forest would itself not be sufficient. And it was difficult even to predict what the outcome of that would be. (Jus was not aware that this harmful addiction could be cured by the Soporific Water.)

With his outstanding intellect, Urfin could well understand the causes of the disintegration that was beginning to take place in his army. Discipline is easy to maintain when soldiers are under the constant watchful eye of their commanders, when they are driven to perform their duties from dawn to dusk, and there is simply no way for dangerous ideas to enter their heads.

But now? The Marrans had fulfilled all their wishes. They were living like gods in warm, comfortable houses, and they were in possession of the boundless wealth of the Emerald Island's merchants and tradesmen. What more could they want? Why did they march through the dusty streets with heavy bludgeons in their hands?

In order to rally the Marrans and fire up their ambitions, it was necessary to place some major new goals before their eyes. Goals such that, in pursuing them, these simple-minded people would throw away all the benefits that they'd gained. The sly, shifty Urfin came up with just such a plan. He went to see Veres in his confinement and said to him: "Tomorrow, I'm going to assemble the soldiers and make a speech to them. Though it may appear to you that it does not adhere strictly to the truth, nonetheless, you'll be bound under oath to substantiate every word I say. If not, you'll be burned in the oven!" The frightened wooden man promised to fulfill everything that his ruler required of him.

Word now spread throughout the Emerald Island and the surrounding area that the Mighty Urfin (Jus no longer styled himself god of fire) was about to make an extraordinary pronouncement to his army. It concerned all of his soldiers, and whoever did not report would have no one to blame but himself.

At the appointed time, all the Marrans assembled on the open field outside the Emerald Island. When Urfin made his appearance, he was accompanied by Topotun the Bear and Veres the wooden courier. He took his place on the tall rostrum, and all the fighting-men turned their eyes upon him. Urfin's face expressed a profound melancholy. After remaining silent for a certain interval of time in order to stimulate further the audience's interest, Urfin began, in a resounding voice:

"Woe, woe! My beloved Marrans, it is my duty to convey to you the most dreadful news!" Excitement spread now, row by row, among his listeners. "Know, my friends, that the commander of the company that I left in Violet Land, the worthy Boice, is dead! That's right, our Boice, a champion in leaping and a man unsurpassed in fisticuffs, is no more! May his ashes rest in peace!"

The hushed crowd waited expectantly. Would he really have assembled such a mass of people merely to report the death of a single Leaper? But Urfin was a skilled orator. Raising his voice, he went on: "But that isn't all! Along with Boice perished his entire company, all fifty of the valiant warriors whose duty it was to keep the conquered territory in submission. They were all killed by the cowardly Winkies, killed treacherously after being lured into an ambush!"

This news made a vigorous impression. Many of the soldiers, who had relatives and friends in Boice's company, began to wave their fists and to holler loud threats.

"The worst is yet to come, my beloved Marrans! The savage Winkies committed outrages against the slain troops: they cut them up into pieces and fed them to the pigs!"

The mob was enraged. Only one man among them kept his head, and he asked boldly: "Isn't it just possible that these are false rumors?"

"False rumors?!" Urfin brought Veres up onto the rostrum. "I have a witness here! This is my courier, and he's only just returned from Winkie Land. Speak, Veres!"

And the little man, stammering, mumbled: "What the Mighty Urfin says is God's own truth!"

Now it just so happened that Annie had switched on the Magic Television only a short time before, in order to watch Jus. She did this every day around noon, and Tim, Strasheela, the Woodman, and Annie's other friends were gathered around the screen.

The scene that unfolded before them that day astounded all the watchers. They trembled with rage as they heard Urfin's outrageous lies. But the affair was far from over. The mob of Marrans thundered and raged. After restoring silence, the dictator addressed the wooden courier: "And what else? What more did you hear? Speak up, my good Veres, don't be afraid!"

"I heard, monarch," said Veres in a trembling voice, "that the Winkies are planning to take the war right into Marran Valley, to slaughter all the old people, the women and the children..." It goes without saying that it was Urfin who had dictated this lie to Veres.

"Oo-oh! Death to those contemptible scoundrels! Vengeance! Vengeance!" The roar of the mob rocked the whole surrounding area. Enraged faces, screaming mouths, clenched fists lifted toward the sky. Urfin looked down on the Marrans, smiling with concealed contentment.

And there, hundreds of miles away, Strasheela and his friends watched the screen with impotent rage, fully aware of their total helplessness. If only they could leap up onto the rostrum alongside Urfin, and force the deceiver to speak the truth...

The drama continued. Urfin made a long speech. Oh, he could really be eloquent when he had to! He called upon the Marrans to avenge their fallen brethren and to save their people from destruction. He appealed to the Leapers' feelings of family kinship, and the Leapers, warlike tribe that they were, still loved their elderly mothers and fathers, their wives and children very much.

The entire army, like a single person, expressed its readiness to set out on the march without delay. Even those who had recently started new families agreed to go. It was with great difficulty that Urfin was able to persuade one company of Marrans to remain behind on the Emerald Island to maintain the king's sovereignty there.

"Well," said Strasheela glumly when the Television screen fell silent, "there's nothing for us to do now but to prepare for an enemy invasion."

It should not need to be said that once Strasheela was released from captivity, he was immediately declared ruler of Emerald Land once again. Kaggi-Karr had relinquished her authority to him and warmly congratulated him on his accession to the highest post. Strasheela, for his part, was deeply touched, and he thanked the Crow for the inestimable services that she had performed during her regency over the land.

"But why just talk about it?!" Strasheela had all but run out of breath in enumerating the Crow's exploits. "I am establishing the Order of the 'Golden Wreath,' and the first person to be honored with it will be our beloved and esteemed Kaggi-Karr. As soon as we settle our score with Urfin, the finest jewelers in all the land will forge this medal; they'll adorn it with the purest diamonds, and it'll shine on our distinguished friend's head..." Kaggi-Karr was so moved that two little teardrops rolled out of her black eyes.

"In addition," continued Strasheela, "in commemoration of Kaggi-Karr's service, and in the name of the people of the Emerald Island, I pledge that any Crow that appears within the confines of the City will be accorded the warmest welcome."

This pledge has been honored on the Emerald Island right down to the present day.

Chapter 35

THE FINAL GAME

Urfin's army raced to Violet Land. The Marrans did not turn aside from the road, and they did not even glance at the farmhouses that lay near the road; the warriors were in a hurry to exact vengeance for their fallen comrades, to save their secluded valley from enemy attack.

No conversation and no singing was to be heard among the files: the warriors' faces were grim. Urfin was clever in keeping their martial spirit up. Fearful that the duped Marrans might learn the truth, Jus issued the following order: "There is to be no discourse with the craven enemy. Attack at once and destroy everything in your path. Kill the traitors without mercy!"

Eot Ling lurked like a rat among the hate-fired Marrans, and he had nothing but encouraging news to take back to his master. "They're ranting and raving," said the Clown. "It'll be a lot of fun once they really get down to business! They're threatening to put a hundred enemies to death for each of their own who was killed!"

Urfin rubbed his hands in contentment. After carrying out reprisals against the Winkies, he would turn westward in full strength and subjugate the Ore-Diggers and the Munchkins. He would find some means of contending with the Dragons and the Six-Paws, and woe to anyone who stood in his way!

In the distance appeared the violet spires and turrets of the Castle, which had been built in times immemorial and modified by many rulers during its long lifetime. In the olden days, when she took over the Castle, Bastinda had enclosed it with a tall, thick wall with iron gates that were always locked. The Witch carried the key to the gate in her pocket, and at night, she hid it under her pillow.

When the Iron Woodman became the monarch of Violet Land, the first thing he did was to demolish the wall and to lay out a park around the Castle. He had nothing to fear, after all, from his subjects, who were passionately fond of their kind-hearted ruler. He had kept up the maintenance of all the outer trimmings and the painting of the Castle, and the place looked so comfortable and peaceful that the Marrans could not help thinking: how can people who live in a place like this commit such a black atrocity?

But Urfin did not give his warriors any time to think it over. The command spread rapidly through the ranks: "Quicken your pace! Throw all your excess baggage by the side of the road and prepare for battle!"

The deadly avalanche poured forward. And suddenly... Slowly but surely, the men's run began to slacken, and slowed down to a walk... and then the army came to a halt.

There were two reasons why they had to halt. The first was a deep ditch that cut across the attackers' path; and on the opposite side of it, they could see arrows sticking out of embrasures in stone towers, aimed directly at the enemy.

And the second reason... Ah, the second was so improbable, so implausible that even the highly experienced Urfin, who had read through numerous books in the Emerald City Library about the history of warfare, stood there open-mouthed.

There was a game in progress in the Winkie camp!

It was strange, unnatural... yet there it was!

Clearly, the Woodman's and Strasheela's forces were relying very heavily on the strength of their fortifications, that they could behave in such a carefree manner in the very face of the enemy. But maybe... maybe the players lacked the willpower to leave off a game that was unfinished, when each of the sides counted on winning?...

The Leapers, who were the most impassioned players in the world, could well understand and appreciate this frame of mind. After coming to a halt, the Marrans lowered their bludgeons and spears and clustered in a disordered mass along the ditch, watching the game with great interest.

The game was completely unknown to them, and no wonder: it was the first time ever that it had been seen in Magic Land, and it was the game of — volleyball!

In case the reader has forgotten, Tim O'Kelly had brought his volleyball along with him. The boy was a passionate volleyball player, and he took his ball on the trip, figuring on playing to his heart's content with the Munchkins and the Winkies. But the whirlpool of events into which destiny had drawn him, had forced Tim to forget about any games. He had remembered it here in Violet Land, during their protracted period of waiting for the enemy invasion.

It is not difficult to acquit oneself valiantly in the heat of battle, when one is actually delivering and receiving blows. It is much more trying to await it from one day to the next, expecting danger to come and seeing it constantly put off... The leaders observed that the Winkies' morale was declining day by day, and this was a very bad thing. What could be done to raise the spirits of the disheartened army? And Tim came up with the answer: volleyball!

The boy organized several teams, explained the rules of the game, and held some practice sessions. (The Winkies quickly wove a net for it and, understandably enough, it was hung considerably lower than is normally the case in the outside world.)

In the beginning, the game was played "on the fly," and it achieved unprecedented success. From sunrise to sunset, the ball flew back and forth in the volleyball court, and it was only the onset of night that dispersed the players. The line of enthusiasts waiting their turn to participate grew incredibly long, and therefore, the leather-workers got out their equipment and turned out more balls by the dozens.

Several teams were formed, and they had the most capricious names: the "Lions," the "Children of Fate," the "Saber-Toothed Tigers," the "Fearless Fellows," the "Winged Monkeys"... And a play-off game for the country-wide championship began.

All fear of the enemy invasion was forgotten. The Winkies changed almost beyond recognition: they were blithe and energetic now, and they even began to do less winking — they simply didn't have the time for it! Ardent sports fans positively thronged around the players.

Tim chuckled. "My Dad was right when he said, 'Sports are a great thing.' And he should know — being a champion who played on the Kansas all-star team!"

The Marrans were not mistaken: a very serious game was being played behind the enemy fortifications. It was the concluding match between the teams that aspired to the top spot. The "Winged Monkeys" (whose captain was Din Gior) were playing "Annie's Invincible Friends" (captained by Tim O'Kelly). When the foe were approaching from the distance, the score was 13 to 13, and each side hoped to win.

14 to 13. The "Monkeys" are in the lead… A hit! 14 to 14! But the score will remain the same for only a few seconds.

The "Invincibles" move ahead. 15 to 14. But half a minute later, the opponents serve, and the score is again tied: 15 to 15.

Could the game really be stopped at a moment like this, even if the sky collapsed onto the earth?!

Each team is putting forward its final reserves of strength. The players are displaying miracles of agility. They're spinning around like tops, they're jumping up and down, they're hugging the very ground, they're hitting the balls in ways that seem downright impossible…

The Marrans were captivated, delighted. Yes, this was a game that was very much to their liking! How well they could have jumped up and down in pursuit of that elusive, sprightly ball! How well they could have delivered stupendous hits! Without even realizing it, the Leapers began to divide up into two parties: one of them rooted for the "Monkeys," and the other for the "Invincibles." They even began to make bets.

The crowd roared, first for the one side, and then the other. 16 to 15, with the "Invincibles" in the lead. One more hit, and the championship would be won…

But what was this? The Marrans were dumbfounded. Could that be Boice?! Yes, Boice came forward to join one of the teams, taking the place of another player. Boice, the one who had been killed, cut up into little pieces, and fed to the pigs! Oh, with what skill he sent the ball flying right over the net!…

But wait a bit! What was it that the Mighty Urfin had said? Maybe that vile wooden man had been deceiving him? Maybe he had been lying about everything else too?... Yet there was no denying, here was one Leaper slicing the ball, while others were laughing happily in the crowd of spectators...

17 to 15! The "Invincibles" have won, and they're now the national champions. And Boice is running toward the trench and greeting his friends happily, waving his arms and inviting them to join in the game!

The eyes of the Marrans turn now upon Urfin. At first they show perplexity and doubt... and then anger and retribution. Urfin could not bear it. He covered his face with his arms in horror, and then he turned tail and ran.

He ran, and he tripped and fell down, then rose to his feet and continued running. Jus's heart was beating furiously in his breast, and he was being torn apart by terror that was unendurable. The fugitive could almost feel a mass of stones whistling through the air toward his back, the indignant retaliators catching up to him with their heavy bludgeons in their hands...

But not a single Marran set out in pursuit of the deposed divinity. They thundered epithets after him: "You faker!... You liar!... Vile slanderer!... False god!..."

It was all over. The wise Carfax had been correct in his prediction. Everyone deserted him, and even the loyal Topotun secluded himself somewhere or other. It was disgrace for Urfin, eternal disgrace, more terrible even than death...

Little bridges were thrown over the trench, and the former enemies dashed toward one another. Plans were already being made for mixed volleyball teams, and the air was filled with balls flying back and forth, and such cries as: "Pay them back... You're out... Pass!..."

[The Marrans would soon be vacating the houses that they had seized and returning home to their valley, enabling the rightful owners to move back in. But] Hannibal and Caesar neighed in unison now and struck the ground impatiently with their hooves, calling on their masters to undertake the long return trip to their own country.

And in time, as destiny willed it, the amazing Mules did indeed convey Annie and Tim home.

THE END

Moscow, 1967-1969

My dear readers!

I had originally intended to conclude the stories of Magic Land and its amazing inhabitants with the adventures of Urfin Jus self-styled god of fire. But I have been receiving so many letters from you expressing the desire to learn the subsequent fate of your favorite heroes, that I have been compelled to take up my pen once more and write a fifth story about them.

That story is called *The Yellow Fog*. In its pages, you'll again meet Strasheela, the Iron Woodman, Annie and Tim, and Charlie Black, not to mention Kaggi-Karr the Crow, Oyho the Dragon, and other old favorites.

Magic Land has been assailed by an unexpected calamity. A giantess named Arachna has awakened from a magical sleep that had lasted five thousand years, in a secluded cave somewhere in the World-Encompassing Mountains. This witch has gotten it in mind to subjugate Magic Land to her authority, to make herself its empress. And when the people, who value their freedom, reject Arachna's demands, the witch sends a poisonous yellow fog to cover Magic Land.

Annie, Tim, and the one-legged Sailor (who just happens to be on hand in Kansas) are called on for help, and they contend with the giantess. In order to counter the mighty Arachna with equivalent power, Charlie Black creates an enormous Iron Paladin named Tilly-Willy. The struggle is a long and difficult one, and Magic Land is on the verge of destruction, but the courage and friendship of our heroes wins out in the end.

Thus it has been, and thus it will always be!

ALEXANDER VOLKOV

TRANSLATOR'S AFTERWORD

The two short novels in this volume comprise the third and fourth installments of master Soviet storyteller Alexander Volkov's "Magic Land" cycle — a saga that he initiated with *The Wizard of the Emerald City* (adapted from L. Frank Baum's *The Wonderful Wizard of Oz*) and continued most brilliantly in 1963 with *Urfin Jus and his Wooden Soldiers*, the first of five original sequels. [Readers are referred to my Afterword in *Tales of Magic Land 1* for further details.]

The two stories presented herewith show Volkov both at his best and at his worst — though these terms must be taken in a relative sense, because even his weakest story is no mean achievement. *The Seven Underground Kings* (1969) lives up in every way to the promise shown by the first two books, while *The Fiery God of the Marrans* (1972) shows some falling-off, and might have been more satisfactory had Volkov been able to go over it and smooth out some of its many rough spots. However, both novels have been extraordinarily popular in the former Soviet Union, ever since their first publication — and I am pleased to be able to offer them in English (to my knowledge) for the first time.

Volkov is in top form in *The Seven Underground Kings*. The previous novel, *Urfin Jus and his Wooden Soldiers*, left a few matters unexplained. Readers will recall that in Chapter 25 of that story, Ellie and her friends travel through an underground passage on their way to rescue Strasheela and the Iron Woodman from captivity, and a hole in the passage wall provides them with the vista of a mysterious underground world in an enormous cavern — the "Land of the Underground Ore-Diggers." But an archer on a flying dragon comes and shoots arrows at them, and they barely escape with their lives! Characters and readers alike are intrigued by all this, but Volkov says no more on the subject. Then later, after Urfin Jus has been defeated, arch-traitor Ruf Bilan escapes his just retribution by fleeing into that same underground passage, where he disappears, and we are left wondering what happens to him. The present story answers both questions in a most satisfying manner.

The early chapters of *Seven Kings* give a fascinating account of the Ore-Diggers themselves and "how they got that way." Fortunately, these people prove to be far less sinister than our brief glimpse of them in the previous novel has led us to expect. They are human beings, just like us. We suffer with them in their exile to the Cavern and in their efforts to tame its hostile environment, and we sympathize with the commoners as their history takes a wrong turn and an excessive number of aristocrats and their followers take to living a life of leisure while the commoners toil to support their lifestyle.

The discovery of the Soporific Water provides respite to the commoners, once its properties are investigated and applied, and it is quite in character that it should be Ruf Bilan who, centuries later, messes things up, so to speak, when he blunders into the magic spring and causes its water to stop flowing. (The man is clearly "bad news" wherever he goes.) The Undergrounders' treatment of Ellie and Fred after their arrival among them may seem unduly harsh, but the people's point of view is quite understandable. Once again, it is Strasheela's wisdom that sets things right in the end. The application of the Soporific Water, though lasting for centuries, is only a "quick fix;" the Straw Man comes up with a permanent solution and gives the story a truly happy ending.

The next story, *The Fiery God of the Marrans*, is, unfortunately, the weakest of all the six in the cycle. The main problem, perhaps, is that Volkov tried to cram too much into one novel: he gives us, among other things, the "origin" of the Marrans and of the Giant Eagles; Strasheela's conversion of the Emerald City

397

into an island; Urfin Jus's preparations for and his actual second conquest of the Emerald City/Island; and, added to all that, he introduces the new Kansas characters Annie Smith and Tim O'Kelly and has them journey to Magic Land on two solar-powered mechanical mules, so that they are conveniently in the right place at the right time to help thwart Urfin. The ingredients are there, but their development is often careless, and the elements don't always mesh, so that the novel as a whole never comes into clear focus.

The episode in which Annie and Tim use the magic whistle to summon the Queen of the Field Mice to Kansas, after which Annie's mother indignantly confiscates the whistle (Chapter 17) was evidently written and interpolated as an afterthought, since other relevant passages were not modified to harmonize with it. Thus, after her arrival later in Magic Land, Annie somehow has the whistle back in her possession, but in the story as we have it, Volkov never explains how it got there; and when she talks to the Mouse Queen now, there's no mention of their earlier meetings in Kansas!

This is a relatively minor matter, easily tidied up in the present translation; but there are many other fine opportunities that Volkov missed, which I have, sadly, had to leave as is. In *Urfin Jus*, Urfin's two viceroys, Cabur Gwyn and Enkin Fled, are briefly but very powerfully sketched, and when it is stated in the present story that Urfin takes them back into his service, it raises expectations that are never fulfilled. The two characters receive at most a few lines of mention, and display none of the qualities that made them so memorable in the earlier tale. (However, Volkov does much better with Guamoko, the Great Horned Owl.)

Carfax the Giant Eagle is one of Volkov's finest creations, but he figures only in the first third or so of the novel before abruptly bowing out, later reappearing very briefly to help the kids in their journey across the mountains. (Fortunately, Volkov uses him and his fellow Eagles to good advantage in the two final stories in the series.) And one would expect regent Kaggi-Karr, a bird of proven sagacity and resourcefulness, to make far better use of the Deadwood Oaks in the struggle against the foe, than merely to hide them away in a forest for the duration.

But in spite of these shortcomings, the story has enough good moments to make it well worth reading. The description of the Marrans' way of life before Urfin Jus's advent among them is very convincing, and Chapter 12, in which poor Urfin tries to lead his unruly Marran soldiers on their first campaign, is one of the most entertaining episodes in the whole series. There's genuine suspense as Annie and Tim try to negotiate Gingema's treacherous Black Rocks while crossing the desert. The Magic Television and the Silver Circlet are worthy additions to the store of magical items in the stories. And the description of the undesirable side-effects of the nukh-nukh concoction provides the story's young readers with a painless yet effective message about the dangers of substance abuse. (If only the real-life drug problem could have a solution as simple as the one that Volkov provides!)

We are glad, too, to see that Urfin's second conquest is not so nearly complete as it was the first time around. He and his army conquer the Winkies and the Emerald City, but their efforts to subdue the Munchkins fall flat — especially since the latter now have the Ore-Diggers, aided by Sixpaws and dragons, fighting on their side. This helps prepare us for Urfin Jus's eventual repentance and reform in the two final stories yet to come.

If Volkov had had the opportunity to go over this novel and make a few discreet modifications, as he did with the first part of *Urfin Jus*, this moderately good story might well have been turned into a truly excellent one.

In my Afterword in *Tales of Magic Land 1*, I pointed out a few parallels (whether deliberate or coincidental) between the Volkov cycle and the American Oz series. A few more may be discerned in the two present stories.

The Soporific Water that figures so importantly in both novels brings to mind the Fountain of Oblivion in the garden of Ozma's palace in the Emerald City. As all Oz enthusiasts know, this Fountain saved the day in *The Emerald City of Oz* (1910), when the villainous Nome King and his evil coalition of Whimsies, Growleywogs, and Phanfasms attempted to invade Oz through an underground tunnel and were inveigled into drinking from the Fountain, thereby forgetting all their murderous plans! (This is the first of several appearances of the Fountain in the cycle.) The Magic Television is really an updated version of Ozma's Magic Picture, though it is not quite so simple to use, requiring a complex incantation to be effective.

When Ellie and Fred travel through a cave to reach the Land of the Ore-Diggers, we think first of all of Dorothy, the Wizard, and their companions and their underground journey in *Dorothy and the Wizard in Oz* (1908). It also brings to mind the situation of the Shaggy Man's Brother in *Tik-Tok of Oz* (1914): the poor man gets lost in a mine in Colorado and ends up in the domain of the Nome King, who enchants him and gives him an ugly face! (Ellie and Fred could have come out far worse than they did!) There is a lengthy underground journey in Thompson's *The Hungry Tiger of Oz* (1926) as well.

A few additional parallels in *Urfin Jus* have been pointed out to me by readers of the first volume. The bearskin coming to life is reminiscent of the story of Dyna in *The Road to Oz* (again!). And with Urfin's Powder of Life, how could I possibly have overlooked the similar powders that played such important roles both in *The Land of Oz* (1904) and *The Patchwork Girl of Oz* (1913)?

Alert readers of both cycles will no doubt be able to spot even more parallels in all the stories.

Finally, a few words are in order to justify the fact that I have made some changes in the text while translating these two stories. The question barely arose with the stories in *Tales of Magic Land 1*, but I had to face it squarely in the current two, especially *Fiery God*.

As with the first volume, I have left the names of the characters as Volkov wrote them, without substituting the more familiar (to Americans) "Dorothy," "Scarecrow," and the like. But, as I pointed out above, Volkov himself slipped up in quite a few other instances in these two stories, and I have, with great diffidence, thrown in a sentence here and there (and omitted one paragraph) to smooth these passages out. To those who feel that I should have kept my hands off, I answer only that the majority of my audience will most likely be reading the novels for pleasure, and such readers will be sensitive to these inconsistencies and discrepancies, with their enjoyment consequently diminished. All of my additions have been clearly signaled as such in the "Notes to the Text," and those whose interest in the stories is of the more scholarly variety, would have no trouble in reconstructing the original state of the text if they should so desire. I have tried to do what Volkov himself would approve of if he were still around to question, and there is not the slightest question that he would have done a far superior job with it!

The translation of these two stories occupied many pleasant evenings for me between autumn of 1988 and spring of 1989. The two remaining novels (*The Yellow Fog* and *The Mystery of the Deserted Castle*) were translated later in 1989, and are currently being prepared for publication as *Tales of Magic Land 3*. I can only hope that some of that enjoyment that I experienced in the course of working on this project, will be imparted to my readers now!

Peter L Blystone
February 21, 1993

NOTES TO THE TEXT

The primary emphasis of these textual notes is a little different than that of the notes in *Tales of Magic Land 1*. The two stories in that volume exist in numerous Russian editions, which display many textual variants among them. By contrast, all the editions that I consulted of the two stories in the present volume are virtually identical text-wise. Thus, most of the notes below refer to changes that I myself have made here and there, where I felt that the text called for "touching up." It is evident that Volkov worked over his first two novels quite extensively, but, unfortunately, left the others as they are. (How I wish that he *had* had a chance to go over them himself, so that my little touch-ups would not even be necessary...)

I wish to take this opportunity to extend my thanks to MARCUS MEBES and PAUL RITZ, for their kind assistance in preparing this new edition of *Tales of Magic Land 2*. This book could hardly have come about without them, and all Volkov enthusiasts owe them a debt of gratitude!

p. 28   *The day finally arrived when King Bofaro breathed his last.* Added by translator.

p. 53   *We will relate that in due course, but we must continue first with events that happened before it.*
Added by translator. The "unexpected event" referred to in the paragraph is obviously Ruf Bilan's unwelcome advent in Underground Land and what he did when he got there, as described in Chapter 16. My addition will make it clear that the reference is *not* to the three recapitulating chapters that he throws in before that.

NOTES TO THE TEXT

p. 56 *Bastinda had an easy time...*

Though Volkov makes no mention of it here, readers of *The Wizard of the Emerald City* will recall that the Witch had the help of the Winged Monkeys in this undertaking.

p. 65 *He sent Guamoko... into the City with the mission of winning over a certain traitor that the Owl had previously found among the citizens.*

The original reads: *...with the mission of finding a traitor among the citizens. And the Owl found him: the turncoat was...* [as in translation]

In the first editions of *Urfin Jus*, Urfin hurls Eot Ling the Clown over the walls of the Emerald City, instructing him to seek out a possible traitor. He does so. That is the first time that Ruf Bilan is mentioned, and Guamoko plays no part in finding him. In the later editions, Ruf Bilan has been introduced previously as a supposedly patriotic citizen, and it the Owl who, while on reconnaissance, learns by chance of his traitorous inclinations and reveals them to Urfin. I made this change in order to smooth out the inconsistency.

p. 222 *"There's the one I need!" exclaimed Jus joyfully.*

At this point, the original has the following additional paragraph:

He recalled how the Clown had aided him at the time of the siege of the Emerald City. Several attacks by the Wooden Soldiers had been beaten off, and Urfin found himself in dire straits. Then Eot Ling went into the City on a scouting mission and learned that a wealthy man named Ruf Bilan hated Strasheela, and Guamoko the Great Horned Owl had persuaded Bilan to open the City gates.

This reference back to Chapter 10 of *Urfin Jus and his Wooden Soldiers* is inconsistent with all the extant versions of the story, and consequently has been omitted in this translation. If there exists any version of *Urfin Jus* in which the two henchmen collaborate in this mission, I have not yet seen it. [*Cf. Note to p. 65.*]

NOTES# NOTES TO THE TEXT

p. 247 *A canal was dug...*

The Russian text calls the resulting body of water a "canal" throughout the story. I have generally translated it by "lake," since, to all appearances, that is what it really is.

pp. 298-299 *Around her neck... restored to her.*
Added by translator.

p. 313 *Keensniffer.*

In the original, *Tonkonyukh*, coined from the Russian words *tonkii* "thin," "fine" and *nyukh* "sense of smell" (when referring to an animal). The other foxes' names are coined similarly:

Longtail: Dolgokhvost, from *dolgiy* "long" + *khvost* "tail"
Fleetfoot: Bystronogaya, from *bystriy* "fast" + *nog* "foot," "leg"
Sharpears: Ostroukhaya, from *ostriy* "sharp" + *ukh* "ear"

p. 361 *I remember you from those times when you summoned me to Kansas, and...*
Added by translator.

p. 393 *The Marrans would soon... ...to move back in.*
Added by translator. By the time of the next story, *The Yellow Fog*, everything seems to be back to normal, and there was no way that I could just leave the poor people homeless and destitute till that time!

www.ingramcontent.com/pod-product-compliance
Lightning Source LLC
Chambersburg PA
CBHW020507020726
47493CB00001B/217

* 9 780578 017075 *